PRAISE FOR

# NOBLE BEASTS

'This is a magnificent novel - vivid, moving and utterly convincing. It is perfectly balanced and the writing is beautiful.'

S.G. MacLEAN, author of *The Bookseller of Inverness*

'Passionate, sensual, profoundly moving, this novel held me enthralled from the first page to the last. It is one of the best works of historical fiction I ever read.'

A.N. WILSON

'A richly woven tapestry of historical detail and evocative description, *Noble Beasts* offers a fascinating and immersive portrait of an artist driven by ambition, passion and addiction.'

JOANNA MILLER, author of *The Eights*

'A gorgeously written, meticulously researched debut, filled with art and beasts, love and longing. I was completely captivated and moved.'

SASHA BUTLER, author of *The Marriage Contract*

'Lucy's prose is elegant and quick-witted, while the love story at its heart is achingly rendered. As beautifully crafted as a Landseer painting . . . a stunning debut.'

EMMA COWING, author of *The Show Woman*

'Intensely moving and deeply evocative . . . a stunning portrait of a man as well as an era. Rendered in luscious prose . . . this is historical fiction at its finest.'

LINDA WILGUS, author of *The Sea Child*

Black&White

First published in the UK in 2026 by Black & White Publishing
An imprint of Bonnier Books UK
5th Floor, HYLO, 105 Bunhill Row,
London, EC1Y 8LZ



A CIP catalogue record for this book is available from the British Library.

Hardback ISBN: 978 1 78530 830 7
Paperback ISBN: 978 1 78530 832 1

*Also available as an ebook and an audiobook*

1 3 5 7 9 10 8 6 4 2

Design and Typeset by IDSUK (Data Connection) Ltd
Printed and bound in Great Britain by CPI (UK) Ltd, Croydon CR0 4YY

FSC www.fsc.org MIX Paper | Supporting responsible forestry FSC® C013604

At Bonnier Books UK, we are committed to publishing sustainably.
Find out more here: bonnierbooks.co.uk/sustainability



The authorised representative in the EEA is
Bonnier Books UK (Ireland) Limited.
Registered office address: Block B, The Crescent Building
Northwood, Santry
Dublin 9, D09 C6X8 Ireland
compliance@bonnierbooks.ie
www.bonnierbooks.co.uk

# NOBLE BEASTS

LUCY WAVERLEY

Black&White

# *Autumn 1828, Glenfeshie, Scotland*

MOONLIGHT STREAMS THROUGH THE WINDOW, mottled by the whispering leaves. It shifts and shimmers over the swell of Edwin's slender muscles, over his tousled golden hair, as though he's underwater. Stirring in his sleep, he looks as he did when they first met. So young. Too young. Hardly more than a boy. She should have known better.

Sick of lying awake, sick of her thoughts, Georgina slips out of the bed. Edwin moves again, paint-stained fingers coming to rest in the hollow where she had been. So peaceful. If only it could always be like this: here, in the hut with the scent of pine and peat smoke, the river rushing through the glen, the hills to hide them. But soon she'll have to go. Back to England. Back to her husband. Because otherwise they lose everything.

Floorboards creak, rough beneath her bare feet as she makes her way over to look again at the fresco Edwin painted on the chimney the day before – a stag, a hind, and a calf. In the rippling silver light, they seem to move, eyes glinting, watching her. A draught curls around her neck. She knows what he's doing: these aren't just deer.

She shivers, creeps back to the bed. Edwin's eyelids flicker but don't open. She curls herself around him, needing the warmth and solidity of his body.

He flinches, murmurs: 'Cold.'

'I'm sorry.' She kisses his hair, inhaling him. 'I couldn't sleep. I had to see your painting again. It's beautiful.'

He rolls over, blinking, sky-blue eyes meeting hers. 'It's us. You, me, and Rachel.'

'I know,' she says.

'No one can stop us being together like that.'

'I know.' She presses her forehead to his, strokes his curls until his breathing slows and she's sure he's asleep again. 'My Endymion, my thing of beauty,' she whispers. 'I'm so sorry.'

# Part I

*Thirty years later*

# *July 1858, Trafalgar Square, London*

'WE NEED LIONS, SIR EDWIN. England expects lions. She's been expecting them for too long. Fifteen years to finish a monument like this is a disgrace.' Lord John Manners from the Office of Works stands by one of the four empty pedestals beneath the Nelson column, irritatingly tall and patrician. His words would have more gravity if they weren't muffled by the cream silk handkerchief he holds over his mouth and nose. Edwin nods, pressing a crumpled piece of cloth to his own face.

Trafalgar Square is unusually empty. The river smells bad every summer, but this year's sun-ripened sewage reeks so much that everyone who can afford to has fled to the countryside. Edwin fancies that even the horses are trying to keep their nostrils closed.

'I thought you invited submissions months ago?' he says, trying not to inhale. 'I heard Milne was your man.'

'Hmph,' says Manners. 'Her Majesty isn't overly enamoured with Mr Milne's lions. Said they were heraldic but not heroic. Not that it's her choice, of course, but . . . you know.'

Edwin says nothing. Manners's secretary, George Russell, son of Edwin's barrister friend William, raises his eyebrows pointedly at him over a garish paisley handkerchief. What on earth is he trying to signal? Silently cursing the stink, Edwin attempts to convey his confusion with a brow twitch of his own, but it doesn't seem to work.

'There must have been others?' He gives up on eyebrow semaphore and gazes across the dusty square, up the sharply cut steps to the National Gallery, soot-streaked but still new enough to gleam in the dirty sunlight. So different from before – before this square, before this London – when the old King's mews stood there (make that the old, old King's). When it was home to menageries and coaching inns. It was here he'd waited for the coach to Woburn that first time, the first time he met Georgina. It smelled of shit then too, but, in his memories at least, it had a more wholesome quality. That's nostalgia for you.

'Ye-es, there were one or two others,' Manners says. 'But they weren't quite the thing either. As her Majesty's secretary put it: very like sculptures of lions, but not very like lions.'

By the fountains, a group of workmen are cooling off: splashing hands, faces, soaking their shirts. Edwin's stomach twists. A man tried to drown himself there last week. Poor devil was dragged out and given a self-righteous harangue on the wickedness of self-murder – as if he hadn't miseries enough. Surely the river would have been a safer bet? But perhaps in its present state it is too horrible. When choosing how to die, certainty isn't the only consideration.

'Sir Edwin?'

What has he missed? A furrow has appeared between George's eyebrows.

'Sorry, what?'

'Will you do it, Sir Edwin?'

'Do what?'

'Model the lions.'

In his surprise, Edwin takes a full lung's worth of foetid air, triggering a coughing fit that brings back the morning's headache. Hardly the response of a great artist, but it buys him some time. He manages to splutter that he's flattered, followed by something about his medium being canvas not clay.

'But surely you *can* work with clay?' Manners pulls out his watch. 'All we want you to do is produce the same effect in a model as you do in a picture.'

If Edwin were able to breathe, he'd laugh himself out of the commission here and now. All we want you to do . . . All! The man has no idea. As it is, he's forced to compose himself behind his handkerchief while Manners checks the time, tuts and says: 'The fact of the matter is we need this agreed before Parliament shuts up shop for the summer or we risk losing the funds. Her Majesty's hints have been clear, but if you won't do it, I shall have to offer it to Milne.'

Queasy after the coughing fit, Edwin glances again at the National Gallery, then back to the two government men. George's eyebrows are motionless.

'I'll need to think about it. I've not been well.' He should say no. He can feel Nelson behind him, peering down from his column, repeating the doctor's bleating warnings. But also a stirring of something else; a flicker of ambition he hasn't felt in years.

'You have one day,' says Manners.

* * *

'The sculptors will beat me to death with blunt chisels if I accept,' Edwin says to William Russell later.

'Devil take the sculptors.' William leans back, his cigar tip glowing red in the dusk. Its smoke mingles with the scent of roses that fills this part of Edwin's garden in St John's Wood, beyond the reach of the river stink. 'Do you want to do it?'

'Of course I do,' Edwin says, pushing both hands through his hair, encountering knots, tangles. When was the last time he brushed it? 'But people will say I only got the commission because the Queen put pressure on the Office of Works.'

'What if they do? Make the damn lions and make them too damned good to criticise. I'm sure Bell says the same?'

'He's not well. I don't want to bother him.' Edwin fixes his eyes on the shrinking scarlet band of sun to the west. Bell is unwell too often these days.

'I'm sorry to hear that.' There's a brief hiss of burning paper, another red glow, a trail of smoke quickly lost in the gloom. 'But you know he'd agree. This isn't any old commission. This won't be stuck away in some fellow's house or even in a gallery. And I can't think of a better way to impress your Scotch girl.'

'Not much at stake then.' Edwin takes the cigar from his friend's fingers and draws on it slowly. He wants to do it so badly, to show them all. William's right. But William doesn't know about the doctor's warning. Edwin hasn't told anyone apart from Bell. *No big commissions. Not until you get the drinking under control.* But he's been feeling stronger since then. Hardly been drunk at all. Maybe the quack was wrong? *It's no laughing matter, Sir Edwin. This will be the death of you if you don't fight it.* If he can win Caroline Stewart-Mackenzie around, have her at his side, surely that will help? And perhaps – he pushes it down, but the thought bursts back to the surface as he watches the smoke shift among the shadowed thorns – Caro's not the only one. A commission this big might be a last chance to show Rachel he's still worth something as an artist if not as a father. That's worth defying the doctor for.

After seeing William out, Edwin returns to the garden. He's no longer thinking of lions. Even the hopes he's been pinning on Caroline drain from his mind as he sinks onto the warped wooden bench. Above the old mulberry tree, the sky glitters with a spray of stars, like dewdrops on a moonlit fern. Only the most committed hypochondriacs fancy themselves cold enough to light fires in this weather and the heavens have benefitted. Tonight, the constellations are almost as clear as in Glenfeshie.

A glass rests coolly in his hand. Whisky. Almost the last of what he and Georgina brought back from their final visit to the Highlands.

He doesn't drink, simply lets the fumes rise and curl into his consciousness like music. Skeins of sweet barley and mellow malt dance above the dark drone of peat. They wind themselves around the scent of old roses – brought here as cuttings from Georgina's garden. The stars blur as Edwin's eyes moisten. A tear traces a warm path down his cheek. More moisture distorts and magnifies the waning moon.

'How could you leave me?' His voice shakes. 'I need you.'

The following morning, his sister, Jessie, and his housekeeper, Mrs Potter, are standing in the dining-room doorway, talking about him. His back to them, Edwin pulls a face as he sits hunched over the sunlit breakfast table.

'What is he doing?' says Mrs Potter in her sharp, nasal voice – as impudent in her fifties as she was at fifteen, when they first clashed in Woolly Simpson's Essex farmyard.

'Reading his tea leaves,' says Jessie. He'd bet a reasonable bottle of claret that she's wearing one of her long-suffering looks.

'I didn't know he could do that.' Mrs Potter's keys jingle, making the hairs on the back of Edwin's neck bristle.

'He can't. Not as far as I'm aware. He's got himself so wound up about these lions that he's even looking for signs from God. Or at least the god of tea – if there is one.' Jessie lets out a sigh, also of the long-suffering variety.

Clenching his teeth, Edwin tightens his grip on the finicky china cup handle, wondering if it will break.

'How long's he been at it?' Another jingle of keys. Edwin's ears itch with annoyance.

'Ten minutes? Perhaps a quarter hour?'

'I can hear you, you know,' he snarls. 'And – in case you've forgotten – this is my house, and I'll sit how I damn well please for as long as I damn well like.'

Mrs Potter draws herself up, masterfully combining a withering look with a perfunctory nod, and shifts a tray of empty bottles and cigar butts onto her hip before clinking off to the kitchen, trailing the scent of stale tobacco. Jessie follows her.

Edwin resumes his scrutiny of the cup. The tea leaves stubbornly refuse to resemble anything useful. The toast crumbs are equally unsympathetic. He can't bring himself to contemplate the ruins of the egg. He stretches out a finger, trying not to see the discoloured patches on the back of his hand, and pokes the unprophetic crumbs around until they resemble a lion. It is not a good lion. He must be a colossal fool to even consider trying to conjure one – no, four – in clay.

He'd almost decided to accept the commission the night before but the demons of the small hours had played havoc with his resolution. In his head, he'd been on a third draft of a letter to Manners agreeing to tackle the lions when paranoia weighed in with a barrage of arguments for both sides. Could he face the critics if he messed this up? Not just one humourless businessman grumbling, but the whole nation? And if he turned it down, wouldn't that be just as bad? Confirmation that he was used up aged only fifty-six, a relic of a bygone age who would be remembered – if at all – as popular but no genius.

*You'll be scurrying to the bottle either way,* the demons hissed, *and you know what that means. Slowly sipping your way to the grave. Or the lunatic asylum.*

The demons laughed. Edwin flung laudanum at them like holy water until they scuttled, muttering, back into the shadows. Then, as a murky yellow dawn began to seep around the bedroom curtains, he'd sunk into a drugged sleep.

The concoction of alcohol and opium has, as usual, left him feeling groggy. Gently obliterating the unfortunate toast lion, he reworks the crumbs into a woman's profile but that won't come right either. Jessie reappears with a pile of letters, catching him in the act of sweeping the whole mess onto the floor. Two canine faces peer hopefully around the sides of her skirts.

'Ned!' she snaps.

'The dogs will eat it – see, they already are.' Eyeing the envelopes suspiciously, he scratches Lassie, the young Scotch collie who is coming on so nicely, behind the ear. Topsey, the wirehaired terrier, is too intent on the scraps to want affection.

Jessie opens her mouth as if to speak, then appears to think better of it.

'What?' Edwin glares at her.

Glaring back, Jessie tucks a strand of sandy-grey hair under her linen cap.

'What?' he repeats, provocatively swiping more breakfast debris onto the floor, to the delight of the dogs.

Eyes rolling heavenwards, she takes a seat opposite him. 'You're impossible when you're like this.'

'You're impossible when you're like this,' Edwin mimics, sifting through the envelopes and ignoring her protests. He groans, first inwardly at one from the Office of Works in George Russell's hand, then outwardly at another from the same place in a more official script. With two deft flicks of the paper knife, he spills their innards onto the table. An examination produces no surprises: Her Majesty's Government, or England, or the public, or whoever it is that has this burning desire for lions, expects an answer today.

He can't think here. For all its high-ceilinged brightness, the room feels airless. The chairs and the table are hemming him in. Even the dust motes dancing by the long windows seem to take up too much space. He needs to clear his head. Standing abruptly, he collides with the table, making both Jessie and the plates jump, almost shaking the cups from their saucers. As the ceramic clatter subsides, his sister's expression is a study in patience.

'Sorry.' He runs a hand over his face.

'Where are you going?' She pours tea from her saucer back into her cup.

'To the zoo. I need to see the lions.'

Before leaving, he steals a final glance into his own cup. Maybe the rattling has spurred the contents into action. Nothing. No letter from Caroline Stewart-Mackenzie either.

Outside, the air is already heavy with stale heat. The Italianate house, with its white stuccoed walls and classically framed windows, skulks in its own shade. The animals currently in residence have cropped the grass to within an inch of its life, exposing brown, bald patches. The pony stares dolefully out from beneath a tree. Edwin returns its gaze with a mixture of sympathy and envy. Making for the side gate, he kicks at the cracks in the earth that widen each day, keeping his eyes on the puffs of dust so he doesn't have to contemplate the eyesore of a school they've built next door where the woods used to be. Maybe the cracks will grow so much he'll be able to crawl into one and hide.

He shouldn't be here. He should be in the Highlands, at Brahan. He would have been there a month ago and could have sorted everything out with Caro if it hadn't been for blasted Royal Academy politics. Why has she not written? Does she think he was making excuses? Is she offended that he's put the Academy before her?

Blinkered cab horses, glistening with sweat, trot on towards the stinking heart of London as he passes the Marylebone Cricket Club. Perspiration already beading beneath the brim of his hat, he swishes his cane against imaginary heather. Caro's last letter was everything he'd hoped for in all but one respect. She wished he could visit sooner and for longer and listed numerous matters of the arts and of the heart on which she held his views to be vital. But she dismissed his proposal of marriage as a joke.

Frustration boiling over, he kicks a large stone into the road, then winces at a sharp pain in his big toe. Damn it. Damn not being twenty-five any more. Damn everything. He limps on towards the entrance of the Regent's Park, through which the gates of the Zoological Society of London are now visible, and drags his mind back to lions.

The carnivore house stretches out like a parody of a palace. Its inhabitants, penned behind Greek columns and iron grilles, loll listlessly in their tiny cells. People mill about outside, gawping, the women in preposterously large skirts, the men with excessively bushy beards. Edwin pushes past, nods to one of the keepers. They all know him and his views on this place, not that they've done much to improve things. He must get Dickens back on the case. Everyone listens to Dickens.

The oldest of the lions tilts its head as Edwin strides up to the bars, then turns its amber eyes on him. Edwin takes in the grey-flecked muzzle, the old scars, the current sores, and the mane, matted but still majestic. An old thrill creeps over him, prickling from the nape of his neck to the base of his spine then the tips of his fingers and toes. The short hairs around the lion's nostrils ripple as it assesses him, whiskers twitching. What can it smell? Oil paint and alcohol? Tobacco and dogs? Is that all he is now?

The lion yawns, then grunts. Enough prevarication. Edwin's own nose wrinkles as the familiar, sweetly rancid breath washes over him. A memory flares: the Royal Menagerie in the Tower of London, seen through the eyes of an undersized boy with an oversized sketchbook. Open-mouthed at the beasts before him, he'd gripped the pencil so hard it jerked across the paper, leaving deep, dark dents that were impossible to erase. Though half a century has passed, he can still feel his father's fingers, gently closing over his own, resting there until he relaxed and was able to draw freely.

A low growl brings him back to the mocking amber gaze of the present.

'Don't be so impatient,' he mutters under his breath, flexing his fingers, switching his cane to the other hand. A young couple nearby pause in their romantic simpering and look at him warily. Perhaps the words hadn't been quite under his breath. As the lovers hurry away, the woman's crinoline swinging like a bell, another memory rises. This one as an adolescent, still small for his age: satchel slung across his back, heart thumping high in his chest, attempting a carefree swagger to get past the one-eyed porter at Cross's Menagerie on The Strand.

'Shouldn't you be in school, Master Landseer?'

'Absolutely not.'

A bark of laughter from the porter, then into the stifling gloom, where heaps of nosegays couldn't disguise the stomach-churning smell of raw meat and dung. Likewise, the farcical jungle scenes on the walls couldn't hide the fact that it was a prison. The beasts' bellows of impotent rage had terrified the horses in the street below and cut into Edwin's soul. The place made his skin crawl, but he'd adored its inmates and wanted nothing more than to draw them, again and again.

Pulling his mind forward forty years, he checks there are no more eavesdroppers.

'How about it?' he whispers. 'One last shot for me; immortality for you?'

The lion licks its yellowed teeth and snorts.

'If I'd wanted that sort of answer, I'd have stuck with tea leaves and toast,' Edwin hisses. Glowering at the beast and the few humans who have strayed near, he tugs out his watch with a twinge of guilt. Is there time for a drink before he goes to see Bell?

The lion snorts again. Stretching one rangy limb at a time, it stands, then shakes its matted mane. Out of the corner of his eye, Edwin sees a passing mother pull her child as close as her skirt will allow, but he remains motionless, watch open but eyes fixed on the wasted muscles beneath the sagging skin, on the old bones holding up the threadbare hide. His mind darts back to the flash of a knife blade, the rasping swish as it pares membranes from muscle, muscle from bone on the studio table. He knows these beasts inside and out: sculptor or not, he knows them better than any other artist in England. He snaps the watch shut.

A rumble emerges from deep within the lion, it rolls its head, opens its jaws, and lets out a roar so profound it vibrates through Edwin's own chest. For one second, two, three, he does not breathe. The smell, so indelibly ingrained, has released another memory, one he has been trying to keep locked up. They were here. Twenty-five years ago. Georgina to his left, hair still as dark as her eyes in those days, a six-year-old Rachel between them, honey-coloured curls shining beneath her bonnet and a new dress bright and white in the sun. She was standing on the tips of her toes to see better when a lion bared its teeth and roared. Shrieking with terrified delight, she had, for once, grabbed his hand, not Georgina's. Back then, he'd been amazed at the strength of his daughter's grip. He can still feel it now – on his hand and on his heart.

Fingers clenched around his antler-topped cane, knuckles white, he blinks, forces himself to breathe.

'All right, damn you. I'll do it. But first I have to convince a Scotswoman to marry me.'

The lion licks its teeth again, slumps down onto its side, and falls asleep.

Edwin rattles his bedroom window open and drinks in woodlands and freshwater lochs that surround Brahan Castle. The breeze slips inside his collar and caresses his neck as he takes in the green of the lawn, the whispering leaves, and the hazy blue of the Ross-shire hills beyond. London, with its August ennui, lions, doctors, and deadlines, might no longer exist. But there's no hint of the hoped-for carriage wheels.

He arrived at Brahan over an hour ago and there's still no sign of Caro. Having spent the coach ride from Inverness composing and recomposing earnest marriage proposals, Edwin was more than a little put out to find she'd gone with her mother to visit Lord Baring, the recently widowed owner of the neighbouring estate.

A midge whines by his ear, sending the wrong sort of shiver down his spine. Batting it away, he turns to the loose-hinged looking glass. Staring back at him is a gentleman of not inconsiderable distinction, unable, or unwilling, to rid himself of the air of a naughty schoolboy. A few days on the Northumbrian moors on the way here have restored a veneer of health, even if the late summer sun has woven more white hairs into the grey. If he squints, he can still see a few threads of the old gold.

The sound of hooves and wheels crunching over the driveway pulls his gaze back to the window. That must be her.

Deep breath.

Bracing himself, he descends the panelled staircase, glancing at the indifferent portrait of Caro's long-deceased father, bowing to Lawrence's romantic likeness of her formidable mother, then lets himself into the drawing room. A fire mutters and fizzes in the grate, split logs and strips of turf shifting as though making themselves comfortable. There's no visible human presence, but air currents carry conversations and cooking smells that mingle with the prattle of cracking bark and the scent of peat.

On a table by a window lie pencils, paper, and a book, weighted open, spine straining. Edwin makes his way over via a sideboard that boasts a spectrum of amber-filled decanters.

They clink as he lifts one. Just a small drink, for courage. Sipping so his glass doesn't overflow, he glances at a sketch on the table. It's Caro's style: a study of ivy – not bad. The book is Ruskin's *Modern Painters*. Twirling a pencil between his fingers, he flicks to a scathing comment about one of his own pictures, tempted to give it a good edit. But the sound of female voices on the other side of the door smothers the impulse to mischief. Caro would almost certainly have failed to see the funny side in any case.

He slides his empty glass behind a marble bust. Brandy slips down his throat; fire and fear seep into his stomach. The voices – very close now – are those of Caro and her mother.

'... I'm thirty-one years old. Don't talk to me like a child. I'm not treating this lightly.'

The brass knob turns, clunks. The door opens.

'You never treat anything lightly, my dear, that's the problem—' Mrs Stewart-Mackenzie, steel-haired and statuesque, stops short as she sees him, lips pursed. Next to her, just as tall, but less forbidding, stands Caro; her large, dark eyes briefly widen with what he hopes is surprise not shock.

'Sir Edwin! We didn't expect you for another hour at least.' Crossing the room, eyes smiling now, she offers him both hands. Relief chases the brandy through his veins.

'I thought I wrote with the time?' His thumbs slide across her smooth palms, and there's a quick return of pressure before she withdraws them, throwing a look at her mother.

'Oh, I expect you did,' she adjusts the ribbon in her dark hair, 'I am sorry. I hope someone showed you your room? It's such a whirl – poor Lord Baring. He's so lost without Harriet. Mama and I have agreed to help when his guests come next week. He's dining here tonight and will be delighted you've arrived. But I am sorry to have neglected you. Will you come and see the gardens and tell me all your news before I go and dress?'

As they make their way down the stone steps to the lawn, Caro looks solemnly into his eyes.

'How are you? Really? You know you don't need to pretend with me.' Before Edwin can answer, she slips her arm through his, adding, 'I can't believe how beastly the newspapers have been about you and your lions, saying you are a terrible choice and—'

'Thank you.' He cuts her off. An account of Fleet Street's views on his flaws isn't an ideal preliminary to a proposal, even by his standards. 'They're not all bad.' He'd been relieved they weren't worse, but her words send a cold trickle of doubt into his thoughts. He blinks it away. 'I've told my sister to feed them to the goats.'

'Oh, you don't have goats now, do you?' A look of horror momentarily distorts her fine features.

'No. But I might get one if the newspapers don't improve.' He can't help grinning at her alarm. A story about the laundry-eating herd Georgina kept in the glen is on the tip of his tongue, but he catches himself just in time.

'Are you sure you're up to it?' Caro says, as they pause to take in the view of the loch.

'A goat?'

She gives him another grave look. It would be a perfect moment. He must stop talking about goats. She might not understand his jokes, but she looks at him like this – as though he matters. And, if he matters to someone so young and beautiful, he can't be completely used up.

'Be serious,' Caro says. 'Are you sure you're up to the lions?'

'Of course I am.' A midge crosses the space between them. 'They've said I don't have to start until spring. Plenty of time to get things in order.' Heart hammering, he pushes Georgina's goats away. 'But there's one thing that would help: one person ...'

Caro brushes aside a strand of hair that the bracken-scented breeze has blown across her face. Her lips drift apart. More midges appear. The old zoo lion flashes into Edwin's mind. Why did she have to ask if he was up to it? He hesitates. It costs him dearly. Mrs Stewart-Mackenzie's voice sails across the lawn.

'Caroline! Lord Baring has arrived.' She looks down on them like an ancient chieftainess, leaning on her stick, shawl fluttering in the breeze.

Cheeks blazing, Caro gives Edwin an apologetic look.

'Caro, in my last letter ...' He grasps at the phrases he assembled earlier, but they fall apart.

'Yes?' She swipes at the midges. Her gaze doesn't leave his.

Mrs Stewart-Mackenzie is still surveying them from the house.

He can't do it.

'It can wait,' he says. 'Go.' He blinks back an image of Georgina shooing a goat away from the washing line. There will be a better time.

Three days later, Caro is sketching by the drawing-room window and Edwin's thoughts are goat free. It would be perfect for another attempt at a proposal, but for the fact that he is trapped on a sofa with an elderly lady writer and a silver teapot that's seen better days.

'I've said it before, Sir Edwin, you're too cruel in your subjects,' says Mrs Jameson, a fiercely good-natured critic and an old friend. She is on one of her favourite hobbyhorses, having exhausted his thoughts on lions the previous evening.

'Blame nature, not me.' Edwin's eyes wander to the decanters, where the afternoon sunlight breaks apart as it hits their crystal sides.

'Nature has beauty and joy too. You are free to choose which to paint, surely?' She extends her top lip, camel-like, into the interior of her cup and slurps.

'Only to a point.' Edwin's tea has gone cold. He is sick of tea. 'People love the sorrow. Tragedy sells.'

Mrs Jameson tuts. 'You used to paint such beautiful pictures: children, families, such happiness. They sold too. I see prints everywhere I go. Your *Drovers' Departure* is still one of my favourites. That young father gazing down at the babe in his arms as he takes his leave of her, the lovers' fond farewells. There's sorrow, yes, but you sweeten it perfectly with the promise of joyful reunions. Why no more like that?'

'The drovers are gone. The children are grown and gone.' His cup rattles in its saucer as he places it on the table, refusing to let his thoughts go down that path.

'But the paintings remain beautiful. "A thing of beauty is a joy forever" as poor Mr Keats put it.' Mrs Jameson smiles triumphantly.

'I wish that were true.' Edwin twists a button on his jacket and endeavours to catch Caro's eye for the thousandth time, but she's intent on her drawing.

'Oh, so cynical.' Mrs Jameson regards him over the brim of her apparently bottomless cup, top lip limbering up for another slurp.

'Not cynical – honest. Keats wrote that when he was twenty-two, twenty-three? I forget.' Edwin drums his fingers on his knee. 'If he'd been doomed to live to my age, he'd have had a different idea of forever. And of beauty.' This is the last thing he wants to discuss. He glances at Caro again.

'Pshaw, pshaw! I'm twenty years older than you, and I say you're wrong. But I shan't argue.'

Lifting the teapot, she feels its side as though checking for a pulse. An expression of deep disappointment settling on her face, she rings the bell for a servant who will bring more damned tea. 'Tell me, Mr Landseer, I mean Sir Edwin, lions apart, what are you working on?'

'A Highland scene,' he says. Caro looks up as the clock chimes the half-hour. 'A pair to that droving picture you like so much, as it happens.'

'Is it joyful?'

'Not remotely.' He usually enjoys teasing her as much as she relishes nettling him, but there's no time. 'It's a flood. A terrible one. I started it during that awful winter back in forty-four but put it aside.'

Caro puts down her pencil and leans back, looking quizzically at her work.

'Why resume it now?' Mrs Jameson rings the bell again, placing her hand back on the side of the teapot in case by some miracle it should have regained its pluck.

Edwin feigns nonchalance, shrugs. 'Something I read in a novel.'

'Oh, do tell. By whom?'

'Lady Rachel Butler.' The name is still strange. Sticks on his tongue. Don't think of her. Not now. His eyes dart from the older woman to the younger, who is stretching her shoulders, about to rise.

'I don't think I'm familiar with—'

'She was a Russell.' He cuts her off. 'Married two years ago.' It was a mistake to talk about this. He shakes his head, tries to disperse the memories that are creeping in. A maid enters. Caro pushes back her chair, stands. 'Mrs Jameson, I'm sorry to break off our talk, but there's something I must speak to Caroline about before I leave tomorrow. Do come and see the picture in London, please. I'll paint a spark of joy into it, just for you.'

Escaping the clutches of the sofa, he blows the old camel a kiss, narrowly avoids tripping over the maid, and succeeds in catching Caro by the elbow before she reaches the door.

'Caro – Miss Stewart-Mackenzie – some air?' he says, embarrassingly breathless.

'I have to dress ...' Her gaze strays briefly to the window then back to him, her cheeks reddening.

'Just a breath or two. The quickest. I promise.'

On the lawn, the air is thick with the sounds of birds gossiping, the warm hum of bees, and midges packed as densely as the crowds on opening day at the Royal Academy's Summer Exhibition. Tone cool, heart racing, Edwin takes Caro's hands.

'This might seem a bit sudden but,' deep breath, keep looking at her, ignore the audience of insects, 'I ... I don't suppose you'd consider becoming Lady Landseer?'

Her beautiful stately features crumple like a letter thrown into the fire.

'Is it that terrible a prospect?' Edwin's stomach twists but he forces himself to laugh, waving away the midges which are attempting to shower him with the kisses he'd hoped for from her. 'I can promise not to get a goat if that would help?'

After a succession of deep breaths and sighs, Caro places a hand on his arm.

'It's not that. It's just ... I didn't think you would ever want to marry. Not after Georgina. That you couldn't mean it ... when you proposed to that French painter, you told me that was a joke?'

'That *was* a joke.' He manages another laugh, almost succeeds in keeping the exasperation out of it. 'Everyone knows Mademoiselle Bonheur is married at least three times over to her art, and as good as married to Mademoiselle Micas. It was a lark to wind up the critics. She thought it a good bit of sport. I told you that.' He hadn't told her how drunk he'd been. But he wasn't drunk now. 'Things have changed. I've changed. You've changed me.'

'I'm sorry.' She buries her face in her hands. For a moment, her bowed head and the curve of her exposed neck are painfully like Georgina. Edwin swallows hard. Gently, he stretches a hand around her shoulders, pulling up her shawl to protect the smooth skin from their airborne audience.

'I did write to explain, but I must have done a poor job,' he says. 'I'm in earnest. Entirely. I don't know what I'd have done without you these past few years. You remember how I was when ... God knows how you put up with me – all the bosh I talk and write. But you were the most beautiful and kindest of stars, when all the others had gone dark. See, I'm talking bosh again. You'd better say something to stop me.'

'I just ... oh, why now? I can't think!'

'Can I at least hope? Or should I pack up my things and drown myself in goats?'

'Oh, no!' She grasps his hand. 'I need time to ...' Her gaze flicks to the house. 'I need to discuss it with Mama.' She blinks rapidly. 'She's been unwell. She's still not strong. I don't know if I can leave her. It's so ... so complicated. You do understand?'

He nods, shrugs, wipes a midge from his eye. At least she's taking him seriously.

'You're coming to Lord Baring's in October, aren't you? May I give you an answer then?' She looks at him with those eyes that make him matter.

'Of course.' Edwin smiles through clenched teeth. 'At least the midges should be gone by then.'

Unable to hold her gaze, he fixes his eyes on the loch, refusing to listen to the voice in his head telling him it's hardly the reaction of a woman in love.

One hundred miles south of Brahan and more than a month further into autumn, Edwin is nestled in a heather-filled hollow in Perthshire, back braced against a moss-covered boulder, damp just beginning to penetrate the seat of his rough woollen trousers. The broad end of his telescope rests on one knee, the other hovers cold and hard in front of his right eye, framing a group of red deer on the opposite side of the valley.

The October air is not yet properly cold but the droplets of rain landing on his cheek have a wintry bite. Beside him, James Hamilton, Marquis of Abercorn and Groom of the Stole to Prince Albert, stretches his long, tweed-clad legs. A friend of half a lifetime and married to Georgina's daughter Louisa, he's one of the few people Edwin can really talk to. A little way off, a ghillie sits scanning the slopes with his own telescope, a deerhound crouching behind him next to the rifles.

'Had a letter from Louisa this morning,' Abercorn says, pulling his plaid more tightly around his broad shoulders. 'She sends her love, thanks you for the picture.'

'How is she? And the baby?' Edwin asks, not taking his eye from the deer, itching to sketch them, to calm his thoughts of Caro and lions, but it's too damn damp. 'How many is that you have now? Twenty?'

'Thirteen,' laughs Abercorn. 'Mother and infant in exceptionally fine form, thank you.'

'Glad to hear it,' Edwin says, adjusting the telescope as the deer wander up the hill into the wind. 'Send her my love back.'

'Of course,' Abercorn says, the long, woody stems of the older heather creaking as he shifts position. He clears his throat. 'She also wrote that Rachel was safely delivered of another baby Butler. Last week. Thought you'd like to know.'

Edwin's view through the glass jerks then yaws like a ship in a squall.

'A girl. They've named her Grace.' Abercorn hands him a hip flask. Whisky rages at the back of his throat and tumbles into his chest.

'Listen, Lanny, come to us in Ireland for Christmas. We'll get Rachel up too, from Dublin.'

'She won't want to see me.' Edwin takes another swig.

'You don't know that. She'll come around. She's always adored you.'

'That was before she knew I was her father.'

Abercorn is about to say something else but Edwin cuts him off, snapping his telescope shut.

'And I can't spare the time. Too many unfinished pictures and now lions to wrestle with.'

'Ah, of course.' Abercorn sounds unconvinced but doesn't challenge him. Instead, he says: 'And the talk is that you're about to bring an end to perpetual bachelorhood? Louisa wasn't sure whether to believe it.'

'I'll let you know next week,' Edwin says through tight lips, fiddling with the leather strap of his telescope case. It's six weeks since he left Caro and he's had barely a line from her, though that's not unusual. For her. But what if she does say no? The face of the old lion flashes before his eyes, licking its teeth and he shivers as a gust of wind brings more stinging rain from the head of the glen.

A few days later, Edwin is back in the North. This close to winter, darkness falls early and fast and has already enveloped Lord Baring's Lochluichart estate by the time he arrives. Dressing hurriedly for dinner, he makes it to the drawing room just in time to steady his nerves with a sherry. Caro's taking her role as understudy-hostess seriously, attending to each knot of guests with self-conscious gravity. A brief apologetic glance is all she can spare him before she is borne away to the dining room on Baron Baring's arm.

They're placed on the same side of the table but several chairs apart. Courses stretch, conversation drags, Edwin catches only glimpses of her, supplemented by bright snatches of her speech between the duller remarks of his immediate neighbours. A note of excitement lightens her usual tone. If only he could see her face.

At length, led jointly by Caro and her mother, the women leave, and port, brandy, and hunting talk take their place. Edwin drums his fingers on the stem of his glass. Baring, looking more chipper than he has in a long while, strokes his moustache and tells an interminable fishing story. It finally ends in a broken rod and victory for the fish, producing a chorus of polite laughter and mumbled hints for bottle-passing from the other banker barons and industrial knights around the table. Too loudly, Edwin mutters that all stories these days are about 'ones that got away' and is challenged to tell something that ends differently. With a fresh brandy and a flourish he doesn't feel, he rattles through a tale of treacherous sheep, snowdrifts, and a lucky shot. He gets a hearty response, but his thoughts are elsewhere, impatient, and increasingly uneasy. It's a relief when Baring, an odd smile showing through his black-and-white beard, suggests they rejoin the ladies.

As they cross the hall, Edwin overhears him tell the butler to bring the champagne. A chill begins to seep through the mantle of talk and drink. In the drawing room, Caro stands by the fireplace. He hadn't noticed earlier, but her dress is a particularly fine silk he hasn't seen before, and the Mackenzie diamonds, which she's worn only once previously in his presence, glitter at her ears and neck. They're insubstantial compared with those Georgina used to wear, but still flash brilliantly as Caro turns her head at Baring's entrance. A shiver runs across Edwin's shoulders. Caro does not look at him.

Standing next to her, the widower calls for silence. Caro places a hand on his arm and, with a tenderness that freezes Edwin to the core, Baring covers it with his own.

It's as though Edwin's watching the rest of the scene through a wall of ice.

When it's over, he somehow makes it out onto the terrace. One hand loosely holds a cigar that Baring has just pressed on him with ghastly exuberance and even insisted on lighting from his own. The other clings to a glass of brandy. He refused champagne.

The golden glow of the party shrinks to the narrowest of chinks as shutters clatter closed. There are soft, slippered footsteps on the flagstones; Caro stands before him, clutching her shawl to her bosom.

'Congratulations.' Edwin spits the word out, takes a slug of brandy. It tastes of nothing.

'I'm sorry. I-I wanted to tell you myself, but W-William wanted to announce it tonight ... and you were late and I couldn't think how ...'

'No, I shouldn't imagine the words trip off the tongue,' Edwin snaps, forcing down a lump in his throat. 'Why on earth did you let me believe I had a chance?'

'I didn't know he was going to ask me.'

'So that makes it all right, does it?' He tries to draw on the cigar, but it has gone out.

Caro shakes her head, keeping her eyes down.

'What was it? The money? The title? Makes up for the fact that he's even older than I am, I suppose.' He throws the cigar to the ground, stamps on it.

'Don't ...' She looks up, eyes reflecting the last threads of candlelight.

'Why the hell shouldn't I?' Edwin snarls. 'Did I ever have a chance? Or were you playing me for a fool the whole time?' His fingers grip the stem of the glass, almost willing it to break. 'Did you think inviting me would put a rocket up him? Force his hand?'

'You don't understand. Don't be like this, please.'

'If old badger-beard moneybags hadn't come along, would you have accepted me?'

'Don't call him that. Don't ask me that.'

'I am asking you.' The brandy is gone, the hot path it traces inside him the only warmth.

'Edwin, stop it. Please.'

He starts to shiver, can't stop. 'Would you?'

There's an agonising pause, then she says softly, 'No.'

At length, he hears himself say, 'Why not?'

She hesitates, pulling her thin shawl tighter over her shoulders. 'I . . . I could love you – I think I really could – but I don't think you will ever really love me.' Her voice hardens. 'And I won't be a substitute for Georgina.'

'But you'll step into Harriet Baring's shoes while they're still warm? She's barely been dead a year. Your oh-so-gallant lover in there is still devastated. You've told me so yourself God knows how many times.'

'Yes, but he's accepted that she's gone.' She bites her lip, takes a step backwards. 'And he doesn't drink.'

Edwin laughs. It sounds like glass breaking. 'Rubbish! He's in there right now soaking his moustaches in champagne.'

A tear glints on Caro's cheek.

'You want me to drink less? I can drink less.' Edwin glares at the empty glass in his hand. 'Dammit! What do you think I am?'

Caro won't look at him.

Weeks later, the memory of that night still feels like a bruise on Edwin's brain: blooming in dark, brooding tones; bleeding into the surrounding matter; excruciatingly tender if touched, even by well-meant sympathy.

Since returning to London, he's spent the days in the studio – painting furiously and drinking strong China tea – or wandering aimlessly around his fog-bound gardens, watching the dogs chase the last leaves spiralling through the dank November air, pulling wilting petals from late roses. Evenings have been filled with concerned friends determined to cheer him up. Other than Jacob Bell, they never admit their reluctance to leave him alone, but their eyes give it away, as do their quiet conversations with Jessie when they think he isn't looking.

Nights have been bad.

Yesterday afternoon, he sent Jessie to Bell's shop for more laudanum. Yesterday evening, Bell returned the visit, bringing the drug in person, looking him in the eye.

'Are you all right, Lanny? Come and stay with me if you need to. I will never mind.'

He'll have given Jessie a lecture about the laudanum too.

At times the studio is a sanctuary; at times it's a prison. Built to his own specifications, it's high-ceilinged, stark, and dark. On better days, soft, natural light falls through the oversized window in the centre of the long north wall. Today, the fog is so dense he's had the gas lamps lit since breakfast. Their hissing is driving him mad, and, bright as they are, they leave deep shadows in the corners where studies, sketches, and abandoned canvasses are stacked. At the far end of the room, near where the Queen's blasted Balmoral boat picture lurks, a weighted velvet curtain covers a stable door. When he imagines escaping, this is the door through which he sees himself fleeing.

Despite the coals smouldering behind him, his breath forms clouds. The white marble clock on the mantlepiece is at least a quarter hour slow – it never was very good at timekeeping, even when it sat in Georgina's sitting room – but still shows the morning's almost over. Edwin tells himself for the thousandth time that he should be able to close the book on Caro, put her behind him. Nothing has really changed in practice, only in expectation. It doesn't help. The hope of having someone with him in the future had made the present bearable.

Taking a palette from the top of a low mahogany cabinet, he slides a pair of spectacles onto his nose and squints at the picture on the large easel – the Highland flood. How could he have misread Caro so badly? She'd been so tender, so understanding, even possessive. How had gouty old Baring crept in and swept her off in a mere few weeks? Selecting a fine brush, he checks its bristles against the light, then coats it carefully in an unctuous, bitter blue. But, bringing it to the canvas, he can't steady his hand. Not for the first time, one thought sidles its way in front of the others: maybe it wasn't just a few weeks.

Inside the cabinet is a bottle of brandy. He wouldn't say it's hidden, but nobody else knows it's there. The palette rattles on the wood as he lays it back down. The brush rolls away; he tries to catch it but only succeeds in getting paint on his fingers. It leaves a forlorn smudge on the floorboards. He doesn't reach to pick it up. Instead, he watches his hand resting on the door that contains the spirit. The lamps hiss. The clock ticks.

Taking a deep breath, he drags his hand from the door and marches himself to the far end of the room.

He searches fervently through the stacks of sketches for God knows what. It's not that he wants to be drinking all the time, just a little more than the daily two glasses of port that sour-faced Doctor Tweedie says won't hurt. It's like with Caro: expectation is the thing. The promise, the hope even, of a drink. Not having the possibility drains what little colour is left from the dreary winter days. And the newspapers don't help, printing more on his unfitness for the Nelson lions. He's told Jessie to buy a goat. Lions, lions . . . lion studies – that's what he needs. Lions still have colour. Somewhere over here should be the old big cat sketches. He must find his dissection drawings too. He'll show them all. Drink or no drink. Caro or no Caro.

There's a noise at the door. Thinking it's one of the dogs scratching to get in, he strides over and opens it. And is confronted by Caro, with droplets of fog clinging to her cloak and bonnet, removing her gloves.

Edwin pulls off his spectacles.

The hissing and ticking intensify.

'You have paint. Here.' The cool, smooth tip of her forefinger caresses his temple. Her voice is steady but her lower lip trembles. She strokes the spot a second time. Before she can make it a third, he catches her wrist and, reluctantly, pulls her hand away.

'Lady Baring.'

The wedding took place a week ago – barely a month after the announcement at Lochluichart.

'Your sister said you were in here.' She speaks quickly, blushing, eyes fixed on his. 'I'm alone. My mother is too unwell to pay calls.'

'And your husband?' He's still holding her wrist. Why hadn't Jessie turned her away?

'His gout is worse. He cannot go out either.' She hesitates, then adds, 'Is this the flood picture?' She tries to curl her fingers around his hand. He drops her arm.

'Yes.' He watches her flinch as her gaze runs over the canvas. 'Why are you here?'

'I wanted to see the picture.'

'Why are you really here?'

'I had to see you.' She turns back to him. 'I can't bear to think of you hating me.' She reaches for his face again. As before, he catches her wrist, but this time can't bring himself to push her away.

'I don't hate you,' he says softly, letting her rest her hand in his.

The clock chimes an hour that passed some time ago.

'I keep thinking how awful you must be feeling,' she says, eyes like Highland pools. 'The thought of you here, alone . . .'

'I've felt better,' he says. Hope flickers in his chest as compassion sweeps over her face, but he won't let her think him pathetic. 'But I'm not alone. There's nothing like misfortune to bring in the invitations. Even my models – the human ones, that is – are asking me to parties. They haven't done that in years.'

'Oh.' A furrow creases Caro's brow.

'Yes. Annie Gilbert even asked me to her birthday.'

The furrow deepens. 'The courtesan?'

He lowers her wrist but does not let go. 'She trains horses and teaches spoilt Society ladies how to ride them. And she's damned good at it. And she's been damned good to me.'

Caro drops her gaze, her hand closing on his. The scent of violets mixes with the fumes of paint and gas. The tips of her fingers reach beneath the cuff of his smock. A shiver snakes up to his elbow.

'I don't think I'll go, though,' he says. 'Courtesans or not, Annie's friends are a little fast for me, sober as I am these days.'

That makes her look up. 'You've stopped drinking?'

'I'm trying.' The ticking and hissing seem louder than ever. He is trying.

She presses his hand, lower lip quivering. 'What if I was wrong? What if I've made a terrible mistake?' Her voice is barely a whisper. 'We leave for France soon. I don't know how long we shall be gone but . . . will you promise not to hate me when I return?'

Damn hope. Damn desire. Bloody Baring. 'Of course.' He presses her close, longing for the touch he's missed so much, his lips brushing her cheek, the scent of violets . . . it's not right. Damn it all.

That evening, Edwin hauls himself to the National Gallery. Royal Academy business waits for no broken hearts or addled heads. After a couple of hours gazing listlessly at a marble greyhound behind the president's chair, he's no wiser as to the cause of the latest panic. Government grumbling about money? Critics carping about standards? Pamphleteers complaining of too many nudes, or is it not enough nudes? Or all of these? It makes no difference. He's so tired.

By the time he leaves, the air in Trafalgar Square has congealed into a murky miasma. Figures loom on the steps and lurch between the dark, dormant fountains; lanterns hover like fireflies; muffled sounds of feet – human and horse – come from everywhere and nowhere.

He makes his way across to the Nelson column. The admiral's invisible. The rest of the square has also vanished. He stares at the empty pedestals, willing himself to see lions there but the past pushes its way through the mist, blotting out future, and present. His body still aches with the echo of Caro's parting embrace, but it's Georgina who swirls through his mind. He closes his eyes and retreats: away from the clammy fog on his face; away from the square, the column, the pedestals; back to the cacophony of the Golden Cross coaching inn that stood here almost forty years ago.

# *August 1819, London*

A DUST-COVERED COACH THUNDERED into Golden Cross yard. Shouts went up that it was the Manchester mail and it was mobbed for news of the riots before even the sweating horses or overdue mailbags were seen to.

Edwin drummed his fingers on his satchel and wrinkled his nose at a waft of dung, sour ale, and acrid pipe smoke. The news made his stomach lurch: hundreds hurt, dead even, soldiers breaking up a meeting of mill workers wanting votes. It was the last thing he needed. He was nervous enough already.

He tried to shut out the yells of grooms, porters, and hawkers, the whinging of other would-be passengers, and stared at his reflection in the dirty tavern window. Would they take him seriously? His new tall hat added a vital few inches of height and almost tamed his honey-coloured curls, his coat was also new – his father had been grumbling about the cost all week – and his cravat was tied with unprecedented neatness (his older sister Jane had laughed so hard at being asked to tie it she'd nearly choked). Did he look more than a tousle-headed boy with a knack for painting pets?

With a cannonade of hooves, another coach clattered in, horses skittering to a halt at a chorus of 'woahs'. Seven o'clock, declared the bells of St Martin-in-the-Fields. George Hayter was late. Edwin glanced again at his reflection in the warped glass.

'Vanity, vanity, Little Ned!' George's voice sailed over his shoulder. Its owner – the most successful and most scandalous of the painters' children Edwin had grown up with – flicked a speck of straw from Edwin's new jacket, then smiled conspiratorially, saying, 'Let's catch you a duke.'

The only seats left on the Woburn coach were on top. Edwin ducked as it rumbled through the perilously low archway into the evening traffic on The Strand. Though George grumbled, Edwin never minded being an outside passenger. As a child, packed off to spend summers in Essex with Jane in charge, he'd merrily told her he loved it because it felt like flying, and people looked so different from above, all hats and hands. Jane smiled patiently, saying she loved it because he was less likely to vomit in the open air than seated inside. At the age of seventeen, both considerations were still important, not that he cared to admit either.

'You met the Duke at the Summer Exhibition, didn't you?' George said, inspecting his nails.

'Yes.' Edwin gripped the wooden rail as the coach swung around a corner. The trunks and boxes behind them strained at their moorings. 'I'm amazed you found time to present me between being rude about every Academician within earshot.'

'You say that as though it were a bad thing? They're far ruder about me.' George laughed and sat up straighter. 'But forget them. Forget the damned Royal Academy. Forget that ghastly business in Manchester. Just concentrate on getting this visit right. The Duke of Bedford might look like one of life's inveterate bumblers, but he's sharper than a sabre and has enormous clout. He's hardly a social butterfly – he leaves that to the Duchess – but if he likes you, he's loyal. If he hadn't set me up in Rome, I would have been ruined by the scandal with Sarah.'

And by a few other things, Edwin thought, but kept it to himself, rubbing the worn leather strap on his satchel between his finger and thumb, watching pigeons streak across the sky to roost. George was ten years his senior, and his father had been muttering about him being a bad influence for as long as Edwin could remember. But even John Landseer couldn't deny George's talent for toadying to the wealthy and well-connected.

'The Duke has an eye for pictures and for painters,' George continued. 'There are always several would-be Michelangelos buzzing around Woburn, but few with as much talent as you.'

'I didn't think you did compliments,' Edwin said, twisting the satchel strap around his forefinger and hiding a blush by gazing down at an enormous Newfoundland dog leading a footman along the side of the road.

'I'm serious. This could make you, Ned. I don't need to tell you that the real power over art in this country is with men like the Duke: they pay, they pull strings – or cut them; they make the fashion.' George leant back on the luggage pile, tilting his hat to shade his eyes from the low sun. 'But if you'd rather spend the rest of your life painting pugs for old women and gundogs for fat squires, you can get off at the next change.'

'Point taken.' Edwin shuddered at the thought of the last fat squire.

The coach trundled on. As the roads cleared, the clatter of hooves softened. New terraces of houses gave way to straggling streets, then fields, farms, and clusters of cottages. Sheep and cattle watched them disinterestedly. The rays of the sinking sun were caught between quicksilver clouds and fields of hayricks. Manchester riots seemed a world away. Even the most rotten, tumbledown thatched cottages looked picturesque. Edwin was still nervous.

It was past midnight by the time the driver dropped them on the edge of the small town of Woburn. The Duke's carriage was waiting. Black and lacquered, it gleamed like a beetle in the light of the gate lodge lamps. An owl screeched as George nodded to a liveried coachman and they climbed inside, where they were met by padded seats and the scents of leather, polish, and cologne.

'Tell me, did I introduce you to the Duchess?' George said as they rolled forward.

'No,' Edwin said, eyes caught by a stone lion on top of the retreating gatepost.

'Oh,' a smile crept over George's shadowed face, 'she's another thing entirely. Get yourself in favour with her and you're made. But for Christ's sake don't annoy her. Don't try to be clever. Or cocky. Know your place.'

'That's rich from you,' Edwin muttered as they drove on through indistinct parkland. Picturing a spectrum of gorgon-like duchesses, he squinted at a group of animals whose eyes flared briefly in the lamplight: too many to be foxes, too low for cattle, but too high for sheep – deer?

'Pull your head away from that window. You look like a dog.' George yawned. 'And it's all Repton.'

'What?' Edwin withdrew a little but continued to stare out into the night.

'The grounds. Humphrey Repton's finest work, apparently, though the Duke was inches from his elbow for most of it. If you want something to flatter him about, tell him how much you like it.'

'Thanks. I'll tell him it's so good it's even picturesque in the dark,' Edwin said.

Ignoring a sarcastic laugh, he leant out of the window again just as the house came into view: a vast hulk of slumbering stone crouching above the silky blackness of a lake. The moon broke free from the clouds, sending a streak of silver rippling across water and windowpanes. Edwin gripped the cold brass buckle of his satchel; he'd worried the strap so much it was in danger of falling off.

'Relax,' said George, leaning back. Edwin could have kicked him but took a deep breath and asked if there would still be anyone about.

'I should think so. They're fond of late hours, especially when there's political drama brewing. Politics is their favourite game.'

They followed an unimpressed footman down a half-lit stone corridor. Pictures, statues, and vases were dimly visible as they swept past, footsteps echoing into the shadows. Even in the darkness, it was palatial – a thousand times grander than the manor house of the strawberry-nosed squire whose dog had been Edwin's last commission. Unable to fidget with his satchel, which had been taken to his room, Edwin twisted a button on his waistcoat. George checked his reflection in a window, pushing a hand through his hair. Coming to a heel-clicking halt, the footman flicked open a pair of double-height doors leading to a small drawing room. A burst of light bounded out, making Edwin blink, and a gust of colder air rushed in from behind them, brushing his ears on its way past.

Candle flames flickered and bowed but the conversation within barely missed a beat. The draught pushed between the pendants of a chandelier, caressed the long earrings of a woman curled on the sofa beneath it, lifted a wisp of thinning hair on the head of a young man next to her, and, finally, ruffled some sheet music on a piano by an open window, before rushing out into the darkness. Almost hidden in the shadows on the far side of the instrument, a female figure reached out to stop the papers following the draught into the night. Lit by the moon, her bowed head, exposed neck and shoulders formed a silver swanlike curve against the blackness.

Edwin's waistcoat button came away in his hand. He cursed under his breath. So much for looking smart.

The woman on the sofa flicked a brief, catlike glance at him, then smoothed the silk of her dress over her heavily pregnant stomach and turned her gaze to a balding man of middle age and not quite middle height. She smiled sweetly, saying, 'You'd allow the mob to vote? Madness. How can you not see?'

Shaking his shining head, the man's glance fell on George and Edwin, who almost dropped the button. Tufts of light brown hair encircled the smooth scalp and nestled behind the man's ears like a laurel wreath, giving him the air of a benevolent Caesar: John Russell, sixth Duke of Bedford. Edwin felt another button come loose. Small eyes crinkling into a smile, the Duke excused himself, crossed the room, and shook George vigorously by the hand.

'Your Grace.' George bowed. 'I've brought you my young animal-painting friend, Mr Edwin Landseer.'

As Edwin bent so low his head was almost level with the buckles at the knees of the Duke's breeches, George added: 'Or the little dog boy, as he's known at the Royal Academy Schools.'

Cheeks burning furiously, but forcing a smile, Edwin straightened up; George smirked and licked his lips.

'An interesting sobriquet, Mr Landseer,' the Duke said, nodding to the footman.

'Yes, Your Grace,' Edwin said, heart pounding but damned if he would give George the satisfaction of appearing bothered. 'The curse of being the youngest. It's a devil to shift – I'm painting mastiffs next so they might at least call me big dog boy.' He regretted the words as soon as they were out of his mouth. What had he been thinking? Even his father wouldn't make a pun that bad to a duke. The next three seconds took a decade to pass. Then his host's eyes crinkled again, this time with laughter.

'Mr Landseer,' the Duke said. 'Your dogs, large and small, are admirable, though I should like to see you try something more ambitious. Perhaps you might find inspiration here? Please consider all birds and beasts at your disposal. Make full use of the place, the park, you know.' He waved a hand at the darkness beyond the windows where the moonlit woman still stood by the piano, now staring towards the group around the sofa, one arm folded across her slim waist, the sheet music crumpled in her hand.

'My dear!' the Duke called. The woman turned. 'Are you going to play, or will you come and greet our guests?'

The woman pushed back her shoulders, dropping the music. For a fraction of a second as she stepped into the glow of the chandeliers she looked on the verge of tears, then she blinked, and a smile spread across her face, stopping just short of her eyes. 'I couldn't possibly play now Mr Hayter has arrived.' The smile flickered as she pushed a dark curl off her forehead. 'He'd only sigh, pick at his nails, and say I wasn't as good as his Italian beauties.'

She held out her hand to George, who kissed it, bending far lower than he had to the Duke.

Murmuring 'my dear Duchess' he denied any capacity for unfavourable criticism, then introduced Edwin, who bowed but was not offered a hand to kiss.

'If you run out of animals to draw, Mr Landseer, you may sketch my sons,' the Duchess said, a brittle note to her voice as she shot a look over his shoulder. At close quarters, she was shorter than he'd thought but had considerable presence. 'They're wild and mildly beastly, but I find them picturesque. The gamekeepers usually know where to find them. But that's for tomorrow. Now you must enjoy a drink and endure some politics.' She rolled her eyes, which were the same intense brown as her hair, passing Edwin a glass from a newly appeared tray. Before he could thank her, she'd turned to speak to someone else, so he swallowed half the glass in one mouthful, silently praying for a guardian angel to stop him making any more bad jokes.

The Duchess rattled through introductions, barely offering Edwin a chance to speak to her, let alone impress or annoy her, and giving him the impression that at least half the room was called William. Leaving him with a dark-haired, long-nosed young man, not intimidatingly tall, whose name she neglected to reveal, she seated herself next to George on a chaise longue. The cat-like pregnant woman glared at her.

'Are you the fellow who painted those fighting dogs?' the young man said.

The ineffectual whirl of introductions had exhausted Edwin's supply of witty things to say about dog paintings. Tiredness and tension tugged at his patience. He was sick of being charming, of performing, but couldn't afford to lose his temper, not here. 'Yes,' he managed with a fixed smile.

'It was capital. Don't suppose you'd do me a copy in exchange for a cigar, would you?' The youth laughed, swigging from an overfull glass. 'I'm William Russell, by the way.'

A groan was out of Edwin's mouth before he could stop it. In horror, his tongue tripped over itself to apologise. 'I didn't mean … it's just that I swear everyone here's called William. Even the women.'

'Fair point.' William Russell grinned, stroking the downy beginnings of whiskers on his cheeks. 'Family name, as you've gathered. The greatest of us all was a seventeenth-century fellow, a political martyr – William, Lord Russell – unjustly executed for treason, head lopped off by opponents of liberty, usual sort of thing. I'm sure the Duke will bore you with him at some point. Looks on him as a sort of saint. He's been muttering about getting a painting of his trial. I suppose that's more George Hayter's line than yours?'

'Unless judge and jury happened to be dogs, yes.' Edwin reinforced his smile with more wine, glancing briefly at George, who was still at close quarters with the Duchess, no doubt attempting to flirt his way closer to a commission.

'I'd pay good money to see that.' William Russell laughed with such heartiness that a genuine smile nudged the false one from Edwin's face. 'As to living William Russells,' he continued, 'or should that be Williams Russell? There are only three of us here, I think, and one female. There's my cousin Young Lord William and his wife Lady William, also known as Bessy.' William inclined his head towards the pregnant woman and the thin-haired man beside her. 'And then there's my father, Old Lord William, woebegone fellow by the fireplace. He's the Duke's younger brother, doomed to penury by family fecundity. You know the Duke has nine sons? Three from his first Duchess, six out of this one. Plus two daughters.'

'All Williams?' Edwin said. Through the weariness and wine, it almost seemed a reasonable question. More reasonable than the Duchess having so many children. Now standing by the door shaking her head vigorously at the Duke, she looked neither old enough nor stout enough.

'Worse.' William wrinkled his nose. 'The shrimp being fleeced at whist in the corner: that's my cousin, Lord Wriothesley.' He stumbled over the word, laughing through wine-reddened lips. 'Ree-oath-slee, also known as Wrio. Another family name, but good God it's hard to say – at least William doesn't make you bite your own tongue, which is perhaps why we're so fond of it. And the girl fleecing him,' he added, draining his glass, 'card sharp that she is, is my sister, Eliza. But she won't mind if you call her William. Clear?'

'As mud, thank you.' Edwin laughed. Out of the corner of his eye, he saw the Duchess leave. At least that removed the risk of offending her.

'Thought it might be.' William grinned. 'Listen, do you like cigars?'

'Probably.'

'Good. I know where my uncle keeps the best ones. This way, but shh.' As they slipped out through a side door, William added, 'By the way, you know George Hayter well, don't you? Is it true he has two wives?'

For a second, Edwin considered a white lie to defend George's reputation, but he was still smarting from the 'little dog boy' introduction.

'Yes,' he said. 'The first ran off with their children a few years ago. And the second isn't quite a wife, but she's in the same condition as Lady Bessy back there.'

William laughed, hiccupped, and led the way to cigars.

Edwin followed, glancing back in case the Duke should be watching, but he was deep in conversation on the sofa with pregnant Bessy or Lady William or whatever her name was. George was leaning in towards them, smirking as he recited something in Italian. The chances of being caught with an illicit cigar looked slim enough.

The next day, Edwin sat beneath an old oak tree, back resting against the cracked trunk. Sunlight glimmered through the leaves and his ears were full of the sounds of bovine snorting and the munching of meadow grass. Half an eye on the swallows and skylarks humming and darting overhead, he opened his satchel and propped his sketchbook on his knees. Twirling a pencil between his fingers, he leafed through the morning's drawings of fallow deer and gundogs with a rush of excitement. The Duke's enthusiasm for them had more than justified getting up early.

As the rough bark pressed through his shirt onto his shoulder blades, he relaxed for the first time since his arrival. The air smelt comfortingly of hay, laced with fresh dung, and that milky, meaty musk particular to cows. There was no danger out here of making a poor impression, and he could draw without anyone interrupting. The throbbing in his temples was almost gone too. William had introduced him to a new kind of headache as well as to the Russell clan.

Gaze alternating between the paper and the rich red hide of the closest cow, he traced the contours of her back, picked out protruding ears, shaded flanks, dips, and hollows, and worked up haunches. The warmth of the afternoon and the buzz of bumblebees were beginning to drag him down into drowsiness, when his subject raised her head, grunted, and lumbered purposefully towards the wooden fence enclosing this part of the park.

A girl in a plain cotton dress was approaching at speed, tartan ribbons trailing from a battered straw bonnet that obscured her face. Reaching the fence, she hitched up her skirts and swung herself over. Half hidden in the shade of the tree, Edwin winced at a ripping sound as she came down the other side. Forcibly freeing herself, she let out a cascade of curses in a Scotch accent. As she reached the cow, she let fly a fresh torrent, the object this time being, as far as Edwin could tell, a rival. He only caught stray words, many of whose exact meanings were a mystery, but their sense was clear enough.

Her bucket-like bonnet quickly took shape on the page next to his bovine sketch, followed by the sweep of her shoulders, the swell of a very fine bosom, and the promise of a slender waist and more curves beneath her loose gown. He'd thought she would have noticed him by this point, but she was still absorbed in her rant, now tying a ribbon to the cow's horns.

'There,' she declared. 'That wanton cat Bessy dropped it last night. It's much bonnier on you.'

Dimly remembering that Bessy was married to one of the William Russells, Edwin felt he ought to alert the girl to his presence before she went further. Hopefully he could allay any initial anger at being observed by making her a present of the flattering sketch (her figure was good, but not as good as he'd made it). He coughed. Cow and bonnet turned. Uninterested, the former went back to her grass. The face beneath the bonnet, however, stared at him aghast.

It was not a girl at all. It was the Duchess.

The whites of her eyes were red and fresh tears streaked her cheeks. A half-spoken word died above her quivering lower lip. If she'd been an animal – dog, horse, even cat – it would have been the most obvious thing in the world to stroke and soothe her until the upset was forgotten. But she was a duchess, which made things awkward. Still, he had to do something. Flinging his sketchbook to the ground and praying it would land face down so she wouldn't see his voluptuous vision of her, he scrambled to his feet.

'What the hell are you doing here?' She glared at him, roughly wiping the back of her hand across her face.

'Drawing a cow, Your Grace.' He tried laughing. She was not remotely amused.

'How much did you hear?' The Scottish accent had disappeared.

Edwin's stomach tried to squirm its way into his boots. His chances of a commission from the Duke suddenly felt a lot slimmer. Before he could answer, the Duchess snapped, 'Oh, what does it matter? You'll tell them anyway – that I'm mad, a jealous old harpy who steals ribbons ... and those things I said about Bessy ... to a cow.' She pressed a hand to her forehead. 'Oh God.'

'No, no ...' Edwin found his voice; whatever he said now could hardly make it worse. 'Not at all mad. Or old. Or any of the rest. And I talk to animals all the time.'

'You do?' She pushed more tears from her cheeks.

'Constantly. I don't swear at them quite as much, but I would if I could do it as well as you.'

The corners of her mouth twitched, almost into a smile.

'You won't tell anyone, will you, Master – Mr Landseer?' She sniffed.

'Of course not. But can I help? You look so ...' Edwin stopped as her lips began to tremble. 'Is there someone I can fetch?'

She shook her head. 'This is for Josephine's ears only.'

'Josephine?'

The Duchess indicated the retreating ruby heifer. 'She's my shoulder to cry on for things I mustn't bother the others with. But I'm being so spoilt and selfish even she's deserted me today.'

She covered her face again, muffling her voice. 'Please. Go. I'm sorry to have subjected you to this.'

Her bosom heaved as she gulped back another sob.

'I can't leave you like this, Your Grace. There must be something I can do?' Edwin said. 'I can listen to more cursing? I could stand in for Josephine? My cow impersonations are the talk of the London stage, I'm told.'

Another sniff. A hint of a smile. But another tear slid to her jawline.

Feeling like an idiot but doing it anyway, Edwin mooed, and, blushing furiously, added, 'Your Grace.'

Her bosom took a break from heaving and shook with a small laugh.

'You are sweet,' she said. 'Thank you. But leave me. You don't want to hear my woes.'

'Oh no, I do . . . I mean, I don't. Not for gossip or anything like that – I mean I want to listen if it would make you feel better, but not because I actually want to know . . .' Edwin tailed off, silenced by the sorrow in her eyes.

'I lost a baby, that's all,' she said quietly, and dissolved into a fresh fit of sobs.

Panicking, Edwin put an arm around her.

'I'm sorry, I'm so sorry,' she said, burying her face in his shirt.

He held her gingerly as her tears soaked through the linen, warm on his skin. Her shoulders shook. The bonnet was awkward. She smelled of roses. What on earth should he do now?

'Maybe you should sit down?' he said. It was better than nothing.

She nodded, wiping her eyes on her sleeve, then, with unexpected suddenness, sank into a heap of skirts on the dry grass. 'What must you think of me?'

Edwin sat next to her, searching frantically for something helpful to say. This would take more than another cow impersonation. He wished his sister Jane were here; she was good at this sort of thing. 'When did . . .?'

'Two weeks ago.' The Duchess hugged her knees to her chest and sniffed. 'I can't cry up there.' She looked towards the house. 'I promised John – the Duke – that I wouldn't upset Bessy. You can't have failed to notice she's *enceinte*. She lost her first horribly last year and we must all walk on eggshells so as not to alarm her and risk this one.' Tears swelled and ripened among her dark lashes. 'Lord knows, I've tried to help her but . . . but . . . she throws it back in my face. Yesterday, she accused me of strutting about like a prize brood mare.' She took hold of the hem of her dress, twisting it around her fingers. 'Well, it seems I'm not worth any breeding prizes after all. My last boy only lived a month. I-I hoped this one . . .' She choked back a sob, knuckles white as she gripped the fabric. 'And I feel so guilty. John's so good to me. We have eight healthy children, who I adore. And I'm only thirty-eight; we could have more . . . What kind of mother am I for not being happy with that?'

Edwin took a deep breath, thinking of the last time he'd seen his own mother weep; the only time he'd seen his father cry.

'I have five brothers and sisters now, but there were others,' he said. 'My mother says a broken heart doesn't love any less, it just hurts more. And it's not like breaking an arm or something, which you can just not use for a while; you can't stop using a heart.'

The Duchess began sobbing again. Unable to sit by and do nothing, Edwin reached across and closed his hand over hers.

'It's all right,' he said softly.

There was a great sniff, another, and another. She gripped his hand back. The skylarks hummed above them, the swallows swooped to snatch insects from the air, the cows shuffled between thistles. The tension in her fingers gradually lessened. At length, it seemed appropriate to offer a handkerchief.

'Thank you,' said the Duchess with a wan smile. 'You've been very kind.'

Gathering up her dress to stand, she noticed his sketchbook on the ground. The blasted thing had fallen open, face up.

'Oh, is that me?' She tilted her head to one side.

'Yes.' Edwin winced.

'You are even kinder than I thought, Mr Landseer.' She blushed.

The Duke's carriage drove them back to Woburn town the following day. George droned on about the big commission he almost had in the bag: the treason trial of the martyred Lord William Russell. Edwin couldn't remember what the treason was but was in no mood to ask.

His mind was full of the evening before: the hot awkwardness of unaccustomed evening dress; conversations flying from cricket and dogs to electoral reform and the future of art; and an image of them all in the dark glass of a long window, lit like a Caravaggio. The Duchess's face had brightened as their reflected gazes met and rested together. Then the Duke's voice had sliced softly through the scene.

'Georgina.'

She'd turned, and the moment was over.

'Ned, stop daydreaming.' George kicked his ankle. 'You might show a bit more gratitude to me, you know. The Duke liked you. He'll commission something, I'm sure.'

* * *

Over the next few years, Edwin made numerous small paintings of dogs and deer for the Duke, and of children for the Duchess. He also revisited Josephine the cow and exhibited her in oils at the Academy. The Duchess accompanied him to most of the heifer's 'sittings'. The shadows of her former melancholy dispersed as Bessy, Young Lord William, and their noisy new son departed for the Continent, and her own body ripened with a new pregnancy. By the time Josephine's picture was finished, the Duchess had a fat pink baby in her arms. When Edwin asked for her considered opinion, she paused in cooing at the child just long enough to smile at him and insist he add a ribbon to the cow's horns. The Duke refrained from commenting on his wife's artistic stipulation, but Edwin caught him raising an eyebrow at the wriggling infant – his tenth son.

The Duke was as generous with his advice and influence as with his cellar and cigars, encouraging Edwin to include more gravity and grandeur in his pictures. As they spent more time together, Edwin's admiration and liking for him grew. He was not a demonstrative man, but there was a profound tenderness in his patience with the Duchess's extremes of spirits, and in the quiet delight he took in his children: from his thin-lipped, buttoned-up heir, Lord Tavistock, to loud, plump baby Lord Alexander Russell. Tavistock rarely acknowledged Edwin as anything above a common tradesman; Alexander, so often in the Duchess's arms, quickly acquired a taste for Edwin's hair, his sticks of chalk, pencils, and brushes.

But a large-scale commission remained maddeningly elusive. Edwin's hopes briefly surged when, following an outing with Tavistock and the Exmoor staghounds, the Duke mused on the idea of a stag-hunting picture. They'd had promising discussions over port and brandy, but before anything was settled the Duke became distracted. By a duel.

When Edwin bumped into William Russell at the theatre a few days later, he'd laughed that it was less a duel, more an early morning picnic with pistols, complete with blankets, camp chairs, and coffee, all laid out beneath the blossom in Kensington Gardens. The bone of contention was an obscure but apparently grave point of political procedure, over which the Duke felt the honour of the House of Russell to have been unacceptably slighted. The caricaturists had a field day. The Duchess was furious. George Hayter was also livid, muttering how selfish the Duke was to risk his own life and the livelihoods of painters who depended on him.

Caricatures of the duel were still in print sellers' windows when George appeared, grey-faced, in the small studio Edwin shared with fellow animal painter Charles Christmas. Cursing the lack of chairs, George leant on the wall by the dirty sash window.

'There's a foul smell in here,' he said. 'Have you been dissecting dead animals again?'

'No.' Edwin eyed a rough-bristled brush critically, then bit it to give it the texture he wanted. 'Not this week.'

George looked to the heavens, pushing a hand through his hair. 'They think the Duke is dying.'

Edwin's brush stopped mid-stroke. The flat sweetness of the paint still clung to his tongue. He usually found the taste oddly pleasant, but now felt sick.

'A paralytic attack. At his place in Devon,' George continued, gazing out into the square below, from which rose the voices of models, tradesmen, other artists, lolling on the scrubby grass in the dusty June sun. They seemed miles away. 'Old Lord William wrote to me. I thought you'd want to know.'

The Duke defied doctors' predictions, first for weeks, then months. By March the following year he had recovered sufficiently for George to resume grumbling about lack of progress with the picture of Lord William Russell's trial without sounding entirely heartless.

Edwin had just celebrated his twenty-first birthday when he received a note summoning him to Woburn Abbey, alone.

The Duke's carriage rolled through the park, past buds on bony-limbed trees that kept themselves tightly closed in the face of bitter April winds. The great house was cold and grey, lifeless as a mausoleum. The Duke himself seemed only marginally more alive. Greeting Edwin at the foot of the marble staircase, his face and frame were gaunt, the laurel wreath of hair had wilted and thinned, and, thanks to another recent attack, the kindly face now resembled a wax model, one side of which had been left too close to a stove.

Edwin struggled not to stare, momentarily at a loss for words. The hopes he'd been nursing for the stag hunt commission flew from his mind. Not knowing what else to do, he forced himself to be cheerful, enquiring with ludicrous enthusiasm about everything from the dogs to the Duke's latest ideas for the gardens.

The sight of the Duchess was almost as alarming: thin, pale, deep purple shadows beneath her eyes.

'Paint her for me,' the Duke said later. 'Sh-show her … show … how beautiful sh-she is to me. I want the life back in her – without her I wouldn't have … I can't … dammit … I want her b-back to herself.'

'I-I'm honoured, Your Grace, but …' Edwin said, cringing at his stuttering in case the Duke should take it as an imitation of his own altered speech. 'But I'm not really … I don't paint portraits.' It sounded pathetic. He'd wanted a commission, but not this – this was too personal. He'd always found portraits hard. If he failed here, there would be no chance of keeping the Duke's support.

'N-Nonsense.' The Duke flung the word out of the functional side of his mouth, a string of spittle escaping from the other. 'You must. You were the only one she would have. Sh-she wept at my mentioning Lawrence. S-said the pressure of being charming to him would f-finish her off. She said you would be kind.' The Duke tugged out a handkerchief and mopped his chin, adding stiffly, 'Just do what you can, will you, L-landseer? And for God's sake, see if you can raise her spirits.'

Often as not, sittings with the Duchess became walks by the lake or drives around the park between sleety showers and brilliant, brittle sunshine. Sometimes in snippets, sometimes in tear-streaked torrents, she poured out her fears for the Duke, and of being widowed and at the mercy of his sons from his first marriage, who she was convinced hated her.

'The beasts would cut me and my children off without a thought. If Wrio were to be the next Duke, it would be different ... What will I do? What will my girls do? I could ask my father, but God knows he has debts enough as it is. Do you know how hideous it is, being a second wife?'

Edwin listened, offered advice when he could, and, when he couldn't, made her laugh.

In the end, the portrait was surprisingly successful, given how frequently sittings had dissolved into tears.

By the end of his visit, the breeze had lost its edge, unfurling leaves softened the outlines of the trees, and crab apples and pears had put out tentative blossoms that matched the delicate pink returning to the Duchess's cheeks.

The Duke stood by his carriage as it was prepared for Edwin's departure.

'Thank you, L-landseer,' he said. 'I trust I don't have to explain how d-deeply grateful I am. Not s-simply for the portrait.'

'It was a pleasure, Your Grace.' Edwin blushed.

The Duchess had thanked him earlier with a kiss on the cheek, after which her own face had flushed scarlet. The spot her lips had touched was still tingling as the carriage rolled past the stone lions guarding the gate lodge.

A year later, watery April sunshine shone on the worn threads of the red Turkey carpet into which Edwin's right knee was pressed. He'd forgotten how dull modelling could be. From the gardens on the other side of the window, he could hear birds, children, and dogs, enjoying the glories of Woburn Abbey on a warm spring day. But he was forbidden to look at any of them: George insisted his gaze remain lowered at all times for this – his long-awaited picture of the 1683 treason trial of William, Lord Russell. He'd also stipulated that Edwin, as Russell's faithful page, wear a blue velvet doublet, padded mustard-coloured breeches that stopped mid-thigh, and the itchiest woollen stockings imaginable. The ensemble gave off camphor vapours that made Edwin's nostrils flare, and he was unerringly conscious of the visibility of his knees.

Close behind his right shoulder, the Duchess yawned loudly. She was dressed in voluminous white silk, sitting at a spiral-legged writing table in the character of Russell's wife, Lady Rachel, who was to be the centre of the work. Edwin only agreed to model because she'd begged him to save her from the boredom of sitting alone. Every time she moved, her dress caressed the back of one of his ankles, sending feelings he was pretending not to have wriggling up to his spine. Mercifully, he supposed, he could now barely feel the dress as that leg was almost numb, offset by a hot thread of cramp crawling through his other thigh.

There was a soft knock at the door and the hope of release coursed through Edwin's grumbling limbs. It opened with a flash of a footman's arm, revealing the Duke.

'A–apologies, Hayter. Do you need Mr Landseer for much longer?'

'Not more than an hour, Your Grace.' George angled his head deferentially. 'Half, if by some miracle he can keep still.'

'Good, good.' The Duke turned to Edwin. 'Landseer, come and find me when you've finished here. I wish to discuss deer.'

'Yes, Your Grace.' Edwin performed an unsteady bow, pins and needles swarming through his right foot and calf, excitement surging through his chest.

'Ned,' snapped George, pointing with his brush as soon as the Duke had gone. 'Back in position. And stop smiling. You're meant to be wracked with worry that your lord and master will be sent to the block.'

The Duchess made a throat-cutting motion, raising her eyebrows. Edwin laughed. George glowered at them both. Foot still prickling, Edwin limped back to his mark on the edge of the carpet and bent over the box of papers he was meant to be on the point of passing to the Duchess. He was unsure of their precise significance as she had been making bored faces behind George's back while he was explaining. For similar reasons, he would have been hard pressed to explain how Lord Russell's plotting to assassinate both Charles II and James II made him a martyr not a traitor.

'And don't roll your eyes!' George said, stepping back towards the canvas.

'And don't blink. Or breathe,' the Duchess whispered, too softly for George to hear.

As the heavy white silk brushed Edwin's heel again, he fixed his gaze on the carpet patterns. A shiver of anticipation scuttled between his shoulder blades. This – finally – could be the commission to see him make the leap from promising young painter to serious artist. It might even help secure his election as an Associate of the Royal Academy when he was old enough.

'Ned!' George snapped. 'How many times do I have to tell you to keep still?'

'It's not my fault.' Edwin stood up, stretched, and defiantly scratched the back of his thigh. 'You try balancing on one knee for hours on end. And my stockings keep falling down. And I'm sure these breeches have fleas.'

'But they suit you so well. Send the fleas to me if they're bothering you,' said the Duchess, with a wicked grin that did something alarming to Edwin's stomach. 'I must say, I like this dress so much I'd share it with a hundred fleas. I almost feel like one of Charles II's mistresses.' She stroked one of her puffed sleeves then tugged at the tight bodice. 'I've always thought I'd make a good Barbara Villiers. Don't you think it would have been fun?'

'I doubt it, Your Grace.' George scowled. 'Itchy wigs, terrible teeth, and the entire court had the clap.'

The Duchess ignored him, continuing to pull at her dress. 'Or perhaps Nell Gwyn? She was the one with the oranges, wasn't she?'

George took two sharp steps away from the easel, a smile rigid on his pale face. 'You, Your Grace, are the centre of the whole composition – more important even than Lord Russell. You represent virtue, loyalty, purity, et cetera, et cetera. There is to be no Nell Gwyn about it.' He exhaled through his nose, tone ominous with ebbing patience. 'I should be greatly obliged if Your Grace would pull that gown up again, *if* it's not too much trouble.'

'I didn't pull it down. It just sits this way. It's too tight.' The Duchess shrugged and squinted at her cleavage. 'You don't think it's too low, do you, Mr Landseer?'

Intensifying his efforts not to laugh, Edwin assessed the situation for as long as he dared deem artistically appropriate, taking in the pressure of silk on soft skin, the smoothness of her neck, the hint of a double chin. Another shiver scuttled across his shoulder blades. This one had nothing to do with the Royal Academy.

'With the greatest possible respect,' George's smile was as immovable as a miniature painted on ivory, 'Mistress Gwyn's oranges seem to be in imminent danger of tumbling out of their basket. If you're struggling to contain them, I'm sure Landseer would be only too happy to assist you.'

Blood rushed to Edwin's cheeks. Catching his eye, the Duchess theatrically heaved her dress up until it almost reached her collarbone.

'There,' she said. 'Forbidden fruit safely out of sight. Even if I can't breathe.'

George tutted as they resumed their positions. 'Eyes down, Ned.'

'Eyes down, Ned,' mimicked the Duchess in a whisper. Edwin bit his lip and endeavoured to focus on the faded gold patterns of the carpet and on the box of somehow important papers. There followed several minutes of near silence. The Duchess yawned, once, twice, three times. The carpet refused to fascinate him. The documents were even duller. He didn't want to get his hopes up by thinking about the Duke's picture. He didn't dare acknowledge the thoughts of silk, collarbone, and cleavage stirring in the pit of his stomach. Then something nudged him in the back at the ticklish spot just below his ribs. Whipping his head around, he saw the Duchess's satin slipper sneak back beneath her writing table. Her face was flawlessly grave, still tilted in the direction George had prescribed, but the corners of her mouth twitched and her eyes flickered towards him for a scant second.

'Ned!' whined George.

'Sorry – flea.' Edwin narrowed his eyes at the Duchess, who flashed him the briefest of grins.

The second time she did it, he managed to stay in pose, but keeping his face and thoughts straight had never been more difficult. The third time, they both collapsed in fits of giggles and George reluctantly agreed that they'd done enough for the day.

Leaving George and the Duchess discussing the cut of her dress, Edwin slipped behind a screen to change, then set off to find the Duke. His footsteps echoed back at him from the stone walls and floor, quickening to a run when he was sure there was no one around to see, then sliding to a halt as he approached the open door of the Duke's study.

'Mr Landseer, at long last!' the Duke said, the nib of his pen glinting as he set it in an inkstand on his desk.

'Apologies for keeping you waiting, Your Grace,' Edwin said, trying to subtly yank the wrinkles out of his sleeve.

'No need, n-no need. I have kept you waiting far longer for this picture. You've been remarkably patient. Do sit.' He grimaced, muttered something about gout, then grasped the cut-glass sides of a decanter and poured a pair of brandies, saying, 'Now, a simple stag hunting picture won't do. It must be worthy not only of my walls but also of your talents.'

'You flatter me, Your Grace.' Edwin sipped; the buttery fire of the brandy on his tongue did nothing to calm the prickles of anticipation in his stomach, or around the spot where the Duchess had kicked him.

'Nonsense. Take the compliment. I shan't let you squander your gifts on empty-headed subjects just because they will sell. Don't mistake me – I know even painters must eat and I dare say pictures of favourite pets will keep you in reasonable claret, but that's all they will do. Do they still call you the little d-dog boy?'

'Not as often as they used to.' Edwin gave his wrinkled sleeve a final tug.

'Well, I hope this picture will help you lose the title once and for all, or at least change it to little dog boy, ARA. You are putting your name forward for associateship this year, aren't you?'

'I can't, I'm not yet twenty-four – this time in two years.' Edwin took another sip, trying to ignore the urge to scratch the back of his knee; perhaps the breeches really did have fleas.

'Ah. Perhaps just Hayter this year then. He's burying the hatchet and putting his name forward, I believe. How do you see his chances?'

Edwin swallowed, surprised. George had recently been even more scathing than usual about the Academy. And, as far as Edwin could tell, there had been no change in the Academicians' views on him or his irregular private life. Even with the Bedford influence, his chances of election were the slimmest. Reluctant to disappoint the Duke, however, Edwin gave a feeble-but-safe shrug.

'It's hard to say.'

'I suppose so.' The Duke sighed. 'Where were we? Ah, yes. Deer. As we've discussed before, an historical context would be more fitting than an ordinary hunting scene. But I don't want yet another Actaeon or Ascanius. My librarian and I were discussing some family history this morning . . .'

Edwin's eye tracked a drop of brandy edging its way down the inside of his glass – would it reach the bottom before the Duke got to the point? Would there be a commission or not? Something about an ancestor, a border skirmish, treacherous Scots . . . the drop slid diagonally as it hit an imperfection – could the Duchess have meant anything by the slipper in the ribs?

'—and it came to me – I want you to paint the hunting of Chevy Chase.'

Edwin's gaze snapped back to the Duke. His heart leapt impatiently as the older man paused, sipped, swallowed.

'You're familiar with the story, I'm sure?'

Edwin nodded more violently than he meant to. Re-enacting Harry 'Hotspur' Percy's ill-fated raid across the Scottish border to hunt the deer of his sworn enemy, Douglas, had been a favourite on the straw-strewn streets of his childhood. Lingering thoughts of fleas and satin-shod toes were eclipsed by knights in blood-spattered armour.

'What do you think?' asked the Duke. 'We'll show the Academy that modern British painters can do more than ape the antique.'

'I think . . .' Possibilities unfurled in his mind, along with memories of fearsome Dutch hunting scenes: tragedy and hope bound together in twisting, sinuous animal forms. That kind of movement would be the devil to capture. But it would damn well be worth it if he could get it right. And he would get it right. Dogs wouldn't be a problem, deer and horses more of a challenge – and men. But he could do it. He was sure. And more than anything, he didn't want anyone else to have the chance to make this picture. 'I think . . . I think it's perfect, Your Grace.'

'I thought you would like it,' said the Duke, eyes twinkling. 'You'll need to see more deer, of course, more than I can put at your disposal here. But you may see hundreds if you'll come to us in the Highlands this autumn. Do I remember you saying you were hoping to be in Edinburgh in any case?'

'Yes—' Edwin's reply was cut off by a rumpus of thundering feet and shrieks in the corridor. Through the open door, he caught a glimpse of the Duchess dashing past, still wearing her Nell Gwyn white silk, pursued by two giggling children.

'She will be delighted to have you with us, of course,' the Duke said. 'You can make some pictures of the children running wild. Only if you can spare the time, that is.'

He leant forward and tilted the decanter once more. Waves of gold washed around the sides of Edwin's glass, and the spot where the satin slipper had nudged him throbbed.

Edwin spent the next two months revelling in the lengthening days and reading about blood feuds in the Scottish Borders. Blizzards of blossom heralded the *Beau Monde's* return to town and his gaze snagged on every party of fashionably dressed ladies as they passed from carriages to milliners and modistes or drove in the park. He repeatedly told himself that he wasn't looking for anyone in particular – certainly not the Duchess – and forced his thoughts to the wider pursuit of patronage and pleasure, with varying degrees of success.

While the air thickened with the first murmurs of summer, he talked artistic nonsense to potential buyers, and theatrical nonsense to actresses after curtain-fall. When nonsense became too much, he sought solace on the high heathland to the north of the city, plunging into bottle green pools, letting the cool silt slip between his toes and shivering as weeds wound themselves around his ankles, then sitting, drying in the sun, looking down on old London, watching the seeds of new canals, villas, and terraces sprout in once familiar fields.

Throughout it all, he made studies for the Duke's picture. The Bedford influence opened doors to some of London's finest private collections, where Edwin copied the writhing, rippling beasts of Rubens and Snyders, two centuries old but never bettered. His own studio was still too small but felt and smelled better thanks to the frequent presence of his sister Jane, who was now Mrs Christmas, having married Edwin's studio-mate, Charles Christmas, the previous December. The Landseers had thought this coming together of name and season the height of hilarity; Edwin's oldest brother Tom still chuckled about it now, six months later. The Christmases hadn't found it quite so amusing.

Jane had been unusually quiet this morning though, staring blankly at the botanical illustration she was working on. Edwin was panicking, unable to find his hat and in danger of being late for a meeting with the Duke to discuss his first sketches for the grand picture, when she took him by surprise and vomited into a brush cleaning jar. She was now sitting on the room's only chair, alarmingly pale. Her husband was staring at the jar with a look of horror.

'I'm all right. Give me room to breathe, Ned.' She leant back, closing her eyes.

'You don't look all right. You're the colour of curdled milk.' Edwin handed her a dented pewter mug of water. Was a vomiting sister an acceptable excuse for being late?

'How are you always so charming, little brother?'

'A great deal of practice,' Edwin said. He needed to go but couldn't leave her like this. He glanced at Christmas, who was still fixated on the jar. What was he expecting to see?

'I'll fetch Mother. It'll only take a minute. She'll know what to do.'

'Don't you dare.' Jane straightened up, fixing Edwin with the look she used to use when scolding him for bringing dead things into the house to draw. 'She'll know exactly what to do. That's the problem. We don't want her to know – not yet. Do we, Charles?'

Coming out of the jar-induced trance, Christmas shook his head, a smile lifting his reddening cheeks.

Jane gingerly placed her hands on her stomach, saying, 'There will be another Christmas this winter, God willing.'

Thinking she was either going to vomit again or was delirious, Edwin reached hurriedly for a bowl. 'Of course there will be another Christmas—'

'Ned, you idiot,' she snapped, grasping the bowl. 'I mean you're going to be an uncle – but not a word until I give you permission.'

The sound of church bells tolling one o'clock rolled through the open window. Edwin kissed Jane with the heartiest of congratulations, embraced his brother-in-law, then scooped up his sketches, snatched Charles's hat, and dashed out of the door, calling over his shoulder that he couldn't be late for the Duke.

He'd almost reached the Bedfords' house in St James's Square when he was forced to wait with a swelling, increasingly irate crowd outside Almack's assembly rooms, home to the season's most exclusive balls. Blocking the street, a convoy of champagne crates fought for precedence over three wagonloads of white roses. Edwin stood on tiptoes to catch a glimpse through Almack's hallowed front doors, which were, for once, open. He'd never been inside – painters were generally too lowly to be admitted – but George Hayter had occasionally slithered his way in to a private function. It looked surprisingly bland.

Various bells announced that it was now half-past one. He was going to be late. The crowd stirred as a cartload of wine from Berry Brothers approached, threatening to make the situation even stickier. Throwing politeness to the wind, Edwin pushed through the press of people and finally made it into St James's Square. For a few moments, it was eerily peaceful. No stray dogs, rough wagons, or hawkers, just the splashing of the central fountain and the sound of a singing lesson drifting from an open window.

Then a voice boomed, 'Beware, Landseer!'

Edwin jumped, and saw William Russell approaching the fountain, stamping out a cigar.

'It's madness inside.' William nodded at the Duke's house. 'Ball fever. It's the Caledonian at Almack's tonight – all Aunt Georgina's Scotch family are going. They're in there, campaign planning. She's short on troops, so I'm being dragged along. I've negotiated my way out of having to wear a kilt but that means I have to wear fancy dress. You can't think of a costume guaranteed to impress every heiress in town, can you?'

'The page's costume for Hayter's picture?' Edwin said as they climbed the stone steps to the front door. 'Those golden breeches . . .'

'Didn't you say they had fleas?' William rang the bell.

'Well-bred fleas. Perfect for Almack's,' Edwin said, as a footman ushered them inside.

'I'm not that desperate. Keep thinking!' William called over his shoulder, disappearing into the small drawing room, from which came the sounds of a heated discussion.

Edwin was shown up to the Duke's study, but the meeting was over disappointingly quickly and mostly consisted of the Duke looking at his watch.

'Very good, Landseer. I look forward to discussing at greater length soon, but for now you must excuse me. I intend to remove myself from danger before the Duchess attempts to lure me to this ball.'

'You're not going, Your Grace?'

'Heavens no.' The Duke closed his watch with a soft click. 'I shall go to my club. Where there are no bagpipes.'

Edwin emerged into the hall, tying his sketches together and silently cursing the Scots and their pipes for absorbing everyone's attention. The voices in the drawing room were now even louder, the door being slightly open. Half in, half out of it, William was talking to Eliza, who smiled apologetically at Edwin.

'Mr Landseer, we have a proposition for you,' she said.

'Landseer, you're coming to the ball,' her brother interrupted, clapping Edwin on the back, and pressing a small card into his palm. 'Forget all I said earlier. It'll be a lark. It's not one of those woeful debutante-and-dowager Wednesday affairs. Aunt Georgina assures me it's a private ball, so private rules, which should mean better drink and decent dancing. Cousin Wrio's sick – at least he says he is – and can't go, which deprives poor Eliza of a partner for at least three dances. It's too late to get anyone else, so the voucher's yours if you'll have it.'

Anti-Caledonian sentiments metamorphosing into something quite different, Edwin turned the card between his finger and thumb with what he hoped looked like the nonchalance of a regular ball-goer.

'Do I have to wear a kilt?'

'No. Fancy dress. Golden breeches?'

'Never again. I'll find something in the Academy's props store.'

'Then you'll come?'

From within the drawing room, the Duchess's voice rose momentarily above the others.

'What have I got to lose?' Edwin said, ribs tingling.

William clapped him on the back again, so heartily he sent several sketches fluttering to the floor. 'Good man! Meet me outside Almack's at half-past eleven? No – wait – are you really going to raid the Academy for a costume?'

'I'm going to try.'

'Take me with you. Wait a minute though, I need to tell Aunt Georgina I've solved her recruitment problem.'

William and Eliza slipped back into the drawing room. Edwin caught a glimpse of the Duchess brandishing a Sèvres tea pot in one hand and a silver strainer in the other before the door closed. As he knelt to gather up his sketches, a footman jogged to the top of the staircase and called down,

'His Grace's carriage in twenty minutes, for Mrs Vernon's.'

Edwin made himself focus on tying the drawings together not the fact that Mrs Vernon's didn't sound remotely like the gentleman's club the Duke had just referred to.

Then William was back.

'Don't dress as anything too ridiculous!' called Eliza as they hurried down the stairs.

Several hours later, a golden fug of gaslight hovered above the sea of ostrich-plumed heads in Almack's grand saloon. Clouds of cologne almost masked the animal scent of hundreds of hot human bodies on a midsummer night.

'Battle dress.' William nodded at the crowds, pulling a lemon sucking face as he drained his glass of claret cup. 'White feathers for the English; dark ones for the Scots, and white roses for Bonnie Prince Charlie, of course.'

'Are we expecting fighting? Or just dancing?' said Edwin.

'Depends how much whisky gets drunk. Might be hard to tell one from the other by the end.'

There was no sign of the champagne that had blocked the street earlier, but the white roses were everywhere: from the orchestra balcony to the hair, dresses, and bosoms of the ladies. William reached inside the ass's head mask he held under one arm (quietly borrowed from the Academy). A pewter flask glinted in his hand,

'Here – take the taste of the punch away.'

The brandy had just begun to dance along Edwin's tongue, when a long, low blast cut through the simmering air, bursting bubbles of conversation until it was the only sound in the room. It seemed to bypass Edwin's ears and lodge directly in his bones. As a flurry of higher notes took flight, the ostrich feathers quivered.

Leaning on his shepherd's crook and pushing himself up on his sandaled toes (sandals and crook also quietly borrowed from the Academy, along with his short Greek tunic and long scarlet cloak), Edwin caught sight of the tops of bagpipes then the ruddy-faced Scotch piper, infinitely more impressive than the soft-skinned royals trailing behind him. Then the ostrich fronds shifted again, blocking his view.

'Heavens, Aunt Georgina's in high feather tonight!' William whistled softly. 'See those diamonds around her neck? They're worth fifty thousand alone.'

Edwin's cloak was suddenly unbearably hot.

'Pounds?' he said, stretching every sinew to see, finally spotting her on the dais behind the piper. She turned to say something to Eliza and her necklace caught the light of the nearest chandelier, flashing with the brilliance of a lightning bolt.

'Guineas. Does it make much difference?' said William.

'No,' said Edwin. It was more than he could hope to earn in a lifetime either way.

He swallowed another tart mouthful of claret cup in the faint hope that it would send his heart back down into his chest. Since returning from Woburn in the spring, it had been increasingly hard to convince himself that his feelings for the Duchess were purely platonic. He forced himself to think of the Duke, but that just brought back the uncomfortable question of who Mrs Vernon might be.

'She's certainly managed to outshine her sister. That's her – gold dress, nose like a cheese knife – Dowager Duchess of Richmond.'

'Sister? She looks old enough to be her mother.' Edwin peered through the feathers at the granite-haired dowager.

'Not quite, though Aunt Georgina is the baby of the family. There was a younger brother, but he died about ten years ago, knocked her for six. The older brother – Marquis of Huntly – is on her other side. Moustache, eagles' feathers in his cap and all that. Odds are he'll be Duke of Gordon soon.' William leant closer and lowered his voice. 'Their father's in the North by his wife's deathbed – second wife, that is. But this lot are refusing to join him out of respect for their mother. This wife was the housekeeper in their mother's time, if you see what I mean. Eliza says that's what they were raving about this afternoon. I try to stay out of it. Russell business is bad enough.'

Before Edwin had time to think on any of this, the first bars of 'God Save the King' floated down from the orchestra balcony and the crowd blocked his view. He braced himself for lumbering patriotic singing. Instead, someone with a deep Scottish accent cried, 'We want Gow!'

More calls for Gow were accompanied by growling laughter.

'What is Gow?' Edwin hissed, trying to get some air under his cloak.

'Mr Gow, there,' William pointed at a slick-haired, dour-faced man holding a fiddle among a group of musicians beneath the orchestra balcony, 'leads the best dance band this side of Edinburgh, according to Aunt Georgina. I don't know what they're like the other side of Edinburgh, but he's damned good.'

The orchestra leader – high above them on the rose-covered balcony, face scarlet over a tight white cravat – shrugged and looked despairingly at the royal party. Several more roses sailed through the air towards Gow, who caught one to loud cheers and bowed. Tucking it behind his ear, he lifted his fiddle and let fly a skein of notes, then the rest of the band joined in, and, after flirting with a jig, a reel, and a hornpipe, the tune morphed into the liveliest version of 'God Save the King' Edwin had ever heard.

Then there was dancing. For a while, Edwin had little choice but to concentrate on not getting the steps too badly wrong. His reeling experience was limited to rough and ready dances during summers in Essex. Bowing, laughing, and apologising to a swan-necked girl who had almost stopped his eyes darting to every diamond flash, he made his way back to William and his shepherd's crook, only to see the Duchess and Eliza approaching.

'Mr Landseer, you're enjoying yourself?' The Duchess's necklace, nestling so perfectly beneath her collarbone, was even more impressive up close. Trying to ignore the tightness in his stomach, Edwin said he was enjoying himself very much.

'I am glad. We were just admiring your costume. The cloak is particularly dashing. What are you meant to be?'

'Endymion, the shepherd prince of Arcadia who falls in love with the moon.' Edwin cringed as the words left his mouth – they had sounded a lot less like a prim schoolboy in his head earlier. And what if she hadn't a clue what he was talking about?

But the Duchess's face lit up. 'Oh yes, Endymion! "A thing of beauty is a joy for ever!"'

'You've read Keats?' He cringed again, this time because of the over-keenness in his voice.

'Of course,' she said, beaming.

Reining in a grin of his own, he said, 'I wanted to bring a sheep and a dog, but William said no.'

'Ha! I wish you had. Such a spoilsport, William. What on earth are you meant to be anyway?'

'I'm offended you even need to ask, Aunt Georgina. I'm clearly Bottom from *A Midsummer Night's Dream*. Why else would I be carrying a donkey's head?'

'But you're not carrying a donkey's head,' said Eliza, softly.

'Damn!' William looked about in panic. 'I must have left it somewhere. Landseer, come and help me find it.'

'Why me?'

'Because you're the one who'll be hauled over the coals by the Academy if I lose it.'

Edwin grudgingly admitted the truth of this, bowed his apologies to the ladies with a flourish of his cloak, then wrenched himself away from the diamonds to go on William's ass hunt.

It took some time and more claret cup, but they found the head. William put it on and went to fulfil promises to dance. Leaning against the saloon wall for a few moments' rest, Edwin was hailed by George Hayter, who, seemingly impervious to the ever-increasing heat, was wearing a tricorn hat and a long black cloak over a pale silk suit. A long-nosed mask dangled, skull-like, from a silver-topped cane he held loosely in one hand.

'Ned, you here? They must be letting anyone in these days.' George lifted a cup to his lips, which were already stained red.

'I could say the same thing. You look terrifying.'

'Prince Leopold invited me.' George's normally pale face was flushed. Edwin wondered just how much claret cup he'd had. 'And this might look terrifying to a cockney brat like you, but it's a genuine Venetian *Carnevale* costume. Remind me what you're dressed as?'

'Endymion.'

'Of course. The shepherd boy ravished in his sleep by the moon goddess. How very apt. Christ, this punch is ghastly!' George shuddered, then tapped Edwin's sandal with his cane. 'Listen, you might be the favourite with the Bedfords at the moment, but don't let it go to your head, and don't do anything stupid.'

'What are you talking about?' Edwin kicked the cane away, feeling even hotter.

'I mean, Endymion, Gods and mortals don't mix. Or if they do, it rarely ends well for the mortal.' The eyes in the shadow of the hat were bloodshot and boasted shadows of their own. The Hayter household must be going through one of its difficult patches.

'I still don't know what you mean.' Edwin glared at the pulsating dancefloor, where couples twirled and thundered in ever expanding and contracting circles, telling himself he was looking for William and Eliza, not the Duchess.

'Oh, I think you do. And don't fall into the trap of thinking you can ever be one of them,' George said.

Edwin made to leave but George stopped him, lifting his cane, the mask swinging from it like a pendulum. 'They flirt with us when they want us to flatter them, to immortalise them; but we're not like them. We're like the piper there. We get privileges – who but a painter can stare so hard and for so long at a duchess or a duke? But that's precisely because we don't signify, see? No threat. Might as well be favourite dogs. Or monkeys. Privileged pets to be cast aside when the novelty wears off. Remember that, Ned.'

'I've never cast a pet aside,' Edwin said, glaring at him.

'But you've never been quite normal. And I'm grateful for it. Believe me. But don't rely on anyone else thinking the way you do – especially not goddesses.' George raised his glass, grimacing at its near emptiness. 'I'm not trying to spoil your night; I just don't want to see you get hurt. Believe it or not, I do have a heart. Here, let's drink to your stag picture. The Duke's told me how excited he is about it.'

Feigning enthusiasm, Edwin drank. Annoyed, and telling himself that George was just jealous, he found Eliza and threw himself into the next few dances with such vigour he almost lost his cloak. Handing her to her next partner, he spotted the donkey's head resting on a bench against the wall and slumped down next to it. He'd just pinned his costume back together and was relacing a sandal when something brushed his shoulder.

'My thing of beauty!'

His brain spun in several directions at once. The Duchess was standing above him, swaying slightly, the strings of diamonds draped over her dress glittering like constellations.

'Don't get up, Endymion.' With a swish of silk, she spread her skirts and sat down. The donkey's head lay on its side between them but even so she was close enough for him to smell the champagne on her breath.

'I have a confession,' she said, eyes lowered towards a garland on the side of the bench, plucking a rose from its centre.

'I haven't actually read all of *Endymion* . . . But I have read the beginning – several times.'

Edwin laughed, heart pounding.

She grinned. 'It's very serious! You mustn't tell my sister. She's always so s-superior about reading and things.' She slurred the 's' of 'superior'.

'My lips are sealed,' he said.

'Your lips are . . .' The Duchess's own lips parted. She shook herself. 'Very kind. You've been dancing?'

'Badly.' Edwin smiled, watching the lights reflected in her eyes.

'I bet that's not true.' She wagged the rose at him. 'But you've had an enjoyable time?'

'Yes, have you?'

'I think so. Yes. No. Yes. It's been a strange day.' She pulled off a petal. 'Did William tell you about my father's wife?'

'He did. I'm sorry.'

'Don't be. I'm not. Well, I am. For him. But he shouldn't have married her.' The petal fluttered to the floor. 'Housekeeper as mistress was bad enough. But wife? I would never have married her. I'm sure you would never have married her. I mean – oh, you know what I mean . . . I mean I know what I mean.' She shook her head, pinched off another petal. This one ripped down the centre, half of it drifted onto Edwin's bare knee.

'I do,' he said.

'You always do. But I don't want to talk about this any more. I don't know why I brought it up. I've had too much champagne – and I want more.' With a lopsided smile, she waved the battered rose at him again. 'And I want to dance and forget all about everything. Come on.' She grasped her skirts and stood. Then swayed. 'Actually . . . give me your arm, I think I might need it.'

Leaving the remains of the flower behind the donkey's ear and leaning on him in a way that provoked some of the least platonic feelings Edwin had ever experienced, she steered a winding course past dancers and spectators. Many of them, like their ostrich feathers, had begun to droop with the heat and the lateness of the hour. Passing the grand staircase, now littered with fallen flowers, she nodded to a footman, who opened a gilded door and let them into one of the private rooms. Inside, illuminated only by a few candelabra, was a small pantheon of high nobility. As they made their way to join her siblings in the Gordon party, Edwin swallowed a wave of awe on passing within inches of the Duke of Wellington, who was holding up a fiddle and talking intently to a member of Gow's band.

The Duchess procured two glasses of champagne, drinking half of hers in one gulp as she handed Edwin the other. The fiddler, having recovered his instrument from Wellington, played a few notes. The Gordons and several others formed into pairs and took up dancing positions. Putting her now empty glass aside, the Duchess took Edwin's arm again.

'Now, Endymion, finish that,' she nodded at his champagne, 'and you can show me just how bad a dancer you really are.'

Edwin attempted to concentrate on the tune as the notes leapt, twisted, and plunged, but it was impossible. The Duchess's breath was hot beneath his ear as she whispered the steps to him, adding,

'You're a liar, you dance very prettily.'

'Only because you're telling me what to do,' he whispered back, inhaling – almost tasting – the salted-rose scent of her neck.

As the fiddler drew the last, lingering chord to a close, their gazes locked. It took the sound of shattering glass and

Wellington bellowing that someone had knocked over his whisky to prompt Edwin to lower his eyes from hers and bow. As he straightened up, heart thumping, William's voice hit him like a bucket of cold water.

'There you are, Landseer! I've been looking for you everywhere. I think I'm in love.'

'Oh, with whom?' the Duchess asked. Edwin forced himself to look away from the rise and fall of fifty-thousand guineas' worth of diamonds.

'Aunt Georgina!' William kissed her on both cheeks and Edwin's stomach gave an envious lurch. 'I didn't recognise you. Your necklace dazzled me.'

'What a thought.' She blushed crimson. 'But who are you in love with?'

'Miss Bridgeman and possibly Miss Campbell ... I'm not quite sure. Anyway, they've both gone home. Eliza too.'

'Gone home? What time is it?' asked the Duchess, blush spreading to her chest as she caught Edwin's eye for a split second.

'Not sure. Four? Five?' William yawned. 'I don't suppose you've seen that damned donkey's head?'

An hour later, the sky was a delicate shade of apricot rising into duck egg blue and Edwin found himself alone, crossing the silent classical frontages that curved along Piccadilly, ears ringing with echoes of music and dancing. Soon busier, straighter streets with narrower houses rose above him, where the morning sounds started earlier and shadows lingered longer. Here, the soot-blackened bricks were adorned with painted advertising messages rather than stonemason's flourishes, and men and vehicles wore a livery of sandwich boards and placards, promoting coffee houses, exhibitions, and freak shows.

Edwin walked in a daze of sublime exhaustion, thoughts drifting at random from dancing, to diamonds, to the Duke of Wellington's smashed glass, then to the Duke of Bedford's study, which seemed to belong to a different life. Everything – time, movement, sounds – had acquired an oddly malleable quality. The sun, flooding now over the rooftops, warmed his face and made him blink. Each drowsy flicker of his eyelids offered an image of the Duchess, which he no longer had the inclination or energy to dismiss.

Inhaling the beery tang of bread proving and the scent of fresh straw and sweet hay, he told himself half-heartedly it was a good thing he wouldn't see her again until the Highland trip in September. Two months would be plenty of time to get over her.

At last, he turned on the aching, blistered balls of his feet into Fitzroy Square, passed the studio, then into Conway Street. In spite of the clunk of the door behind him, the house remained asleep. From the hallway, he could hear the snores of at least four of the eight resident Landseers. As usual, his brother Charles in their shared bedroom had taken the role of principal soloist.

Deciding against going to bed, he left his crook in the umbrella stand and slipped through the whitewashed door, down and round the curl of the stairs to the kitchen. His stout white terrier, Brutus, wagged his stump of a tail and wove himself around his ankles in his own version of a reel. Music and laughter still haunting his ears, Edwin liberated a hunk of cheese from the larder and sank onto the cool floorboards next to the dog, back against the wooden doors of the dresser. Watching the sunlight begin to stream through the dusty windows onto the high shelves of dull pans, he gave half the cheese to Brutus. In his tired brain, snores blended with bagpipes and he was dimly aware of the dog licking the remaining cheese from his increasingly limp fingers while Keats's lines ran through his head, draping themselves like strings of diamonds over a figure as bright as the moon:

*A thing of beauty is a joy forever*
*Its loveliness increases, it will never*
*Pass into nothingness, but will keep*
*A bower quiet for us, and a sleep*
*Full of sweet dreams, and health, and quiet breathing.*

# Part II

# *May 1859, London*

'HOW ARE THE LIONS?' BELL RASPS.

'Fine,' Edwin lies.

He sets the canvas on the easel, but the damned thing is in the wrong place. Trying not to make too much noise, he nudges the apparatus closer to the sofa on which Bell is propped up.

'Is it a year yet?'

'Not quite. There's a dead lion in the studio right now, if you must know. Fresh from the zoo. Well, it was fresh . . .' He gives the easel another shove with his foot; why won't it co-operate? 'It reeks now. Young Keyl's making casts of it. I only obeyed your summons to escape the stench.' Another lie. This time one Bell can't possibly believe. They both know why Edwin's come. That he'd never have refused.

Unable to meet his friend's eye, Edwin unfurls a leather roll of brushes with an over-hasty flick of the wrist, sending them skittering onto the floor. Most are stopped by the thick pile of the rug, but one makes it to the polished boards and rolls under the sofa. As Edwin kneels and reaches for it, Bell grasps his wrist with a feebleness that makes him want to yell and weep.

'You know I hate painting portraits,' Edwin says, his voice shaking on the final word; he keeps his eyes fixed on the thin little brush that had tried to escape and hide.

'Thank you,' Bell says.

Edwin can only manage a grunt as he stands, roughly brushing non-existent dust off his trousers, then from his eyes. Counting slowly along with the clock as it strikes three, he regains a modicum of composure. He tries not to look at the medicine bottles on the table, labelled in the thick, upright script of Thomas Hyde Hills, Bell's colleague in the chemist's business for more than twenty years, who's lived with him here at Langham Place for almost as long. Snapping open his paintbox, he adds colours instinctively to the palette; there's no time for sketches, no time for thinking. No time to be throwing brushes around the room like a cursed fool.

Bell closes his eyes, which even now look as though they are laughing thanks to the diagonal creases at their outer edges. That look had been there from their very first meeting. It remained through the days of Bell's boyish awe – embarrassingly close to adulation – as Edwin gave him drawing tips. That was before Bell's expulsion from Sass's drawing school for singing forbidden French songs had curtailed his artistic career. The look was there through meandering talk over the chemist's counter of dogs, horses, and the *haut ton*, while Bell mixed cures for the blue devils and headaches that proved to be unavoidable side effects of Edwin's success. Bell's eyes glinted merrily through country house parties, over port-stained shirt fronts and ill-contained laughter; through parties here at Langham Place, where Hills and Bell held court, matched painters to models, and everyone let their hair down and secrets out. Some secrets at least. Even through the darkest moments – when the blue devils seemed unconquerable – Bell's eyes looked as though they were smiling. Even now.

Edwin grits his teeth. His eyes trace the contours of Bell's sunken cheeks; his hand puts back what life he can into the canvas version. Bell won't want Hills to have a picture that resembles a death mask. Edwin's hand shakes, he adds too much white to the palette, swipes at it roughly. Pauses, collects himself.

Hills enters with a creak of floorboards, heavy tread muffled by the carpet. He nods to Edwin, then busies himself with Bell, plumping cushions, adjusting blankets, stoppers clinking in and out of bottles as he measures doses. Grimacing from the taste or the pain or both, Bell leans forward, opens his mouth, and swallows, all with pitifully perfect timing. Edwin knows how familiar the movements must be to both. He rolls a brush between his finger and thumb and continues, adds shades of gold, ochre, a hint of Indian red.

Hills leaves, Bell dozes. Edwin paints on as the silent room echoes with three decades of friendship. The walls, hung with one of the best collections of modern painters' work in London, are layered with stories, laughter, crises, triumphs. Edwin reaches into his pocket and touches the brass key, turns it over. He's always had one, ever since Bell moved here. If he called and Bell was out, he'd turn a painting to face the wall to let him know. Bell did the same at St John's Wood. The last time that happened was months ago.

When Bell wakes, Edwin says, 'Baron Marochetti told me they have an excellent lion cast in Turin. The Government has requested a loan of it for my beasts. Makes me feel quite important. Some compensation for having to wallow about in so much clay – it's a devil to get out of the fingernails.'

'You have actually begun then?' A hint of a smile threatens to push Bell's cheekbones through his paper-thin skin. Hills said he barely eats now.

'Of course.' Edwin has to pause, blinks hard, focuses on the brush between his fingers. 'If Keyl's casts are good, and we get this Italian model, Trafalgar Square will be a zoo in no time.'

'Jessie says you've been unwell again.'

Edwin shrugs, his brush darkening the shadows that show the firmness of Bell's jaw.

'We all have. There's been a plague on all Landseers. Did she tell you Charles had whooping cough?'

'She says you've been brooding.'

Edwin shrugs again, runs his eyes over Bell's coat, stares fixedly as he mixes blood red with burnt umber, then draws in impenetrable Mars black.

'Give Caro up.'

'I can't. Not while there's still hope.'

'Hope?' The word cracks as it leaves Bell's lips.

'Girls turn chaps down all the time. They expect to be asked three or four times, don't they? Always happens that way in novels.'

'Don't be a fool. She's married someone else.'

'The new divorce laws – it's not like before. If you knew what she'd said, what she'd written . . .'

'Priceless: while Dickens and Bulwer scramble to keep themselves out of the divorce courts, Edwin Landseer scrambles to get himself in.' Bell coughs, his features twist horribly. Cut to the quick, Edwin downs palette and brush and fumbles with a jug, eventually managing to hold a glass of water to Bell's lips.

'Give up Caro. And the Duchess. Forgive her. Forgive yourself,' Bell rasps. 'You'll never finish those lions if you keep spiralling back into all that.'

At the sound of a slow step and a dull clink of glass, Edwin turns. Hills is staring at him. His heavy features wear the same resentful look as when Edwin and Bell used to stagger into Langham Place, late and laughing, and find Hills in dressing gown, slippers, and cap by the embers of a fire and a candle that had worried itself to a stump. Lifting the bottle labelled laudanum, Hills says, 'Try not to talk too much, Jacob.'

Edwin counts the rusty drops as they fall into a liqueur glass between Hills's fingers.

'Can't hurt now,' Bell says, taking the glass.

Picking up his palette again, Edwin resumes work while more pillow plumping goes on. At length, as Hills pulls a blanket higher over Bell's sleeping form, he takes up the most delicate of the brushes – the one that had tried to hide earlier – and dabs it in luminous lead white, adding the faintest of highlights to the forehead, the bristles caressing the canvas with all the feelings he can't put into words.

'Done,' he says, his voice so low it's almost drowned by the clock striking five.

'See?' Bell whispers without opening his eyes, 'you can work quickly when you really want to.'

While the carriage is brought round, Edwin waits with Hills in the study. Hills is already well into a glass of brandy and begins to fill another but Edwin shakes his head, not trusting his voice to hold firm.

Hills continues to pour. 'You look as though you need it. I'll write a label to prove it's medicinal if you like.'

Edwin closes his eyes. The glass chinks against his teeth, sending a dull thud through his skull as the vapours swirl around his mouth.

'How long?'

'A week? Maybe two?'

A fortnight later, Bell is gone.

A week after that, Jessie hands Edwin a letter from the Office of Works expressing regret that it will not be possible to obtain the anatomical lion cast from Turin – the thing's been broken up and is possibly in Sardinia, possibly at the bottom of the sea.

Another week and she hands him a note from Caro, announcing her return from honeymoon and summoning him to dine. Before he has time to give in to temptation, he writes a reply telling her he cannot come, leaves it on the hall table for the post, then hurries to the studio.

Locking the door, he stares at Keyl's lion casts. They will not do. He should have been there to supervise. Should have done it himself. The old lion had rotted too quickly. He paces up and down between easels and shadows, panic crawling up his spine.

How is he meant to do this – without the casts? Without Caro? Without Bell?

He stops pacing, glares at the bottle that's been on top of the cabinet for some days now. Reflected on its green, sloping shoulders is part of the Highland flood picture, which occupies the main easel in the centre of the room. Humans and animals stare desperately at him, made grotesque by the curve of the glass. A raging torrent threatens to destroy everything they hold dear. In front of them, his own dark silhouette lurks: the imp in the bottle. Next to it is the novel Rachel wrote: *Jessie Cameron: A Highland Story.*

Rachel.

Rachel. Who he saw at the Queen's ball just before Bell died.

Rachel. Who saw him and hurried away.

Edwin seizes the bottle. The reflections waver and disperse as he upends it into a glass, but they regroup as he puts it back down and reaches for the book. Now a lion sketch, resting on a smaller easel, ripples, seems to snarl over his shoulder as he turns the pages. He was a fool to read the novel when it was published; an even bigger fool to read it again now. It brings back the glen in all its stern splendour: autumn days that once seemed endless; the whisky stills, the turf-roofed houses, the people. So much of it swept away.

It's always this way: memories rise like bubbles, shimmering in sunlight, then they drift into the shadows and burst against the rocks hidden in the darkness.

The deepest shadow is Georgina's death.

He told her not to go to Nice that winter. They could have gone to Brighton, Margate, anywhere. But she promised she would be back before he knew it, even said they might tell Rachel the truth when she returned if it all went well.

But she hadn't returned.

*She wouldn't have gone if she really loved you,* growls a voice from the darkness. *She wouldn't have insisted on keeping things hidden.*

'That's not true,' Edwin snarls back.

He will not think about it. He will not. Thinking about it makes it real. It will burst the last bubbles – the ones in which she is waiting for him at the huts in the glen, scolding him for being late. He can't face that. Not yet. Not alone.

He lifts his glass, grateful at least for the numbing comfort of the wine. It won't last, but it's better than nothing.

Friends had been so kind. But he'd pushed them away. Even the Queen. He shudders at the memory of her face as he yelled at her, that he couldn't take any more relentless sympathy, that she had no idea what it was like. Even the dachshund at her heels had looked at him as though he were a demon.

He'd only been able to face it – or begin to face it – with Caro by his side. She listened, let him talk and weep, gave such good advice. He hadn't wanted her to be a substitute for Georgina. No one could ever be a substitute. He just wanted someone to stop him talking to the beasts in the shadows.

But he hadn't told Caro about Rachel, or that damned letter. He'd told Georgina to burn it. Why did she never listen?

# *September 1824, Scotland*

THE TRIP TO SCOTLAND DID NOT BEGIN WELL.

Edwin had arranged to sail on the fashionable new steamer, the *James Watt*, at the end of August with Charles Leslie, an old friend and newly elected Associate of the Royal Academy. He'd planned to cut a dash in Edinburgh, visit his literary hero, Sir Walter Scott, to whom Leslie had an introduction, then head on alone to the Highlands to study deer and join the Bedfords.

But, from the moment they floated clear of the forest of swaying masts crowding Blackwall Dock, he was humiliatingly seasick. Convinced a bilious death was only a heave away, he abandoned ship when they put in at Scarborough with half the journey still to go. He spent the next few days hunched miserably on a succession of lumpy coach seats, rutted roads jarring his bones and churning his still-spasming stomach as he gazed out of filthy windows at windswept moors. Sometimes he wondered if this was what they'd looked like in Hotspur's time and tried to make mental notes for the Duke's stag hunting picture; mostly he concentrated on not vomiting. At least it stopped him thinking about the Duchess.

By the time the final coach lumbered into the salty, gull-filled streets of Edinburgh's port town, Leith, the only thing on his mind was sleep. After fourteen hours of blissful oblivion on a hard hotel bed, he woke hungry for the first time in almost a week. Giving kippers a wide berth, he fortified himself with tea and toast, then set about rearranging the plans that had been upset by his lack of sea legs. He wrote to the Bedfords, who he was now in danger of missing. He'd already missed Scott. Everyone to whom he explained his predicament seemed to think it hilarious or profound (or both) to quote Robert Burns's infernal words: *The best laid schemes o' mice an' men gang aft agley.* If he heard the line one more time, he would scream.

Thank God he hadn't missed the deer: they were still waiting for him at Blair House, seat of the Duke of Atholl, to whom the Duchess had arranged an introduction. His stomach quailed at the prospect of another two days of stuffy coaches to reach Blair, but once they were moving, glimpses of wooded slopes, waterfalls, and distant mountains turned nausea into wonder. As they set off in a dawn mist on the second day, his heart rather than his stomach leapt as he saw his first wild Scottish deer – a hind and a well-grown calf – blurring into the blue-tinged forest edge.

With whitewashed walls and narrow windows, Blair House looked more like a barracks than a ducal seat, but Edwin couldn't have cared less. He was soon so engrossed in drawing that nothing else mattered. It even took the edge off his anxiety about rearranging the rendezvous with the Bedfords. There was a quick grace and a wildness to these deer, even those near the house, that their park cousins of the South lacked. He'd never seen anything so free. After a few days scrambling around steep, tree-clad slopes, sketchbook and pencil employed at every opportunity, he couldn't close his eyes without seeing white-tipped antlers, russet haunches, and wide apart, watchful eyes, and couldn't sleep for dreaming of the larger, truly wild herds, deep in the glens that he was determined to find a way of seeing.

Other sketchbook pages filled with drawings of the sturdy Highland ponies, with their bold broad muzzles and deep jowls, which Edwin could hear and smell from his small bedroom above the stables. He was eyeballing one – a hairy grey mare who looked at him sarcastically from behind a thick mane – when his host appeared. Tall, broad-shouldered, and as heavily jowled as the ponies, the Duke of Atholl was as different from the Duke of Bedford as Blair was from Woburn. With him was John Crerar, his head forester, who also bore a pony-like aspect.

'Landseer,' Atholl said, leaning on his stick as though it were a claymore. 'Crerar tells me you want to see some deerstalking for this picture of yours. We've had precious little of it this year; I'm out of action – damned pony trod on my damned toes,' he tapped his foot with the stick, 'and the guests have been too lazy, only interested in the damned grouse.' A harrumph set the jowls wobbling. 'But there's an Englishman – name of Scrope – has taken Bruar Lodge. Crerar's out with him tomorrow. He's agreed to have you and your pencils along. Bit of an amateur artist too. Says he knows your father – Landseer the engraver, that him?'

'Yes, Your Grace.'

Atholl's jowls juddered again as he nodded. 'Better ride over this evening. Scrope likes an early start. Crerar will point you in the right direction. Oh, and,' Atholl pulled a letter from his pocket, 'I've just had this from the Duchess of Bedford. Asked if you were still here. Says she's paying me a visit in the next few days.'

'Thank you, Your Grace,' Edwin said, elation and trepidation at both pieces of news chasing each other like over-excited spaniels around his brain.

The start at Bruar Lodge was the sort of early that involved waking in total, disorientating darkness. Having fumbled with buttons and boots and groped his way down the bare boards of the stairs, Edwin found Scrope – ruddy-faced and obscenely wide awake – in the sparsely furnished dining room, presiding over a platter of cold partridge, a dish of scrambled eggs, and the smell of toast.

'I hear you came by steamer, how was it?' Scrope asked, shovelling egg into his mouth.

'Torture,' Edwin said. Of all the things to be reminded of at this ungodly hour. Buttering a slice of toast, he gave as brief an account of his journey as politeness would allow.

'Commiserations!' Scrope shovelled in more egg. '"The best laid schemes", eh?'

Edwin grimaced and poured himself a cup of tea.

'A day on the hill will sort you out.' Scrope beamed. 'This your first time in Scotland?'

'Yes.' Edwin wriggled his foot to shake out a crease in his sock and make his new boots less uncomfortable. 'Though I grew up with my father's prints of your Scotch scenes – my sister would pretend they were scenes from Walter Scott's poems when she read to me.'

'Ah, Miss Jane! Such a promising girl. She even helped your father with one of the plates, a loch view, if I remember rightly.

But you were the one he wouldn't stop talking about, though you can't have been more than five or six years old.' Scrope's fork flashed as, chuckling, he speared a slice of partridge. 'You threw an almighty tantrum because a cab horse outside the window moved off before you'd finished drawing it. Had to be hauled away by your mother!'

'I'm sure that wasn't me.' Edwin glared at the leaves floating darkly in his tea, remembering the drawing with surprising clarity. He'd been convinced it would be the best he'd ever done – until the fool of a man moved the horse.

A click of canine claws and a gentle cough from the doorway announced the presence of John Crerar, tamping a plug of tobacco into the bowl of a clay pipe. A couple of deerhounds stood next to him, long muzzles twitching at the scent of breakfast.

Crerar looked up briefly from the pipe. 'Ready, gentlemen?'

In the courtyard, chimneys and treetops were beginning to solidify against an inky, moonless sky. As directed by Crerar, Edwin hauled himself onto the nearest of a group of ponies tethered beneath the outline of an archway. As his thigh muscles reminded him that yesterday's four-mile ride from Blair to Bruar was more time in the saddle than he'd had in months, he ran his fingers through the pony's wiry mane and patted her neck, more to calm his own nerves than hers.

A breeze whispered through unseen leaves and birds chattered maniacally about the approaching dawn. There was a whickering and snorting as Scrope swung himself onto another pony, all the while addressing Edwin in a stage whisper loud enough to be heard back in Edinburgh, pointing out rifles, telescopes, and panniers of provisions. Pipe bowls glowed red then were emptied onto the moss-covered cobbles. A dog whined. Edwin shifted his satchel over his shoulder, straightening a kink in the strap.

It wasn't how he'd imagined a deer hunt. Head full of ballads and warriors, and several glasses of port, he'd taken in little of Scrope's extended explanations the night before. Now, rather than setting off at a crazed canter, they plodded along. Crerar and a skinny youth led the ponies while a pale dawn seeped into the sky then sunrise added a golden glaze to the undersides of scattered clouds and lingering shreds of mist.

The gilding was long gone and they'd climbed above the treeline by the time they dismounted. Crerar and Scrope drew out brass telescopes and mumbled to each other about deer in the distance. There was no horn blowing or wild hunting cries, just more pipe smoking. Only the trembling deerhounds betrayed any excitement. Unable to make out even a single beast, Edwin sat on the damp ground, watching his pony rip up mouthfuls of waxy grass, his own fingers tugging irritably at gnarled heather stems. If he was this bad at spotting deer, he might as well have stayed at Blair. Especially if the Bedfords might be there.

'Do you see them, Mr Landseer?' Crerar ambled over. 'Just there, between the big rock and the burn.'

Edwin shook his head. It was ridiculous. There were hundreds of big rocks and thousands of burns tumbling down the hill. Scrope joined in with enthusiastic, unhelpful directions.

'Here.' Crerar handed him the telescope. 'Rest it on your knee. That's it. Now, do you see?'

Redoubling his efforts to ignore Scrope's jabbering, Edwin closed one eye and peered through the glass. The useless thing was black, then green with a dark crescent, then a green dot encircled by gloom. What if the Duchess arrived and he missed her again?

'Take your time, lad.' Crerar's soft lilt mingled with sweet pipe smoke. 'Relax.'

Edwin drew in a breath slowly, blinked, then settled back to the eyepiece. Damn her. Damn the telescope; still black, but the green circle was larger. And larger. He twisted the tube, rocks came into focus, a burn — and there they were. A hundred, more ... He never was any good at counting. It didn't matter.

'Your face, laddie!' laughed Crerar. 'Anybody might think it was a hill full of naked lassies.'

'I'd rather see this,' Edwin said, not daring to move for fear of losing the view, relief and awe washing away thoughts of the Duchess. 'But no need to tell the lassies.' There was nothing like this, nothing even close, in London, in the menageries, even at Woburn.

'You won't see a herd like that anywhere else.' Crerar's voice was like a whisper in church. 'My father, my father's father, and his father before him, have all been part of it. Generations of work have made Atholl what it is. I've seen them every day of my life and I could still sit and watch all day.' He gently prised the telescope from Edwin's hands. 'But now we have work to do.'

They left the ponies with the skinny boy and continued on foot, a new severity in their silence. Even Scrope's stage whispers stopped. There was wiry, trouser-tugging heather and bright, boot-sucking moss. There was crawling through bogs and burns, gritting teeth to stay silent even as spring water shocked knees, belly, and groin, always hoping against hope that his sketchbook – wrapped in oil cloth in the satchel on his back – would stay dry. They slid on their stomachs across red-tipped grass and were set upon by clouds of inquisitive midges, before finally creeping to a halt behind a rocky rise.

As Scrope crawled to the top of the slope and leant in to the rifle, Edwin's heart hammered so loudly he was amazed the deer hadn't heard it and fled. He'd hunted rabbits and dissected carcasses for anatomical studies, but this was different – deer were different. More beautiful, more fascinating. A stab of guilt made him momentarily as uncomfortable as the icy water, but his mind wouldn't stop racing.

The boom of the rifle eclipsed everything. The ground vibrated as the deerhounds thundered past, a blur through the sharp-scented powder smoke. Crerar and Scrope followed. Ears ringing, caught in the wave of dogs and men crashing down the hillside, Edwin ran, leapt, stumbled, moral qualms muted by a visceral compulsion. Heart pounding, chest heaving, he reached the others by a stream at the bottom of the valley. The stag lay, dead, on the bank, thick, bright blood shining on its shoulder, glossy as paint on a palette: so intensely red against the browns and greens; terribly beautiful and beautifully terrible.

Still gasping for breath, unable to take his eyes from the sight, Edwin felt a gentle touch on his shoulder.

'Here, lad.' Crerar offered him a flask wrapped in worn leather. 'There'd be something wrong with you if you didn't feel it. He was a noble beast.'

Bringing the flask to his lips with one shaking hand, Edwin wiped the sweat – and tears – from his face with the other. Then reached for his sketchbook.

Scrope rode back with Edwin to Blair the following morning. As their ponies trudged around the last bend in the track and the house came into view, there was a shrill yell of 'Lanny!'. Heart soaring, Edwin saw Lord Alexander Russell wielding a wooden sword and bearing down on him as fast as his three-year-old legs would carry him. Skirts bunched in one hand, half jogging, half walking behind, was the Duchess.

'I'm sorry,' she panted, scooping Alexander into her arms and making a face at him that provoked shrieks of laughter. 'I've tried to teach him Landseer, but he can't,– or won't,– say it. He's been so excited. Wouldn't stop talking about you the whole of the ride through the glen. And then you weren't here. Such impudence!' She grinned, blushing scarlet as she set her squirming son back on the ground.

'I didn't know you were coming.' Trying not to look too pleased, Edwin dismounted with as much grace as he could summon from his complaining muscles, then kissed her hand far more fleetingly than he wanted to.

'Pah! That's a feeble excuse.' She parried a lunge from Alexander's sword, then turned to Scrope, who had also dismounted and was holding the reins of both ponies. 'You must be Mr Scrope? Atholl speaks highly of you. My husband was wondering if you'd care to join us at Forest Lodge for a day's shooting?'

'I'm sure I should be honoured, madam, but, but I regret to say I'm not sure who your husband is.'

It took all of Edwin's self-control not to laugh at the indignation on the Duchess's face.

'My husband, *Mr* Scrope, is the Duke of Bedford. I am the Duchess, but you may call me Your Grace.'

Unable to keep a straight face any longer, Edwin feigned a coughing fit and bent down to talk to Alexander about swords while Scrope garbled apologies then beat a hasty retreat to the stables with the ponies.

'You should really call me Your Grace too, you know,' the Duchess said, taking Edwin's arm as they walked to the front of the house. 'Heaven knows why I let you get away with such slackness. But I'm sorry not to have given you more notice. We've been at sixes and sevens – my father's housekeeper-wife died, so I went to see him, poor old thing. And he had some business with Atholl but refuses to travel himself – mourning for the housekeeper I suppose – so I said I would attend to it. So here I am. Attending as well as anyone ever attended to anything. I even managed to get Atholl to agree to John, the Duke, I mean, having a few days' shooting. So we're in Forest Lodge, just up there,' she pointed to a steep-sided glen, 'and we get to see you in spite of your best efforts to avoid us. I'm kidnapping you. Honestly, late to Edinburgh, not here yesterday . . . but I'm rattling on worse than the children. What have you been doing?.'

'Well,' in an act of great disloyalty, Edwin's face betrayed him by grinning, 'first I was embarrassingly seasick, now I'm embarrassingly saddle-sore, and yesterday I embarrassed myself by crying when Scrope shot a stag.'

Her eyes danced with his for a moment.

'I've missed you,' she said softly.

That afternoon, Edwin and Scrope rode alongside the Duchess's two-wheeled dog cart, which contained herself, Alexander, and various provisions she'd commandeered. Blair House was long out of sight, and she and Scrope were debating whether the Tweed or the Spey was the better river for salmon fishing, when Scrope held up a hand.

'What ho, did you hear that?'

'Yes,' declared Alexander. 'Hear what?'

Edwin, who'd been alternating between scrutinising the trees for deer and watching a lock of hair work its way loose beneath the Duchess's bonnet, said he'd heard nothing except the river.

'A roar.' Scrope's stage whisper was back in action. 'I thought I heard a stag roar, my little Lord.'

'Lions roar. Not stags, silly,' said Alexander, playing with one of the tartan ribbons trailing from his mother's bonnet.

'Don't call Mr Scrope silly, darling.' The Duchess planted a kiss on Alexander's hatless head, her eyes flicking to Edwin. 'And stags do roar. When they're in love.'

Edwin told himself it couldn't be more than idle flirting. So there couldn't be any harm in enjoying it.

'Ha! My dear Duchess – Your Grace – I've never heard it put like that before. Love!' Scrope chortled. 'My young lord, the red deer are beginning their mating season; we call it the rut. Because they are in love as your noble mother so poetically puts it, the stags – the boy deer – leave their herds and pine for their ladies. Some say it's the first cold weather that makes them . . . err . . . or that eating wild mushrooms gives them . . . err . . . notions.' Scrope's colour changed from sun-bronzed to crimson. Edwin pressed his lips together to hide his amusement. 'Others think that the hinds – that's the lady deer, my lord – coming into . . . err . . . season has an . . . err . . . drives the stags mad with . . . err . . .'

'Love,' said the Duchess, with a delicate flick of the reins.

'Yes, Your Grace.' Scrope lifted his hat, wiped his brow. 'And that's when they roar!' He bellowed like a bad-tempered ox, sending Alexander into fits of giggles. 'And then they fight over their fair ladies, sometimes to the death, just like the knights of old.'

By the time Scrope finished explaining further theories on the romantic life of red deer, Forest Lodge was in sight, Alexander's silky chestnut head lolled sleepily against his mother's arm, and the lock of hair Edwin had been watching had completely escaped the bonds of her bonnet and lay curled on the smooth skin of her neck.

Forest Lodge was almost as sparsely furnished as Bruar, but the presence of so many Bedfords made dinner chaotic, cacophonous and brilliant. By the time the servants removed the final plates, the candles were half their original height, and talk had wandered from deer to grouse, to types of heather, whisky, and the best materials for boot soles. At the sound of a chair scraping, all eyes, not least Edwin's, turned to the Duchess's end of the table, where she stood, her own eyes narrowed, lips curling into a smile.

'Now, gentlemen,' she adjusted a green tartan ribbon tied beneath her bust, 'I fully accept that – in England – ladies are expected to retire when the port is brought out.' She stepped to the sideboard, from which she took a bottle. 'But this is Scotland, and this is whisky. So, I trust there are no expectations that I shall retire. Mr Scrope,' she placed the bottle in front of him, 'has been asking me about illicit whisky stills. I've always preferred the term private to illicit, but try this. It's from a still run by a delightful old poacher on my father's lands above the Spey. Liquid rent is one of his favourite traditions, though I'm sorry to say it's on the wane.'

'Why's that?' Scrope shuddered as he passed his nose over the neck of the bottle.

'Taxes.' The Duchess sat down and held out her glass for him to fill. 'Money-grubbing government. Grossly unfair, making it easier for vulgar industrialists to make bad whisky and harder for decent Highlanders to—'

The Duke coughed. 'My dear. Politics.'

The Duchess swallowed a mouthful of whisky, raised an eyebrow and blew him a kiss.

'Anyway,' she continued, 'I'm sure I saw a still during our ride here, not far into the glen. I shall be leading an expedition to find it tomorrow, should anyone wish to see one at close quarters.' Her eyes shone in the candlelight as she looked directly at Edwin. 'It would make a fine picture, if you need a change from deer, Lanny.'

The way she said 'Lanny' made him shiver.

The expedition took place the following afternoon, with a stiff breeze driving ragged clouds across a pale sky. The party consisted of Edwin, the Duchess, Eliza, and Wrio. Scrope dithered loudly, then elected to join the Duke in pursuit of grouse. As the River Tilt splashed beside them, the Duchess took Edwin's arm, ostensibly to stop herself slipping. Edwin asked her question after question about fish, hills, and whisky stills, ostensibly for artistic purposes, watching her eyes dance and cheeks dimple as she described the Highland summers of her childhood.

'I can't tell you how good it is to be here and away from Woburn,' she said, adjusting her thick plaid shawl. 'Bessy's back. I thought motherhood and a year in Europe might have softened her, but she's worse than ever. And John is so damned passive about it all – disappears to the library or the gardens or says he's going to his club ...' She kicked at a splinter of stone, sending it skittering off the path into a patch of marsh grass. 'Am I being unreasonable? Can't he just tell William it's not acceptable? She spreads gossip about me and my children, countermands my instructions to the servants, criticises everything—'

'I've told you before, you can always come and mix paints for me.' Edwin pressed her hand. 'Or why not stay here? I couldn't imagine anything finer.'

'You like it then?' She returned the pressure, making his stomach twist with guilty delight. 'I always maintained you were more sensible than you looked. Mind what you wish for though – if John keeps telling me I'm fussing over nothing or that it's all in my head, you will find me on your doorstep. But enough, I promised myself I wouldn't rant. Let's find this still.'

They left the riverbank and began to climb a steep slope, where the Duchess swore she'd seen signs of whisky production. Eliza and Wrio were some way behind.

'What do you think of those two?' The Duchess gazed back at them, shielding her eyes as the sun burst from behind a large cloud.

'I like them both very much.' Edwin pulled the collar of his coat up against the strengthening breeze, which was pulling the yellow leaves from a clump of birch trees, scattering them over the figures below.

'I didn't quite mean that.' The Duchess kept her eyes on her son and niece. 'I worry they want to be more than just cousins.'

Edwin gazed with new interest at Wrio, who he'd always thought too strait-laced for love affairs. A gust snatched Eliza's thin cotton shawl and deposited it on the ground a few feet away from her. Wrio scampered after it.

'She's a wonderful girl.' The Duchess pulled her own shawl tighter. 'But … cousins? And neither of them will have any money. Old Lord William hasn't a bean to give her. John will give them something, of course, but … one day he'll be gone and it will all be up to Tavistock.'

Having retrieved the scarf, Wrio slipped on the wet grass, then, laughing, limping, presented it to Eliza. Perhaps Edwin had underestimated him.

The Duchess muttered something in Gaelic, cupped her hands around her mouth and called, 'Come on you two!'

'Is it much further?' Wrio called back, now leaning on Eliza.

'No.' The Duchess placed her hands on her hips.

'You always say that,' said Wrio.

'I do not. Come on.'

'Perhaps we might go back, Aunt Georgina.' Eliza glanced at her cousin. 'Wrio's hurt his ankle and I'm getting cold.'

'And it's going to rain,' added Wrio, testing his injured ankle with a theatrical hop.

'Chickenheart!' The Duchess folded her arms. 'I've known the weather here my whole life. It's not going to rain. Go back if you must. We're going on.'

As soon as Wrio and Eliza were out of sight on their way back, it began to rain. Hard.

'Damn, damn, damn!' laughed the Duchess. 'There goes my bonnet and my pride! Quick, under here!' She stretched her plaid over her head like a tent. 'I might have been wrong about the weather, but I swear I'm right about the still. We can sit out this shower there – there might even be some whisky. Look! There, just before the burn. I knew it!'

'Where?'

'There! Quickly or there really will be no hope for my bonnet.'

Huddled close beneath the shawl, they half ran, half slipped as the rain came down even harder.

'Here we are!' the Duchess declared triumphantly. A thrill shot up Edwin's arm as she pulled him towards a dark, cave-like opening, adding 'duck!' just too late.

'Ouch!' He blinked, pain crawling from his forehead like hot needles across his scalp. A dim vision, part-cave, part-cottage, swam before his eyes. 'What was that?'

'A tree trunk. Let me look . . . You're bleeding.'

'What was it doing there?'

'Holding up the roof. Will you stop moving?' She placed a hand firmly on the side of his face.

She was so close. He could smell roses, could feel the memory of her pressed against him at the ball. Desire fought with dread, and won. He barely had to move for his lips to find hers, soft, yielding. There was an electric pause, then an increase in pressure as she kissed him back. His whole body sang. It lasted no more than two, perhaps three, seconds, before he pulled himself away, the rushing of blood in his ears almost louder than the burn outside.

'Your Grace,' he said, trembling like a deerhound as their eyes locked.

After some of the longest moments of Edwin's life, the Duchess blinked, licked her lips, and said, 'I thought I told you to stay still?'

'Sorry,' he said, heart pounding. 'I promise not to do it again.'

'That's almost certainly a good idea.' She straightened her shoulders, took out a handkerchief and pressed it to his forehead, the corners of her mouth twitching with a hint of a smile.

Edwin winced. '*Almost* certainly?'

She laughed, lowering her gaze. 'It's not that I'm not flattered. And it's not that I wouldn't want to . . . it's just . . .' She met his eyes again, balling up the bloodstained handkerchief in her fist.

Pulse still racing, Edwin said nothing.

The rain began to penetrate the roof of loosely woven pine branches. The Duchess shook herself as a drop landed on her nose. 'We should go further in. Mind that idiotic head of yours.'

Head stinging, heart galloping, Edwin felt his way in the gloom, fingers tingling as they slid over wiry roots, wet earth, and rough stones, finally coming to a halt on damp wooden boards. What the hell had he just done? Had she really kissed him back? The burn roared louder than ever. The Duchess knelt and reached behind a bench.

'Aha!' She stood up, brandishing a bottle. 'We could be here for a while. The least we can do is make ourselves comfortable.' Easing out the stopper, she said, '*Slàinte mhath!* Good health!' Drinking, then gasping 'it's a strong one', she handed the bottle to Edwin.

It was like swallowing fire.

'How's your head?' she said.

'Stings a bit, but not half as much as drinking that.'

'Let me see. Sit down.'

'Just now . . .' Edwin said, wincing, darts of pain and pleasure shooting to his fingertips as she touched his forehead. 'I'm sorry.'

'Are you?' She raised an eyebrow.

'Almost certainly,' he said with forced levity, passing her the bottle.

She took a long swig. 'You're infuriating, you know that? There I was, righteously indignant about my father bedding servants, my brother seducing governesses, my husband and his fancies . . .' Another swig. 'Of course, in public I don't mind: one is not *allowed* to mind as long as it's discreet – minding makes it a problem. But that doesn't mean . . .' She pushed the bottle into Edwin's chest and sat next to him. 'Then you come along and make me feel like a colossal hypocrite.'

'I really am sorry.'

'Stop apologising. If I were a man, I should have insisted you do it again. And again. It's not the kiss. A kiss doesn't signify, as my father's so fond of saying. It's the way you . . .' She waved a hand then dropped it to her side, where it rested against his. Warm, soft. 'My heart somersaults when I hear your name. And when I see you . . . everything somersaults.' Her little finger twitched, stroking the side of his hand.

Pulse pounding low in his stomach, Edwin began, 'I—' but she cut him off.

'And it's ridiculous! I'm old enough to be your mother. It's madness. I tell myself so, many times a day. Poor Josephine has had a lot to put up with . . .' Their little fingers curled around each other as she turned to him and added, 'but I want nothing more than to be kissed by you.'

A gust of wind lifted the mesh of branches a little, letting in a spray of rain and briefly illuminating a crimson blush covering her face and neck as the rest of their fingers slid together. He knew he should withdraw his hand. He knew what would happen if the Duke found out. The burn raged. The rain drummed on the branches. He tasted whisky on her lips, then her tongue. Out on the hill, a stag roared. Scrope's just-shot beast flickered briefly in his mind before he became utterly lost in the scent of peat smoke in the Duchess's hair and the taste of roses on her skin.

Back in London, autumn was fading to winter and guilt flitted around the edge of Edwin's thoughts like a midge that had followed him back from the Highlands. With the Bedfords gone to Brighton until Christmas (for sea air and stultifying boredom, the Duchess said), it was possible to ignore it – most of the time.

By day, there were plenty of distractions. He worked up his Scottish sketches. He tried to stop Jane – round-bellied and tired now – from fussing and tidying the studio. He dined with her and Mr Christmas, and George Hayter and his wife-in-all-but-law, Amelia. And there were plays and parties, and the new challenge of avoiding his eldest brother Tom's musings on the merits of Miss Pocock, a shrill, yellow-haired young woman who worked in his favourite confectioner's. The last thing Edwin needed was someone else's love-struck ramblings when he was unable to share his own with anyone but Brutus the terrier.

There were nights, however, when the horror of what he'd done buzzed like a hornet, drowning out even his brother Charles's snoring. No matter how often he repeated the Duchess's phrase 'a kiss doesn't signify', Edwin couldn't fool himself into thinking the Duke would see it that way. Especially because he badly wanted to believe it did signify.

December came and went without Jane's baby making an appearance, but it did bring an invitation to Woburn for Twelfth Night, stirring both hot and cold currents in Edwin's blood. He kissed Jane goodbye and told her not to let their father – who had spent Christmas lecturing them about Near Eastern antiquities – persuade her to name the child something unpronounceably antique if it arrived in his absence. She set his cravat straight and said she would do her best. Then he hurried with George through the fog to catch the mail coach.

The Abbey was bright and brimming with colour and warmth. Branches and berries covered walls and chimneys, and fires roared in every grate. Russells were in abundance, from the young Alexander, who ran from room to room refusing to go to bed, to William bearing purloined cigars, and Eliza and Wrio, who spent a suspicious amount of time near the mistletoe or walking out together in weather that kept everyone else indoors.

The Duke and Duchess were caught up in preparations for an imminent visit from the King's brother and heir, the Duke of York. Edwin hardly saw them until the evening of Twelfth Night itself, when the children, still in costume after performing a new play in the Duke's private theatre, were ecstatically stripping the foliage from the walls ready to burn on the midnight bonfire to prevent bad luck. He'd resigned himself to the fact that what happened in the Highlands didn't signify at all, which delighted his conscience but dealt grievous blows to his pride and heart. Then, while everyone else was gasping with delight at flames and fireworks, there was a lingering kiss in the dark under a sprig of mistletoe the Duchess had refused to give to the fire. The glittering explosions in the sky were nothing compared to the stirring in Edwin's veins.

After a week of festivities, the mistletoe was finally discarded and Edwin returned to a damp, dingy London. The door to the house on Conway Street opened before he'd finished scraping the slick grey mud from his boots. His mother stood behind it. Wearing black. She shouldn't have been wearing that much black.

Everything seemed muffled. Shuffling footsteps, lowered voices. Edwin watched a cup of tea go cold as he listened to his mother explain, while his father paced behind her, stick thudding arrhythmically on the floorboards.

The baby – a boy – had been born without breathing shortly after midnight. The mother – Jane – had been gathered to God as the church clocks chimed one. The embers of the Woburn bonfire would still have been warm. He'd been laughing under the mistletoe. Mistletoe that should have been burnt to prevent bad luck.

'Why didn't you send for me?' he said.

'What could you have done?' his father snapped, bringing his stick down hard.

'I could have been here. With Mother. With you.' Edwin glared at him.

'And waste a chance to keep in Bedford's good books?' The stick crashed against a chair leg.

'That's not important. Not as important as this.' Two pale faces, his younger sisters, peered around the door. He tried to smile at them.

'Don't be impertinent.' The stick thumped down again. The faces disappeared.

The house and the studio became at once stiflingly claustrophobic and unbearably empty: cluttered with black cloth and sympathy, punctuated with fathomless shadows and echoing holes in conversations where Jane ought to have been. Edwin tried to paint – needed to paint – but nothing would come right. He took Brutus and walked miles with the grief-stricken Charles Christmas. They wore their boot soles thin around the lanes north of the Regent's Park, up onto the heath at Hampstead and back through drizzle and mist until the cold, hard light was gone. The fields here were full of stories of Jane – sketching, teasing, telling him off for getting covered in mud or caught in brambles, drawing caricatures of them all – but Edwin wished he could offer his widowed brother-in-law more than memories for comfort.

The Duke sent a note of condolence. He would understand if Edwin couldn't finish the small portrait of Alexander he'd promised in time for the Academy's Summer Exhibition. A cold trickle of shame slid between Edwin's shoulder blades. He wrote back instantly, assuring the Duke the picture would be finished on time. As if that would somehow lessen his guilt.

The weeks rolled on. Jane would have told everyone to stop wallowing. She would have told Edwin to stop staring at ghosts of dried raindrops on the window and work. In her absence, Edwin's father, brandishing his ear trumpet, performed this task. John Landseer's visits to the studio became more frequent. Charles Christmas came in less and less. Edwin agreed to let his father stay, provided he remained on the other side of the canvas and refrained from critical comments. The injunction had little effect, but Edwin found an odd comfort in listening to him rant about the current bees in his bonnet, from historical errors in novels to the state of the roads. It helped distract from the needling thought that the Duke had written but the Duchess hadn't. Perhaps kisses signified nothing after all and he ought to be grateful to have got away with it.

Neither Edwin nor his father mentioned Jane. One of her shawls still hung from the back of the studio door. Edwin pretended not to notice that his father always touched it on his way out.

April brought the deadline for Summer Exhibition submissions. Edwin helped George deliver the finished picture of Lord William Russell's trial to Somerset House. Seeing the image of himself and the Duchess for the first time in months, he could almost feel the itchiness of the stockings and the satin-slippered toes in his ribs. The sittings at Woburn – only a year since – felt like a lifetime ago.

'Wish me luck.' George chewed a fingernail as the porters loaded the painting onto a trolley with several others. 'You've deposited yours?'

'Yes, all given up,' Edwin said, kicking a stone which skittered after the trolley and earned him a black look from a porter. The only letter he'd had from the Duchess was a curt thank you for the portrait of Alexander, saying he'd asked too little for it. He'd read a hundred hidden meanings into her words, mostly ominous, and eventually thrown them into the fire in frustration. 'You are putting yourself forward for Associate this year then?'

'Yes. It's pride-swallowing time. The bastards had better hang it in a good spot.' George stared up at the windows of the exhibition rooms. 'Drink?'

Edwin nodded. He didn't want to face the empty studio or go home. The prattling object of Tom's affections was liable to be there at this time of day, delivering sugar plums.

Once they were ensconced at a corner table in a cellar off The Strand, George ran his hands through his hat-flattened hair, and asked awkwardly if Edwin wouldn't mind standing the first bottle.

'To be honest, Ned,' he said, as wine sloshed into his glass. 'I'm only standing for election because I need the money – getting closer to that golden RA would give my coffers a much-needed boost. Sarah's hounding me to pay for children she won't let me see and Amelia needs money for children I see too much of. Prince Leopold's away, so no tin from him, and I've spent what Bedford paid me up front for the Russell picture.' He sipped through tight lips. 'If this doesn't come off, I'll go back to Rome. The wine's better there and people aren't so damned sniffy about exactly how married one is to the mother of one's children.'

'How is Amelia?' Edwin asked. 'I hardly see her these days.' The last time he'd seen her had been at Jane's house. Charles Christmas no longer gave dinners.

'Bored. Suffers with nerves. Says I never take her anywhere, that I must be ashamed of her – but where can I take her? It's not my fault Society is what it is.'

'I'm thinking of moving out. You can bring her to dine with me.'

'This is news. Where to? The menagerie at Woburn? A kennel in St James's Square?'

'Very droll. There's a barn to let in St John's Wood I like the look of.'

'I'm sure Amelia would be overjoyed to dine in a barn.'

'There's a cottage too.' Edwin took a large swig. 'It's got a few acres. The barn will be the studio and I'll be able to keep all sorts of animals.'

'St John's Wood, you say? Another classic Ned Landseer scheme – other men stable their high-class whores up there, and you'll have a harem of donkeys and dogs. When are you flying the nest?'

'I haven't decided if I'll take it yet.' Edwin swirled the dregs in his glass.

'Can you afford it?'

'Depends how the Exhibition goes.'

They ordered more wine.

'It's all about tin.' George declared, as the second bottle neared emptiness. 'If you're in cash, you can keep as many mistresses as you like. Give little parties for them with your friends, who don't mind because they do the same. But if you're a tin-less wonder like me, woe betide you. I'll bet the Duke of Bedford never has complaints from any of his women.'

Edwin put his glass down more forcefully than he'd intended, sloshing dark red drops onto the ring-stained table.

'Don't look so shocked. Even the Duchess knows. I believe Mrs Vernon's the current favourite, but Lady Sandwich was *maitresse du jour* for a while. This can't really be news to you? They're all at it.'

'Really? Not the women though?' Edwin's stomach twisted as though he were back on the Edinburgh steamer.

'How can you be such an innocent? Some of them rampantly so. Mostly the older ones – heir and spare done, time for fun, so long as it's kept decently quiet. Lady William's convinced our dear old Duchess of Bedford has no end of lovers. 'S why I was worried she was setting her cap at you last year.'

Feeling more seasick than ever, Edwin mumbled what he hoped sounded like nonchalant agreement.

'Speaking of which, she wrote to me last week.' George raised an eyebrow. 'She and Eliza are determined to master etching. She wants you to give them lessons once they're back in Town. Maybe she is after you.'

'Ha ha.' Edwin's cheeks burned. To get off the subject, he said: 'Did you hear Tom's to be married?'

'No. You are full of news today. Not something I'd have put money on. I don't mean to disparage your brother, but . . .'

'I know, I know. Everybody loves Tom: no one more than me, but even I'll admit he's deuced eccentric. And looks like a cross between a beer barrel and a kitchen mop.'

'Who's to be Mrs Mop?'

'A Miss Belinda Pocock. Works in his favourite sweet shop. We've had nothing but puns about sweethearts for weeks. If I weren't already thinking of moving out, it would have tipped me over the edge.'

The Summer Exhibition opened and Edwin's paintings were hung reasonably well, as was Lord William Russell's trial, though George complained it was too high. One of Edwin's pictures sold for three hundred guineas – the most he'd yet received for a single work. He signed the lease on Punker's Barn, St John's Wood, the same week.

He also gave the Duchess and Eliza their first etching lesson. As he guided the needle in the Duchess's hand, she leant in, sending his anxieties scurrying away, and made him describe every detail of the cottage, the barn, and the land, then appointed herself his official adviser for improvement works, saying she would visit soon.

Away from her presence, with little more than a promise of gardening advice, doubts crept back in. While making the most of the long days to work on the Duke's picture (still in the old studio, still with his father muttering in the background), George's words hovered ominously in Edwin's head. Were there other lovers? George himself had flirted openly with her on that first visit to Woburn. If there were others, would that, in some twisted *beau monde* way, mean the Duke might not actually mind? And did that make him just a passing fancy? He found himself scratching out parts of the painting and having to redo them, mixing colours with angry swirls, telling himself he didn't care and never wanted it to be more than a casual thing anyway.

But the following week, when the Duchess arrived at the overgrown, unhinged gate of Punker's Barn, Edwin couldn't help sliding his fingers between hers as he inhaled the rose scent that always clung to her.

'How did you find something so wild so close to London?' she said as they paused in the shade of an old mulberry tree, looking out over the meadow.

'It wasn't always this wild. It went to seed after the last tenant farmer died and the rest of the land was sold off. My sister used to bring me and my brothers sketching around here when we were boys. She always said it was the kind of place she'd like to raise a family.' Edwin swallowed. 'When I saw it was available to rent . . .' He stopped, had to bite his lip.

The Duchess squeezed his hand. 'I was so sorry to hear about her death. I wanted to write but John insisted on doing it. I didn't argue because, well, you know . . . it would have looked suspicious. But my heart broke for you. You were very close?'

Edwin nodded. 'She was the only one who could snap me out of my stupid tantrums. She was so funny. And she wasn't afraid to tease me or make it abundantly clear when she thought I was being an idiot.' He had to stop again.

The Duchess's grip tightened. 'If it would help,' she said, 'I can promise to tease you and point out when you're being an idiot?'

Edwin laughed, attempting to wipe away a tear without her seeing. 'Jane would be delighted. Thank you.' He took a deep breath. 'So, what do you think?'

'Well,' she said slowly, a finger stroking the inside of his wrist, quickening his heart to a canter. 'I'd thought St John's

Wood was filled with kept women in vulgar, new houses, but I love this. I've been saying for months that brambles should be the new fashion in gardens. And as for holes in the roof, I'll have some installed at Woburn immediately.'

'There aren't that many holes, and, I'll have you know, I'm intending to farm blackberries.' Edwin pulled her close, his spine crackling with desire. 'And I only plan to keep wild women, Your Grace.'

She poked him in the ribs, mumbling 'idiot' as his lips traced the curve of her neck, then adding, 'And – you win – don't call me Your Grace, at least not when we're alone. It does sound ridiculous.'

'What shall I call you then?' The rose scent was strongest in the hollow at the base of her throat. He could drown in it, forget everything else.

'Whatever you like,' she murmured. 'But Georgina will do.'

'All right, Georgina.' He tried it out, feeling a rush of reassurance. 'And there are no brambles under the tree.'

Basking in the warm hum of bumble bees beneath the low, leafy canopy, they explored contours, textures, and tastes, fingers and lips lazily roving, probing beneath folds of fabric . . .

'Cooee!' A high-pitched female voice came from the direction of the gate. 'Neddy!'

'Damn!' Edwin hissed.

'Who's that? Not a kept woman, I hope?' the Duchess whispered, a fingernail resting tantalisingly on the rim of his navel.

'Heavens no.' Edwin rolled onto his back, breathing heavily as he fought to bring mind and body under control. 'It's my brother Tom's awful fiancée – I said he could bring her to see the place, but I told them half past four. It can't be three yet.'

Scrambling to his feet, he hurriedly tucked in his shirt, pulled on his jacket and looked about for his hat. 'I'll see if I can get rid of her.' He looked down at the Duchess – Georgina – who was rearranging her dress. 'Do you need any help with . . . laces? Or that sort of thing?'

'No, thank you,' she smiled. 'I'm perfectly capable of shifting for myself.'

'Neddy!'

Dismissing a voice in his head that asked how many times she might have done this sort of thing before, Edwin ran off, removing grass from his hair and cursing Miss Belinda Pocock.

Two months later, on a sweltering September day, Edwin watched as the rector blessed Miss Belinda Pocock and turned her into Mrs Thomas Landseer.

Everyone said it was just what the family needed after poor Jane. Everyone also said what a surprise it was that Tom was the first to marry. Then everyone speculated which brother, Edwin or Charles, would be next.

Edwin wished everyone would shut up.

But he was happy for Tom, who'd beamed through the service with his barrel-like chest threatening to burst out of his embroidered waistcoat and his mop of flaxen hair waxed almost to obedience.

'Oh, it won't be Neddy next,' cackled Belinda, making Edwin clench his teeth so tightly he worried he might break one.

'Why not, my sweet?' asked Tom, still smiling on the whole world, squinting as the sun came out from behind a towering dark cloud.

'Oh, he's young, you know.' Belinda curled a finger into one of her yellow ringlets. 'I'll wager he has a few wild oats to sow in that meadow of his first.'

For an awful moment, Edwin could have sworn she winked at him. But the light was in his eyes and he couldn't be sure. An instant later, the sun went back in, sending the temperature plummeting and showing Belinda looking as though butterscotch wouldn't melt in her mouth.

By October, Belinda Landseer couldn't have been further from Edwin's thoughts. He sat on a three-legged stool in a smoke-filled cottage, deep in the Cairngorm mountains. He could hear Georgina's laughter outside as his gaze alternated between his sketchbook and the heavily lined face of Anna Mhòr, who was hunched over a cauldron at the open hearth and was so old she had been a tenant since Georgina's mother's time. The folds in her pale linen cap and flannel dress caught the late morning sun that fell through the open door and mixed with the hazy air. There were no windows. The rest of the room, which constituted the entire dwelling, was blanketed with varying degrees of darkness.

A movement took his attention momentarily from the old woman – a mouse, its coat almost an exact match for the dirt floor, scurried across the shaft of light between the door and the fire then disappeared into a dark corner. Eyes hovering on the shadows in case it returned, Edwin sipped from the wooden cup of whisky and honey Anna Mhòr had pressed on him. For a second, the mouse poked its nose back into the light, then seemed to rethink and retreated. *The best laid schemes of mice and men:* there was no escape from Burns.

His own schemes were, thank God, in better shape this year than last. Old Mr Bell, the Oxford Street chemist, had mixed him a syrupy caudle to prevent sickness on the coach, which had rendered him blissfully unconscious for much of the journey. Edwin suspected Mr Bell had been generous with his 'dash' of opium. Since arriving in Scotland, groggy, but well-rested, he'd secured a commission for a large sporting portrait from the Duke of Atholl before travelling further north to join the Bedfords at Invereshie House on the River Spey. Georgina (calling her by her name, if only in private, still thrilled him) had persuaded her brother, the Marquis of Huntly, to put in an order for a similar portrait. Later that afternoon, they were due to take the cart a few miles down the river to Huntly's shooting lodge at Kinrara to discuss details, but Georgina insisted there was time to ride into the glen to visit her mother's old tenants first. The Duke declined to join them in either visit, saying he didn't fancy Huntly's fast Tory crowd and would rather talk proper politics and snooze with his own guests.

There was a brief eclipse as Georgina ducked through the doorway.

'Anna Mhòr?' Her voice rang out, the Scottish lilt strong. 'Is Mr Landseer bothering you?'

Anna Mhòr gave a smile that showed more wrinkles than teeth, said something in Gaelic, then shuffled across to refill Edwin's cup, offering another to Georgina.

'What did she say?' Edwin asked, chalk moving swiftly, eyes not leaving the page.

'That she likes having such a bonny young man around and that I'm welcome to leave you here permanently.' Georgina drank then licked her lips. 'And if you don't put that down soon, I shall leave you here. You must be nearly finished, or have you just been sipping whisky and daydreaming?'

'Anna Mhòr said if I drink this every morning, I'll live to a great age and never have rheumatism. And she ought to know: she told me she's a hundred years old.'

'Nonsense,' Georgina snorted. 'She hasn't a clue how old she is. But I suppose she was ancient even when I was a girl.'

'She told me she remembers the Jacobites in forty-five.' Edwin took out his pocket knife and began paring the black chalk in his porte-crayon to a sharper point. 'And your lady mother kissing recruits to raise a regiment in the Nineties. Not to mention a few stories of you.'

'Hmph. Don't believe anything unflattering. And why are you sharpening that? I thought you were nearly finished.'

'I never said that.' Edwin checked the point and began drawing again.

There was a rustle of skirts and the smoky light shifted as she moved to look over his shoulder. 'Are you always like this?'

'Probably,' he said. The area behind Anna Mhòr needed to be darker. The corner of the box bed, just visible in the far corner, also needed more definition … light strokes, a few bolder lines … more shading of Anna Mhòr's features.

'Are you even listening? Can you please be finished soon? I have to visit Mrs Collie, then we must leave or we won't get to Kinrara in time to dine.' Her finger traced the seam down the back of his coat. The chalk jerked, giving Anna Mhòr an unintentional antler.

'All right.' Edwin arched his back as her touch reached his waist. 'Just a few more minutes.'

Anna Mhòr poked the fire, sending more smoke swirling into the tar-coated thatch.

After what was probably not much longer than a few minutes, Edwin kissed the old woman's hand in farewell, making every wrinkle blush, and emerged into the sunshine. Georgina stood outside another turf-covered house, hands on her hips, talking to a small, sandy-haired girl. Her posture exactly mirrored that of a hen sheltering beneath the low eaves of the house behind her, tail fanned out to shield her chicks from an inquisitive puppy. Edwin reached into his satchel and retrieved the porte-crayon and sketchbook he'd just put away.

'Oh no you don't!' Georgina swept over and snatched the porte-crayon. 'No more drawing. We have five miles to ride.'

Watching the hen ruffle her feathers and peck at the puppy, Edwin reluctantly slid the sketchbook back into his bag.

'If we make good time, we can stop on the way – to sketch or whatever you please. But only if we leave now.' Her fingers brushed his as she handed him back the chalk.

Edwin forgot about the hen.

Having made good progress, they stopped, tethering the ponies near a tumbledown stone shelter where recent heavy rains had carved new river channels and undermined peat banks, exposing twisted roots and long-hidden rocks.

'You puzzle me, Lanny,' Georgina said, as they sat on a spread plaid, backs against the ragged stones of the shelter wall. 'You say you don't like painting people, but you must have drawn half the population of Badenoch since you've been here.'

'It's not people I don't like,' he said, eyes slowly tracing her profile against the blurred background of late flowering heather. 'It's portraits.'

'What on earth is the difference?'

'I don't know. People doing things, that's interesting. It's easy enough to get into their heads, show what they're feeling, but portraits are . . . unnatural?' He wound a waxy blade of grass from the base of the wall around his finger. 'A person just, well, being a person sitting to a painter is hard, for me at least. I never know what they're feeling other than boredom, because that's what I'd be feeling myself. The moment I start painting a portrait of someone, they become so self-conscious about not looking awkward, it becomes awkward.' The grass snapped.

'And it's easier to paint the feelings of a dog being a dog, is it?' Georgina took off her bonnet and wriggled closer to him.

'Much easier,' he laughed, sliding his arm around her. 'Dogs aren't pretending to be something they're not.' As Georgina rested her head on his shoulder, he added, 'And I don't feel the need to impress them – I don't feel I'm pretending to be something I'm not.'

'Surely you don't worry about that?' She looked up at him.

'I do.' Edwin leant back on the rough rocks, pulling up more grass with his free hand. 'I wish Atholl and your brother hadn't asked me for portraits.'

'Ha! I thought you'd have been thrilled, but no. What pesky beasts, these dukes and marquises, having the temerity to ask painters to actually paint pictures. For actual guineas, no less. Next they'll be serving you warm champagne or refusing to let you flirt with their wives.'

'Heaven forbid,' he said, kissing her.

'You're not flirting with any other wives, are you?' she said, idly turning one of his waistcoat buttons.

'Not right now.' He took her fingers and kissed them one by one.

She sighed contentedly, stroking his hair. 'You mustn't worry. You've already impressed everyone. I'm sure you'll do a good job.'

'I don't want to be good. I want to be brilliant. I want to be the best. And I know I can be, just not with portraits.'

'Ooh, is that a flash of ambition?' Her eyes glittered.

'What if it is?'

'It's very attractive.' She kissed him, slowly. 'More please.'

Maybe it was the influence of Anna Mhòr's honey and whisky, maybe it was the dry-sweet scent of heather and the majesty of the hills, or perhaps it was her lips behind his ear and on his neck, but something loosened his tongue. Between kisses, he told her all the dreams he didn't dare confess to anyone else: how he wanted to be spoken of in the same breath as Rubens and Snyders; how he wanted everyone – from the President of the Royal Academy to the crossing sweepers on The Strand – to know his pictures; how he wanted to make them feel all the joy, sorrow, and wonder he saw in the world.

What he didn't tell her was that – more than all the rest put together – he wanted to do more than just kiss her.

They made it back to Invereshie with just enough time to get to Kinrara. As they left in the cart, the Duke and Old Lord William were sitting on the lawn in the late afternoon sun, wearing straw hats, drinking champagne, and reading newspapers. In other circumstances, Edwin would have insisted on delaying to sketch them but the thought of being alone with Georgina drove out all others.

Three days later, they made the journey in reverse. The view was almost identical, but everything had changed. As Invereshie House came into view, the cart lurched into a pothole, throwing them together. The contact lasted a second or two longer than strictly necessary before Georgina righted herself and reinstated an inch of propriety between them. Intensely aware of her closeness, Edwin gathered the reins and stared fixedly at the pony, willing himself to focus on the muscles and bones working beneath the rise and fall of its rump, and the twitching of its ears. He stared so intently at a matted patch in its shaggy mane that he only narrowly avoided another hole, but it was useless. The faint rustling as she smoothed her dress drowned all other sounds – thudding hooves, rumbling wheels, rushing water.

The Duke and Old Lord William sat on the lawn no more than fifty yards off, shielded from the low sun by the same straw hats and now also from the wind by heavy plaids. Edwin sat up straighter and braced himself for the jolt as the pony came to a halt. Helping Georgina down from the cart, he set his face into a smile and somehow came out with a stream of light-hearted small talk as they crossed the lawn, heads held high, to join the Duke. It was disturbingly easy to pretend nothing had happened. Then, announcing that she was going inside to dress for dinner, Georgina planted a kiss on her husband's cheek. The stab of jealousy Edwin felt was all the sharper for being unexpected.

'Landseer, join us for a drink? We've plenty of time before dinner.' The cheek that Georgina had just kissed crinkled into a smile. 'Tell us of your adventures with Huntly. How were the grouse?'

Edwin accepted a glass of champagne, staring at the straw-coloured bubbles and listening with surprise to the naturalness of his own voice describing the visit, laughing, impersonating Georgina's brother, even Georgina herself. It was a relief when the Duke and Old Lord William fell into a long discussion about shooting that didn't require more than perfunctory input from him.

Suddenly exhausted, he stretched out on a blanket next to a black-and-tan setter. Lifting his glass, he caught the scent of Georgina on his wrist and his thoughts were borne away by the rumbling of the river, along its stony channel back towards Kinrara, where the last rays of the sun formed a golden haze, caught mid-air by the dust of decaying leaves.

He looked back to the Duke, whose bald head was now free of its hat: contented, entitled, carefree. A man who'd done so much for him as a patron – even as a friend. His stomach lurched.

It was an insane thing to have done.

Waves of memory had been crashing over him all day. Another engulfed him now, in which desire and horror were so closely tangled it was impossible to prise them apart. Moon-dappled darkness on mercifully silent floorboards. Fingers curling, caressing, lips pressing. Clothing crushed, breeched, kicked aside. The thunder of the river and the bellow of a stag. The thrill of flesh on flesh, prolonged almost to agony, before finally becoming flesh in flesh. Closing his eyes, he suppressed a shiver then drained the rest of the champagne. Feeling a shadow across his face, he looked up with a start to find the Duke standing over him, bottle in hand.

## *1826, London*

IT WAS THE FIRST ANNIVERSARY of Jane's death. Edwin had just returned to St John's Wood after spending the day with his mother and younger sisters. The sitting-room fire spat and hissed but failed to make inroads into the cold. His new housekeeper had placed a handful of letters on the side table. Recognising the Duke's controlled script on one, Edwin cautiously slid his finger under the seal and unfolded it. He hadn't heard from the Bedfords since they left for France at the end of October.

It began innocuously enough: paintings and people seen in Paris; apologies for not having responded sooner to Edwin's letter; would the stag hunt picture be ready for the Academy this spring? He began to skim over the second side, when a reference to 'the Duchess's doctors' brought him up short. It took a few glacial seconds for the next words to sink in.

She was pregnant.

'*Of course,*' the Duke wrote, '*at her age, such things are not without dangers. So here we shall remain until the doctors give her leave to travel or the situation resolves itself.*'

It was as though he'd been kicked in the stomach by a horse. He'd last seen Georgina in October. It was now January.

There was a crash from the hallway, the door burst open and George stormed in. Throwing his hat onto a chair, he glowered at the useless fire and said,

'Bastards!'

Edwin scrunched the letter into a ball, feeling lightheaded.

'Sanctimonious, hypocritical bastards!' George kicked the sofa.

'Stop it! That's not paid for,' Edwin snapped.

'I've just been told those bloated fools at the Academy didn't let me in because Amelia's not my wife and I have the temerity to live with her openly. If I crept in and out of dressing rooms and whorehouses like the rest of them, I'd be ARA right now. Happy fucking Twelfth Night.'

'Yes.' Edwin steadied himself on the back of the unpaid-for sofa.

George looked at him for the first time since entering. 'Damn, it's Jane's anniversary, isn't it? I'm sorry. To hell with the Academy. Let's get drunk. Very drunk.'

'Yes,' Edwin said again, forcing himself to breathe as the crumpled letter dug into his palm.

# Part III

# *May 1860, London*

THEY'RE STANDING IN FRONT OF Edwin's Highland flood picture, which has been given the place of honour at the Summer Exhibition. They're not exactly fighting off crowds, but most people do at least stop, stare, and lower their voices. Edwin supposes it's hard not to. Most pictures look washed out when hung in these halls, hemmed in by so many others. They lose vitality due to colour clashes with neighbouring works, flashy frames, badly dressed crowds. Not this one. It takes a lot to diminish ten feet of darkness and despair. Edwin almost laughs when people tell him it's beautiful. Perhaps they think they're being polite.

To his right, Caro is gazing at the painted family huddled on the turf roof of a cottage, their dogs, sheep, goats, and hens with them. They're surrounded by fragments of a doomed way of life – a Jacobite shield and dirk, a bottle of illicit whisky, a green and navy Gordon plaid. Caught by the torrent raging below them, horses, cows, carts, even trees are being swept away. Mrs Jameson would have shaken her head with wholehearted disapproval, though to appease her Edwin had included a look of joy on the face of a cat devouring a broken egg laid by a terrified hen. But she isn't here. Edwin was deeply saddened to hear of her death in March. Another friend gone.

'I don't know what to say.' Caro dabs her eyes, the Baring monogram a flash of red on her lace-edged handkerchief. She looks up again at the terrified young mother, who is clutching an infant in her arms. 'What that poor woman must be feeling . . .' She puts a hand to her own stomach, which all the world can see is nearly ripe even though it's covered by a ludicrous mass of dress. Lord Baring, on her other side, takes her handkerchief-wielding hand.

'A great work, Sir Edwin, very powerful. The President was most complimentary,' he says.

Edwin clears his throat. He should have known Baring and his stupid beard would be here with her.

'How kind,' he says. 'I'm sorry it's affected Caro – Lady Baring – so much.'

'I weep so often now.' She lifts her head, sets her jaw like a tragic queen. 'Dr Quain says it's quite normal as confinement approaches.' Another touch of her hand to her stomach, as if they needed reminding. To rub salt in, Baring's hand follows hers.

Edwin turns away, pretends to scan the crowd; he was right to have that brandy before coming down. The faces are annoyingly blurred. His eyes are dry and aching again but he's damned if he's going to wear spectacles in front of everyone. Then one face – cloudy as it is – stops him short. He blinks, squints.

'Sir Edwin?' Baring. Why did Baring always have to blunder in?

'Yes, what?'

'I was saying I would like a portrait of Lady Baring. Once the child is born, of course, God willing.'

'Yes, of course, God willing, of course.' Edwin blinks again. 'A portrait? Frank Grant's your man. Or Jonny Millais.' He glances at Caro, who holds his gaze for a second then turns back to the picture.

'What about you, Sir Edwin?' says Baring.

'I can't take on anything new while the lions are in my care.'

Caro, without removing her gaze from the canvas, purses her lips and says, 'You're painting Annie Gilbert.'

'That's not new,' Edwin says with half a smile; at least she's still jealous. 'And it's not a portrait – she's just modelling. So is her horse.'

Someone hails Baring and he turns to talk to a man with a face like a potato. Caro turns to Edwin and leans in, saying, 'How are you?'

'Fine.' Over her shoulder, he catches sight of the profile that stopped him before. His chest tightens. 'How are you?'

'Oh, I am . . . so very happy . . . and so very melancholy. Life seems to be all doctors. I miss our conversations. Would you paint me? It would mean so much.'

But Edwin doesn't hear any more because Rachel is standing behind Caro. Her face is obscured, but he's sure it's her.

'Will you? Sir Edwin?' Caro places her hand on his and he hauls his gaze back to her.

'Yes, yes, all right,' he says, heart battering against his ribs. It is Rachel. The good-looking man at her side with the weedy whiskers – that's Lord James Butler, her husband.

'Thank you,' Caro whispers as Baring rejoins them. More bland pleasantries issue from the mouth-shaped hole in Baring's beard and he declares that they must be getting on. Edwin watches them leave, already cursing himself for not saying no.

When he turns back to the flood picture, Rachel is only a few feet away, separated from him by a crinoline's width. She turns to take in the canvas and sees him. She pauses, wrinkles her snub nose the way she's always done when not sure what to do, then says with perfect politeness,

'Sir Edwin. We were just admiring your picture.'

'Lady Rachel,' Edwin says. 'Lord James.' He bows.

She wrinkles her nose again, glancing towards the door.

'It's a very fine work; quite the best thing here,' says James. He seems like a good egg. Edwin wishes he could know him better. 'Is it Glenfeshie?'

'It is, my lord, and you're most kind.' Gazing at Rachel, who's staring pointedly at the canvas, and willing her to look at him, Edwin adds, 'But it was the flood scene in Lady Rachel's novel that gave me the spur I needed to finish it. I have her to thank.'

'I'm sure you're welcome, Sir Edwin.' Her jaw is rigid and her eyes don't leave the painting, but tears are gathering above their lower lids. 'Forgive me,' she says, hastily pulling out a handkerchief. 'So many memories. I'm afraid we must go.'

They blur and melt into the crowd, which seems nothing more than a badly painted backdrop of flat, featureless figures. The only thing that seems real is the painting. So many memories indeed. He'd hoped finishing it would purge them and allow him to focus on the lions. But it has only stirred up more.

James Abercorn was the one who told him Rachel had discovered the truth. He and Louisa had been in Nice with Georgina. After her death, they'd travelled back through France with Rachel.

Abercorn was alone in the drawing room in Belgravia when Edwin called on that airless May afternoon. Wouldn't meet his eye. Kept folding and refolding a pair of black gloves.

'Lanny, there's something you need to know. The Duchess left papers. A letter. Concerning Rachel.'

The floor had lurched.

'It said the Duke ... the Duke was not Rachel's father.'

The air had frozen in Edwin's lungs.

Abercorn ran a hand across his face. 'We all knew you and the Duchess were ... well ... close. And more than close recently. Even Rachel knew that. But that was all she knew. Of course, we'd heard gossip but dismissed it as just that. Rachel had no idea.'

'Had?' Edwin heard his own voice say. 'Have you shown her the letter?'

'Not me. The executors. They thought she ought to know.'

'I need to talk to her.' Edwin forced himself to breathe. 'Where is she?'

'Now is not the time.'

'Where is she?'

'She's too upset. It was a great shock. And so soon after her mother's death ...'

'I'm not leaving until I see her.'

Edwin shakes his head. He will not think about this. Not now. Not here. He glares at the paintings, at the crowds. Wills the flood to sweep him away to oblivion. But the damned scene comes back anyway.

Rachel in the Abercorns' drawing room: jaw set, eyes wet. He'd expected her to rail at him, to shout, scream even – that's what

Georgina would do ... would have done. But, when she first spoke, her voice was barely audible.

'You lied. You've made my whole life a lie.'

'I never meant to hurt you ...'

Then she had shouted: 'I don't care what you meant. You are *not* my father. You *betrayed* my father in the worst way possible. And now you've taken my mother from me too – I don't know who she was any more! All I had left of her were memories, and you ... you've destroyed those! I hate you! I hate you!'

# *Spring 1826, London*

A FORTNIGHT BEFORE THE SUMMER EXHIBITION deadline, Edwin's mother insisted he dine with the other Landseers at Conway Street, saying it was too long since she'd seen him.

'You're looking thin and grey, Ned,' she said as he refused pudding but helped himself to more wine. 'Are you unwell? I worry about you up there all alone.'

'It's painting at night that does it,' said Belinda, licking her finger and passing the cream jug to Edwin's father. 'You should see the number of candles he gets through.'

'You'll ruin your eyes. A painter can't be without his eyes,' said his father. 'You should get up earlier. Then you wouldn't have to paint so late.'

'I have to paint late because I'm subject to constant interruptions during the day.' Edwin glared at Belinda, who'd developed a habit of calling in unannounced. She said she was visiting friends nearby, but it seemed to Edwin her primary purpose was to annoy him and gossip with his housekeeper while she waited for Tom – an engraver like their father – to finish for the day. 'It's just to get the Duke's picture done,' he added with a yawn. 'I can't stand for Associateship if I don't exhibit anything. And I can't sleep so might as well work.'

'Well, you should be able to sleep. I never have any trouble sleeping,' said his father, unhelpfully.

'Me neither,' laughed Belinda. 'Do I, Tommy?'

Edwin clenched his teeth and stared at the ceiling, trying to blink away the paralysing panic that was creeping up his spine again. They had no idea of the horrors that kept him awake: visions of the Duke's fury, of scandal at the Academy, but most of all of Georgina and the baby. And of Jane and her baby.

The stag hunt was the only picture he submitted that year. Nothing else was remotely ready. He was now twenty-four and theoretically eligible for election as Associate, but would a single picture be enough? George, who hadn't gone to Rome in spite of his grand pronouncements, had put his name forward again and bombarded the Academy with eight works.

'One last roll of the dice,' George said, downing a glass of wine after they'd seen everything taken in to Somerset House. 'Did I hear the Bedfords are returning soon? Is the Duchess still pregnant?'

'Yes,' said Edwin. 'And yes.'

He ordered more drink.

A week later, Edwin received a summons to the Bedfords' villa at Campden Hill in Kensington. The Duchess was back. The Duke remained in Paris.

Intermittent drizzle dampened his new white top hat – so much for being the height of spring fashion – but every time his horse (also a novelty) quickened her pace, Edwin found himself leaning back in the saddle until she slowed. The sooner he got there, the sooner he would have to face up to . . . what? What on earth was before him? Not knowing made it ten times worse. If he got away with this, he would live like a monk for the rest of his life.

He slowed the horse again at the village by the gravel pits. Undeterred by the damp, a group of children hurtled down the side of the road, pulling a wooden cart in which the two smallest rattled along, splashing through puddles, shrieking with laughter. What he wouldn't give to be that carefree. From the shelter of a doorway, two women looked on, one shouted at the children to be careful. The other gazed at a baby in her arms.

'Oh God,' Edwin whispered to the horse.

The higgledy-piggledy houses petered out as he turned into a quiet lane lined with old elms. Bluebells and wild garlic made splashes of brightness in the shadows around their roots. Ordinarily, the sight would have filled him with the sense of freedom that followed submission day each spring. Not today.

On arriving at the Bedfords' vast red-brick villa, he was shown to the Duchess's sitting room, where he found Eliza. Attempting to drown his nerves in tea as they talked trivialities, he began setting out etching apparatus for the lesson that was the ostensible reason for his visit.

'How was the journey from Paris?' he asked, extracting a book of Highland sketches from his satchel, trying to steady his breathing.

'Aunt Georgina will tell you it was fine.' Eliza glanced at the door. 'But she'll be lying. Lanny, she listens to you, will you tell her she must rest?'

Edwin almost dropped a case of etching needles. 'Surely it's not that bad?'

'We couldn't believe she insisted on coming back for the birth.' Eliza took the case from him, lowering her voice. 'The French doctors said it was madness. I know she wasn't happy there. She and the Duke had been ... arguing.' Her cheeks flushed; Edwin shivered. 'But she was so ill. I lost count of the times they said she would lose the baby, but in the end, she told them to get out and said she was damned if she'd be confined under their care. Did you know she can swear as well in French as she can in Scotch?'

'No, but it doesn't surprise me.' In spite of the terror coursing through his veins, Edwin felt a glow of admiration.

'The Duke's doctor, Woolryche, was no help, of course. And now we're back, she's ignoring the English doctors as much as she ignored the French.'

A loud 'take it away! Stop fussing!' from the hall announced Georgina's approach.

And there she was: pale as paper, thin-faced but enormous elsewhere. Her eyes were underlined by shadows as purple as the wisteria creeping around the window frames, but as they fell on Edwin, they shone.

'Lanny!'

He kissed the hand she held out. The monastic vow made earlier disintegrated like a cobweb.

'I'm sure Eliza hasn't told you half the fun we had in Paris yet. Lying on a sofa for – how long was it? Months and months and months I think. Those damned doctors. I could have guillotined the lot of them. I cannot express my sheer delight at being home.' Her eyes hadn't left his for a second. 'But people will keep fussing. Would it be too beastly to ask you to take a turn about the garden with me before we begin drawing, or whatever it is I said we'd do? I've been cooped up for so long.'

'Isn't it raining, Aunt Georgina?' said Eliza, looking up from a sketch she'd been examining.

'No.' Georgina placed her hands on her hips and arched her back. It was hard not to stare at the size of her belly. Jane hadn't been that big. 'It has stopped.'

As soon as they were beyond the eyes and ears of the house, she burst into tears. Edwin steered her to a bench and made her sit.

'I'm so glad you're here,' she said, accepting his handkerchief. Dabbing her eyes with one hand, she pressed the other into the small of her back and stretched.

The panic Edwin had felt earlier when planning what to say was nothing compared to the dumb blankness that now gripped him.

All that came out was: 'Is it . . . mine?'

He'd never seen her so angry. His 'I didn't mean . . .', 'That's not what I . . .' and 'Will you listen?' were lost among the expletives.

'What the hell do you take me for? Do you think I play at St George with any randy little stripling that comes along? No one has so much as touched me for years – apart from you. Even John hasn't laid a finger on me since Alexander was born! I cannot believe you would even think . . . let alone say . . . You can leave right now and don't think about coming back – and you can forget about your precious commissions too!'

'Georgina,' he snapped, fiercely enough for her to take notice. She glared at him, cheeks and eyes blazing. Feeling his own colour rising, he paused, then plunged. 'I said the wrong thing. Don't string me up for not knowing how to talk about . . . If you must know, I . . . I don't have a clue about this sort of thing. I've never . . . there's never been anyone else. You were the first.'

They stared each other down. Both breathing hard.

'Well, you should learn to say what you mean,' she muttered, then gasped sharply and put a hand to her side.

'What's wrong? Should I fetch a doctor?' Edwin said, anger evaporating.

'No, no,' she grimaced. 'Here, give me your hand.'

Cautiously, he did so. She placed it on her belly, which was unexpectedly taut beneath the gathered cotton. It was his turn to gasp as something from within pummelled the place beneath his fingers.

'I'm still extremely angry with you. But that's *your* baby.' She slid her hand over his. There was another pummelling. '*Our* baby.'

Head awash with feelings he couldn't name, Edwin watched his fingers move as the child kicked again. Eventually, without moving his hand, and only because he couldn't avoid it any longer, he said,

'What about the Duke?'

Georgina shifted, stretching her back again. 'He knows it's not his, but he doesn't know it's yours. I convinced him there was a moment of whisky-induced madness with one of Huntly's friends at Kinrara. I've never seen him so furious. I was terrified he would banish me to some godforsaken French town until it was born, then make me give it up and pretend nothing had happened. Or worse, make me get rid of it before . . .' She pressed her hand more firmly over his. 'But – thank God – too many people already knew. I have blessed, blundering, indiscreet Dr Woolryche to thank for that. And then I was so ill . . . I know the Duke wanted me to lose it. That would have solved the problem for him. But the illness shocked him. It shocked me, to tell the truth.' She squeezed his fingers. 'Anyway, he's calmer now. We've agreed there will be no fuss. No scandal. As far as the world is concerned, this will be just another Russell.'

As the baby kicked again, a drop of rain fell onto the back of Edwin's hand. More followed, hitting the clematis behind them and releasing a warm, honeyed scent that couldn't have been more at variance with Edwin's mood.

'Always at the mercy of the weather,' Georgina said. 'We'd better go in or I shall be locked up again for disobeying doctors' orders. And I must be on my absolute best behaviour now. You too. We need to keep the Duke happy at all costs.' She accepted his arm, stood up awkwardly. 'If he were to find out ...'

The Summer Exhibition opened at the beginning of May. The stag hunt met with high praise but the reviews did little to ease Edwin's anxieties. The doctors urged Georgina to begin her confinement. She refused, saying she'd birthed eleven babies and knew her body a damn sight better than they did. She was remarkably lively and amusing in company, but Edwin saw the tension and tiredness in the way she set her jaw and closed her eyes when she thought no one was looking.

The Duke remained in Paris, where Mrs Vernon had joined him, until almost the end of the month, by which time Georgina was acutely anxious. On the rare occasions they were alone, Edwin pressed her close, feeling the child moving within her with a mixture of awe and terror, and whispered that everything would be all right, trying to convince himself as much as her. In the sanctuary of his studio, he muttered to himself and the dogs, cursing his inability to help, concocting wild schemes of elopement, but always coming back to the stark reality of the situation: they would lose everything if they ran.

When the Duke did finally return, he seemed in disconcertingly good spirits and invited Edwin to lunch at his club before viewing the long-awaited stag hunt at the Academy. Sir Thomas Lawrence, the President, led a flurry of nodding and bowing as they entered Somerset House, congratulating the Duke on looking so well and complimenting Edwin on the picture.

'You should be assured of his vote at least,' the Duke whispered, smiling as William appeared with Georgina, who had insisted on coming in defiance of doctors' orders. He took his wife's elbow – the picture of husbandly devotion – and they made their way through the exhibition.

Beneath the breezy conversation Edwin somehow managed to sustain with William, his stomach lurched. How had he been such a fool? Everything he'd ever worked for was there for the taking, but the Academicians wouldn't elect him in a thousand years if the scandal broke. Seeing the Duke and Georgina together, however, he had to admit scandal couldn't have looked less likely. Her conciliation campaign was clearly going well. Her husband held her tenderly, whispered to her – even her neck and shoulders appeared to relax as she leant on him. Perhaps it was going too well. Then Georgina clutched a hand to her side, and Edwin's stomach twisted again as the Duke's arm tightened around what had been her waist, and he asked if she wished to leave. Paler even than usual, she nodded.

Left alone in the crowded galleries, Edwin watched the Bedford party depart, gritting his teeth as people made idiotic comments about how virile the Duke was – at his age – but how dangerous it was for the Duchess – at hers.

On a humid, cloudy day a fortnight later, Edwin rifled through the *Morning Chronicle* at a newsstand. Ignoring advertisements and election news, just as he had every day for the past week, he combed the close-packed type until he found the births, marriages, and deaths. How long could a baby take to make its way into the world? He wasn't expecting Georgina to write, but . . . would anyone have told him if the worst had happened?

He blinked and read. Then blinked and read again. Joy and relief exploded in his chest and surged through his limbs. The last entry in 'Births' read:

*On the 19th instant, in St James's Square, the Duchess of Bedford, a daughter.*

As soon as he got home, he took a bottle of Kinrara whisky into the garden and, with Brutus nosing his elbow, sank to the ground in the shade of the mulberry tree.

The following week, the Duke invited him to a small, informal dinner at St James's Square. Georgina wasn't present, having finally submitted to doctors' advice to rest, but Sir Thomas Lawrence was. The Duke made no bones about giving Edwin every opportunity to impress the man whose presidential voice could determine the Academy elections. Gratitude magnifying his guilt, Edwin swallowed an extra glass of champagne, forcing himself to focus on Lawrence and make erudite artistic conversation, though every sense was straining for a hint of Georgina and the baby, who must be somewhere in the house.

When food, port, and cigars were finally finished, they left the dining room. Crossing the hall, they came upon her in a bedgown and wrapper, curls escaping from an ineffectual turban, eyes sparkling. She looked young, pink-faced and very, very beautiful. And in her arms was a tiny bundle: white linen, lace, and a yellow-tinged snubbed nose.

'May I present Lady Rachel.' She blushed from chest to cheekbones as her eyes held Edwin's for a scant second. 'It seems she doesn't like to sleep when there's a party going on. Mr Landseer, would you mind awfully – I must fix my hair – could you hold her ladyship for a second?'

Edwin's chest hammered as she passed him the bundle, so warm and soft and fragile. Blood rushing in his ears, he looked down at his daughter. She gazed briefly back at him with unfocused blue-black eyes that were drifting shut in spite of her alleged reluctance to sleep.

'Don't panic, Landseer, I'll take her,' the Duke's words sliced softly into his brain.

Edwin swallowed hard, blinking to clear his vision as Georgina's husband stroked the cheek of the now-sleeping infant. He had no choice. He handed her over.

He hadn't known a heart could burst with love and break at the same time.

That autumn in the Highlands even the raindrops seemed tinged with gold. Most of it was spent deep in Glenfeshie. Georgina had had an encampment built in an old forestry clearing near where the river spread into shallow, braided channels. Commanding a view of the hills at their most majestic, it comprised a collection of plank-walled cabins with sturdy stone chimneys, which she referred to as 'the huts'. Each was sub-divided into two or three rooms and large enough to sleep as many people as Georgina decreed necessary. In the centre was a larger, undivided hut that served as dining room, drawing room, dance floor, and everything else in between. On the edges of the clearing were a couple of old blackhouses, built of turf and tarred branches on stone footings, one of which was assigned to Edwin.

The afternoon after his arrival, he sat against the sun-warmed planks of the largest hut listening to shrieks and laughter as the children played and splashed in the bright, cold river. Georgina – skirts hitched up – had joined them and was directing the building of dams and supervising fishing. Even the French governess, who sat blowing soap bubbles with a clay pipe for Alexander, had removed her stockings and was cooling her feet in the water. The Duke was back at Invereshie House with Old Lord William and other shooting guests.

In Edwin's arms, curled warmly against the linen of his shirt, lay Rachel. She had turned from a tiny, curled-up creature into a plump, snub-nosed cherub, whose smiles were like sunlight after a squall and whose eyes were now the same sky blue as his own. Her wide, dark pupils travelled between his face and her own fingers as she clasped fistfuls of his shirt. Bubbles floated over their heads while he told her stories about deer, about the people of the glen, and about her mother, until her tiny lips pouted and parted in a series of yawns and her lilac-veined eyelids started to close. He'd never wanted to capture a moment more but didn't dare reach for pencil and paper lest he wake her, so he traced her features over and over with his eyes, etching them into his mind, along with her solidity, her warm milky smell, and her soft, contented breathing.

He could – and did – capture everything else: the hills; the heather; the people; Georgina nursing, gazing down at Rachel. But no amount of sketching could keep the leaves on the trees or stop the weeks passing. All too soon October was half over, the weather forced them back to Invereshie, and preparations were being made for the grand trek south. Having packed up his easels and few possessions, and dressed for one final dinner,

Edwin wandered onto the sweep of cropped grass that ran down to the river, fighting a wave of sadness.

'Lanny?' Georgina appeared from the direction of the stables. He waited as she caught up with him, holding her skirts clear of the wet grass. Glancing back towards the house, the windows of which reflected the sinking sun, she motioned him to walk on. She didn't take his arm. As soon as they reached the privacy of a stand of birches by the water, she turned.

'Don't panic, but my brother knows.'

Edwin's sadness turned to horror. 'Are you sure?'

'He just told me he was glad to see I was a true Gordon after all – adding a pretty little bastard to the family collection. Then he asked if she was able to hold a paintbrush yet.'

'How did he find out?'

'I don't know. Servants gossiping? The rows in Paris were volcanic. Everyone there must have heard.' She flushed. 'If he's heard the Duke isn't Rachel's father, it's not hard to put two and two together. He knows there's only one person I could have had in my bed at Kinrara last year.' She pulled her shawl tighter then reached for Edwin's hand. 'But he won't tell anyone. We just need to be even more careful.' She squeezed his fingers and the breeze wafted the scent of roses across Edwin's face, but fears that had lain dormant for the past few months were stirring.

'How can you be certain?'

'I trust him. He's never let me down before.'

'Before?' Edwin resisted her attempt to pull him close.

'With . . . other things.' She tried again.

'Other lovers?'

'No.' She dropped his hand, a scowl flashing across her face. He scowled back.

'What the hell made you say that?'

Edwin bit his lip. 'I don't know.' Damn George Hayter and his damned gossip.

Georgina shook out her skirts, then with one hand on her hip, looked him in the eye. 'I don't know what you might have heard. I won't lie. I have had flirtations in the past, but they were nothing serious.' She continued to hold his gaze.

Edwin blinked, refused to fill the silence.

Hands on both hips now, she said, 'My husband is definitely the father of all my other children, if that's what you're wondering.'

He still said nothing. Her eyes began to moisten. He was on the point of apologising when she forcibly took his hand, saying, 'They weren't like you. There's never been anyone like you. I love you.'

'You love me?'

'Yes, you fool. I thought that was obvious?'

'I'm not just some flash in the pan?'

'How on earth could you think that?' Edwin's skin purred as she slid her arms around his waist, then added, 'And this is where you say you love me. And if you don't, I shall push you into the river.'

'You wouldn't dare.'

'I would. Say it.'

The more she pressured him, fingers digging into his back, the more it silenced the demons. She poked him sharply in the ribs, then, with her lips so close to his ear it set every hair shivering from the nape of his neck to the base of his spine, she whispered, 'Say it, my Endymion.'

'All right,' he laughed. 'Desperately, uncontrollably, wildly . . .' Another jab in the ribs. 'I love you,' he said, with all his heart.

* * *

On a wet London night near the end of November, Edwin sat in the Garrick Club next to William.

'What's the time?' he asked, twisting a playing card between his fingers.

'Two minutes later than last time you asked, if that.' William tapped the ash from his cigar. 'They'll let you know as soon as the results are out. Will you leave the cards alone? That's the second ace you've destroyed.'

'Will you just get your watch out?' Edwin put down the dog-eared card and drummed his fingers on his knee. 'Leslie said election meetings are normally over by half past ten.'

'All right, all right.' William leant back and extracted a battered silver watch from his waistcoat pocket. 'Ten minutes before eleven. Happy now?'

'No.' Edwin looked at his empty glass and threw himself back into the studded leather armchair. 'Can we get some more brandy? How long would you say it takes to walk here from Somerset House?'

'I don't know. Be patient,' William said. He waved his cigar at a passing servant. 'Excuse me, might we have another brace of brandies? And another deck of cards.'

Edwin realised he'd picked up the ace again. He screwed it up and shrugged.

Before the servant had made it halfway across the room, a breathless, beaming Charlies Leslie appeared in the doorway.

'Ah, Mr Russell,' he drawled, ostentatiously avoiding Edwin's gaze. 'I'm looking for a newly elected Associate of the Royal Academy of Arts. I'm told there might be one on these premises by the name of Edwin Henry Landseer . . . ARA.'

'Huzzah!' yelled William. 'You – ignore that order for brandy: we need champagne!'

Edwin threw down the crumpled ace, lightheaded with relief.

'Who else got in?' he asked, steadying himself with a hand on the table. He'd got away with it. Now they would take him seriously. No more Little Dog Boy.

'Jack Gandy,' Leslie said, accepting a cigar from William's apparently inexhaustible store.

'And George Hayter?' Edwin said, also taking a cigar.

'Ah, Hayter.' Leslie shook his head. 'I'm afraid not, but he fared better than Benjamin Haydon. He was your teacher for a while, wasn't he? Poor silly ass didn't get a single vote. At least George got a few.' Leslie sat back, puffing his cigar alight. As they raised their glasses into the clouds of smoke, Edwin dismissed a twinge of guilt at the thought of George and Amelia. Georgina was right. Secrets and lies were better than open scandal.

A few days later, Edwin was waiting for his brother Charles, just returned from a stint as official artist on a diplomatic expedition to Brazil, at the old banker's house on Pall Mall that had been left to the nation as a public gallery. It was too cold to linger outside so he'd gone in and was attempting to bring feeling back to his fingers in front of Hogarth's self-portrait with a pug. He was picturing Brutus by his own side in a picture, when a familiar voice soured the scene.

It was the vote-less, luckless, history painter Benjamin Haydon, accompanied by a stout man in a green cravat. Almost a decade had passed since Edwin's father had sent him to Haydon's studio, where his brothers were already pupils. The memories still made him ache with boredom. The man hadn't changed much: thick lips and thin hair then, thick lips and even thinner hair now. His voice was also as grating as ever.

Not wanting to talk to him, Edwin tilted his hat to hide his face and went back to Hogarth's pug, praying Haydon would be gone by the time Charles arrived.

But Haydon never had been able to keep his voice down: 'It's yet more proof that the elections have nothing to do with merit. It makes the Academy the laughing stock of Europe.'

'Too true,' said the green cravat man. 'Same with the newspapers. All about influence – and deep pockets.'

Haydon brayed in agreement. 'We need art which improves and uplifts. But what do they do? Simper to connoisseurs with portraits and pet painters. Talent means nothing without toadying. Take Landseer.'

Edwin stiffened, narrowing his eyes at Hogarth, who stared implacably over his shoulder. Where was Charles? It would serve Haydon right if he walked in right now.

'John Landseer never toadied to anyone in his life! Quite the reverse,' laughed the know-it-all companion.

'Not the old man – the boy, Edward. They've just elected him ARA. I spend years striving to advance the cause of High Art and what do I get? Not a single vote. But that ungrateful whippersnapper toadies to Bedford and saunters straight in. He's no better than he ought to be, take it from me: I taught him everything he knows. Now he gives himself airs, dresses like the worst sort of dandy. He's nothing more than *The Monkey who had Seen the World*.'

Hogarth's pug looked embarrassed. Edwin clenched his fists as Haydon and his companion chortled their way out of the room. He knew the fable all too well – a common monkey gets made a pet by a great lady and fawns all over her to obtain gifts and favour. Of all the deluded, self-important fools, Haydon was the worst. Taught him everything he knows? He'd always thought the man delusional, but this sealed it. He tilted his hat back to its proper angle – it was fashionable, but hardly 'the worst sort' – then marched out of the room. Clattering down the steps, he almost ran into Charles, who spat a lump of tobacco into the gutter.

'Ah, Ned, shall we go in?'

'No,' Edwin snapped, catching sight of his reflection in a window, searching it for hints of dandyism. He was not a toady. Damn Haydon. Damn him to hell. He'd show him and that snivelling friend of his. He'd show them all.

# *October 1860, London*

AN ORB OF LIGHT SURROUNDS the lantern swinging from his hand. Cigar smoke drifts into the darkness beyond its edges where pictures slumber on their easels.

'What about this one?' Edwin says, stopping by a clay model of a lion. 'I know, I know, the fur needs work – ignore that – but the pose works well, don't you think? Majestic but not too static . . . Or do you think it's too heraldic?' Clamping the cigar between his teeth, he crouches to peer more closely. Through the free side of his mouth, he says: 'But would it work scaled up? Twenty-foot long?'

Patting the beast on the head, he staggers a little – but only a little – as he eases himself upright and draws on the cigar, lets the rich smoke swirl around his mouth, roughly caressing his tongue, before blowing it out in a steady stream.

'Next!' he says, and the light follows him a few paces deeper into the gloom. 'Now, this one I think we will have to . . . smash.'

There is a soft knock at the door.

'Ned? Who are you talking to?' Jessie's face appears around the edge, all chiaroscuro and concern.

'The dogs. Topsey's being very rude about my clays.'

'May I come in?'

'Yes, if you don't mind me smoking.'

'I'm used to it. And it's your house, as you're so fond of saying.'

'It's your house too.' He takes her arm. The terrier Topsey rubs her wiry head against her ankles. Lassie continues to pad by Edwin's side. 'Topsey was particularly critical about this one – it's her.' He reaches down to pat the head of a life-sized model on the floor.

'You hardly need to tell me.' Jessie takes the lantern from him and squints. 'It's her to the life. You should have taken up clay long ago.' Her breath steams into the chill air.

'Glad I didn't.' Edwin puffs, trying a smoke ring, which wobbles and hovers above the clay dog like a halo. 'Horrible stuff. Makes the skin on my hands so dry it feels about to flake off. But – don't tell anyone – I did enjoy doing Topsey. Do you reckon they'd accept four colossal terriers for Nelson?'

Jessie laughs and squeezes his arm. 'Why the lamp? Is the gas not working?'

'It hisses at me. And this way I only have to look at the things I want to see. Come on, you might as well have a gawp at the worst.'

Edwin peels off the wrappings and they look at the serious lions. Two of them on a work table, about the same size as Topsey. The lamp makes thin whistling sounds. More cigar smoke swirls into the shadows.

'Now, ignore the paws, but I think I can train them up to the job. I'm rather pleased with the muzzle on this one.' With a laugh, he holds the cigar up to the open jaws, puts it as close as it will go, but his hand shakes and slips, makes a mark in the clay.

'Ned, careful,' Jessie says.

He waves it off, pretending not to be annoyed with himself. 'It doesn't signify. I'll fix it. Hold this.' He hands her the cigar, which she holds as though it might explode, then begins to stroke and guide the clay back into shape.

'Very good. I like it even better than before,' she says, leaning in and holding the light closer.

'Not afraid to put my hand in a lion's mouth, see?' He laughs. 'Not afraid of anything,' he mutters, catching sight of the shattered fragments of the third lion on the edge of the blackness, kicked into a corner with the broken brandy bottle. He takes the lantern and cigar from Jessie and steps a few paces back from the table. The evidence of his earlier tantrum is swallowed back into the darkness.

# *1827, London*

SPRING WAS FIZZLING OUT IN a succession of drizzle-filled days and dreary evenings when Edwin gave his first dinner at St John's Wood. The guests of honour were his youngest siblings, Emma and Jessie, who were celebrating having pictures accepted for exhibition at the Academy. A fire wheezed and smoked in the grate and the candles on the table flickered in a draught that continually threatened to cast the whole company – his brothers, sisters, George and Amelia – into darkness. No one seemed to mind. At a shriek of Belinda's laughter, Edwin reached for the claret bottle. Even at the other end of the table, Tom's wife was too loud. He'd put her next to Charles, who was still telling interminable stories about Brazil, hoping they'd cancel each other out.

'Neddy!' Belinda called. 'I was just saying what lovely thick nappies you have.'

'What?' Edwin winced, surprised her voice hadn't broken all his new glasses.

'Your dinner nappies,' she cackled, flourishing a linen napkin perilously close to a candle. 'So fancy!'

'They're finer than the ambassador had in Brazil,' said Charles, slurping his way through more wine.

'From Woburn, if I'm not mistaken,' George smirked. 'Have you been pilfering Ned?'

'No.' Edwin was grateful for the lack of light to conceal his burning cheeks. 'The Duchess gave them to me. They're old.'

'They don't look old to me. They're ever so thick. Feel that weave, Tommy.' Belinda reached across the table, blithely oblivious to the risk of setting herself and the napkin on fire. 'If your duchess has any more, get some for us, will you?'

'She won't. And she's not my duchess.'

The fire hissed, belching wet soot onto the hearth as a volley of raindrops landed.

'I thought you'd fixed the roof, Ned?' said Tom, who sat between their younger sisters, Jessie and Emma.

'I have,' said Edwin. 'I didn't say anything about the chimney. It's waiting until I sell another picture.' The candles flickered again.

'Might you invest in shutters at the same time?' said Tom, chewing on a mouthful of mutton and glancing at an ill-fitting window frame.

'Or curtains?' said Emma, pulling a face as she took a sip of wine.

'Not if people keep nagging me,' Edwin said. 'Anyway, I like looking out at the trees. It reminds me of the Highlands.'

'But it's dark,' said Emma.

'But I know the trees are there.' He grinned at her.

As if in answer, a twig squeaked against a cracked window pane.

'I like it,' said Jessie, firmly placing her hand over the top of her glass as Tom brandished the bottle in her direction. 'It's romantic.'

'It's damp and draughty, but that's synonymous with romance to young ladies these days,' said George. 'Pass that wine will you, Ned?'

'Don't mind him, Jessie,' said Amelia, to Edwin's left. 'He hates winter. I hope he'll be in a better mood when we go to Florence.' Noticing her glass was empty, Edwin took the bottle from Tom and served her before passing it to George.

'Do you know when you're leaving yet?' he asked.

'The Duke of Bedford's arranging things. He's been so kind. The Duchess too. I'd have liked to thank them in person, but George tells me that's not possible. He says he has tried but ... you know how it is.' There was a brittle note in her voice as she raised the glass to her lips. It wasn't the first time Edwin had refilled it. She'd drunk as much as Belinda, though with quieter results. He wasn't sure how hard George had actually tried, but didn't doubt the Bedfords' reluctance to meet his mistress.

'How are the children?' he said, allowing himself briefly to wonder what Rachel would be doing right now. Would she be asleep?

'They're well – I mean as well as children ever are. Sweet, noisy, exhausting ... It's so good to be out. Thank you, Edwin.'

'It's a pleasure.' He squeezed her hand, draining his own glass and pushing down an image of Rachel sleeping in his arms. 'Next time, I might even get a proper fire going.'

She blinked. Smiled. Wiped a tear from her cheek.

'Mrs ... err, that is ... Miss... err, my dear lady,' Tom butted in, peering around her other side. 'My Lindy says to ask for tips on how to manage children. You never know when a little Landseer might show up.' His broad face puckered into a grin. Edwin motioned to George to send the bottle back.

Amelia flushed. 'I'm not the person to ask, I've never felt like a very good mother—'

'Don't be in too much of a hurry, Tom,' George cut in. 'You can't imagine the havoc the wretches wreak. They're a damned drain on the purse strings too. And as for being able to concentrate on work: there's a reason so many painters are unmarried.' He laughed and the others – except Amelia and Edwin – followed suit.

'Speaking of which, in a way, did you hear the latest on Ben Haydon?' said Charles, smearing his napkin with a dark streak of mutton grease from his mouth.

'No.' Edwin put down his glass.

'He's avoided debtor's prison by the skin of his teeth. The bailiffs were about to cart him off to King's Bench but he squealed so loudly that Lord Egremont coughed up an advance for a new picture.'

'Shame. It might have knocked some sense into him,' said Edwin. 'Did I tell you what he said about me being the monkey who'd seen the world?'

'Yes,' groaned several voices.

'Well, begging is better than toadying, I suppose. In his twisted mind.'

'Don't be harsh, Ned. I'm sure it wasn't his intention to beg,' said Jessie.

'No. He just wastes money he doesn't have by painting huge canvases nobody wants, and then expects to be bailed out. And it's not just rich patrons he taps when the bailiffs come knocking, it's us too – you remember when Father gave him half of my silver medal prize money?'

'Give it a rest, Ned. You never liked him because he refused to pat you on the head and say how wonderful you were when he was teaching us,' said Charles.

'Not true! He didn't teach me—'

Tom cleared his throat loudly. 'Have you seen the latest recruits to the zoo?'

'Yes,' drawled George, upending the wine bottle into his own glass before passing it along. 'Bedford tells me he's donating a llama.'

'Ooh, I'd love to see a llama. What *is* a llama?' said Belinda, grabbing the bottle. "Ooh, Ned, I read such a funny piece that said your duchess was donating a cuckoo!'

Edwin froze.

'A cuckoo? Why would they want a cuckoo in the zoo?' asked Jessie.

Belinda cackled. 'Oh, you sweet little duck, Jess, it's a naughty joke, you know, about one naughty bird sneaking its baby into another bird's nest. It means—'

'Where did you read that?' Edwin glared at her, only just managing to keep his voice steady.

'Oh Lord, I don't know. *The Satirist*, I think?'

'Filthy scandal sheets,' he snapped. 'I'm amazed you let her read that sort of thing, Tom.'

'Hoity toity!' she cackled. Charles joined in.

'I have no control over her,' Tom said, beaming as Belinda blew him a kiss.

'They've actually carted Ben Haydon off to prison this time,' said Charles a month later. His teacup chinked against its saucer like a chisel chipping into Edwin's skull.

'What for? Painting terrible pictures or boring people to death?' Edwin said. His head felt like it was full of broken glass.

'Don't be so disrespectful.' His father put down another cup with even greater noise. Edwin winced. Why must they all be so loud? He'd been out with William the night before and had only dim memories of arriving back at his parents' house on

Conway Street, where he was staying while building work went on at the cottage.

'Edwin? Edwin? Are you listening to me?' His father again. Couldn't they leave him alone? The Duke had commissioned a small portrait of Georgina and he had a sitting with her at St James's Square that afternoon. In his current state, he wasn't sure he would survive the journey, let alone be able to hold a brush.

John Landseer showed no mercy. 'Poor Haydon's in King's Bench for debt. Think of his wife and children. You should be putting your hand in your pocket to help, not kicking him when he's down. He's done a lot for art.'

'Poor Haydon. Poor, poor Haydon,' Edwin said, thinking of someone else's wife, and his own child, who he hadn't seen in a month. The jokes about the cuckoo had died down, but Georgina was still terrified of gossip. 'All he's done for art is carp on about how frivolous modern paintings are while painting oversized, overambitious shockers himself.' And call me a monkey, he thought, briefly resting his forehead on his hands and breathing very slowly. Speaking wasn't a good idea.

'Ned, are you unwell?' his mother said.

Someone made another skull-chiselling noise with a teacup.

'I think I need some air.'

'You need not to come in at all hours, roaring drunk,' said his father.

'I was not drunk.' Edwin stood, leaning on the table for a few breaths. 'At least, I was not roaring.'

'No, you were reciting poetry,' Emma giggled. 'It was very funny.'

'Thank you.' He smiled at her, then turned to his father. 'See – not guilty. Not roaring. Now, if you'll excuse me, I really must get some air.'

In the street, the air had too much nightsoil about it to be described as fresh but was better than nothing. Old John Bell the chemist had better be able to mix something to save him or the afternoon's sitting would be entirely wasted. A fleeting glimpse of Georgina the night before came back to him, making his stomach twist. It was the first sight of her he'd had in a fortnight. Her father, the Duke of Gordon, was in town and she'd been caught up with dinners and balls to which Edwin was not invited. He'd been walking home, having left William at the club, and there she was, on the steps of a grand house. Light, music, and conversation cascading from the windows. Kissing cheeks, laughing, getting into her carriage. If she'd seen him at all, he would have been no more than a figure in the shadows – beggar, pickpocket, pimp? But she hadn't even glanced in his direction. His father was right, he'd had too much to drink, but at that moment his head had been icily clear.

It was anything but clear as he reached Bell's shop. Swallowing hard, he gazed at the jars and bottles displayed in the window. The shelves inside were lined with more. Bottles and jars, jars and bottles, like a kaleidoscope . . . His stomach flipped. Things were becoming urgent. The clang as he pushed open the door failed to summon anyone to the counter. Leaning on the polished wood, he pushed down one side of a set of scales. The brass pan wobbled then fell, landing with an awful noise. Gravely endangering his stomach contents, Edwin bent to pick it up.

'Don't worry, I'll get it.' A slim young man appeared from the back room, stepped smartly around the side of the counter, and retrieved the fallen pan. Edwin had rarely been more grateful to anyone.

'I was looking for Mr Bell,' he managed.

'He's not here. Perhaps I can help? I'm his son, Jacob. You're Edwin Landseer, the painter, aren't you?'

'I was yesterday, but God only knows who or what I am today. Do you have anything to turn the clock back so I can stop myself drinking at midnight?'

'No.' Young Bell's eyes crinkled with amusement. 'But I can mix you a tonic – what symptoms? Headache?'

'A thousand of them.'

'Nausea?'

'In spades.'

'Fatigue?'

'I'd lie on the floor and sleep right now if the room would stop spinning.'

'I'd recommend a chair rather than the floor.' Jacob indicated a shiny leather seat next to the counter. 'And drink this.'

'What is it?'

'Water.'

Edwin sat and stared at the water. Bell reached for jars, weighed ingredients, and pounded something in a pestle and mortar.

'I saw your pictures at the Academy. The monkey was excellent.' The clanging of the mortar joined the list of things that made Edwin's head hurt. 'Is it true you painted a dog into one of Turner's?'

'Yes.' Edwin rolled his eyes to the ceiling, cringing at the memory. Another Associate had dared him to. Fortunately, Turner had approved of the dog.

As the youth laughed and tipped whatever it was he'd ground up into a flask, Edwin noticed a pile of drawings next to a jar of leeches. Giving the bloodsuckers a wide berth, he gingerly pulled the papers closer. On the first page was a study of an antique sculpture, surrounded by caricatures of modern men.

'This is good. And very funny. Is it yours?'

Young Bell blushed and looked down, stirring his mixture furiously. 'They're just scribbles. Nothing special. Here,' he handed Edwin a beaker of something that fizzed softly, 'this should bring you back to the land of the living.'

'Urgh.' Edwin pulled a face. 'You draw better than you mix drinks.' A spark of memory flickered into life – Old Bell had a son at art school. 'Ah, you must be the one at Sass's academy?'

Bell blushed again. 'Yes.'

'Why aren't you drawing now then?' Edwin winced as the words left his lips. 'Oh God, I sound like my father. I mean … ignore me.' With difficulty, he swallowed another mouthful of Bell's tonic. 'How long before this stuff gets my brain working again?'

Bell regarded him with a mixture of concern and amusement. 'If you can keep it down, a quarter hour? And, if you must know, Sass has banished me for a week to think about my behaviour.'

'How did you behave?' Edwin tried another tentative sip.

'I sang French songs. Old Sass hates the French and he hates singing, so French songs are doubly forbidden.'

'Sounds doubly important to sing them then,' Edwin said. As he embarked on a further sip, a clang at the door announced the return of Bell Senior.

'Edwin Landseer ARA!' The chemist swept off his low-crowned hat. 'You're looking less than well. What's the trouble?'

'Brandy,' said Edwin.

Old Bell nodded and tutted unhelpfully. 'Is Jacob looking after you?'

'Impeccably.'

Bell junior coloured again and busied himself clearing up.

'Good, good. Your father was in the other day. Telling us what a travesty it is that your pictures are hung so low – says they're your best yet. Tells me he's going to take the hanging committee to task.'

'He'd better not.' Edwin drained the cup, screwing up his face at the aftertaste.

'Don't be too hard on him. He was bursting with pride about how well you're doing. Always is.'

Caught out by the report of unexpected paternal praise and another wave of nausea, Edwin failed to formulate a response.

'Will you tell him I'll have his order delivered tomorrow?' Old Bell continued.

'Of course.' Edwin eased himself into a standing position, the hammering in his head not quite as loud as it had been. 'Can you put this on my account?'

'I'm surprised Jacob hasn't asked you to pay him in drawing tips.'

'I'd be more than happy to. Come up to the studio any time,' Edwin said. Bell junior thanked him and flushed his deepest shade of scarlet yet.

By the time Edwin reached the Bedfords' house, most of the broken glass seemed to have cleared from his skull and the queasiness had retreated. But his delight at recovery was short-lived. William, grey-faced, met him in the hall and explained in hushed tones that the Duchess's father had died in the early hours of the morning.

'He was eighty-three, but it was a bit of a shock. He's been dining out all week, even went to Clapham yesterday afternoon – I mean, no one expects a man to spend his last afternoon on earth in Clapham, do they? Then last night he was taken with some sort of attack. Aunt Georgina was with him at the end. She's in a bad way.'

As if on cue, Georgina appeared, pale, puffy-eyed.

'Lanny,' she sobbed, falling into Edwin's arms.

'It's all right, it's all right,' he whispered, but felt a shiver of dread as he caught a look of astonishment on William's face. In a much louder tone, he added, 'Can we take her to her sitting room? She's fainting.'

'Yes, yes. Come on, Aunt Georgina.' William's eyebrows returned almost to their resting height.

Edwin glared over Georgina's shoulder at a wide-eyed maid. 'Fetch some smelling salts and some water,' he growled.

'And some brandy,' said William.

Georgina was still sobbing when they laid her on her sofa and – with some difficulty and a pang of guilt – Edwin prised her arms from around his neck. Damn not being able to comfort her, but the look on the maid's face, and on William's, had put the fear of God into him.

'Where's the Duke?' he asked, wrenching his eyes away from Georgina. Damn everything.

'Woburn.' William ran a hand through his hair, not meeting Edwin's gaze. 'They've sent word. He'll be here later.'

A knock at the door was followed by a firm 'Mama' and fifteen-year-old Lady Louisa Russell entered, accompanied by a maid with a tray.

'Mama, I thought you were trying to rest?' Louisa said, putting her arms around her mother.

'I hadn't thought she was that close to her father,' Edwin said quietly to William, stomach twisting with more than last night's drink as he accepted a brandy and water.

'She hated what he did to her mother but adored him.' William shrugged and sipped. 'It was complicated. I suppose fathers are. I know mine is.' Running his hand through his hair again with an anxious look, he added, 'Look, you'd better come back another time. I'll make your apologies to Aunt Georgina when she's calmed down. If you're feeling half as bad as I am after last night, you'd probably rather be in bed anyway.'

Edwin arrived back at Conway Street to find his own father bending over the drawing-room table, examining a pile of papers with a magnifying glass.

'Anything exciting, Father?' he said, peering over the thread-bare shoulders of his father's housecoat.

'Eh? Oh, Ned. What was that? Look! A new treatise on cuneiform tablets!'

'Oh. Lovely.' Edwin filled the words with as much bonhomie as he could muster. 'Look, I'm sorry for what I said about Haydon earlier. Did you say there's a collection to get him out? Will you give this from me?' He placed a bank note on the table, then wearily climbed the stairs and sank onto his old, narrow bed, eyes open, thoughts churning.

Unable to stomach Society after her father's death, Georgina travelled to the Highlands early, leaving before July was over. Edwin travelled with her, using the need to work on a whisky still picture commissioned by Wellington as justification. The Duke planned to follow when business and doctors allowed.

Edwin and Georgina travelled in one carriage, the children and maids in another. Having spent the early part of the journey in a caudle-induced doze in spite of the ruts baked into the roads, Edwin woke to see Georgina wiping her eyes.

'I was thinking about my father,' she said in response to his groggy expression of concern. 'These hills always remind me of coming home to him after a season in London with my mother.' She balled up her handkerchief. 'I wish I'd seen more of him. If only he hadn't married *that woman* ... Why did he have to *marry* her?'

'Perhaps they were in love?' Edwin muttered, blinking as moorland came into focus through the open window, blazing purple with heather and foxgloves. The North. He must have been asleep longer than he thought. He couldn't fault Old Bell's mixture for banishing nausea but wished it didn't make him feel quite so drowsy or drunk.

'But did they have to marry?' Georgina went on. 'They could have continued as they were. It wasn't as though he needed an heir. It was an insult to my mother's memory.'

'Maybe the housekeeper wanted to stop living in sin?' Edwin thought of the look of hope on Amelia Hayter's tired face as she left for Italy a few months previously.

'Pah. She'd been happy to live in sin for twenty years. And they never went anywhere or saw anyone even after they were married. He should have known how much it would hurt us.' She wound her handkerchief around her fingers. 'I suppose my mother shouldn't have married *him* in the first place. But when the most eligible bachelor in Scotland asks you, it's hard to refuse. Her father was only a baronet, you see, but her mother was ambitious. So was she. She used to say: Georgy, one doesn't marry a duke for love.'

'Did you?'

'Did I what?'

'Did you marry a duke for love?' Edwin asked; As Georgina hesitated, he wished he hadn't.

'I married a duke because my mother told me to.' She laughed, but not with her eyes. 'I did think I was in love. But I was very good at fancying myself in love with whoever my mother put in front of me. I'd spent the previous two years being in love with John's brother. Did you know that?'

'Old Lord William?' said Edwin, unable to hide his surprise.

'No. Francis. The fifth Duke. John was never meant to be duke, you know. Francis was his older brother. My mother was a great matchmaker; her life's work was to see her daughters marry well. She'd already bagged two dukes and a marquis-to-be when it came to my turn. Bedford was quite the prize. She ordered me to fall in love, and I did. Then she ordered me to do whatever it took to secure an engagement, which I also did.' She blushed and looked away. 'I was only eighteen – she told me that was how things were done, that it wasn't a sin if marriage followed.' Edwin reached for her hand, but she pulled away, winding the handkerchief tighter, adding with a brittle laugh, 'And Francis was quite the dashing rake. And then – after I'd let him ... but before any engagement could be announced, he died. It was so sudden. It was the closest I've ever seen my mother to panicking. If word had got out, my reputation would have been ruined.' She looked up, jaw set. 'So off we went to Paris – it was during the peace of 1802. Everyone was there, thinking we'd seen the end of those ridiculous wars – and she set her traps and instructed me to fall in love with Napoleon's stepson Eugène de Beauharnais.'

Edwin failed to suppress a laugh. 'Really? So you were nearly Napoleon's daughter-in-law?'

She smiled, relaxing a little. 'Not very nearly. It wasn't one of her more successful attempts, or mine. But John came along in the middle of it all. He'd been with his brother when he died and brought a message for me. He was the sweetest, most compassionate ... He'd been widowed the year before and was so quietly melancholy. I didn't need my mother to tell me to fall in love with him. So yes, I suppose I did marry a duke for love.'

Needing – but not wanting – to know, Edwin said, 'Do you still love him?'

'I . . .' She squeezed his hand, hesitated again. 'Not in the way I love you. He's more like a brother now.'

Edwin bit his lip, jealousy burning away the drowsiness caused by Bell's mixture. 'Would you have married me if I'd come along twenty years earlier?'

'I'd have run away with you in a heartbeat.' She leant in to kiss him, but he stopped her.

'Would you run away with me now?' He gripped her hand harder than ever.

She looked at him the way she had when he'd first kissed her at the whisky still.

'Would you?'

She pulled her hand away and began twisting her handkerchief again. 'I . . . if things were different, in a heartbeat but . . . the children . . . the scandal. Who would even think of marrying the girls? There's enough gossip already after my parents, and my sister—' She stopped abruptly.

'Richmond?'

'No. A different sister. I can't talk about it.'

She leant in and kissed him with a suddenness and fierceness he'd never known, but he still felt crushed.

'Don't spoil what we have,' she murmured, fresh tears in her eyes. 'Please.'

'It was only a joke.' Edwin forced a smile. 'But I shall pretend this is an elopement until the Duke arrives.'

Her expression told him she knew as well as he did that it wasn't a joke at all.

The weather being fine, they made their base at the Glenfeshie huts. Every morning, in the chill air of dawn, Edwin slipped from Georgina's hut to his own, the dew soaking his boots as he pulled his jacket close over an unfastened shirt, leaving dark footprints in the glistening grass, watching the deer browsing in the mists that rolled through the glen.

Three weeks after their arrival, they were joined by Eliza and Wrio (recently ordained and every inch a serious young clergyman, until he laughed or blushed, both of which he did frequently when looking at Eliza). The Duke had remained in the South, having decided to sample the waters of newly fashionable Leamington Spa, as had Mrs Vernon.

That same day, Rachel took her first unaided steps, tottering briefly on the earthen floor of Edwin's hut before overbalancing into his arms, imprinting her delighted, dribbling face even more deeply onto his heart.

'Thank God for Leamington Spa,' he whispered that night, as the river rushed through the starlit darkness. 'I can carry on pretending to have eloped with you.'

'God bless Leamington Spa,' Georgina murmured, arching her back in ecstasy.

September's greens and yellows mellowed to russet and ochre as October arrived. Edwin's footsteps crunched over frost in the dark rather than through dew at dawn. It became too cold to stay in the huts, so they moved back to Invereshie.

By the end of the month, Rachel was toddling from Georgina's arms to Edwin's across the drawing-room rug.

The Duke was not coming. He sent word he was expecting Georgina to join him in Brighton, where he was staying with Young Lord William and Bessy.

Though Georgina put off leaving for another three weeks, the days of the would-be-elopement were numbered. By late November, when the hill tops were white and the rowans and birches stripped bare, Edwin had learnt the location of every creaky floorboard between Georgina's room and his own, Rachel was able to say 'Mama', 'shh', and 'Lanny', and it was time to go south.

When Edwin arrived back in London filled with December gloom, it was to the news that the works on his house – and long-awaited new studio – were finished, that Benjamin Haydon had yet again received no votes in the Academy elections, and that, in Italy, George Hayter's Amelia was dead. Poisoned with arsenic.

# *November 1860, London*

DUST EXPLODES OFF THE PAINT-SPLATTERED floorboards as another clay model crashes down from the workbench – paws, mane, jaws lie shattered in a pool of flickering amber light. Reaching for the bottle, Edwin almost knocks the candle over, feels a blazing surge of pride at catching it, steadying it – who's drunk now?

A scalding streak of wax solidifies across the back of his hand as the whisky melts a trail through his insides. Whining and scraping at the door; the dogs – they mustn't come in. They can't see this. More scraping. They should be in the sitting room with Jessie. What is she doing? Why doesn't she stop them? Pain sears across his hand where the wax is hardening, pulling hairs from scorched skin as he clenches his fingers around the shepherd's crook. He glares at the next model, filled with loathing, raises the crook …

'Ned! Stop!' Charles's voice. How did he get in? Rancid smell of chewing tobacco.

Barking, Lassie at his legs. He hesitates. Charles grabs the stick.

'Get off!' Panic. Staggers. Swings an elbow at his brother's ribs. Misses. Stumbles. Arms pinned. Can't breathe.

'Ned, it's all right. Give me the stick.'

'Go away!' Squirming. 'Take your hands off me!'

'Ned, stop it! Stop it!'

'Let go!' Wrenches the stick back. Wave of anger.

'These are good – leave them be!'

'They're not. They will not do. They will not!' Raising the stick, but damned Charles has damn well got hold of it again. 'Let go—'

'No. These are good. You can work with them.'

Lassie licking the back of his hand. He can't meet her eyes.

Sobbing.

'Let go. Let go.'

More sobbing.

'Let me fail.'

# *1828, Woburn Abbey*

A BAD BUSINESS FOR GEORGE HAYTER in Italy,' said the Duke, shotgun resting in his gloved hands, words steaming in the January air as they paced along a line of leafless trees.

'I haven't heard the details, Your Grace,' Edwin said, eyes on the Duke's two favourite pointers crossing and recrossing each other's paths, noses down, trying to find what little scent there was in the frost. 'His letters have been rather cryptic.'

'I shouldn't imagine he's in spirits to write much, poor man. There are the worst sort of mutterings about him. The last thing I wish to do is spread gossip, Landseer. I only tell you because I know it will go no further.' The Duke stopped, sniffed the air, then continued. 'Friends in Florence tell me Hayter is blamed for the woman's death. It seems they quarrelled. I believe there was jealousy over a model. Some say she took the poison purposefully to destroy herself. Others – and this is strictly between us – others say he drove her to it. Some even accuse him of having given it to her, but that's preposterous.'

A twig cracked, wings flapped, and a cock pheasant burst from the dead leaves and dormant brambles. The Duke twitched, lifted the gun halfway to his shoulder, then shook his head and let the bird go. Its copper plumage glowed against the drab scene, tail feathers streaking behind as it disappeared into the skeletal trees.

'I'm sorry, Landseer. I never met the woman. Did you know her well?'

'Well enough,' said Edwin. Her fate seeped into his bones with the chill of the day. Before he could say more, another bird, a pale hen pheasant, clattered out of the undergrowth. This time the Duke's gun came smoothly to his cheek. There was a click, a hiss, and a bitter-scented explosion. The hen folded in the air then hit the frozen ground with a thud that juddered through the soles of Edwin's boots. George had been here so many times, yet they didn't even know Amelia's name.

'Yes. I knew her,' he said. It was inconceivable that George would have deliberately injured Amelia, but the idea that she had destroyed herself was disturbingly easy to believe. He should have seen what the secrecy and shame were doing to her. He hadn't understood it then but was beginning to understand it all too well.

'A very bad business,' the Duke repeated, shaking his head.

The sun set over a blank frost while back at the Abbey champagne bubbles rose in front of warm fires. Edwin, still in damp, muddy shooting clothes, painted faces and touched up scenery for the play the Russell children were to perform that evening, while Georgina topped up his glass and tried to keep Rachel from being too 'helpful'. He was onto the final backdrop, adding leaves to trees with swift, loose brushstrokes, when, in spite of Georgina's best efforts, small fingers met wet paint.

'I'll take her to the nursery,' she said, wiping a green handprint from her cheek and carrying a protesting Rachel away. 'I won't be long.'

Having repaired the damage, Edwin stretched his shoulders in an attempt to throw off the stiffness from the cold and regain some semblance of festive spirit. He was about to finish the last of the trees, when he heard voices in the auditorium. The speakers were hidden by the scenery, but he recognised the tones of William, and Georgina's daughters, Georgy and Louisa.

'William, are any of your smart friends coming? Mama hasn't invited any young men,' said Louisa.

'Lanny's young. I'm young,' said William. 'I hope you're not calling us old?'

'You don't count,' said Georgy.

'Whyever not? What's wrong with us?'

'You're you, and Lanny – we love Lanny – but he's only a painter.' Georgy again. Edwin's brush slipped, smudging a branch.

'Painter he may be, but he's worth two of most of my friends.'

'That doesn't signify. We need young men to sigh over and fall in love with. What would Papa say if we were to go around falling in love with painters?' Both girls laughed. Edwin took a deep breath.

'I see what you mean,' said William.

Edwin put down his brush and picked up his glass.

'Anyway, I see your lady love has arrived,' said Louisa.

'Don't talk about Miss Campbell like that,' said William.

'You're blushing!' the girls shrieked together.

Edwin drained his almost-flat champagne in a silent toast to Amelia Hayter then slipped out by the side door, leaving the Russells to their inane chatter.

The performance – a farce acted by the older Russell children, with appearances from Georgina and Dr Woolryche – was declared a resounding success. Spirits numbed if not restored by several glasses of wine, Edwin laughed as loudly as anyone, but his eyes went as often to Rachel sitting on the Duke's lap, playing with his watch chain, as they did to the stage.

Afterwards, he and William smoked cigars and sent balls rumbling around the billiard table.

Stretching to line up a shot, Edwin said, 'So what's this romance of yours I hear so much about? Is it Emma Campbell?'

'It is.' William ran a hand through his hair. 'I've never met anyone like her for beauty or brains. Or making me look an idiot. It's making me deuced nervous, to tell you the truth. She has me thinking all sorts of illogical things. Is that what it's meant to feel like?'

'If you believe poets.' Edwin sent a ball spinning into a pocket.

'It'd put paid to my dreams of untold riches, though – she's as penniless as I am. Her uncle's the Duke of Argyll, but I know better than anyone how far ducal uncles don't go in terms of tin. But – and here I surprise myself – I don't think I mind. Is that normal? Am I crazy to even think of it?'

'Damned if I know,' Edwin said, swearing as he missed his shot.

'Bad luck.' William knocked back the contents of his glass and picked up his cue. 'You know what? If I pot this last ball, I'll ask her to marry me. If I miss, the quest for an heiress continues.'

William pushed back his hair, pushed up his sleeves, then slid the cue back and forth an inordinate number of times. Edwin leant against the wall and closed his eyes. He was exhausted but wasn't ready to face a night with thoughts of Amelia Hayter. Or Georgy Russell's words about painters. There was a soft thud as William's cue collided with the ball. Had he been a fool to think he could ever be more than a hired brush to these people? There was another thud and a muffled rattle. He opened his eyes. The table was clear.

'*Amor vincit omnia!*' William grinned.

'What?' Edwin was too tired to even try to understand.

'Love conquers all! I shall brace myself for poverty and poetry. And practice begging from my cousins. At least I don't have to worry about whether my father approves – he hasn't got any money not to give me. I suppose I should ask the Duke? Now, how on earth does one go about proposing?'

'I'm the last person to ask,' Edwin said, staring at the empty table.

William's proposal was met with approval by everyone, most importantly by Emma Campbell. Settlements were drawn up by the ducal uncles and a date set for the middle of May, with the marriage to take place from the Bedfords' house in St James's Square.

With less than a week to go, William sat on the new bench in Edwin's garden, wiping away tears of laughter as Edwin finished a story about his father embarrassing him at a recent breakfast with Sir Walter Scott by lecturing the novelist about minor historical inaccuracies in his books.

'Thank you for that. It took my mind off the wedding for almost a quarter hour.'

'Not having second thoughts, are you?' Edwin refilled William's glass and sat back to watch the lingering light of the first warm evening of the year, almost daring to relax. The cuckoo gossip had died down and Georgina's visits to St John's Wood had resumed, both in her capacity as self-appointed head gardener, and for final sittings for her brother's sporting portrait, in which she'd insisted on featuring, and which was now finished and on show to the public at Somerset House. She even brought Rachel when she could. Occasionally, Edwin let stories of elopement spin out in his head, but, as he always told the dogs afterwards, that would be madness.

'Second thoughts?' said William. 'Lord no. Just can't stand the fuss. My old man's even come back from Switzerland to help pile on the pressure. He's moping around St James's complaining how expensive everything is. Is that my fault? If I were in charge of the price of claret it would be a darn sight cheaper.'

Removing a cigar from the case in his pocket, Edwin cut it and touched it to the candle that sat on an upturned log next to the wine bottle, puffed it alight, then handed it to William. 'This is the last I have – it's yours. Calm those wedding nerves even more.'

'Too kind of you. We'll share.' William put it to his lips and raised his eyebrows. 'This is a corker. Where did you get it?'

'A gift from the Duke.'

'You must be in high favour; I wouldn't dare pilfer anything this good. He turns a blind eye to my snaffling the lesser ones, but if he caught me with my hands on these I'd lose my head – or at least my allowance, which would be infinitely worse.' His cheeks hollowed as he puffed contentedly. 'I nearly forgot to ask, how was the Exhibition opening?'

'Oh, fine, fine,' Edwin said. 'No one laid into the Gordon picture too heavily.'

'It's got a few tongues wagging though, you painting Aunt Georgina,' said William.

Edwin breathed in too sharply. 'Wagging about what?' He coughed.

'Just tittle-tattle, mostly. But Bessy said she'd heard you were ... well ... more friendly than you ought to be.' William laughed awkwardly and refilled his glass. 'I've never heard the Duke bawl anyone out so violently. Said he'd never heard anything so ludicrous. She was quite cowed for once.'

The evening no longer felt quite so warm.

William sipped and cleared his throat. 'I know you're great pals and all, but ... there isn't anything in it, is there?'

'Christ no.' Hand shaking, Edwin passed him the cigar. 'The Duke's right. It's a ludicrous idea.'

'It is,' said William, with palpable relief.

The next day, Georgina was in the middle of telling Edwin where to plant the rose cuttings she'd brought from Campden Hill, when she grasped at his arm, staggered, and would have landed among the thorns if he hadn't caught her.

With an ominous lack of protest, she allowed him to help her inside.

'I'm praying it's just the heat,' she said, sinking onto the sofa. 'Or the wedding. Eliza's bridesmaid's dress is still not right,' she fanned herself with her gloves, voice rising, 'and she has no mother to help. If I let her down ...'

'Calm down. It'll be all right. Drink this.' Edwin handed her a glass of water.

She'd looked alarmingly pale in the sunlit garden. Here, in the small, dark sitting room her complexion bore an alarming resemblance to curdled milk.

'Oh, Lanny,' she ran a hand over her face, 'I think I'm pregnant.'

They stared at each other in silence. The birdsong coming through the open window became brittle.

Edwin swallowed. 'How sure are you?'

'I could be wrong. But . . . I'm quite late.' She shrugged. 'But I'm forty-six. I'm always late these days. I'd hoped I was past all this.' She put her head in her hands. 'What a cursed mess.'

Edwin poured two glasses of brandy and sat down heavily next to her. 'I assume the Duke won't be expecting it?'

'Unless I can convince him it's an immaculate conception, no.' She sipped. 'And that bitch Bessy's damned rumour-mongering . . .'

'Shall I arrange a passage to Calais?' Edwin gave a humourless laugh. 'Or will we need to go to the colonies?'

'Don't joke.'

'I'm not.'

'Well don't be serious like that then.'

'I can't . . . oh it doesn't matter.' Edwin downed his brandy. 'Is it still . . . you know, early?'

'Yes. I think so.'

'Then it might resolve itself?'

She bit her lip and closed her eyes. 'Yes.'

Edwin squeezed her hand. 'And if it doesn't,' he said. 'Charles Leslie tells me America's not all bad.'

'Don't be ridiculous,' she murmured, resting her head on his shoulder. 'You'd be too seasick to survive an Atlantic crossing. I'm not even sure you'd make it to Calais, and then where would I be?'

When she felt strong enough to return to wedding preparations, Edwin helped her into her carriage, making her promise to send word of how she was the next day. He'd just turned to go back inside in search of the dogs and a drink to dilute the dread pooling in his stomach, when he heard the jingle of another horse drawing to a halt. The word 'cooee!' flew through the air like a knife.

'Neddy!' Belinda called, as an oily-whiskered man helped her out of a gig. The man made a clicking noise with his teeth, saluted her goodbye then whipped the horse into a sudden trot, disappearing down the road. Edwin pushed both hands through his hair and tried to breathe slowly.

'Tommy was wondering if you had any sketches of lions or tigers he could borrow?' Belinda said, straightening her dress.

'What the h—what does he want them for?'

'Some natural history thingummy he's doing. Did I just miss your duchess? I'm sure that was her carriage leaving, wasn't it?'

Edwin exhaled through his nose. 'Come and have a look. You can't stay long though. I'm terribly pressed.'

'All work and no play makes Ned a dull boy,' she said, toying with one of her carriage-spring curls as she followed him inside. 'You'd better not try and back out of coming to the play on Friday for Jessie's birthday.'

'I wouldn't dream of it,' he said through clenched teeth.

He found some lions and a tiger or two, then marched her out, ringlets swinging with indignation at being denied tea and gossip with Mrs Eames.

As soon as he was alone, Edwin poured himself a very large whisky and sank onto the studio floor. Brutus shuffled in, laid his elderly head in Edwin's lap and sighed. Bran, his deerhound, padded over and stretched out in a patch of sunlight. Bran's likeness looked down, wild-eyed, from the canvas above them, battling a wounded stag in a raging Highland burn, both in danger of being swept over a precipice. The whisky did nothing to stop Edwin's mind racing. That morning he'd hoped this picture would secure him election as a full RA. Now his chances looked on a par with those of the stricken beasts.

The morning post brought no news from Georgina, but there was a note from William asking Edwin to meet him at his lodgings as a matter of urgency. Heart in his mouth, stomach in his boots, Edwin went.

'Two days to go and this happens!' William dragged a hand across his face. 'I swear my family is cursed. First Aunt Georgina collapses, now the Duke's ill too.'

'Is it serious?' Edwin said, blood thundering in his ears.

'Damned serious for me,' said William.

'I mean for the Duchess,' Edwin snapped. 'And the Duke,' he added, forcing himself to speak more calmly.

'Woolryche says there's no danger to life, but I almost wish there were – devil take the pair of them. They're not coming to the wedding and the Duke's said we can't have the lunch at St James's Square now . . . what on earth am I'm going to do?'

'You still have the bride and the licence, don't you?'

'I do,' said William, head in his hands.

'Well, that's all you need.' Edwin tried to sound reassuring. 'The rest is just frippery. I've never heard of a marriage declared invalid for lack of lunch. Surely there's somewhere else you can hold it?'

'Not at this short notice.'

'Couldn't you postpone?'

'No, no ... my father's itching to get abroad again, some terrifyingly grand Campbells have come down—'

There was a soft knock at the door and a maid bobbed her way in, blushing.

'Lord Rizth ... Lord Wristly ... Lord Reowsthly Russell to see you, Mr Russell, sir,' she said.

'Thank God. Show him up, show him up!' William raised his eyes heavenward.

With a clattering of boots, Wrio appeared, cheeks flushed above his clerical collar, chestnut hair flattened by the top hat he carried in one hand.

'Eliza told me what happened,' he said, breathless. 'I've just been to see my brother Tavistock. He says you can use his house after the service.'

William leapt up and planted a kiss on his cousin's forehead. 'Wrio, I hope they make you a bloody archbishop! You're an angel.'

Wrio blushed, muttering that it was the least he could do.

'Is there any news on the Duke and Duchess, Wrio?' said Edwin, only just managing to keep his voice steady.

'I don't know,' said Wrio. 'Mama hasn't been well all week. Eliza said she fainted yesterday afternoon while they were trying to fix her dress. Woolryche was there and took her off to Campden Hill. Then Woolryche said my father was also unwell, but that's all anyone will tell me.'

* * *

As Edwin stepped through his front door half an hour later, Mrs Eames the housekeeper handed him a note in Georgina's handwriting.

*He knows. Burn this. Burn everything.*

Most of Georgina's letters and several sketches had been reduced to blackened, curling flakes in the studio fireplace by the time the knock came.

Mrs Eames closed the door softly, leaving the Duke standing behind a battered chair, jaw set, eyes narrowed.

'Your Grace, I—' Edwin's stomach twisted.

'Don't speak.' The Duke held up a hand.

'I just want to—'

'You *want*? I don't care what you *want*. You are not entitled to *want* anything. Not after the way you've behaved. After everything I've done for you, you repay me by … by …' The raised hand grasped at nothing, balling itself into a white-knuckled fist.

'Let me explain—'

'There is nothing to explain. Nothing! You've been fucking my wife. Do you think I need a description?'

'Is she all right?'

'I told you not to speak! This is hard enough, damn it, don't make it harder.' The Duke pressed his fist to his temple, where a vein was throbbing. 'And no – she is not all right. She's no longer with child, if that's any concern to you. She is hysterical. She swears she will leave me if I forbid her to see you. Or k-kill herself.' He glared at Edwin. 'See what you've done?'

'What I've done? It's not my fault.' Edwin said, agonisingly conscious that it was. 'It's you—'

'Silence!' the Duke thundered. 'I will not have this! I will not!'

Edwin bit his lip so hard that sweet, rusty blood seeped between his teeth.

'I will not have a scandal – I will not, you hear me? You will give her up.'

'No.' Edwin clenched his fists, nails biting into his palms. 'I love her.'

'You love her?' The Duke let out an awful, wheezing laugh. 'You're as deluded as she is. What on earth would you know about love?'

'I know enough,' Edwin said, heart thudding.

'Be quiet!' The echo of the Duke's voice faded into the rustling of leaves from the garden beyond the open barn doors. The Duke leant on the back of the chair, breathing heavily. For a chilling moment, Edwin thought he was about to have another stroke, then saw a tear slip down his cheek.

'I will not have this. I will not. I will not lose her,' the Duke said through clenched teeth. 'We may not be in the first flush of love. But there is more to a marriage than ... than lust; more than someone like you could possibly understand. Try to take her from me and you will regret it.'

Unable to meet his eye, Edwin stared over the Duke's shoulder at the half-painted canvas. The doomed stag gazed desperately at him. How could he have been so stupidly naive? He tasted blood again. His stomach lurched. How could he have thought it wouldn't all come crashing down?

'You put me in an impossible position.' The Duke's voice was shaking now. 'I could ruin you. And I would do so without hesitation but for the fact that it would destroy her too. And, unlike you, I do not live solely for the gratification of my own selfish desires. I have the honour of my family to consider. My children. The girls above all. A scandal hits daughters hardest – not only do they lose their mother, but her sin also tarnishes them. If you refuse to bring an end to this ludicrous ... this ...' he shook his hand as though trying to free it from a cobweb, 'then for their sake ... for Christ's sake ...'

'I didn't—' Edwin started but the Duke cut him off, slamming his fist onto the back of the chair.

'Do you ever do as you're told?' he hissed. 'Have you any idea how hard this is for me? At least have the decency not to interrupt.' He swallowed with a shudder. 'I am far from happy about this, believe me, as far from happy as one can be. I'd hoped you'd act like the gentleman I once took you for, but ... but ...' The Duke screwed up his eyes and brought a hand to his forehead. 'Continue with her if you must. Just, for God's sake, do not take her away. Don't ruin her. I beg you.'

The last syllables hovered in the humid air.

Rage, Edwin had expected, but not begging. His heart quickened. If the Duke was so worried, perhaps there was a chance. If he could just get to Georgina at Campden Hill, would she come away with him now?

'I shall require your solemn oath – though God knows what that is worth any more – that you will never so much as think about eloping. If she leaves me, it will be the end of you. I shall ruin you both. You will be outcasts and she will never see her children again. Think what that will do to her.'

'I wouldn't be the one stopping her seeing them. That would be you,' Edwin said, scrabbling to keep the new, insane hope intact.

'It would be the world. It would be the law. It would be God's judgement,' the Duke growled. 'A woman who abandons her husband and her family has no right to her children. They would remain with me. All of them,' his eyes flashed, 'including Rachel.'

Hope crashed to the floor. Edwin couldn't breathe.

'It was you then?'

Unable to speak, Edwin nodded.

The Duke grunted, struggled to swallow. The vein in his forehead pulsed as he leant on the back of the chair, chest heaving. When he looked up, his eyes were brimming with tears and fury. 'As far as the world is concerned, as far as the law is concerned, as far as she is concerned, she is *mine*. She is never to be told otherwise. I will not have that kind of shame brought on the name of Russell. Or on her.' A muscle in his cheek flickered. '*She* has done nothing wrong. Do you understand me?'

Edwin couldn't think. The world swirled around him.

'Well?' said the Duke. 'Now I wish you to speak you remain silent? Will you give me your word?'

The leaves rustled softly as the breeze brought in the scent of dying blossoms and the promise of thunder. Edwin could have bellowed like the beleaguered stag on the easel, but could find no words.

'It's quite simple, Landseer,' the Duke said, steadier now. 'It's an offer most young men would jump at – one I never thought I would find myself making. I will tolerate you being my wife's lover if you swear not to elope with her.'

'And if I give up my daughter,' Edwin said, his mouth dry.

'She is *not* your daughter.'

It was Edwin's turn to blink back tears. 'Does Georgina know about this?' he said.

'No. But if you accept the conditions, you may tell her yourself. She is still at Campden Hill.'

Edwin clasped his arms across his chest and willed air into his lungs. 'And if I refuse?'

'I think I've made that perfectly clear, Landseer. If you love her at all, you'll accept. You wouldn't break her heart by taking her children from her, would you? And Rachel – you must realise I can give her a better life than you can ever hope to. As my daughter, she will want for nothing. What chance would she have as the illegitimate offspring of a disgraced painter?'

Edwin felt sick.

'Would you condemn her? To poverty? To shame?'

Edwin looked back to the wild eyes of the half-painted stag in the raging water. He thought of Benjamin Haydon, in debt and in jail; of George, in his Italian disgrace; of Amelia; and of Georgina and Rachel. He couldn't make them live like that.

'And there's your own career,' the Duke continued. 'With my support, you could be one of the greatest painters of our age. Would you throw all that away? I can set you up in Paris, or Rome, or Florence, if you decide that, after all, you can give Georgina up?' There was no need to add that he could close off those places just as easily.

Edwin felt as though an iron band were tightening around his chest.

'Well?'

'I need time.' He pushed his hands into his hair, wanted to pull it all out, to scream.

'No. You agree now. Or you are ruined. Unless you'll give her up?'

'Never.'

'Well?'

A memory of a picture seen years ago rose unbidden in Edwin's mind. Of all things, one of Benjamin Haydon's. *The Judgement of Solomon*: the king giving his verdict to two women fighting over an infant, his sword poised to cut the child in two, the true mother renouncing her claim so the child could live.

He let out a long, slow breath and finally met the Duke's eye, hating himself. 'All right.'

The Duke held his gaze for a moment, then turned on his heel and left without another word.

Edwin had just returned from Campden Hill, perspiring and dust-covered as afternoon began to turn to evening. He was watching a last packet of letters curl and burn, when the studio door opened and his brothers, his sister Jessie, and Belinda bustled in.

'Lord love us, it's hot in here!' Belinda fanned herself with Tom's hat.

Edwin shivered.

'Ned, you're filthy. Are you not ready?' Tom said.

Edwin stared at him.

'Tommy, the fire's lit, no wonder it's hotter than the devil's ar— you-know-what in here.'

'Ned, I like this easel. Where did you get it?'

'Ned, are you not going to change?'

'We'll be late if we don't shift soon, Tommy.'

'Can I borrow this, Ned?'

'Tommy, if we go now, we can squeeze in a cheeky gin or two.'

'Ned, are you coming?'

It was too much. Edwin pulled his hands across his face and swallowed the urge to scream.

'Neddy . . .'

'What?' he said through clenched teeth.

'The play. You said you'd drive Jessie in that gig of yours as a birthday treat, remember?' said Tom.

'Oh, is that today?' Edwin leant on the back of the chair where the Duke had stood only a few hours before. 'I'm not feeling . . . I think I might have to give it a miss.'

'Nonsense. It's meant to be a hoot! We'll take a cab, but Jessie's been looking forward to you driving her like a fine lady for weeks.'

'I don't mind, really,' said Jessie, but her face told another story.

'Of course. Sorry. I'll just change. Give me two minutes.'

In his bedroom looking glass, Edwin watched his head emerge from the neck of a clean shirt, fingers smoothing hair, working at buttons and studs, but he felt no connection to the fashionable figure before him: the dandy, the toady, the man who'd just sacrificed all self-respect, who'd just agreed to give up his daughter.

'Ned! Come on!' called Charles.

The Edwin Landseer who'd managed to wash and dress in two minutes also managed to drive his two-wheeled gig to the Lyceum, making Jessie grin with delight. Edwin saw him reflected on the gleaming sides of the carriages of true fine ladies, in shop windows, and in the spectacles Tom put on when the curtain went up. He hated that Edwin Landseer.

An idiot on the stage let himself be gulled into buying a bottle containing a demon in the ludicrous hope that it would bring him wealth and women. Did he not know how badly these things always ended? It was a stupid play. Sure enough, the dissipated old alchemist who'd sold the bottle to the idiot cackled that the thing was cursed and that anyone dying in possession of it would be damned to hell.

Edwin closed his eyes.

Georgina had said they would make it work. But had he just made an even worse bargain than the fool on the stage?

'You're hardly being discreet coming here like this,' she'd said, an attempt at a smile on her pale face.

'I don't care.' He clutched her hand as he sat on the edge of her bed. 'I had to see you. Did you really say you'd elope with me if he tried to keep us apart?'

'Yes.' Her grip was as strong as his.

'But the children . . . would he really take them? It's barbaric. Surely he wouldn't?'

'My sister's husband did,' she said quietly. 'I suppose you're too young. You wouldn't remember the Duchess of Manchester scandal.' She stared up at the plaster mouldings on the ceiling. 'She was my sister, Susan. My mother found her a duke to marry – Manchester. And she dutifully did. But he was a beast. She was desperately unhappy. For years. Then she fell in love,' she swallowed, 'with one of the gamekeepers. Manchester said she was never to see him again, so they eloped. And that was it. She was cut off. No one was allowed to visit her, not even family, not even her children. It broke my mother's heart and my father's, but they still refused to see her.' She returned her gaze to him. 'Oh Lanny, you can't imagine what she suffered. She died last summer, just after my father. I-I broke ranks and saw her just before the end . . . Only John knows.'

'Why didn't you tell me before?'

'I can't talk about it. I'm so ashamed – of my family, of myself for not standing up to the rest of them. I should have damned them all and had her to Woburn. But . . . you don't know what fear they can put into you. If she were a man, it would have been different, of course. Look at my father. It's not fair. None of it is fair.'

There was an explosion on the stage. Edwin opened his eyes. Smoke streamed across the boards and a demon in a lurid green costume laughed maniacally as he tormented the hapless hero.

'Ned – sweet?' whispered Tom, shoving a package of sugar plums into Edwin's face, their syrupy sides stuck to the thick brown paper.

Edwin shook his head, stomach flipping.

To his left, Jessie flinched, clutching his arm as the demon disappeared with another bang and more smoke. Edwin pressed her hand, catching sight of Belinda on Tom's other side, blushing, waving to someone, then whispering something in Tom's ear that sent a smile flooding across his broad face. A pang of longing for Georgina filled his chest.

Shifting in his seat, sweating one moment, shivering the next, he wished he hadn't come. He could have given Jessie the drive another time. She wouldn't think it such a treat if she knew what he'd done. He loosened his cravat and tried to shut out the stage, the crowd, everything.

Georgina had stroked his hair and said it would be all right. That now she was able to think more clearly she saw how lucky they had been. So lucky. That it would be madness not to accept the Duke's offer.

'And,' she said, 'I feel terrible about hurting him.'

'He has Mrs Vernon,' Edwin said.

'I know.' The stroking stopped. 'But it's not the same. We've been together so long, he's . . . I can't put it into words. He's a part of me.'

'Ned, wake up!' There was a rustle of paper. The plums were back.

'I'm not asleep,' Edwin groaned.

Judging by the volume of the actors' voices, the play was coming to its climax. The demon, in his ludicrous costume, pranced and cackled. The bottle had somehow come back into the possession of the alchemist, whose crimes had caught up with him and who was now about to be executed for sorcery. Edwin shifted again in his seat.

He knew he'd behaved badly in regard to the Duke. Very badly. He knew he had no right to feel aggrieved. Georgina was right. They should count their blessings. He could still see her, and Rachel. And he could paint, keep his house, his studio. And – fresh guilt trickled into the ocean of shame in which he was already swimming – the Duke wouldn't live forever.

The demon let out an unearthly cackle, and, with a thunderous crash and a shower of emerald sparks, the alchemist was imprisoned in the bottle and taken down to hell.

# Part IV

# *November 1860, London*

Tongues of flame surround the cauldron that hangs over the furnace. The ferocity of the molten metal inside makes the gaslights on the walls look feeble. Edwin's face and hands prickle in the heat. The air itself wavers and seems to be in danger of melting. It doesn't take much imagination to see himself in the flames, crumpling, blackening, curling like paper, melting like wax.

'Sir Edwin! Do not stand so close! You will singe your whiskers,' calls out Baron Marochetti, his half-Italian, half-French accent giving him an air of European suavity even when yelling over the foundry din. 'And they are such fine whiskers, it would be a shame to lose them, would it not, Lady Baring?'

Caro nods solemnly to the sculptor, not venturing to make her voice heard over the clamour. Georgina would have bellowed that his whiskers needed trimming anyway. The Baron has been given the lucrative contract to cast the lions. He won't be quite so keen to preserve the whiskers when Edwin tells him he can't deliver the clay models on time.

'And you, Lord Baring, must also have a care – keep that beautiful beard away from my flames,' Marochetti continues, dabbing his brow with a lilac silk handkerchief. Baring shuffles goutily backwards, leaning on Caro.

'The final part of our tour of my little factory: these cauldrons – we call them ladles – they are where the magic happens,' Marochetti says, shielding his eyes from a cloud of scalding air as more flames belch from the furnace. 'From them, we pour the bronze into the mould, like so.'

They all squint into the steam as a team of men, armoured in padding to protect them from the heat, tilts one of the ladles on its gibbet-like frame and glowing metal writhes into a sand-covered mould.

'This one is small but some are very large – very, very large. For Sir Edwin's lions, we shall have to use the largest of all. So big a man could bathe in it, but I really would not recommend such a bath, Lady Baring, oh no!' The Baron laughs.

Caro looks horrified.

Baring strokes his beard and says perhaps they've seen enough and might return to the Baron's studio to discuss the marble busts he would like to commission of Caro and himself. Marochetti nods, bows, and leads them through the double doors and away from the hellfires.

For a few moments longer, Edwin watches the seething bronze try to leap from the cauldron, and shudders. While all eyes are elsewhere, he unscrews the lid of his flask, brings it to his mouth, and replaces it in his pocket as smoothly as if it were a handkerchief and he were blowing his nose.

He can't put off breaking the news to Marochetti much longer: the lions are nowhere near ready for casting. He has tried to sweeten the pill by arranging for James and Louisa Abercorn to join them here later this afternoon. A connection with one of Prince Albert's closest courtiers ought to mollify the snobbish sculptor, at least partially. He's also delivered up the Barings – making it clear to Marochetti that he was the one who suggested they commission these busts. Caro was delighted by the idea when Edwin mentioned it during a portrait sitting, which was more than could be said for his allusion to divorce. She'd met that with horror. Too great a scandal, she said, patronisingly pressing his hand with great solemnity – as if that wouldn't have occurred to him – adding that her husband was too old to be left in charge of their daughter, Maisie, should she leave him. Edwin had been crushed, but not quite as much as he'd feared.

In the bone-chilling air of the alleyway between the foundry and the row of studios, there is no one to see him. He takes another, longer, swig, then heads inside to witness the first steps towards the Barings' immortalisation in marble.

Having poured brandies and water for Baring and Edwin, Marochetti makes a great fuss of Caro, saying she's looking so well he must make a sketch or two for the bust immediately. Baring readily agrees and limps over to a red velvet sofa. As he slurps his brandy and stretches, his gouty foot unwittingly kicks the head of a tiger skin rug, making it wink at Edwin, who sits on another sofa opposite.

Keeping half an eye on Caro, Edwin leaves his own glass untouched – she notices things like that – and marks the way she tilts her head and solemnly fixes her eyes on the sculptor, the way she places a hand on his wrist. All ominously familiar. It might not be soft smiles or tinkling laughter, but it's still flirting. Not that Baring seems to notice. He's too busy wincing and flexing his foot.

'The old enemy?' Edwin says. Coveting another man's wife is one thing; failing to show sympathy for his gout is quite another.

'Yes.' Baring grimaces, drips of brandy glistening on the tips of his moustache. 'Doctor Quain has recommended increasing the dose of colchicine, but I'm not keen on the side effects, if you know what I mean. The – ahem – WC.'

'All too well.' Edwin smiles wryly as the tiger winks at him again. 'Have you tried ginger? Or extract of black cherry?'

'Ginger yes; cherry no. Does it work?'

'No.' Edwin shrugs. 'Bell used to say it was the height of quackery. But it tastes a damn sight better than colchicine and is easier on the WC.'

Baring's beard ripples with a low laugh.

Caro's dark eyes snap over to them.

Edwin almost reaches for his glass, then remembers. The flask is there, comforting, heavy, nestling in his pocket. For later.

Gout talk and solemn head tilts have just resumed when there's a knock at the door, immediately followed by the entrance of James and Louisa Abercorn. Edwin stands with as much alacrity as his own joints will allow.

'Baron Marochetti, Lord Baring, Lady Baring, you know the Marquis and Marchioness of Abercorn?' he says, smiling as an expression of annoyance flits across Caro's face. Louisa Abercorn, Georgina and the Duke's second daughter, is at least Caro's equal in beauty and her superior in both rank and fashion.

They nod, bob, and say the usual meaningless things that matter so much, then Marochetti says he needs a few more minutes with Caro, following which the new guests will have his undivided attention.

'That's a fine beard you have there, Baring,' says Abercorn, sitting next to him while Edwin makes way for Louisa's skirts. 'I'm deuced tempted to grow one myself but can't while I'm at court. Albert has a theory that a smooth chin is the only thing that sets us apart from wild animals.'

'Well, he's right. Did you ever see a beast with a shaven chin?' Edwin smiles, catching his hand halfway towards his glass again. He grips the arm of the sofa.

'I might have known you'd side with him. Probably gave him the idea in the first place,' Abercorn laughs. 'But I'm angling for release from royal service, and if I'm successful, I shall spend my first months of freedom cultivating facial shrubbery.'

'Oh, well, yes,' Lord Baring says warily, as though unsure whether he's the butt of a private joke.

Drumming his fingers on the velvet, Edwin catches Louisa's eye and they both have to stare at the tiger skin rug to avoid laughing. She resembles both her parents, but when amused her likeness to Georgina is always uppermost.

'Her Majesty is well, I trust?' says Baring, brow still furrowed in puzzlement.

'Generally well, though in floods of tears when I last saw her. Your fault, Lanny,' Abercorn says, with what Edwin desperately hopes is mock severity.

'My fault?' Unfinished royal commissions gallop through his mind. She wouldn't be blubbing over the lions, would she? Christ. And when was he going to tell Marochetti? His fingers drum faster.

'She hasn't told you?' says Abercorn.

'I'm out of favour at court these days.'

'Hmm . . . She implied you were the one making excuses not to attend, but that's by the by.' Abercorn strokes his smooth chin. 'She and Albert went to Glenfeshie last month, rode over from Balmoral in mufti and poked about in the old huts. They're all tumbling down; those deer you daubed on the walls are half washed away. She wept so much when telling us, even the Prince was surprised. What on earth have you told her about the place?'

'Just stories.' Edwin's fingers stop. 'I'm surprised she remembers.'

'Oh, Her Majesty remembers everything,' Abercorn says, prompting Baring to begin a dull anecdote about the Queen once remembering a poem.

'I wrote to Rachel about the huts,' says Louisa to Edwin only, while Baring's story meanders on. 'From her reply, she was almost as upset as the Queen.'

'I saw her at the Exhibition.' Edwin lowers his voice. 'She can't even look at me, Louisa.'

'Lanny, give her time.'

'What if there isn't time?'

'What on earth do you mean?'

'I mean . . .' Why did he say that? Idiot. He swallows, fidgets with a button on his waistcoat. Doctor Tweedie's words: *get it under control or it will kill you.* He told Tweedie not to be a melodramatic old woman. Perhaps less politely than he might have done. He releases the button, stares at his untouched brandy. It is under control. It is. He doesn't need to tell Louisa. And what could he say that wouldn't make him sound an even more melodramatic fool than Tweedie? Sometimes I think I'm drinking myself to death? It sounds insane. And he absolutely can't afford that.

'I mean I have given her time,' he says, gripping the button again. 'Seven years. She needs to know my side but she won't let me talk to her. If I . . . if I write it down, would you persuade her to read it – beg, plead, bribe? Whatever it takes?'

Louisa nods but before she has a chance to speak, Caro wafts into the space between the sofas.

'Marquis, Lady Abercorn, I'm afraid we have pressing business elsewhere and must leave. I am sorry.' She says it as though they'd come to see her and says it to Abercorn only, barely glancing at Louisa, who raises an eyebrow at Edwin.

Baring hobbles towards the door, leaning on his wife's arm as Marochetti shows them out.

While the Baron is still out of earshot, Abercorn says, 'That was her? Wasn't it?'

'Yes,' says Edwin, finally lifting his glass. *Under control, is it?*

'She's not quite what I expected,' Abercorn says. 'Nice to see you're all getting along though.'

'Oh, we're all fast friends. Lord Beard and I are great gouty pals,' Edwin says.

Over the rim of his glass, he sees Louisa flash a subject-changing look at her husband.

'And it's so interesting to see where your lions will be cast,' she says.

'Ah yes, Lady Abercorn, the lions!' Marochetti swans over and takes the place recently occupied by Baring on the sofa. 'Sir Edwin, I must ask you, are we still expecting them for . . . when? Easter, did we say?'

'About that . . .' Edwin cradles the glass on his knee. It is under control. It is.

'Yes?'

'I need more time.'

'How much time?' Marochetti's voice is as smooth as his suit, but his teeth flash, wolflike, between words.

'I can't quite say . . . it's not my fault . . . the Sardinian government . . .' Edwin puts the glass back on the table to stop himself turning it around and around.

'The what?'

'The Sardinians – they have some casts I need but are being damned slow in handing them over.'

James Abercorn looks at his nails. Louisa examines the braiding around the pocket on her jacket.

'So you need how many weeks?' Marochetti drops a sheet of sketches of Caro onto the table with a shrug. 'I can rearrange some pieces.'

'Not weeks.'

'Months?'

Edwin waits – Marochetti is almost there.

'Years?'

'Not more than one. Probably.'

He tries to make it sound like it's no great matter but even Louisa looks surprised. Marochetti shakes his head, hissing something in Italian. In the silence that follows, Edwin glowers at a sketch of Caro on the table. It would serve her right if he were to draw her a beard to match her husband's.

Marochetti shows his teeth again. 'Marquis, I don't suppose you could interest the Prince in a large bronze statue of any sort? I have an unexpected hole in my casting schedule. Perhaps Her Majesty would care to commission something for that fourth plinth in Trafalgar Square?'

# *April 1829, London*

LIFE LURCHED AWKWARDLY ON. But there were two lives now: the private life, in which Edwin and Georgina snatched moments together in the rose walks and shrubberies at Campden Hill and in the sanctuary of St John's Wood; and the public life, in which he was hailed as the rising star of British art, and in which he increasingly filled nights with parties, plays, and cards, while Georgina attended balls and dinners to which he could not go. He continued to be part of the Bedfords' set in London and the country, eating at the Duke's table, entertaining his guests, drinking his wine. The latter formed a screen through which Edwin watched Georgina as the Duke's devoted wife, and Rachel as the Duke's daughter, sitting on his knee and planting kisses on his shining, patrician scalp. And calling him Papa. It stopped the knife going all the way into his heart.

True to his promise, the Duke hadn't withdrawn his patronage, but when discussing a painting, he now used the same tone as he used to order his carriage or a drink. He also had a policy of superciliously ignoring gossip, which seemed to be working.

As the spring buds swelled on the trees at Campden Hill, Georgina was more annoyed by rumours about Eliza and Wrio than about herself.

'What can I do? The Duke will be in town next week to see the new house and he's bound to want this business about Wrio settled.' She stabbed a needle into the handkerchief she was embroidering. 'So much for seeing the world, becoming a man . . . I was sure six months in Europe would have got Eliza out of Wrio's system, but now the first thing he does when he's back is propose to her – damn!' She cursed as her needle came unthreaded.

'Why's that a bad thing?' said Edwin, sitting on the morning-room floor with Rachel untying his bootlaces. 'They've both told me they love each other – in confidence of course – so if they ask, I'm not the one who told you.'

'Because they're first cousins. And neither of them will have any money.'

'Cousins marry all the time, and I thought the Duke was giving Wrio a living near Woburn? Tavistock will hardly turf them out if . . . when he's duke . . . Eliza's his cousin too.'

'Yes . . .' She gave up on her sewing. 'But it's such a poor parish. The Duke doesn't see the issue. He forgot what it was like to be a younger son years ago. And what if there are, you know, problems with the children? My sister was telling me—'

'Plenty of cousins marry without problems, as you put it.' Rachel clambered onto Edwin's lap and began to play with the brass buttons on his waistcoat, smiling and babbling at him. The sunlight made her flaxen hair look gold. He would give anything to stop time at that moment. 'Think how lucky they are to have the chance to marry for love.' He traced a curl with his finger. 'Don't ruin it for something your sister said.'

Georgina leant down and kissed Rachel, then kissed him. 'I'm not sure saying wise things like that suits you. But you have a point.'

A week later Edwin needed to deliver a picture to the Bedfords' new town house in Belgrave Square. Delaying as long as possible in the hope that the Duke, who was back in town, might have gone to his club by the time he arrived, Edwin called in to Bell's chemist's on the way. At the ring of the doorbell, young Jacob, now boasting faint whiskers on each cheek, looked up from a ledger.

'What's this? Late Academy submission?' Bell peered at the cloth-wrapped picture under Edwin's arm.

'Nothing so exciting. Lord Alexander Russell on a pony. Just back from the engraver. I was expecting to see your father, is this not one of your Sass days?'

'Herr Sass and I no longer see eye to eye,' Jacob said, with an air of embarrassed amusement.

'Sorry to hear that. You're welcome to pick my brains for painting tips, for what they're worth.' Edwin stifled a yawn.

'I suspect their worth depends on where you were last night.' Bell finished a line in his ledger with a flourish and a grin. 'I have other artistic plans for now, but I appreciate the offer. What can I get for you?'

'Something to make a baby sleep.'

'A baby?' Bell dropped his quill. 'I hadn't heard you were, err, married?'

'Good Lord no – not mine. It's my brother's. Newly arrived this month.' Tom's baby boy was nowhere near as pretty as Rachel had been; Edwin thought proudly that she hadn't cried at night either, then the pride soured as he realised he hadn't been there.

'Ah, of course, silly of me.' Bell blushed and hurriedly reached into a row of bottles behind him. 'This is very effective, I believe.'

'Excellent. I might try it myself.'

'I can give you something stronger. Exhibition deadline keeping you awake? I hear rumours you'll be a full RA before the year's out.'

'Something like that.' Edwin grimaced. He was quietly confident, but all too aware that any resurgence of rumours of another sort would instantly scupper his chances.

Bell reached up to a higher shelf, retrieving a darker bottle.

'Phenomenal, thank you,' Edwin said. Still trying to delay the inevitable, he added, 'I'd better settle my account too, it's been a while.'

He fingered the lid of the bottle as Bell turned to his page in the heavy ledger and totted up the figures. To sleep would be a fine thing.

'How do you do that so quickly?' he said.

'Easy when you know how.'

'Well I don't. It takes me days to go over my accounts and then they're still wrong.'

'I'd happily look over them for you.' Another blush.

'Would you? I'd be eternally in your debt. My father's always telling me I should pay more attention to them.'

'Honestly, it would be no trouble.'

'Wonderful, right, I'd better deliver this picture.' He couldn't put off facing the Duke forever, but as he had a hand on the door, an idea shot into his head. He turned back to Bell. 'If you're serious about helping with the accounts, why not come over tonight? I'll bribe you with dinner. And you can tell me about these other artistic plans. Maybe I can help.'

It would take his mind off Georgina being at yet another ball to which he was not invited.

The lease on the Bedfords' St James's Square house had expired, and, in anticipation of his daughters' imminent Society debuts, the Duke had taken on the largest of a row of terraced mansions in newly fashionable Belgravia. Its smooth stucco frontage gleamed even in the cloudy afternoon light, but the opposite side of the square was still a building site. Edwin missed the warm old bricks of St James's.

'Mr Landseer.' The Duke looked up as Edwin was shown into his study, which was already sumptuously furnished, but smelled of sawdust and varnish. 'I find myself in the unexpected position of being grateful to you for making Georgina see sense about Wrio and Eliza.'

'Oh, that . . . yes, Your Grace.' Why couldn't the Duke have gone to his club, or his mistress's, like any self-respecting aristocrat?

'I have to confess, she is more, how can I put this . . . manageable when you are around.'

A footman knocked then placed a tray of letters on the Duke's desk. Edwin recognised Benjamin Haydon's handwriting on the top one. So did the Duke, uttering the history painter's name with a curse almost worthy of his wife.

It was so unexpected, Edwin laughed. The Duke eyed him angrily for a moment, then shrugged.

'The confounded fool keeps writing to me saying the Government should commission more paintings. I've told him repeatedly it's out of my hands, but it doesn't deter him. He bombards Wellington too. If he were to spend as much time painting as he does writing letters, he might find himself in less straitened circumstances.'

'It's an addiction, letter writing,' said Edwin, testing the waters. 'My father suffers from it too. He must make his views known. It doesn't matter who gets hurt, or bored, in the process. I asked him to send a picture to Scott a few months ago and he sent it with a four-sided letter grumbling about historical errors in *Ivanhoe*.'

There was a flicker of the benevolent Caesar expression Edwin missed so much, so he plunged into the story of his father lecturing Scott over breakfast, at the end of which the Duke half smiled, drew in a long breath, and said,

'Would you have time for a sherry? I would appreciate your thoughts on where we should hang the pictures here.'

The sense of relief was overwhelming. It continued long after Edwin left Belgrave Square and throughout dinner with Jacob Bell, during which he entirely forgot about accounts and almost managed to forget about Georgina. That night, without even having recourse to Bell's tonic, he slept better than he had in months.

Three weeks after Wrio and Eliza's wedding, and the morning after the Academy dinner to mark the closing of the Summer Exhibition, Edwin sat at his own breakfast table nursing a pot of cold, stewed tea. Warm, fat raindrops pummelled the windows as he mulled over gossip from the night before, weighing up his chances of being elected a full Academician. His only real rival was Charles Eastlake, a friend of Turner's. But Eastlake was away in Rome and Edwin had made the most of his absence to flatter and amuse the RAs on whom the election depended – the monkey had given one of its most charming performances. And the rumours about his private life were no longer on everyone's lips.

He was looking for hints about his prospects in the leaves at the bottom of his cup, when Lucy Potter, the daughter of a family friend who he'd recently taken on as a maid, marched in. With one hand on her hip, she ushered in his brother Charles. For once he wasn't chewing anything.

'Ned, I need to talk to you.' Charles glanced at Lucy, who was ostentatiously brushing a group of decanters with a feather duster. 'In the garden.'

'It's a bit wet.'

'Somewhere else where we can talk privately then?'

'Here?'

'But . . .?' Charles looked even more pointedly at Lucy, who gave the decanters a last flick and flounced off. As she closed the door, he produced a letter from his pocket.

'This was delivered this morning. Addressed to me. It's anonymous.'

'What is it?' The dregs of last night's wine began to curdle in Edwin's stomach.

'It's about Tom.' Charles pursed his lips. Edwin relaxed a little, but the relief was short-lived. 'It says Lindy's been . . . that the baby's not Tom's. That he's the child of criminal intercourse.'

'That's preposterous.'

'It says everyone knows Lindy's been carrying on, that the world says Tom's a fool.'

'Nonsense . . .'

'I'm only repeating what this infernal letter says. According to this, she's been seen meeting a man named Robinson near Regent's Park for, well, improper purposes.'

Edwin felt sick. The number of times she'd arrived at his house unexpectedly. And that man with the oily whiskers ...

'Have you told anyone else?'

'No.'

'Good. Don't. No need to worry Tom yet – this will crucify him if it is true, and it might not be. It might just be some deranged sort of prank.' It sounded ridiculous even as he said it. 'I'll come back with you. We'll talk to Belinda. Whatever you do, don't tell Father.'

When they reached Conway Street, Edwin's hopes of it being a joke, which had never been high, sank even lower. Belinda wasn't home, but there was another letter, this time from Robinson himself, declaring that he was indeed baby George's father and stating his intention to take the infant and Belinda to live with him. Tom had seen this one. So had their father.

The moment Belinda returned, she was escorted into the drawing room, where they were all waiting for her: John Landseer glowering over a pile of Babylonian artefacts on the table; Tom sitting next to him, ashen-faced, mechanically sipping a brandy and water.

'It's all lies!' Belinda wailed when confronted. 'I told him to sling it and he's trying to get back at me.' Her reddened eyes clashed with her yellow curls. 'Tommy, you know it's not true, don't you?' Tom said nothing. 'Why does no one believe me?'

'Why should we?' snapped Edwin. 'How could you do this to Tom, who's never hurt anyone in his life? All those times I heard a carriage draw up at my house just as you left, that was him, wasn't it? Calling on me as an excuse ... I wouldn't be surprised if you even used my house while I was out. Mrs Eames told me she's seen you—'

'That's rich! Given what she must have seen from you.' Belinda glared at him. 'You've got some nerve. I'd have thought you of all people would have been on my side—'

'Why on earth should Edwin be on your side?' growled Edwin's father.

Belinda narrowed her eyes. 'Because your precious Ned's been up to much worse than anything you're accusing me of, that's why.'

Edwin's blood ran cold.

His father turned to him. 'What in heaven's name is she talking about?'

'He's been at it with his duchess for years.' Belinda tossed her hair.

'Be very careful before you say anything more, my girl. If this is some malicious lie to save your own skin—'

'Ask *him*,' Belinda spat. 'They've got a little girl and all.'

Edwin watched, speechless with horror as she let fly rumour after rumour, sticking to her guns in spite of his father's thundering refusals to countenance them. Finally, John Landseer turned, one eye beginning to twitch. 'Edwin, this isn't true, is it?'

'It's as true as anything.' Belinda put her hands on her hips. 'Everyone's talking about it, it's only this blessed family that's too deaf to hear—'

'Silence!' John Landseer slammed a hand down on the table, rattling the fragments of a stone lion, not taking his eyes from Edwin. 'Well?'

'It's . . .' Edwin's chest tightened. He'd had no idea there was still so much gossip. There was no way he could get away with denying it. 'It's not like *this* . . .' He looked at Belinda and Tom and seeing the devastation on his brother's face, was unable to continue, feeling more wretched than he'd ever felt in his life.

'See?' said Belinda, eyes blazing.

'That's enough from you. Get out!' bellowed John Landseer, fingers clenching and unclenching on a lion fragment. Belinda stared open-mouthed at Tom, down whose face tears were now silently streaming, then, gathering up her skirts, she ran from the room.

'Father, I—' Edwin began.

'You can get out too,' his father hissed, gripping the lion fragment so hard his knuckles were as white as his hair. 'You're as bad as she is – worse. I won't have you in this house.'

The look on Tom's face was etched into Edwin's mind so deeply whisky didn't even begin to blur it. The empty bottle lay next to him under the mulberry tree, where he was sitting with Brutus when the rustle of a dress made him turn, half expecting Georgina. It was his mother.

'Are you going to make me sit on the ground too?' she said.

'No, no.' He rubbed his eyes. 'How's Tom?'

'Still very upset. He says he will stand by Lindy though. But I didn't come here to talk about him.'

'You're wasting your time with me.' Edwin used the tree to help himself stand. 'I'm a lost cause.'

'What she says is true?'

'Yes.' He was too drained, dunk, and guilt-stained to deny anything.

'All of it?'

'All of it.' He forced himself to meet her eyes, braced for anger and disappointment, but found only sympathy.

'Oh Ned. Does the Duke know?'

Edwin nodded, shrugged.

They sat in silence on the bench, Edwin with his head in his hands and the dogs at his feet. The sun wove itself between a patchwork of clouds, a warm breeze murmured through the leaves and a pigeon cooed. Edwin's mother began to stroke his hair the way she used to when he was a boy and he'd had a fight with his father, or someone hadn't liked a picture.

Eventually, still stroking, she said, 'Your daughter, what's her name?'

'Rachel.'

'What a lovely name. How old is she?'

'Three. Next week she'll be three.'

'Does she know you're her father?'

'No.' He rubbed his eyes, voice cracking. 'It's better this way. She's better off as a duke's daughter. What kind of a father would I be anyway?'

'Oh, Ned. Don't say things like that.'

'I've been so stupid. You must hate me. I don't blame Father for banishing me.'

'I could never hate you, my Ned, never. All this . . . it must be so hard.'

He tried to shake off the tears, to joke. 'I have plenty of things to make it easier. Champagne, parties, commissions . . . and I've only myself to blame.'

'That doesn't mean it hasn't hurt you. If anything, it must hurt more.'

He sat up straight and took a deep breath. 'There are times I just want to run away from it all, but I can't bear not seeing Rachel grow up. I didn't think it was possible to love anyone this much.'

'And do you love her mother too?'

'Yes.'

'Truly? Though she's so much older than you? And another man's wife?'

'Yes. And I hate lying. And being a sordid secret. But I'd hate being without them more.'

She smoothed his hair again, muttering what sounded like a prayer, then was silent for a while. Eventually, she said, gently, 'What's she like? This granddaughter of mine.'

Edwin told her. In spite of everything, once he'd started – describing Rachel's sky-blue eyes and golden hair, the way she wrinkled her nose, her laugh – he couldn't stop, talking until the clouds had turned lavender in the evening light.

'Thank you,' he said as he embraced his mother and handed her into a cab to go home. 'What about Father?'

'He'll calm down eventually,' she said. 'He always does. Give him time.'

A month later, John Landseer still showed no sign of calming down. He wrote to everyone: to lawyers, to Belinda's father, and to Robinson, who turned out to be a money lender from one of the shadier City courtyards, and who doggedly clung to his claims concerning Belinda and baby George.

He did not write to Edwin or consent to have him back in the house.

Tom continued to stand by Belinda, and things might have resolved themselves quietly had the scandal sheets not got hold of it, and if Edwin's father had been able to resist the temptation to pen a reply. But he couldn't resist, and the whole thing was made horrifically public. The rumours about Edwin, Georgina, and Rachel also came back with a vengeance. The irony of Tom being cuckolded while Edwin cuckolded the Duke was too ripe for the satirical commentators to ignore. Even the Bedford influence couldn't silence the gossip, which caught and burnt like wildfire around Society drawing rooms. Edwin's chances of election as a full Academician went up in smoke and his spirits sank to the bottom of the sludgy, stinking Thames.

'So it was true then?' said William, as Edwin let him in to the studio, where a pair of hooded peregrines rested on perches, brought inside to avoid the dirty raindrops that were pelting the windowpanes.

'Yes.' Edwin poured William a drink.

'You might have told me.'

'I'm sure you can imagine why I didn't.'

'I suppose. But really? My aunt?'

Edwin shrugged and slumped down onto the chaise longue, picking up a half-full glass of wine. 'I understand if you want nothing more to do with me, but please don't make me grovel. My capacity for grovelling is all used up.'

William sipped his brandy, then shook his head and sat down. 'Lord, Lanny, I'm not about to drop you. What if you were to shop me to my uncle about all the cigars I've purloined over the years?'

'Thank you. You don't know what that means to me.' Edwin met his gaze over the rim of his glass and held it.

'Exhibit A.' William offered him a cigar. 'What are you going to do now?'

'Hide in the Highlands until it's died down a bit, once I've finished these birds. The Duchess is already there.'

'With the Duke?'

'No. He's pinned down with gout. Staying in the South.' The Duke had been furious but was sticking rigidly to his policy of refusing to dignify rumours with any form of reaction.

'Is that wise?'

'Wisdom be damned.' Edwin drained his glass and refilled it with brandy.

The weather had been even worse in the North and, when Edwin finally arrived in Glenfeshie, he was met with a scene of devastation that matched his mood. Heavy rains on ground already saturated by a wet summer had swollen the rivers to monstrous proportions and they'd flayed the land, in places to the bone. The waters had risen so fast and with such fury there had been little time to save possessions and no time to save harvests. Scores of trees had been uprooted, new channels scoured deep into the peat, and river crossings and roads washed away.

'Anna Mhòr says they're the worst floods she can remember,' said Georgina the night of Edwin's arrival, as she lay beside him, her hair spread across his chest. The moonlight illuminated the contours of her body, echoing the hills beyond the hut's small windows. 'We can rebuild the houses and the roads, though it will take a deal of work, but it will push even more of the younger folk into leaving the glen. I worry they'll never come back. Rents are so high; wages are so low.'

'Can't your brother do something?' Edwin asked, tracing a finger along her collarbone.

'He can't – or won't. He's in so much debt he says he's tempted to emigrate himself. The only money to be made up here these days is from leasing places to English tourists to shoot grouse or gawp at waterfalls.' She shrugged. 'But that doesn't help Anna Mhòr and the others. I do what I can – I've made her son Peter into head forester to oversee the deer, but it's a drop in the ocean. I want the old days back so badly. I want the drovers, the whisky stills . . .' She rolled on top of him, eyes huge and shining in the darkness. 'You will keep painting them, won't you? Capture them. Before they're all swept away?'

'I will.' Edwin pulled her close and held her as if he feared she would be swept away too.

There was less fishing, shooting, and lazing that year. Instead, there was shifting earth, stones, and timber. It was exhausting but cathartic. With each stone, Edwin vowed he would repair the breach with his father and Tom, and would rebuild his reputation with the Academy. He would show them. After a fortnight, he stood on the banks of the River Feshie with Georgina's son, Lord Henry, and Anna Mhòr's son, Peter, surveying the work. It had been back-breaking: sweat plastered his shirt to his back and a collection of dead midges to his forearms, his fingertips were raw, palms blistered. Everything ached. But he suspected this would seem easy compared to fixing things with his father and brother.

# *January 1830, London*

ON A BLEAK JANUARY MORNING, Edwin glanced to where his father stood among the small group of engravers gathered with the students, Associates and Academicians for the funeral of Sir Thomas Lawrence, late President of the Royal Academy. John Landseer held his gaze for a moment before shaking his head and turning to his neighbour. They'd barely seen each other, let alone spoken in the six months since the Belinda business. Edwin wasn't giving up, but he wasn't going to grovel either. Bowing his head and removing his hat as the coffin was carried through the courtyard of Somerset House towards the waiting hearse, he gripped the brim with frozen, black-gloved fingers. He'd show the old man he wasn't a complete wastrel. He'd damn well make sure he was elected a full Academician. He'd work his way to President if he had to.

'End of an era,' said someone as the undertaker's horses began their slow walk and the artists shuffled into line to follow Sir Thomas on his last journey through the slush to St Paul's.

'It'll be the King next,' said someone else, to a chorus of non-committal muttering as the front of the column filed through the archway onto The Strand.

Edwin stepped around a pile of rancid, half-melted snow and placed himself next to his father. For a hundred yards or so, the only sound between them was John Landseer's stick tapping the slick cobbles.

'Still cold,' Edwin said.

The stick didn't miss a beat. 'I've known it much colder.'

They walked on. Past crowds gathered in spite of the weather to pay their respects to the greatest portrait painter of the age, who'd made fat princes look like heroes and heroes look like gods. Past St Clement's Church onto Fleet Street, the green copper dome of the cathedral now visible against the leaden grey sky.

John Landseer suddenly raised his stick, pointing it towards the Thames, almost hitting Edwin in the face. 'Icebergs,' he grunted.

'What?' Edwin straightened his hat.

'Long while since I've seen icebergs in the river. You should go and look.'

'I think it would be frowned upon if I skipped off to see them now.' Edwin stared straight ahead.

His father harrumphed.

Edwin kicked a pile of slush. 'I might go and look afterwards.'

Another silence. Then his father slipped on a kerb. Edwin caught him by the elbow, ignoring his protests. They walked the rest of the way to St Paul's without speaking, but arm in arm.

Back at Somerset House after the service, drizzle turned the remaining snow into thick, brown puddles, and warm wine turned talk to the vacancies left by Lawrence's death – the

Academy needed a new president and would also have to elect a new Academician. Still smarting from having lost out to Eastlake for the last vacancy, and not wanting to hear residual gossip, Edwin escaped outside onto the terrace overlooking the Thames. Leaning over the balustrade by a stone lion, he turned up his collar and pulled his coat about him. In the river below, slabs of ice slid over each other on top of grey waves. His father was right: it was worth seeing. Footsteps approached, but it wasn't John Landseer. It was Charles Leslie, his companion on that first trip to Scotland.

'They're muttering about you in there,' said Leslie.

'What am I meant to do about it?' Edwin shrugged.

'Get your head down and work, Ned. That's the key. Get everyone talking about your paintings, not your private life, and you'll be joining us as Edwin Landseer RA this time next year, I'd bet my palette on it.'

'I am trying,' Edwin said, glaring at the lion's weather-worn face.

Edwin painted until his wrists and eyes shrieked with fatigue, but that summer all art was overshadowed by the King's failing health. Every day, the great – if not the good – gathered outside St James's Palace to hear the latest bulletins. Society nerves were balanced on knife edges. No one wanted to commit to anything knowing a new monarch and potentially a new government were on the horizon.

Georgina was even more on edge than the rest, this being the year she planned to bring out her daughters Georgy and Louisa as they turned eighteen and seventeen respectively. The Duke and Edwin found themselves unexpectedly united in urging her to calm down, but she was determined to throw everything into their first season with three grand balls. Edwin teased her that she was turning into her own mother. She failed to see the funny side and burst into tears, sobbing that he didn't understand how important it was to secure the girls' futures.

The Duke continued to turn a blind eye to Georgina's visits to St John's Wood. He also continued to ignore the still-smoking rumours, holding to his line that they were so ludicrous as not to merit acknowledgement, let alone denial. In turn, Edwin refused to acknowledge how deeply he was cut by the insinuation that he was a laughable prospect for a lover, no matter how many times he told himself it was the only option. For now.

The date for the first ball arrived. The King was still in the land of the living, so number six Belgrave Square was garlanded and gilded to within an inch of bad taste. Restless and annoyed that his pictures hadn't made the splash he'd hoped at the Summer Exhibition, Edwin stood with Georgina in the dining room, sipping champagne as she supervised the final decorations: wreaths of flowers, swathes of green and navy Gordon tartan, and scallop shells from the Bedford crest, plus two frozen sculptures, which the pastry cooks had almost finished carving into the shape of a Bedford lion rampant and a Gordon stag's head.

'Is the ice too much?' Georgina held out her glass for more champagne.

'Not at all,' said Edwin, pouring and peering closely at the lion. 'They could use a little finishing though.' He picked up a chisel and reshaped a section of the lion's muzzle, adding a chunk of the ice to his glass, where it fizzed and cracked.

'You beast!' Georgina hit him with a list she was holding. 'If you break that, I'm liable to lose not one but two irreplaceable chefs.'

'But it looks better, don't you think?' He eyed the lion critically, still holding the chisel. 'And my champagne was getting warm.' He lifted the glass to his lips, glancing at her over the rim, and was appalled to see her eyes filling with tears. Again.

'It's taken them all day, and they kept saying how hard it is to sculpt a lion standing like that, and they nearly walked out when the tip broke from the antlers ...'

'Shh ... shh ...' Edwin put the chisel down and held her. 'I'm sorry, I was joking. It'll be the best ball of the season, until your next one, of course.'

'I hate balls, I hate all this,' she said, her voice muffled against his waistcoat. 'I wish we could run away to the Highlands and be shot of it all.'

'So do I, so do I,' he said, wishing she meant it.

She wiped her eyes and finished her champagne (into which she had let him add another chunk of ice). 'I shall be fine once it starts. I promise. Now I'd better dress. I'll see you at about eleven o'clock.'

Edwin, who was not invited to the grand dinner before the ball, went off to kill time at the club.

Several hours later, the ice sculptures were melting and Edwin was sick of dancing and small talk. Out on the balcony with William, he dipped a frozen antler tip into yet another glass of champagne.

'Let's go somewhere else. I can't face another dowager asking me to paint her damned pug.' The ice cracked. A large flake sheared off and slipped through his fingers.

'Not the kind of business you're looking for?' said William.

'Hell no.' Edwin stared back through the open windows. Georgina stood on the other side of the ballroom, glittering with diamonds. Desire and frustration smouldered in his stomach. She'd been the life of the party to everyone but him – because that was the damned bargain they'd struck. But tongues were wagging like tails by a butcher's cart anyway. He'd lost count of the number of ageing, overbred, lavender-scented females desperate to discuss lapdogs and watercolours with him, who fell straight to gossiping behind their fans as soon as he'd bowed and moved on, with variations of: 'so that's Georgie Bedford's pet' and 'so young!' and 'but so ornamental, my dear, and isn't he amusing?'

He dipped the ice antler into his glass again. Damned thing still wouldn't fit. Throwing it at the dowagers wasn't an option, so he hurled it into the garden below.

'As long as it's not too scurrilous, or as long as Emma doesn't find out, I'm in,' William said. 'Where shall we go?'

'God, I don't know. Anywhere.'

Several drinks later, they'd just left the Athenaeum, and were wondering where to go next, when a shape slinking into a dark alley caught Edwin's eye.

'Look!' He pointed, buoyed up by brandy and a win at cards.

'I'd rather not,' said William, who'd matched him in drinks but not luck, stamping his cigar butt into the gutter.

'What a beauty.' Edwin ignored him, blowing a smoke ring and standing at the entrance to the alleyway. 'That face.'

'If you don't get garrotted in there, my aunt will murder you for sniffing around Haymarket for whores.'

'It's a dog, not a girl, you idiot,' Edwin laughed; the last few drinks had filled him with a restless boldness.

'Leave it. It'll be some mangy old thing – and I should like to live to see the other side of thirty.'

'And that lack of romantic spirit is why you were doomed to be a lawyer, not a poet, my dear William. Come on.' Taking another pull on his cigar, briefly gripping the street corner for balance, Edwin plunged into the darkness.

'Lanny!' William's footsteps echoed behind him, but Edwin was intent on the dog, its pale stump of a tail a beacon in the gloom as other shapes shifted in the shadows. A human grunt that could have been passion, could have been pain, came from ground level. Edwin ignored it and pressed on towards the faint glow of a tavern doorway. There was a strong smell of piss, overlaid with stale beer and sour smoke. But no lavender. No dowagers.

'Lanny!'

'Don't be such an old woman,' Edwin snapped. He felt alive for the first time that night, for the first time in weeks. 'Here, here . . .' he crooned to the dog, making a clicking noise with his tongue and taking out a handkerchief. 'Look – cheese.' He unwrapped a handful of cheddar swiped from Belgrave Square that he'd intended for Bran. The dog turned, regarding him with one good eye, one clouded. The stump wagged faster. It was mesmerising, the marked skin, the muscles beneath, and the network of scars – a dog that could tell a thousand stories.

William was still whining about getting murdered. Edwin called him a chicken, and had just squatted down to dog level, holding out a piece of the cheese, when an intense odour of unwashed human descended. There was a man standing above him – a man made of even more scars than the dog, and also of darkness, of thick stubble, and a knife.

'Well, well,' said the stubble. 'Pair of pretty young gents like you ought to watch theirselves in a place like this.' The knife blade – along which he ran a dirt-encrusted finger – was the brightest thing in the alley.

'I told you,' William hissed.

Heart thumping, but still riding high on brandy and defiance, Edwin fed a piece of cheese to the dog.

'I was admiring this beauty,' he said, letting the dog lick his fingers.

'You must be very drunk or even more stupid than you look. Or are you escaped from the madhouse?' A gob of tobacco-laden spit landed on the ground, as glossy as the patent leather of William's dress shoe, next to which it lay. William shuffled back against the wall.

Edwin staggered upright. 'I'm a painter. And I want to paint your dog.'

The man pinched the end of the knife and snorted. 'Painter?'

'The best damned dog painter this side of . . . this side of . . . wherever we are. It doesn't matter what side we're on . . . or of . . . But I'm bloody good. And I want to paint him.' Edwin pointed his cigar at the dog.

The man laughed, but it wasn't a nice laugh. 'Cocky little shit.'

'Look. I'll damn well prove it.' Edwin leant against the wall for support as his head swam, then fished in his pockets for pencil and paper.

'Lanny!' William hissed again. 'We should get out of here. I'll see if he'll take my watch and let us go . . .'

'Shh . . . I need this dog.' Edwin's fingers closed on a porte-crayon. He must have some paper somewhere.

'Go on then,' the man leered. 'And if I don't like what you draw, I'll do my own picture. On your face.' He pinched the tip of the knife again. 'Won't be such a pretty boy then, will you?'

Edwin squared up to him. 'Fine. But if you do like the picture, you'll bring him to my studio.'

William whimpered.

Edwin found a crumpled calling card and crouched down to dog level again. 'Hold that, just there, by his mouth.' He thrust his cigar at the knife man, who was so surprised that he obeyed. Chalk skimming across the card, blood pounding in his ears, brandy repeating on him, Edwin followed the dog's gaze in the gloom and fought a wild urge to laugh.

'There!' He finished with a flick of the wrist and held out the tiny drawing in the dim light.

'Jesus Christ,' the man laughed. 'You'd give that Landseer a run for his money – I seen a print of his fighting dogs in the Red Lion.'

Edwin grinned, lurching into a standing position. 'That's my card – bring him to me. Then he can see prints of himself.'

William tugged at his sleeve, hissing, 'What in the name of hell are you doing? Come on, before he remembers his knife.'

When they'd regained the broad, gaslit safety of Pall Mall, William let out a loud sigh. 'This is the last time I ever agree to a nighttime stroll with you. What the hell is Aunt Georgina going to say?'

'Don't care,' Edwin said, veins still fizzing. 'I'm not her bloody lapdog.' He lifted a fresh cigar from William's coat pocket. 'Where next? I need a light. Let's ask him?' He pointed across the street to a policeman, who stood outside the palace by the board displaying news of the King's failing health.

'No,' snapped William, pulling him in the opposite direction with what felt like far more force than necessary. 'That's enough fun for tonight.'

By the end of the June, Georgina had managed to hold a second ball, but, to the relief of Edwin and the Duke, the King's death forced the postponement of her third and final event. When it did occur, all energy for gossip was used on the question of whether the new King William and Queen Adelaide would manage to produce an heir, or whether the eleven-year-old Princess Victoria would be pressed into action.

In August, Georgina shifted her campaign from London to Scotland. The Bedfords had leased a new Highland base, better suited to marriage broking. The house, known as The Doune of Rothiemurchus, sat on a bend in the River Spey just north of Georgina's brother's estate at Kinrara. It possessed a loch, a ruined castle, myriad ghosts and legends, and was closer to the military road so the Duke could be confident of being no more than a week behind political news. It was still close enough to Glenfeshie to permit frequent visits to the huts, which was where Edwin joined the party.

The day after his arrival, the drovers came through the glen.

Feet damp in unlaced boots having just left Georgina's hut, he was gazing at the fir trees bristling on the horizon against the dawn sky, when he saw not deer, but cattle, scores of them, streaming over the hill like ants. He ran to his own hut for his telescope and sketchbook, emerging just as the new sun kindled the underside of the clouds.

He drew, barely blinking so as not to miss a moment, as more and more came, slowly flowing down the old drove track. The sun crested the rise behind them and gushed into the glen, prompting stirrings in the servants' huts. Figures emerged humming, whistling, collecting eggs, filling kettles and jugs at the river. Smoke rose from clay pipes and cooking fires.

The shadows were already shortening and the dew was drying when there was a shout from Alexander – knees proud beneath his kilt, fishing rod in hand, landing net slung over his back.

'Lanny! Mama says are you coming in for breakfast? And are you going to get dressed at all?'

As Edwin entered the dining hut ten minutes later, Rachel gave him a jam-smeared grin, and Georgina looked up from a sheet of paper.

'There you are! You don't mind having a few guests bunk up with you tonight? The Bear's holding a ball on his side of the river. The Duke is bringing additional troops from The Doune this afternoon, and I can't exactly put the young men in with the girls.'

'The Bear?' Edwin ruffled Rachel's golden curls and helped himself to the last boiled egg.

'Mr Ellice.' She wrote two names next to a roughly drawn rectangle on the paper. 'You must have seen him in Town – made a fortune in Canadian furs, has to duck through every door – he's taken the lodge and shooting over there—' She waved a hand at the sideboard. 'Lovely man. Has a very promising son too, about the right sort of age.'

'Known as the Bear Cub?' Edwin knocked the top off his egg.

'He is! You are clever, even if you do sit around in your night-shirt half the morning. Now, are you fishing or shooting today?'

'Neither. I want to follow the drovers. And I thought you might act as my guide.'

She smiled his favourite smile.

They took ponies and panniers filled with whisky and oatcakes, which they doled out to the drovers while Georgina asked for news of old tenants from her parents' time. Edwin sketched until he was out of paper. Then they left the cattle and plodded slowly down towards the huts, looking back occasionally at the line of beasts climbing to the pass, beyond which lay the glens of Atholl, the great cattle markets of the Borders and, eventually, England.

Georgina told so many stories of when she was a girl and the droves were even larger that Edwin laughed that she was becoming like Anna Mhòr with her tales of Bonnie Prince Charlie.

'It's not funny. It was very beautiful and very moving,' she said, giving him a dig in the ribs that made his stomach leap like a salmon. 'It always brought me to the verge of tears, seeing how sad those men were to go – especially when they had to leave babes in arms. But it was hearing the muttered promises of what they would do when reunited that always tipped me over the edge.'

'I know how they feel,' said Edwin.

She slid her hands into his. 'We will always come back here, I promise.' As he kissed her, she added, 'Always.'

That night, after much reeling and more wine, Edwin sat up late discussing whisky, dogs, and deerstalking. His companions were the Bear Cub and a willowy student, who'd inherited vast estates and become Marquis of Abercorn at the age of seven but was one of the most unassuming young men Edwin had ever come across. When the Bear Cub began to snore, Abercorn, apologising like a schoolgirl, asked if Edwin knew of any attachment between their sleeping friend and Lady Louisa Russell.

'Perhaps. She thought it damned impressive that he ate two kippers for breakfast yesterday.' Edwin yawned. 'But don't worry, I'll put in a good word for you.'

Abercorn was soon asleep too. Edwin took the remains of the bottle of whisky outside. The sky was a meadow of stars, the moon low over Georgina's hut. The glow of candlelight came from one of her windows. She and the Duke must still be awake. Edwin watched, and drank, until the light went out.

The next morning, Abercorn polished off three kippers in front of Louisa. Edwin couldn't stomach more than toast. He declined to fish or shoot and took his copy of Scott's *The Bride of Lammermoor* to a sheltered spot by the river, intending to read and sketch out ideas for illustrations Scott had recently commissioned. He was just settling in when Neville, Alexander's retriever, appeared at his elbow, followed by Louisa.

'Oh, Lanny. Sorry. I didn't realise anyone was here. He's not too wet is he?'

'He's fine. I thought you'd have gone fishing with the others – or are you not in the mood for more of the Bear Cub's thoughts on trout?'

'No,' she said. 'I've had a surfeit of trout.'

'You're welcome to join me, but you might have to model.'

'Model . . . I . . .'

'Nothing risqué – it's for a Walter Scott illustration.'

'What would I have to do?'

'Pretend to have swooned after being attacked by a mad bull.'

She laughed.

'It's a very serious and tragic scene.' He grinned, taking off the plaid he'd been wearing around his shoulders against the morning chill and spreading it out so she could sit. 'I'm sure the Bear Cub would impersonate the bull if you like. Or I could ask James Abercorn – he's not really stout enough for a bull, but I'm sure he'd fall over himself to do it.'

'I can imagine perfectly well without them.' Even in the shade of the trees, the blush that swept over her face as she seated herself next to him was obvious.

'So, do you like him, then? Abercorn? He'd be delighted—'

'I don't know him.' The blush deepened. 'Lanny, Don't think me stupid, but I'm terrified by all this talk of marriage.'

'Of course I don't think you're stupid. Marriage is notoriously terror-inducing. Have you told your mother?'

'No. She's what I'm scared of. I don't want to disappoint her. She has it all planned out for Georgy and me. The husbands will be rich and of impeccable family and we are to be utterly in love with them. That's the bit that worries me most – though it sounds crazy. She says she won't let us marry without love. It's such an awful lot of pressure.'

'Don't you want to marry someone you're in love with?' Edwin said, glancing at Georgina and Rachel, who were playing hide-and-seek behind some laundry hanging outside the huts. The Duke had gone shooting with The Bear.

'What if I get it wrong? What if I choose to fall in love with the wrong man and end up with a beast or a bore? What if the man I should have chosen comes along when it's too late? What if I become like . . . like Mama's sister?'

'I hardly think that's likely. You've always had impeccable taste,' said Edwin, digging a stone out of the earth with his fingers. Rachel's laughter bubbled across the clearing. Georgina had promised they could spend the afternoon together painting more deer on the walls of the huts. 'Anyway, you can't choose to be in love with someone. I dare say you can fool yourself for a while, but if you're really in love, you're in love in spite of all the reasons against it, not because of the reasons for it. If we could choose to be in or out of love, life would be a damn sight easier.'

'Would you have chosen not to fall in love with my mother?'

The question knocked the air from his lungs. 'What?'

'Papa told us – me and Georgy – just before the first ball.'

Edwin hesitated, clutching the stone; Louisa's face wasn't as easy to read as her mother's. 'What exactly did he tell you?'

'That you and Mama are . . . have a special friendship.' She blushed again. 'He said now we're old enough to be in Society, he didn't want us to hear gossip and think ill of her . . . but . . . but he said these things happen. That there are different types of love. He said he was telling us so we would know not to talk about it.'

'What a way to prepare you for the ball.' Edwin turned the stone over and over.

'It didn't make much difference. I was so nervous anyway,' she said softly. 'I was shocked at first – angry even – but Papa said it was good for her to have you.'

Good for her to have him? He wasn't some sort of spaniel.

'You're very understanding,' Edwin said through clenched teeth.

'And he said that there's no danger of her running off with you and leaving us.'

'Ha! No danger.' Edwin flung the stone towards the tangled pine roots at the water's edge with such force that Neville, who'd been lying next to him, leapt up and padded back to Louisa.

'I'm sorry, Lanny. I didn't mean to ... I'm sure it can't be easy. But that's what I mean. Falling in love seems to make everything so complicated.'

Over by the huts, Rachel was trying to conceal herself behind a sheet. Louisa hadn't mentioned her; presumably she didn't know. Small mercies. Spotting Edwin from her hiding place, Rachel waved, a grin lighting up her face and taking the edge off his anger. He waved back, bringing a finger to his lips in a sign that she shouldn't give her hiding place away.

He turned to Louisa and shrugged. 'Marrying someone you're not in love with will hardly help though, will it?'

With impeccable timing, Neville chose that moment to bark at a pair of ducks who had drifted into the dark tangle of roots.

'Anyway,' Edwin silently thanked the dog for breaking the tension, 'if you do decide to fall in love, you could do a lot worse than Abercorn.'

She coloured again. 'He has legions of mamas after him, and all the prettiest girls.'

'But he's more taken with you than any of them.'

'You can't know that?'

'He as good as told me last night,' Edwin said, spirits improving in spite of himself as a look of delight flashed across her face. 'Why do you think he ate three kippers for breakfast this morning?'

'I assumed he was hungry. I didn't think kipper-eating was a sign of love?'

'It could be if someone told him you thought the Bear Cub very manly for eating two of them the day before.'

'You didn't ...'

'I might have done. Don't you think that's devotion though? Will you give him a chance?'

'All right.' She smiled. 'But please tell him he doesn't need to eat any more kippers.'

The party returned to The Doune and kipper consumption returned to normal levels, but before Abercorn went south to commence his final year at Oxford, Louisa had promised to write to him. The Duke also took his leave of the party early, departing for London with the more politically minded guests to throw his weight behind plans for an electoral reform bill.

The day after his departure, Georgina led an expedition back to the glen.

First light and birdsong filtered through the thin linen curtains in her hut while Edwin sat cross-legged in the rocking chair by the bed. His pencil traced the silver-threaded hair spread across the pillow, the curve of her cheek, her lips, her shoulders . . . She swallowed, the lips parted, the eyelids fluttered.

'Dammit,' he whispered. 'Don't move. I so rarely get to see you like this. I always have to sneak off. I want a souvenir for when I'm old and lonely.'

She made to pull the sheet up.

'Leave it just as it is . . . please,' he said.

She pouted.

'If you keep your face like that, I'll work this up into a portrait and exhibit it.'

She pouted more.

'I will.'

A drowsy smile straightened her lips and she reached an arm lazily towards the sketchbook.

'I'll show you when I'm finished. If you stop messing around.' Edwin pulled it closer to his chest as she pulled another face. 'You're lucky you're even more beautiful when you're being an idiot.'

Narrowing her eyes, she propped herself up on her elbow.

'No, no ... lie down again ... I'm almost done.'

She rolled onto her back and began to pull the sheet down.

'Georgina ...'

The sheet shifted another couple of inches.

'You're making it very difficult to concentrate.' He tried not to laugh.

'You're enjoying it,' she licked her lips. 'That's the most lecherous grin I've ever seen.'

'This is a frown of concentration.' He lost the battle with laughter. 'But I might be enjoying it a little.'

With a flick of Georgina's foot, the sheet landed on the floor.

'Christ!' Edwin almost dropped his pencil. 'All right. I am enjoying it. I take back what I said about exhibiting this ... What are you doing? Give me back that pencil ... Georgina!'

As winter arrived, Queen Adelaide was not pregnant in spite of King William's best efforts, but Georgina was. Rather than enduring the journey to England, she remained in Edinburgh on doctor's orders; Edwin remained with her, though she'd told him to go south. When the situation 'resolved itself' a week before Christmas, the Duke didn't hold back in expressing relief. Outwardly stoic, Georgina said he was right: even she couldn't ignore the dangers of childbirth at almost fifty. But, at her bedside, Edwin gripped her hand and watched tears slide onto her pillow from her closed but twitching eyelids, while more slipped silently down his own cheeks.

It was kept quiet enough that it neither alarmed the suitors for the young ladies Russell, nor the Royal Academy. When the RAs met in February, Edwin was elected a full Academician, but as the celebratory drinks got going at Somerset House, he found himself on the terrace watching the grey-green waves of the Thames, leaning on the stone lion and thinking of lives that would never be.

'Your mother's out,' said his father, shuffling into the hall as Edwin stepped through the Conway Street front door the following week.

'I know. It's you I want to see.'

'Well.' John Landseer pushed his spectacles up his nose. 'Now you've seen me.'

'Well.' Edwin stopped halfway through pulling off a glove. 'If you're going to be like that.'

'Like what?'

Edwin pulled his glove back on and was back at the door when his father cleared his throat and mumbled, 'Well done.'

Edwin paused, fingers on the handle.

'A Royal Academician before you're thirty,' John Landseer muttered. 'I hope you realise what this means. Not to be sniffed at.'

In danger of contradicting himself, he pulled out a handkerchief and blew his nose loudly. Edwin nodded with the barest inclination of his head but had to swallow a lump in his throat to say, 'I'm working on a new picture for the Duke. I was hoping you might sit for me. I need a *pater familias* and I thought you'd be rather good at it.'

As he'd suspected, there followed a deal of muttering about being too busy with letters and pamphlets, but eventually John Landseer said, 'What manner of picture?'

'Cattle drovers in the Highlands – taking leave of loved ones as they set off for the markets in the South. The sadness of separation. And a lot of livestock.'

'Hmph. Finicky, cabinet-sized thing, I suppose?'

'No. Large. Majestic. Like a history painting.'

# *1831 to 1835*

IT TOOK EDWIN THE BEST part of four years to finish the droving picture – and his father complained incessantly throughout his sittings – but when it was done the papers called it the finest of its kind ever painted in England. Edwin accepted the praise with a pinch of salt, but he still accepted it.

Georgina took nearly as long to finalise the match between Louisa and Abercorn. But when it was done, their wedding, with fireworks, pipers, and feasting at Gordon Castle, was said to be one of the finest ever held in Scotland. She then turned her attention to her elder daughter Georgy, but was urged by the Duke, Edwin, and not least Georgy herself, to approach the business with less urgency. It was only when she caught pneumonia the winter after Louisa's wedding that she agreed to take their advice.

* * *

Edwin continued to look on, teeth gritted, through the screen of champagne and small talk, as Georgina swanned through Society on her husband's arm, or with other male friends, but never with him. Their relationship must have been privately dissected in every drawing room in London, but admitting to it in public was still unthinkable.

In spite of this, or he sometimes thought because of it, Edwin found his social and artistic abilities were increasingly in demand in Town, country, and the Highlands. The latter were busier than ever with parties of southerners variously equipped with firearms, paintboxes, and poetry – sometimes all three. All pursued their quarry with the ferocity of a swarm of midges on a still summer afternoon, whether they were after grouse, deer, or the sublime and beautiful.

The huts at Glenfeshie remained a sanctuary even from these new tourists, and Edwin returned annually with immense joy and relief. Guests came and went, the Bedford children and cousins grew, flew the nest, then flocked back with children of their own. Georgy continued unmarried and, as far as Edwin could tell, content. Louisa and Abercorn exchanged glances over breakfast whenever kippers were present, and soon Georgina had a growing brood of grandchildren to distract her from matchmaking.

The Bear and Bear Cub continued to hold balls across the river. When the weather was fine, the sound of pipes and fiddles skirled into a sky so thickly streaked with stars Edwin would have had to use a pallet knife to paint them. When it was less fine, the rain drummed on roofs of canvas, beating time for dancing feet, while the river thundered in the background.

Though the whole glen came to the balls, the gaiety couldn't hide the fact that the population was dwindling. Georgina's plans to improve the shooting and stalking for her sons provided some new sources of income, as did her building projects, but they couldn't stop the snuffing out of the old ways of life and the drying up of distilling and droving. Edwin drew the Highlanders with renewed intensity. The subject came up frequently over dinners in the grandest of the huts and at The Doune, but it rarely lasted long in competition with the parliamentary reforms underway in England, discussion of the day's game bags, or the week's weather.

And Edwin too had other things on his mind: watching Rachel grow, teaching her to paint deer on the walls of the huts as they told stories together, listening, laughing, spellbound by the tales she wove. And he watched Georgina sleep in the moonlight or felt her breath warm on his neck as she woke him with whispers of 'Endymion', and they wrapped themselves around each other before it was time to step out into the mist once more. Instead of imagining they had eloped, Edwin now imagined they were a family.

The Duke's health was declining, slowly but steadily. Through those morning mists, Edwin saw a future in which he didn't have to leave at dawn, in which he could be a father to his own child, and in which Georgina would be his wife. He laid bets with himself that if he saw deer during those dew-drenched walks in the half-light, it was a sign she would marry him, that they could be fully together at last. He would often wander an extra mile just to catch sight of a hind, and painted his hopes into the frescos in the huts.

# *June 1861, London*

THE CANAL FLOWS, SLOW AND streaked with weeds, at the bottom of Edwin's garden. He peers down onto the towpath from the top of the brick-built embankment. Black now but once golden, it flanks the dark water where it emerges from the tunnel, shepherding it around the corner as it continues towards the Regent's Park and the zoo.

There it is again – a shadow that shouldn't be there.

He'd put up a fence to stop the animals falling down, but sometimes they get out. It's not goat-proof, but this is no goat. Escapees from the zoo also appear occasionally. He'd been out here trying to clear his head when he noticed it, felt it watching him muttering to himself, going in circles trying to finish the letter to Rachel. What did he want to ask of her? Acknowledgement? Absolution? Love? And now this whatever-it-is creature is distracting him.

The shadow slinks along, hard to see in the bright, stinging light. Very large for a stray dog. Definitely not a cat. Edwin lifts an ink-stained hand to shade his eyes as it approaches the end of the path and the mouth of the tunnel.

When he first moved here, it was still new – three hundred yards of manmade blackness, no towpath inside. There have always been rumours of ghosts. Unquiet spirits of bargemen who'd slipped while propelling the boats with their legs on the ceiling, dragged down into darkness. They've never bothered Edwin before, but now, as the shadow stops, he shivers.

And then he sees – no, feels – the eyes. Lion's eyes. Hears a growl, but it's drowned out by water slapping against the sides of a barge emerging from the tunnel. There's a sound of something hitting the water, more ripples, and it's gone.

'Neddy!'

He jumps, heart thumping, cold sweat trickling down his chest. It's only Belinda, her white ringlets bouncing, carrying a bunch of peonies.

'Neddy, there's a great big wagon just arrived. Driver says it's lion casts? From Italy? Won't hand them over to anyone but you.'

'Thank you,' Edwin says, excitement not fear now quickening his pulse. 'Thank you.'

'You all right? Look like you've seen a ghost,' she says, sorting through the flowers. 'And had a fight with an ink bottle,' she adds, taking in the state of his hands.

'No to the ghost. Yes to the ink – the bottle won,' he says, walking back towards the house with her. 'You haven't heard any reports of missing animals from the zoo, have you? No . . . no lions escaped?'

'Not that I've heard. Your goat got at the laundry again though. Mrs P's furious.' She pulls a drooping leaf off one of the stems in her hand. 'Can I take these for our place? I want to make a little party for George tonight; he got another medal at the Society of Artists – a real chip off the old block.' Is there still a slight edge to her voice when she mentions how her son is so like Tom, or is it his imagination?

'Oh, yes, I saw. He's doing marvellously. Yes to the flowers too.'

'Come and join us? It'll be a lark. No good you moping around here on your own.'

'I was planning to mope with these lion casts.'

'Go on, just a little drinky? And can I borrow some of your nappies?'

'Napkins. Yes. Ask Mrs Potter,' Edwin says. He buys napkins in the full knowledge that she will take them and either destroy or sell them. It's a donation to Tom's household. Part of his ongoing attempt to atone for wounding him so deeply during the Robinson affair, though Belinda and Tom forgave him long before their father did. He still hasn't quite forgiven himself.

After Belinda's 'little party', which was surprisingly enjoyable, he inspects the casts. They lie around the studio like the ruins of a lost civilisation – a paw here, a haunch there, muzzle, flanks, muscles ... His father would have said it looked like the British Museum. Then would have given him a lecture on what poor specimens they were compared with the achievements of antiquity. John Landseer's stick is still in the stand by the barn doors; his ear trumpet sits with his snuff box on a side table next to his old chair. It's almost a decade since it's been used. If Edwin doesn't look, he can imagine the white hair still catching the light in the afternoons, his father's muttering mingling with the breeze outside and the domestic noises within.

*Stop gazing out of the window, Ned.*

*Don't be so flippant.*

*You'll never amount to anything if people think you're not serious.*

And the final conversation. Not in here. Across the hall in the bedroom his father used for the last year of his life.

'I'm sorry, Ned. Did I push you too hard? I only wanted the best for you, you know. I only ever wanted the best for you.'

The voice is so real he can smell pipe smoke and old books, but when he turns, there's only a shadow, and an ear trumpet on the table.

He knows how the letter to Rachel must end.

There's a comforting physicality to clay: thick and slick under his fingers, cool in the heat of the July afternoon. He pushes the pallet knife through it, moulds it, scores it, feels a ripple of pleasure when he executes the deft flick he's learnt that takes the formless, flat substance and creates cascades of fur.

Both dogs take themselves into a pool of sunlight just outside the open studio doors, where they soak up the heat. Noises float over the wall – children playing, shouting, a hoop clattering to the ground. It's working. The images are flowing from his mind to his hands without getting stuck and distorted or broken in between.

The letter to Rachel is finished, sitting heavy in his pocket, corners jabbing into his chest, ready to be given to Louisa Abercorn this afternoon.

*Or to be fed to the goat.*

He shakes his head, rubs his fingers together, plunges them into the jar of cloudy, lukewarm water and wets the top of the lion's mane – teases it into a curve, pinches it to a soft-nosed peak – then reaches for the glass next to the jar, which is already dappled with drying fingerprints. The wine is sweet and rich on his tongue: he dares to think he can do this.

At the sound of carriage wheels on gravel, the dogs snap from lifelessness to a yelping frenzy, scrambling up and skidding around towards the front of the house.

'Lanny!' comes Abercorn's voice. 'Are you in your den?'

'I am!' Edwin wipes his hands on his smock. Braces himself, clinging to optimism as leaden panic swirls around his knees. Imperfections he hadn't previously noticed in the model bloom before his eyes.

'Wonderful! It's an actual lion!' Louisa says as they appear around the corner, pausing to gaze at the clay before she kisses him. Hope bobs back to the surface.

'Don't go smashing this one, Lanny,' Abercorn says.

Mrs Potter brings a table and a tray out into the garden. As they drink tea, talk turns to the old days. The weight of the letter pulling his waistcoat down beneath his smock, Edwin glances at the lion, then out over the meadow, where one of the dogs is snaking hypnotically through the long, uncropped grass. The lion will work. The letter will work.

*Or make things worse.*

Ignoring the voice, and a glare from Mrs Potter, Edwin breaks a biscuit in two, drops half for the dogs.

'Will you come to The Doune this year?' asks Louisa. 'It's not the same without you.'

'I don't know.' Edwin watches Topsey snaffle the biscuit before poor old Lassie's even stirred, so he feeds her the other half, then realises with a start that, if they're both with him, there's something else in the grass. A fox? A cat? The towpath creature? He thought he saw it again the other day, reflected in an evening bottle, but when he'd turned, it was gone. Ignoring a prickling at the back of his neck, he says, 'I was going to stay with Breadalbane, but Lady B's unwell, gravely so. I might go to Lochluichart with the Barings.'

'Is that wise?' Abercorn strokes his new beard.

'Almost certainly not,' Edwin says, squinting over his friend's shoulder, but whatever it was that had been making the grass shake has gone.

They talk more about the old times, about the children.

They don't mention Rachel.

Too hot, Edwin shrugs off his smock, runs his finger along the edge of the letter, wishes for something stronger than tea. It's not until they're on the point of leaving that he plucks up the courage to hand it to Louisa.

As he listens to their departing carriage wheels on the gravel, he sees something stir the grass again. He shivers, shuts his mind to the voice that says:

*It won't change anything, you know.*

## *1836, London*

'NED, I'VE GOT A NEW PATRONESS FOR YOU. Whatever you do, don't fuck this one.'

George Hayter was back. The scandal of Amelia's death had dwindled to occasional mutterings. It had hardened rather than humbled him.

'Such a prettily phrased offer,' Edwin said, making a series of charcoal marks on the canvas in front of him. 'But I'm too busy. I'm up to my eyes in work.'

'You'll make time for this one.' George pushed his fringe – increasingly peppered with grey since his return from Italy – to one side.

'I wouldn't be so sure. Who is it?' Edwin glanced briefly at a sketch pinned to a smaller easel then swept the charcoal in a long arc.

'Leopold's sister, the Duchess of Kent, for her daughter the Princess Victoria. A birthday present.'

Edwin glanced at the half-dozen unfinished paintings that filled the studio, turning the charcoal between his fingers an inch from the canvas. 'When's the birthday?'

'The twenty-fourth.'

'June?'

'May.'

Edwin let his hand drop to his side. 'That's only two weeks away.'

'It's just a small spaniel. Nothing to the great Edwin Landseer RA. I've told her you'll be at Kensington Palace this afternoon. And before you say you can't, remember King Billy isn't long for this world and this plump little princess will be Queen before we know it. Prince Leopold says she's already a great admirer of yours – as crazy about dogs as you are. This is one to drop everything and everyone for.'

Edwin had already put down the charcoal and was removing his sleeve covers. 'I know, I know. I'm going. And thank you.'

Having braced himself for palatial splendour grander even than Woburn, Edwin spent the afternoon at Kensington Palace shut in an airless storeroom with feeble light, a smell of drains, and, for a long time, no dog. The severe-looking German baroness supervising him expressed her annoyance that he wasn't beginning the picture immediately. Pointing out the absence of the dog failed to mollify her. She merely huffed that the picture was to be a surprise and it was not a quick matter to seize a spaniel from a sixteen-year-old girl without her knowing.

'She is showing her drawings to her cousin Albert and the dog is sitting between them. You must be patient. Paint as much as you can for now,' she said, then sidled out of the door, poking her head briefly back around the edge to ask if Landseer was a German name. Edwin said he didn't know. The head sniffed disapprovingly and disappeared, and its owner locked him in.

Edwin stared at blank walls, blank sheets of paper, blank canvas. This was ridiculous. He should have said no, royalty or no royalty. Innumerable commissions back at the studio needed his attention more than this pampered – and so far invisible – spaniel. Hadn't he spent the past decade trying to prove that he was more than a pet painter? And why the hell had the German woman locked him in?

After an interminable period of more blankness, a key groaned in the lock and the Baroness slunk in sideways, glancing furtively behind her before depositing a confused dog on the floor.

'What? You still have not begun?' she said, brushing dog hair from her dress.

Edwin ignored her and bent down to the dog, which looked as wearied by the whole business as he felt.

Above them, the Baroness cleared her throat. 'You have half an hour. Then I shall return for the dog before he is missed.' About to lock the door once more, she added, 'Are you sure you are not German?'

Just about keeping his temper, Edwin said he really didn't think he was German and got to work. At least the dog was good company.

By the time the Baroness returned, he'd made a detailed oil sketch and a firm friend of the spaniel. He received an approving nod and his liberty.

'We require the finished picture in one week. And accept my apologies for asking if your name was German, Mr Landseer, I have now realised that, of course, you are Dutch.'

Badly in need of a drink and some sane company, Edwin made for Campden Hill, only a few minutes from Kensington Palace.

Georgina and her daughter Georgy were in a flurry of ball preparations, Rachel, the Duke, and a heavily pregnant

Louisa, were in the library surrounded by half-empty teacups. He told them of his royal adventure. Rachel, sitting at the Duke's feet with a white rabbit, laughed so hard she gave herself hiccups, and made Edwin repeat his impressions of the Baroness over and over.

'Did you – hic – talk to the Princess?' she asked.

'No – that was the cruellest part.' Edwin grinned. 'I was shut away for the whole time like some sort of Rumpelstiltskin, only I was expected to produce pictures of pets, not spin gold.'

'You've met her, haven't you, Papa?' Rachel twisted to gaze up at the Duke, who had been listening with his usual understated amusement.

'I have. She is nowhere near as clever as you, my dear,' he said. 'And I think you are taller than her.'

Rachel sprang up and kissed his shining head.

'Papa,' she hiccupped. 'You're such a flatterer, but I love you.'

Edwin winced and sipped his tea, which was stewed and cold. What was left of his good humour drained away and a headache was building behind his eyes.

There being no place for him among Bedford balls or dinners that night, he went home but thoughts of Rachel saying 'Papa' to the Duke, and of Georgina at her ball made work impossible. His headache was worse. He needed fresh air and fresh company. He picked up his hat and cane and went out to find Bell and William.

Much later, they ended up at Gore House, the home of Lady Blessington – described by George as the daughter of an Irish drunk who'd used her wits and her tits to capture an earl. Now widowed, she'd established herself as the leading hostess of Society's literary underbelly. Her gatherings buzzed with writers, artists, and politicians, who brought their most brilliant conversation, but not their wives.

'Lanny! It has been a looong while,' purred Alfred, the Comte d'Orsay, currently Lady Blessington's lover, rumoured to have been her late husband's lover, and – for a short spell – the husband of Blessington's daughter (but never *her* lover). Whenever Edwin lamented the complexity of his own personal life, there was always a crumb of comfort in the fact that others had it worse. D'Orsay adjusted his glittering waistcoat and skintight trousers, kissed Edwin on both cheeks, and, with a slow smile, said, 'Are you still fucking your duchess?'

'Fuck off,' Edwin said, wishing he hadn't already drunk so much.

'Witty and charming as ever, my friend. I can see why you are in such demand at all the best houses.' D'Orsay took the cigar from Edwin's fingers and blew a perfect smoke ring. 'Come, I won't have you looking so sad. Have some more champagne and I will introduce you to the most beautiful ladies – or gentlemen, if that takes your fancy these days. That boy you arrived with . . .'

'Bell? Don't talk rot. He's a friend. Helps me with my accounts.'

'Ah.' D'Orsay blew another smoke ring and patted Edwin's hand. 'I see the way he looks at you. He is not thinking of accounts.'

'Fuck off.'

'Ah again, that wit. Worthy of Versailles. You are sure you are not French?'

'I'm Dutch, according to that lot at Kensington Palace.'

'That explains much. That duchess of yours, she is very like a Rubens. All that glorious golden flesh.'

'Go to the Devil.' Edwin took back his cigar, thinking of the glorious golden flesh dancing in some glorious golden house without him.

They sat and smoked. D'Orsay talked. Edwin drank and looked around for Bell and William. William had been an old woman about coming, saying his wife didn't approve. Your wife's not your keeper, Edwin said. But there he was – must have got over his scruples – laughing with the novelists Bulwer and Disraeli, both almost as dandified as d'Orsay. And there was Bell, stuck with Benjamin Haydon, apparently unchanged by another spell in debtor's prison.

Edwin couldn't remember the rest of the night. He was unable to contemplate laying a brush on Princess Victoria's spaniel until the middle of the next afternoon.

The following week, the Princess turned seventeen and was delighted with her surprise present. She sent Edwin a gushing message of thanks. Georgina was overjoyed for him, but his moment of glory was cut short by the death of her brother, the last Duke of Gordon.

The following year, shortly after her eighteenth birthday, the Princess became Queen, much to the annoyance of Rachel, whose eleventh birthday party was cancelled as a result.

Three months into this new reign, Edwin and the Duke sat in wicker chairs on the grass in front of the drawing-room windows at The Doune. Before them, the lawn sloped down to a bend of the Spey, where yellowed birch leaves fell like rain. The Duke leant towards the champagne bottle between them but flinched, flexing his fingers and swearing under his breath.

Edwin lifted the bottle and refilled their glasses.

'I'm a useless old fool. Unable even to pour my own drink.'

'Not a bit of it, Your Grace,' Edwin said, turning up his collar against the breeze. 'It's just the weather turning – we should go in. This wind can't be doing you any good.'

'That doesn't signify.' The Duke took a sip of champagne. 'I shall stay out here until the light goes. I intend to see as much of the place as possible lest it be the last time.'

'Nonsense.' Edwin refused to let his voice betray the foreboding that was even souring the wine. 'There's plenty of pluck in you yet.'

'There isn't, Landseer, there isn't. The vital forces ebb a little each day. I might have another year or two, but no more.'

'You'll feel different once you're out of this damp air and basking in the sun in Nice.'

'You sound just like the Duchess,' the Duke sighed. 'But it can do no more than patch me up, no matter what Woolryche says. I find I mind less than I thought I should. I simply wish not to be a burden. This is no longer my world. This age of steam locomotives and stucco. And the coming men – and women for that matter – so judgemental; no one takes the time to understand any more. But I mustn't ramble on. I have a request.'

'Your Grace?'

'I wish you to paint me. For the Duchess.'

Edwin took several moments to gather himself before saying, 'It would be an honour.'

'Thank you.'

They both stared out into the valley, where the setting sun swelled and reddened. Edwin groped for words but found none.

'I don't fancy any of the other fellows doing it. I want her to know a part of me will still be with her. I dare say people these days wouldn't understand our … arrangements. Such things are not as common as they were. Modern matrimony is rather unforgiving. If it had been a fling, that would have been different. But you make her happy. Which brings me to a second request: look after her for me.'

Edwin blinked as the sun blurred, guilt and hope becoming increasingly entangled. He nodded, forced a laugh and said, 'You'll have to linger a while longer. I'm too busy to take sole charge of her at the moment.'

'I shall do my best.' The Duke raised his glass.

Royal commissions came thicker and faster than Edwin would have liked, delaying the Duke's portrait, but by the following summer it just needed a final sitting.

'You don't mind if the shutters are part-closed, do you, Landseer? You still have enough light?' The Duke leant back in his favourite armchair as a footman brought the wooden panels together across the long windows, leaving slender strips of sunlight across the shelves in the Belgrave Square library. 'Keeps it cooler, you see.'

'I'll manage, Your Grace. Don't worry,' said Edwin, opening a roll of brushes, quietly relieved; the bright sunshine outside had given him a headache like hot needles around his eyes.

'I hear George Hayter's star is still in the ascendant at court?'

'It is.' Edwin took in the lines around the Duke's eyes. The shadows beneath were deeper, the cheeks thinner.

'And yours too: my sources tell me you're in line for a knighthood.'

'Not likely, Your Grace,' Edwin said, intent on capturing what was left of the Duke's laurel wreath of hair. He had heard something, but didn't believe it for a second. 'I wouldn't trust the palace rumour mill if I were you. George is cocksure of getting one though.'

They'd moved on to other artistic gossip – Ben Haydon and his latest encounter with the bailiffs, the Academy's new home in Trafalgar Square – when Rachel entered at a run, skirt bunched in one hand, a book in the other.

'Papa, Papa! Thank you, oh, thank you!' She flung her arms around the Duke.

'Careful, my dear, Mr Landseer is trying to paint me.'

'Sorry, Lanny – but look what Papa did for my birthday! It's my story! As an actual book! It's the most wonderful thing anyone has ever done.' She held out a slim volume bound in soft blue leather.

'I'd better not touch it. My hands are covered in paint. Would you show it to me?' Edwin's heart twisted with jealousy. His own gift of a portrait of her reading was clearly forgotten.

'Isn't it beautiful? See: *Memoirs of a Dormouse*,' Rachel traced the gold lettering with her finger, eyes shining, 'by Lady Rachel Russell.'

'If you wrote it, does that mean you're a dormouse?' Edwin made himself smile.

'Yes, that will be my pen name! My first novel shall be published anonymously as by Dormouse,' she grinned, 'and you shall illustrate it, Lanny.'

'I might.' He smiled again. He could never not return one of her smiles. 'But the Queen keeps asking for things: draw me a monkey, sketch me that hippopotamus, paint me riding bareback like a circus girl.'

Rachel giggled, eyeing him sceptically. 'You're not really painting the Queen like a circus girl?'

'No, but she is keeping me awfully busy.'

'Busy? You'd never be too busy for me, would you?'

'No, Dormouse, I wouldn't,' Edwin said. The Duke's eyes met his over Rachel's dark golden ringlets, sad, stern.

'Are you coming to Brighton with us next month?' Rachel continued. 'Louisa's going to have her baby there, Mama says.'

'I hope so,' Edwin said. The Duke's gaze was still on him.

'You must come! It'll be so dull without you. I'll have no one to tell stories with.'

'I'll do my best, but the Queen wants me to—'

'Fiddlesticks to the Queen! Tell her a dormouse has ordered you to Brighton.' She stamped her foot, then looked around, smiling even more broadly at the laughter she'd provoked from the two men.

Edwin's nerves were increasingly strained. He was behind with commissions, constantly interrupted by callers. He told Mrs Eames he was not at home to anyone but family or Georgina, but the Queen kept sending notes requesting his presence at the palace to paint more pets. How many animals could one woman have? In the evenings, when he hoped to catch up, there were so many dinners, lectures, and plays, he struggled to remember where he was meant to be. He was sure people were complaining behind his back about him cancelling at the last minute, but it was so difficult. Sometimes Georgina was unexpectedly free; sometimes he felt suddenly panicked, unable to go out and be the witty, charming Edwin Landseer they were expecting; sometimes he simply forgot.

And there was money: in what now seemed a moment of hubristic madness following good reviews at the 1838 Exhibition, he'd commissioned more works on his house and employed a valet, and had no idea if he could pay for them.

Worse still, he had a permanent headache and his eyes were increasingly sore.

He confessed the problem with his eyes to Bell, who was leafing through accounts and letters while a portrait of Bell's dogs, the bloodhound Countess and the terrier Scratch, took shape on one of the easels.

'Can you see all right?' Bell looked up.

'Yes, most of the time. Just this damn stinging and the headaches – always headaches.' Edwin clicked his fingers to hold the terrier's attention.

'You need a holiday.'

'I've just had one.'

'Did it help?'

'No.' He'd made it to the Highlands for a fortnight. The weather had been terrible. He'd barely seen any deer, and London had felt twice as oppressive on his return.

'In that case you need a doctor. Tweedie's good. Are you still not sleeping?'

'No.'

'Laudanum not helping?'

'It is, but it makes it so hard to wake up again.'

'You're taking too much – careful, or you won't wake up at all.'

'If I take any less, I lie awake and fret about being bankrupted by these building works.'

'Leave that to me.' Bell straightened one pile of papers and moved on to the next. 'As long as you remember to send your bills promptly and don't agree to any more stupidly low fees, you'll have money to spare. Those print copyrights will start to come in soon—' Bell cut himself off, holding up a letter. 'Lanny, this says you're meant to be at the palace today?'

'I told them I couldn't make it.'

'Whyever not? You're only painting my dogs, for goodness sake. You can't just tell the Queen you don't feel like seeing her.'

'I really couldn't face it. I'm too used up to work.'

'But you are working?'

'This isn't work.' Edwin bent down to scratch Countess behind the ears, then ruffled Scratch's fur after she let out a jealous, cat-like yowl. 'I'm painting this for you even if I'm slung in the Tower for treason. It's a pleasure. I don't know where I'd be without you.'

'You're an idiot.' Bell blushed.

Edwin was lying on the sofa in his small sitting room, eyes closed and covered with a damp cloth, trying to banish the needling, stinging sensation. There was a knock and the sound of Claridge, his new valet, clearing his throat.

'Mr Landseer, sir? Mr Hayter to see you.'

There was a smart click of leather soles on the floorboards, followed by a skull-shattering handclap. 'Time to wake up.'

Edwin peeled the cloth from his eyes.

'Little Vicky is cross with you, Little Ned.'

'What have I done now?' Edwin blinked gingerly.

'Apart from taking too long with her pony picture, and not dropping everything each time she shakes her rattle, she knows about you and the Duchess.'

'Christ, who told her?' Edwin sat up, grimacing.

'Lady Tavistock? She's one of Vicky's bedchamber brigade and is still thick with Bessy.'

'I can't deal with this right now.' Edwin's head throbbed. 'I suppose she's going to drop me?'

'Hardly. She's cross but desperate to know more; *entre nous*, I think she's jealous. She'd grown keen on the idea that you were her pet – probably because you're the same height as her.'

'I'm not anybody's pet,' Edwin growled. 'And I am not the same height—'

'Pet or not, you'd better do whatever she asks until she calms down, or you can kiss goodbye to her patronage. And to a knighthood.'

Edwin's eyes got worse.

'Did you see the doctor?' asked Bell, having found Edwin lying in the darkened sitting room for the second time in a week.

'No.' Edwin winced.

'Why the hell not?'

Edwin shrugged and bit his lip. 'What if he says there's something seriously wrong? What on earth will I do then?' It kept him awake at night. Along with everything else.

'There's far more likely to be something seriously wrong if you don't see him.' Bell opened the curtain a chink. Edwin flinched. Bell sent for Doctor Tweedie.

'Rest, Mr Landseer, you need rest,' Tweedie pronounced. 'Take a few weeks off. Go to the sea. No work and plenty of sleep.'

'Not possible.' Edwin closed his eyes to ease the soreness. 'I have to paint parrots and pineapples at the palace – on pain of death. And I can't sleep. Can't you give me something?'

The doctor tutted and shook his head but wrote out a prescription anyway.

Being jolly to the Queen and making jokes about her parrots was worse than wading through a peat bog. She babbled away with the spaniel, Dash, on her lap. Dog and mistress were uncannily alike – both small, with dark silky hair and pop-eyed expressions. If the Queen were to put the animal in a pink-and-cream silk dress, they would look like twins. Edwin wouldn't have put it past her. He squinted at the scarlet streaks he was applying to the canvas as she asked myriad questions. What about the Abolitionists' campaign? What about the Chartists? He didn't think there would be revolution, did he? What did he think of the design for the Nelson monument? Wouldn't the statue be too high for people to see? Would he be sculpting the lions guarding it?

Forcing smiles between brushstrokes, Edwin managed to say he hoped the Abolitionists would prevail, but would be grateful if any Chartist revolution could be put off at least until after he'd finished his pictures for the Exhibition; he hadn't thought about the Nelson monument, at least the pigeons would enjoy it; and, no, he absolutely was not going to sculpt the lions.

'Oh, but I thought you adored lions?'

'I do, ma'am.' He stifled a yawn and blinked to freshen his eyes. 'I just have too much canvas to cover before I decide to start chipping away at stone.'

'Oh. I love lions,' the Queen said, seemingly to the dog. Then she began to talk about Van Amburgh, the American who was causing a stir at Drury Lane by staring big cats into submission on stage. Half of London was in awe. Half thought him vulgar and cruel. The excitement on the Queen's face, making her eyes bulge even more than usual, proclaimed her to be in the former camp. She'd seen the show seven times, she said. Edwin's heart sank. He sensed her next words before they skipped off her tongue.

'Dear Mr Landseer, I should so love a picture of Mr Van Amburgh and his lions.'

Head beginning to throb, Edwin summoned every last ounce of charm to dissuade her, even offering to paint more of her damned pets, but she wanted lions and wasn't going to give up until she got them.

She took Dash in her arms and said, in a very unqueenly voice, 'Oh, Dashy! Wouldn't it be marvellous if Mr Landseer could have our lion picture ready for the Exhibition? Wouldn't it be so clever of him?'

'Yes, ma'am,' Edwin said.

'Yes, ma'am,' croaked the parrot. 'Yes, ma'am.'

Edwin gave it a very black look.

'You must learn to say no, or it will be the death of you,' Bell said, when Edwin told him. 'But at least it will pay for your building works. How long have you got?'

'Six weeks,' Edwin said, head in his hands.

He managed it, with newly installed gaslights hissing late into the night. Van Amburgh was irritating, arrogant, and strutted about in the costume of a Roman centurion (which Edwin's father, looking at his sketches, said was not historically accurate). The beasts – lions, tigers, a leopard, and a cheetah – were unutterably sad. Edwin painted them with every ounce of nobility oil could give and allowed as little as possible to Van Amburgh.

Having despatched the thing to Trafalgar Square for the Exhibition, he lay on the chaise longue in the studio with his head on Georgina's lap.

'I never want to see another lion as long as I live. Or leopard, or tiger, or—'

'Shh.' She stroked his hair, one touch giving more relief than all the laudanum he'd swallowed over the past few weeks. 'What does Her Majesty think?'

'I don't care. I never want to see her again either.' He wanted to lie here, with Georgina, forever.

'I'm delighted she's no longer my rival for your time or affections. But what did she say?'

'She loves it. Will no doubt want more.' He tried opening his eyes and winced at the dagger-like April sunshine.

'Shh.' Georgina stroked more gently. 'Did you see the doctor again?'

'Yes. He says it's just overwork.'

'They hate me. Did you read the reviews? Did you see?' Edwin slammed down *The Examiner* review so hard that the other guests who had lingered late at Gore House all turned. 'Should be ashamed of myself, shouldn't have accepted the commission. In poor taste and poorly executed – that's what they said! Should I be ashamed of myself, d'Orsay?' Edwin waved his glass at the blurred Frenchman.

'I think it is time for you to go home, my friend. Before you do something you *will* be ashamed of.' D'Orsay eased the glass out of Edwin's hand and passed it to Bell. 'It is just a bad review.'

'It may have been poor taste, but that's not my fault. It's not my taste. It's *hers*. I'll tell her to boil her head – crown and all – next time she asks for anything. But poorly executed? Was it?'

'Lanny, you're shouting,' hissed Bell.

Struggling to focus, Edwin glared in his general direction. 'I rushed it. Maybe it was badly done. Was it, Bell?' He reached for the table. 'Put that bloody bottle back, d'Orsay, you damned French—'

D'Orsay shook his head. 'I think you have had enough.'

'I'll say when I've had enough.' Edwin swiped at the bottle, missing as d'Orsay moved it further away. 'Bastard.'

'You have your carriage, Bell?' said d'Orsay.

'Yes. Let's get him up. Come on, Lanny.'

'I can walk perfectly well, thank you.' Edwin pushed them away and fell over the table.

Outside, hooves thumped among cinders and sand, and lanterns lurched down the darkened Rotten Row. Leaning on the wheel of Bell's carriage, Edwin felt his stomach lurch. 'Oh God. I think I'm going to be sick.'

Afterwards, somehow, he got into the carriage.

'I'm sorry.' Grimacing at the sour taste in his mouth, he stared blankly at the rump of Bell's horse between the lanterns. 'I'm a liability.'

'You're not,' said Bell. 'You just can't take criticism – or drink. Forget about the papers. They're flexing their muscles against the Queen as much as against you. Mark my words, the masses will snap up prints of your lions. Most of them don't care a straw for what the critics say they ought to like. They buy what they actually want to look at.'

Edwin groaned, beginning to feel sick again.

'And one very important person told me he thought the picture was capital.' There was laughter on the edge of Bell's voice.

'Who? Must be pretty damned brave to go against those reviews.' They were approaching the end of Park Lane. Could he manage not to be sick again? Home was a long way off.

'Wave to him if you like,' Bell laughed, pointing at the cold stone-clad bulk of Apsley House, which loomed to their right. 'It's Wellington.'

'No?'

'Yes.' Bell grinned. 'And – you'll love this – he likes it so much he wants you to paint one for him.'

In spite of the mounting nausea, Edwin couldn't help joining in with Bell's laughter. Then the nausea became too much.

'I need to get down,' he managed to say.

A few seconds later he was vomiting into a bush in full view of Wellington's windows. The compulsion to lie down and stay there was overwhelming.

'Look,' he heard Bell say. 'You're in no state to go home. Stay with me tonight. It's closer. You look frightful.'

Edwin was too tired and wretched to care where he went.

Bell turned away while he was sick again, then drove the short distance to his house on Langham Place. In the sitting room, they came across a sleeping, nightcapped figure by a slumbering fire.

'You've met my friend, Tom Hyde Hills, haven't you?' whispered Bell.

'Oh, yes,' said Edwin, bumping into a chair as the sleeping, plumpish young man woke and glared at him.

Bell showed him into a bedroom.

Edwin tried to curl up on the bed.

'At least take your shoes off,' Bell said.

Edwin was dimly aware of someone sitting on the bed, removing his shoes; someone holding a glass of something vile to his lips, and someone pulling a blanket over him, whispering, 'Good night, Lanny.'

# *November 1861, London*

CHARLES LEANS OVER THE EDGE of the green baize table in Edwin's billiard room, takes his shot, misses, winces. Edwin lifts a decanter, sloshes more wine into his glass. Charles pulls another mealy-mouthed face. Edwin fills the glass to the brim, then takes a large gulp before making his own shot, potting the ball Charles just missed.

'That was a jolly dinner, I thought,' Charles says slowly.

'No it wasn't,' Edwin says, leaning over to line up another shot. 'Why did you invite *him*?'

The ball rattles into the pocket.

'Who?'

'You know who I mean.' Edwin straightens up, steadies himself.

'Dr Tuke?' Charles won't meet his eye, pretends to be concentrating on the table but he's not even looking at a ball. 'Hills invited him. He's a nerve specialist. They're old friends.'

'Don't lie to me. He treats lunatics and drunkards.'

'Nerves. He's a nerve specialist, Ned. Your nerves are shot, you said so yourself. We just wanted to see if he could recommend anything. A rest cure perhaps. As I said, he's a friend of Hills. He was a friend of Bell too.'

'Don't you dare talk to me about Bell!' Edwin slams his glass down on the edge of the table. 'And if you think I'm mad or a drunk, say it to my face.'

'Nobody thinks you're mad, Ned.' Charles takes a step back, eyes on the precariously balanced glass. 'We just think a rest might help. Tuke runs a very comfortable retreat. In Chiswick.'

'Retreat?' Edwin slams his cue down too. 'It's a madhouse.'

'I was only mentioning it. As an option.'

Edwin glowers at him, takes another swig of wine and reaches for the decanter.

Charles takes a deep breath. 'Tuke said you'd feel better if you drank less.'

'*You'd* feel better if you drank less,' Edwin sneers, refilling his glass.

'Don't be childish.'

'Don't be—'

'Ned!' Charles snaps. 'You can't carry on like this. Do you want to drink yourself to death?'

'Maybe I do.' Edwin glares at him. Rachel hasn't written back.

'Do you have any idea . . .?' Charles looks as though he might cry; what the hell does he have to cry about? 'What does it take to get through to you?'

Edwin raises his glass in a mock toast and downs half the contents, unable to stop himself in spite of the horror on his brother's face, and the shame in the pit of his own stomach.

'It'll be your own fault if you're declared insane again. You know that, don't you?' Charles shakes his head. 'And we might not be able to keep it so quiet this time.' Throwing down his cue, he hurries from the room.

Edwin hurls the glass at the wall, where it shatters, leaving a dripping, blood-red stain.

# *October 1839, The Doune*

THEY WERE ALL IN THE drawing room dressed for dinner when Edwin arrived at The Doune.

'Landseer! At last,' said the Duke, rising stiffly from the sofa to greet him. 'We were beginning to think you had been caught by the Chartists.'

'Just a broken spoke on the coach at Perth – a riot might have been more fun.'

'At least you're here now, though you look quite used up.'

'I would have been here a month ago but for the Queen.' Edwin accepted a glass of champagne. 'Her German cousin's visiting and she's decided to be in love with him. She's all whim and fancy and has had me painting love birds and love tokens.' He downed half the glass. It was nectar.

'I can only imagine. I trust you'll recruit health and strength while you're here,' said the Duke, who looked far from well himself. 'If you wish to begin tonight, we dine at seven.'

As the others fell back into conversation, Georgina crossed the room to greet him.

'You really do look exhausted,' she said. 'Don't give a thought to dinner if you're too tired.'

'Do you know what I would really love?' Edwin said, wanting to collapse into her arms. 'A whisky and a bath. Then I can finally wash off the soot from the train. I've never felt so filthy.'

'Would you like a view of the hills with the bath?' She smiled.

'That would be music to my eyes.' He smiled back.

Not long afterwards, Edwin rested his head on the rim of a copper tub, knees drawn up to his chest, and let out a long, slow breath. The splashing of the river beyond the open window and the sight of the dark hills did as much to banish the dirt and tension as the lukewarm water lapping around his waist. He closed his eyes and breathed in peat smoke, sweet heather, and roasting venison. Perhaps he would go down to dinner . . . then, from the door behind him came a soft click, a light step, and the scent of roses.

'Your whisky.' A fingertip caressed the nape of his neck.

'Careful, or I'll pull you in here with me . . .'

Edwin didn't make it down to dinner. Georgina did, but only after the bell had been rung three times.

Having slept until almost noon the next day, Edwin was walking on the lawn with Georgina beneath quick high clouds, when a footman came running.

'Your Grace! Your Grace! It's the Duke.'

The colour drained from Georgina's face and Edwin's insides went cold as she grasped his arm.

'Your Grace!' The footman called again.

'Come on.' Edwin clutched her hand and hurried her across the damp grass.

The Duke was at his writing desk, head lolling unnaturally, one side of his face drooping. A newly lit fire leapt over young logs in the grate behind him. A pen lay on the desk next to his limp fingers, a dark blot of ink spreading beneath the nib.

'Johnny . . .' Deathly pale, Georgina knelt and cradled the distorted face. 'Johnny, it's me. It's Georgy. Everything will be all right. I'm going to look after you.' The eyelid on the good side of the Duke's face flickered and his lips moved but no sound came out. Edwin's heart was racing and there was a ringing in his ears. He heard himself tell the footman to go for Woolryche and Abercorn.

Woolryche appeared. Georgina continued to stroke the limp fingers and whisper words of comfort as they carried the Duke to his bedroom. Edwin told himself it wasn't happening. This wasn't what he'd wished. Not like this. Not now.

Georgina wouldn't let go of the Duke's hand.

Woolryche took Edwin aside. 'He's alive, but God only knows for how long. Will you tell the others?'

It was the hardest thing he'd ever had to do. Especially with Louisa, who was close to confinement with yet another child. And Rachel, who yelled and stamped her feet and told him he must be lying before her sisters calmed her down. Then Edwin went in search of someone to send after Abercorn and the Duke's sons, who had gone shooting.

When he returned to the Duke's room, Georgina was still sitting next to the bed, holding one unresponsive hand; Rachel sat on the bed itself, holding the other. She was chattering through her tears but frequently had to stop to gulp down sobs.

'Dearest, darling Papa, best of all papas, it's not time to go yet. I have so many stories still to tell you—' she swallowed, 'and you promised you would always listen to them . . . always.' Another sob. 'Will I tell you one now?'

She began a nonsense tale of the dormouse and a doll.

Edwin stood in a corner, unable to do anything but watch. It was a new depth of wretchedness: jealous of the love shown to a dying man – a friend – who he'd been cuckolding for fifteen years. What sort of monster did that make him?

A low, cold voice in his head whispered: *They'll never love you the way they love him. She's never asked you to call her Georgy. You've never really mattered. You are just a toy.*

Edwin blinked, refusing to listen.

Now holding both the Duke's hands, Rachel choked on the ending of her story.

*See how much she loves him? You're a monster to even think of taking that from her.*

The Duke never regained consciousness.

# Part V

# *December 1861, London*

THE HOUSE IS DARK AND FULL OF SILENCE. The windows shudder in their frames as Edwin slams the door but the sound is quickly eaten by the shadows. The servants have the day off. Jessie's still at Tom's house. He's meant to be there too. But there's been an argument. He can't remember how it started. He does remember shouting.

He remembers Charles yelling, 'You're drunk. Again!'

He itches with anger. At Charles for being right. At himself for being like this. At the others for trying to help. Because that means they know what a mess he is.

Fumbling on the shelf above the kitchen stove, he finds a candle, matches. Breaks two. Useless fool. A third fizzles out, burns his fingers. Damn damn damn. Finally, some light. Stumbles on the cellar steps. Wants to cry. Why shouldn't he cry? Finds a bottle. Makes his way down the hall to the studio, shadows closing in behind.

He'd hoped Rachel would have written back, at least sent a message – a sign, anything – for Christmas. But she hasn't. So to hell with it being Christmas Day. To hell with Dickens.

To hell with Scrooge and his spirits. They're nothing compared with his own demons. Nothing compared with knowing you are the demon.

Bottle under his arm, he jiggles the key, shoulders the studio door open, receives a chill slap in the face from the air inside.

Why should Rachel acknowledge him anyway? If she has any sense, she should run a mile. It's his own fault for agreeing to the Duke's terms in the first place. For choosing his career rather than his child. For thinking they'd be free when the Duke died. For thinking he could avoid the bottle imp.

The wine is too cold. To hell with that as well – it's still drink and he can't face this picture without it. Taking another swig, glancing at Georgina's clock on the chimney piece, he crosses to the far corner of the room and yanks the cloth off the Balmoral boat picture. It flickers as the dust settles in his small circle of light – the Queen, young, happy, stepping ashore, gazing at Albert.

Through the fog of drink and anger shines a vision of the day the Queen suggested it, so clear he could be back there. A dazzling September afternoon on the shores of Loch Muick, the sky hazy, the water glassy, reflecting the hills in perfect detail, then rippling like silk where the Queen's boat slid through it. She and Albert and their brood had been like an ordinary family there. She'd wanted him to capture that. But he'd failed. That day his thoughts had been filled with Georgina, of getting back to her at The Doune, and realising the dream he'd clung to for so long.

He's barely been able to look at this picture since Georgina died.

And now Albert is dead too.

And Edwin Landseer is going to fail again – with the lions.

Cold wine trickles down his throat. Hot tears roll down his cheeks. His breath mists and dissipates with the memories into the darkness. Then a sound cuts through the clouds.

Clicking. Claws on stone flags. Another click. From the kitchen?

Grasping the candlestick, hugging the bottle, feeling his way along the wall, he reaches the back hallway. Cupboards loom: the panelled one – filled with napkins, cloths, candles – and the glass-fronted one – filled with bowls, pans, copper moulds. He stops. There's a reflection in one of the lower panes. A glint of eyes. Something is behind him. The hairs on the back of his neck prickle, a coldness creeps down, down, between his shoulder blades. And then there's a growl. He flinches, drops the candle – which goes out – and stumbles over a bucket, heart pounding, ears ringing with the metallic clatter, terror cascading down his back in the darkness.

Then – oh blessed relief! From the other end of the hall, Lassie barks. Fresh tears flow down his cheeks as she bounds up to him, and he buries his fingers deep in her fur as she licks his face.

What a fool. What a cursed old fool.

He staggers back to the kitchen; Lassie keeps close. Lights another candle, slumps onto the table, glaring at the reflection of the fool in the half-empty bottle. Swigs again. Finds a pen, paper, ink. Draws himself. Thank God he can still do that. Draws himself as he really is. A Christmas scene – sprawled on the table, bottle in hand.

# *January 1840, London*

ONLY THREE MONTHS AFTER THE unhappy events at The Doune, Edwin's mother's death hit him so hard he struggled to string two thoughts together. When he could, they spun off uncontrollably. It felt like a punishment for having wanted the Duke to die.

'I'm so sorry, Ned.' George embraced him awkwardly then sat on the edge of the sofa.

Edwin shrugged, sat down heavily, and buried his fingers into the fur of the sheepdog Luna, who hadn't left his side for days. Eventually, he managed to swallow and say thank you.

'What was it? Influenza?'

'No. Her heart.'

'Sudden then?'

Edwin nodded. Luna shuffled even closer.

'How's your father?'

'Horribly quiet. Not even complaining about the Queen's wedding.' Edwin covered his face with his hands and exhaled slowly, then, pushing his hair behind his ears, said, 'I've arranged the funeral for Saturday. Will you come?'

Luna whimpered and rested her head on his knee. Thank God for dogs.

'Of course. Have you heard from the Duchess?'

'She's still with Georgy and Rachel in Ireland at Abercorn's place – consoling herself with Louisa's new baby.'

'I hear there's trouble at Woburn. Young Lord William tells me the old duke left a shocking mess with his will. And I'd no idea how much the old rascal spent on grasses and grottoes. There will have to be serious economies.'

Edwin raised his eyes to the window; silver clouds scuttled across the night sky. 'He always said Georgina would keep Campden Hill and Endsleigh.'

'From what I hear, she'll have a fight on her hands. Duke Francis is feeling pinched.' George took a walnut from the bowl on the table. 'What are the two of you going to do anyway? Is she happy to play the merry widow without his protection?'

'I'm going to ask her to marry me,' Edwin said, taking Luna's face in his hands, stroking her behind the ears. 'As soon as she's back.'

'You're not serious?'

'Deadly serious. It's the only thought keeping me going right now.'

'You're mad. There'll be one hell of a scandal.'

'I don't care. Anyway, so many people more or less know. How can it be scandalous to do the right thing?'

'You don't understand Society, Ned. You're not thinking clearly. First the Duke's death, now your mother . . . Wait a bit.'

'She won't be back for a month or so, but I'm not waiting any longer than that. I'm sick of waiting, of lying. I've waited half my life.'

'Then you should be able to wait and lie a bit longer.'

'No.'

George shrugged, took another walnut. 'And you think she'll say yes?'

'I damn well hope so.'

'What will the Queen think? You know she and Melbourne have been gossiping about you.'

'I couldn't care less.'

Head throbbing, Edwin leant back on the sofa, closed his eyes, screwed them tighter shut as thoughts of his mother welled up. He *did* care what she would have thought. He blinked to clear the gathering tears. A sliver of a moon winked through a gap in the clouds. It had to be a sign. Georgina was still his moon goddess. He could bear all of this if he could finally be with her. And be a father to Rachel.

Two months passed. His mother's death was less raw, though no less sore. Edwin buried himself in work. By the middle of April he had submitted a string of paintings for the Exhibition that he prayed would make up for the previous year's Van Amburgh disaster. And Georgina was back.

Immediately on her return from Ireland, she'd marched to Woburn to do battle with her stepson, the new Duke of Bedford, but was outgunned. Duke Francis refused to accept her claim to Endsleigh, the house in Devon she and the old duke had built together, but had confirmed she'd been left Campden Hill for her lifetime, and that he would pay an annual allowance for herself and her unmarried daughters. She'd arrived back at Campden Hill, William reported, like a general leading a retreat: head held high and with a considerable baggage train.

Edwin walked with her through the rose garden. The buds swelled with promise and the spring sunshine lent the scene a soft glow, but Georgina was oblivious to his matrimonial hints. She wouldn't stop talking about cows and the injustice of her friend and neighbour, Lord Holland, refusing to let her keep one in his grounds at Holland House.

'How else am I supposed to get milk? I can't get it sent up from Woburn any more and there's no room here.'

'Can't you just buy milk?'

'Buy milk? Like a …'

'Like an ordinary person?'

She scowled. 'Do you have space for a cow?'

'Yes,' he said. 'In theory, but I would have to charge a very high rent … unless …' It wasn't a conventional lead in to a proposal, but when had she ever been conventional? Heart kicking wildly against his ribs, he plunged: 'Unless you agreed to marry me.'

'What?'

'Marry me. And I'll let you keep all the cows you want at St John's Wood.' He laughed to hide his terror.

'You're not serious?'

'Of course I am. Just because I'm laughing, doesn't mean I'm not serious. See. I'm not laughing now. I can get down on one knee if you like. Will you marry me?'

Her eyes widened and sparkled; her bosom, buttoned up in mourning, swelled; her lips parted but no sound came from them.

Edwin's heart screamed in his ears. 'Say something – please – I've never been more terrified of asking anything in my life.' She let him take her hands, but still didn't say anything. 'For God's sake, don't leave me in suspense. Put your foot on me and snuff me out … or make me the happiest man alive.'

'I … I … But …' The sparkling of eyes and swelling of bosom intensified. 'Where will we live? What will we live on?'

Edwin squeezed her hands. 'We'll work all that out. I'll paint every pampered poodle and child of fashion from here to Timbuktu if I need to.'

'Are there many poodles between here and Timbuktu?'

'I've no idea. That's not the point. Will you marry me?'

'It's still so soon after John ... what will people say?'

'They can say what they like. They can say you only married me for the cow. We don't have to listen. And it's nearly six months.'

'That's still quite soon. I hadn't thought ...'

'Well think now. And say yes. I love you, Georgina, I've loved you for almost twenty years and I don't want to hide it any more.' He kissed her. As her lips reluctantly let go of his, he said, 'So? Do I have to kiss you again?'

'Yes – and yes,' she laughed.

After he'd kissed her again, she added, 'But only if we call our first cow Josephine.'

Blankets were spread between the rose bushes at Campden Hill. Georgina sat in a shaded corner holding the latest baby Russell – William's second son – on her lap, cooing as he sucked on the black ribbons trailing from her bonnet. William was playing a noisy game of hide-and-seek with his two eldest children, much to the annoyance of his father, Old Lord William, who was attempting to doze in a wicker chair.

Edwin lay on a blanket on the sunny side of the rose garden, refusing to let his latest headache stop him talking to Rachel, who was making a daisy chain next to him.

'It's so good to see Mama happy again,' she said, softly enough that only he could hear. 'Babies always have a miraculous effect on her.'

'Yes. I remember her with Alexander. And you.' Edwin tilted the brim of his straw hat to stop the sun stinging his eyes.

'What was Sandy like as a baby? I can't imagine him as anything but a big, bluff soldier now.'

'He was fat, funny, and pink.'

She grinned. 'And what was I like?'

'Oh, you were horrid: like a pig.' Edwin laughed.

'Beast!' said Rachel in mock-horror and threw the half-made daisy chain at him. 'What was I really like? Louisa's children are all so different, it makes me so curious – how children with the same parents can be so unalike.'

Carefully unhooking the daisies from his waistcoat buttons, Edwin said, 'To begin with, you were red and wrinkled like a monkey. Then you were a plump golden cherub. Then you were a puppy. Then, somehow, you transformed into a dormouse.' Sliding the flowers into his pocket, he gazed at her bowed head, at the dark blonde curls beneath her straw bonnet. 'And when you were happy, you were the best company in the world. But when you didn't get your way . . . but you don't want to know about that . . .'

'Beast again!' She grinned, looking up from a new chain. 'You must tell me.'

'All right.' Edwin smiled, lowering his voice. 'You were as stubborn as your mother and would throw enormous tantrums if you didn't get your way.'

'Not true.' She pursed her lips, pinching a daisy stem.

'Oh, I remember very clearly. Once, you were four years old and I'd let you help paint the scenery for a play at Woburn – when I say help I mean you made a mess and didn't do a thing I asked—'

'Such a tyrant.'

'You were the tyrant: this brush, Lanny, not that one! No! Paint it lellow not blue! And when your nurse came to take you to bed, you had such a fit that Georgina – your mother, I mean – had to carry you away, kicking and screaming, flipping like a salmon.'

'Hmm.' Rachel pouted at her daisies, then met his eyes and laughed.

William let out a bull-like bellow on being discovered behind a tree by his elder children, causing everyone to jump. Even his dozing father startled into an upright position.

William knew. Edwin had told him. He was sceptical, as was Bell, but had fished a cigar from his pocket, saying it was an early wedding present.

'It's so good to have people here again,' said Rachel, when the commotion had died down. 'I miss Papa more when it's quiet. I know Mama does too. Georgy spends so much time visiting Wrio and Eliza, and I expect she'll be married herself soon – there's a beau called Romilly waiting in the wings. So it's just Mama and me. I wish you would come and see us more.'

'I would if I could, Dormouse,' Edwin said with feeling. 'But this is the first afternoon I've not been trapped at the Academy in weeks. If they ever threaten to put me on the hanging committee again, I shall go and become a hermit in the glen.'

'Poor Lanny, here's a crown for your efforts.' Rachel draped her second daisy chain on top of his hat. 'But you must promise to visit us more when you're free.'

'I will,' Edwin promised. 'It will all be done by Friday.'

A host of unsaid words filled his chest. She had a right to know about the marriage plans. Surely, given the promise she'd just extracted, she would be pleased? But Georgina insisted on being the one to broach the subject. He had reluctantly agreed, conceding that even at nearly fourteen, Rachel was still capable of throwing a tantrum, and he'd never been any good at dealing with those.

Head throbbing again, he closed his eyes, folding his fingers around the flowers in his pocket. It would be all right. Once the Exhibition opened, they would head north by train then coach to Scotland, where they would marry. And nobody would be able to do a thing about it.

At two o'clock on Friday morning, the Exhibition hang was finally complete. Having placed the last picture, Edwin and Cook and Deering, the other two RAs sentenced to be hangmen that year, wandered out into a dark Trafalgar Square. The only other souls present were a drunk slumped by one of the gallery's fluted columns and a cat weaving its way from shadow to shadow. Both man and cat startled at the loud pop when Edwin sent a champagne cork flying.

'Do you think they'll hate us?' said Cook, swigging from the bottle.

'Who?' asked Deering, taking the wine from him.

'Everyone,' said Edwin, watching the cat slink closer.

'Oh yes, I'm sure they'll all complain. But what could we do? There isn't enough space.' Cook passed the champagne back to Edwin.

Only a column away now, the cat crouched, eyes flaring in the light of a streetlamp, intent on something in the darkness.

'Here's to having finished.' Edwin shivered as he drank, sending a silent prayer into the moonless sky. The ghosts of Van Amburgh's lions breathed down his neck. He couldn't tell if he was more nervous about the reviews or that something would go awry with the elopement. It would be all right, he repeated to himself, taking another swig. Just a few more days.

The cat pounced, seizing a mouse. It didn't kill it, but toyed with it, before slinking off into the shadows with the petrified creature in its jaws.

# *June 1862, London*

EDWIN WAKES WITH A START. A wave of nausea crashes over him. He's drenched: hair and forehead dripping with cold, sour sweat; sheets and nightshirt freezing, plastered to his skin. The snarls of the lion in his dream reverberate in his ears and, if he blinks, he sees its teeth.

'Jessie!' He fumbles for the small brass bell on the bedside table, shakes it violently, then pulls up the sodden sheet, which does nothing to stop the shivering. 'Jessie!'

By the time she arrives, he's huddled in the centre of the bed, hugging his knees, staring at the lion pacing through the fog that has seeped out of his dream into the room.

'Ned.' Her hand reaches through the mist, touches his forehead. The beast won't touch her. It has come for him.

'I don't think I'm well,' he says. Icy droplets of sweat rake their way down his back and chest. Like claws. 'I need Bell.'

'Ned.' She tries to take his hand. 'I'll send for the doctor.'

'No! I want Bell.' Edwin jerks away, gripping the sheets as the lion's stare bores into him. Teeth chattering, he glares back.

'He . . . he's gone. Remember?' She places her hand on his forehead again.

The lion's shoulders tense; it crouches. His heart races out of control.

'You're burning up. You need the doctor.'

The lion leaps. The bed shakes as it lands only feet from him; he can smell it – musky, sweet, rotten.

'No!' he yells. 'Get off!'

Jessie withdraws her hand abruptly.

'Not you,' Edwin manages to say.

The lion narrows its eyes. Struggling to breathe, Edwin presses himself back into the clammy mess of bedclothes as it crawls towards him.

Jessie's turning towards the door.

'Don't leave me!' He daren't look away from the muzzle, the scar on the lion's cheek, the amber eyes. Its breath is hot on his neck.

Jessie doesn't leave. She lets him cling to her until he's able to whisper, 'Don't tell the others. Please. I'm not mad. I'm not mad. I'm not.' He stares into the eyes of the lion that is sitting on his bed.

'Ned . . .'

'Please!'

'You're not mad.' She presses his hand. 'But you are ill. You must see a doctor.'

'Not the mad doctor.'

There is no long-suffering look. Just pity. From his sister and the lion.

Dr Tweedie arrives. The lion bares its teeth and stalks around him, growling, but Tweedie doesn't notice and measures out a dose of laudanum, handing it to Edwin. The lion slinks back to the shadows.

Edwin asks for a drink, and is told no.

There is pulse-checking, tongue flattening, bleeding. The lion paces along the far wall of the bedroom.

Edwin demands a drink, and is told no.

Tweedie takes his pulse again and places a cold stethoscope on Edwin's chest.

Edwin shouts that if somebody doesn't fetch him a drink this instant he will set the lion on them. The lion stops pacing and licks its lips.

Putting his instruments back in his bag, Tweedie says, 'I won't beat about the bush. It is *delirium tremens*, Sir Edwin.'

Edwin grits his teeth and stares straight ahead.

'You have to stop drinking so much. A glass or two a day at most if you absolutely must – light wines only, no spirits.' Tweedie snaps the bag shut. 'And I'm sure you don't need me to tell you that another attack could kill you.'

'I don't need you to tell me anything.'

Tweedie shakes his head, tells Jessie it's the illness talking, not the man – he's in the grip of a demon, apparently.

The lion waits until they're gone. Until it's dark. Until Edwin has clambered out of bed and is rummaging through the drawers for the bottle of whisky that should be there, then it says, 'So you do want to die then?'

'You can leave me alone too,' Edwin snarls.

The bottle is not there, dammit. He must have a drink. He needs a drink. Jessie must have found it. Or Lucy Potter. Or did he drink it? It doesn't signify. There's another one in the studio. His head spins and his nightshirt sticks to a fresh sheen of sweat on his chest. Shivering, he shrugs on his dressing gown, steadying himself on the door.

'How the mighty have fallen,' says the lion, head tilted to one side, reminding him oddly of Caro. 'The great Sir Edwin

Landseer. Such a promising child, such a talented young man. Look how you've wasted it. Now you're a laughing stock. A national joke.'

'Shut up,' Edwin hisses, trying the handle. It opens. At least they haven't locked him in this time.

'The papers are full of it – nobody believes you'll ever finish this. You're already a failure. But if you die trying, that makes you a tragic failure: a noble sacrifice to your art. Remember Benjamin Haydon?'

'How could I forget?' Edwin glares at the lion, which pads alongside him from shadow to shadow in the hall.

They pass Jessie's room in silence, pass the sleeping dogs in the kitchen, reach the studio. He lights a lamp, sets it on the chimney piece, finds the bottle, breaks the wax off the stopper, and places it on top of the cabinet.

'So, you are choosing tragedy?' The lion's breath strokes the back of his neck as Edwin's fingers close around the glass, like taking the hand of an old friend.

On the chimney piece, next to Rachel's novel, Georgina's clock strikes one. Both are reflected in the bottle. So is the lion.

Edwin breathes, braces himself. 'Not yet. I have unfinished business.'

The lion paces, circling him. 'Your business is finished. It was finished a long time ago. Raking it up again now won't help. You can't change anything.'

He sees himself kissing Georgina – his wife – the soft dark shoulders of the hills behind her, the years they should have had together in front of them. What would she do if she were here? Why is she not here? Why? She said she would always help.

He tightens his grip and, glaring at the lion, raises the bottle to his lips. The old fire kindles in the back of his throat and the pit of his stomach. He knows what she would do.

'*Slàinte mhath*,' he rasps, then puts the bottle down and picks up a brush and a palette.

The beast circles him. He mixes colours, swigs again. If he's going to hallucinate lions, he's damn well going to make use of them. He's promised the new Board of Works he'll have something lionlike ready by next spring and he damn well will.

'You'll never last that long,' sneers the lion.

Edwin swears at it in Gaelic.

The beast snorts.

Edwin paints, something stronger than whisky now flowing through his veins.

As the clock strikes four, soft, grey light begins to slip through the window and the lion lies down and sleeps. Edwin blinks, stretches his shoulders. The bottle is still more than half full. He puts it back in the cabinet then unbolts the stable doors to the garden. Sharp, sweet birdsong dances above a low grey mist. Cool dew soaks his bare feet and clings to the heads of tall grasses, which bow and sparkle in the silver light. And there, moving through the meadow like a nymph, is a roe doe, her dark eyes fixed on him.

# *May 1840, London*

THINGS MIGHT HAVE GONE TO plan if it hadn't been for the murder.

The Exhibition opened. The critics said he had triumphed. The ghosts of Van Amburgh and his lions were defeated by Edwin's picture of d'Orsay's poodle as Lord Chief Justice, which was declared the star of the show. He and d'Orsay celebrated late into opening night. The poodle came too. It won a surprising amount of money at cards.

Then, two days before the planned elopement, William's father, Old Lord William, was murdered, his throat cut while he slept.

It threw everything into chaos.

The Russells gathered at Belgrave Square, now occupied by Duke Francis. Georgina insisted Edwin come with her, saying she couldn't face it without him. Duke Francis looked less than pleased when they arrived together.

Edwin sat and smoked in the garden with William while Georgina did what she could to console Eliza.

'Didn't expect to see you here,' said William. 'Shouldn't you be getting married?'

'We've put it off,' Edwin said awkwardly. 'Could hardly go gallivanting off at a time like this.'

'Thank you.' William stared at the growing ash tip of his slim cigar. 'It's good to see you. A bit of normality with all this . . . Christ,' he ran a hand over his face, 'it's the type of thing I don't even believe in the papers. I can't take it in. You heard what the police think?'

'That it was the valet?'

William nodded. The ash grew longer. 'He'd been stealing from my father for a while, they reckon. The man must be insane. My father never had anything worth stealing, let alone . . . let alone killing him for.' The ash was about to fall onto William's knee. Edwin gently took the cigar from his hand and tapped it off. 'Thank you.' William sighed.

'Wish I could do more.'

William shrugged. 'Saving my trousers from burning is better than nothing.' He took the cigar back. 'You're still going to elope with my aunt then?'

'Yes.' Edwin drew on his own cigar. 'We've agreed next month. God willing. I won't make you call me Uncle Edwin though.'

Three laudanum-filled weeks later, Edwin was scowling, sore-eyed at the Queen's equestrian portrait, which would still not come right, when Georgina arrived at the studio unexpectedly. The dogs squirmed around her skirts in a whirl of tails, ears, and noses. Similarly delighted, Edwin took her hands, but, when he went to kiss her there were tears in her eyes.

'Duke Francis knows,' she said. 'About the elopement.'

'So what?' Edwin's chest tightened. He gripped her hands harder. 'It's nothing to do with him.'

'He's told my sister Richmond.'

'It's nothing to do with her either, or any of them.' Dread began to creep up his spine.

She pulled her hands free. 'They've forbidden it. They'll cut me off if we go through with it.'

'But that doesn't matter,' he said, heart thudding. 'I can support us. You know that. It won't be like Woburn, but it'll be comfortable enough. I'll increase my prices. Bell's always saying I should.' His stomach lurched but he ploughed on. 'And the Queen . . . George says she'll give me a knighthood if I can finish this blasted horse picture.'

'Francis knows about Rachel. He'll let the whole story come out.'

'Let him. I'm sick of lying. I want her to know the truth.'

'But that will ruin her life!'

The words sliced into him like cold steel. 'Who will marry her if they know?' Georgina said, despair on her face and in her voice. 'She's used to being a duke's daughter. How will she cope with suddenly being . . .'

'Being a painter's daughter? Being my daughter?' Edwin said, forcing air into his lungs. 'Being my daughter will ruin her life?'

'I didn't mean it like that.'

'How else could you mean it?' He couldn't breathe.

She said nothing.

'You're ashamed of me. I'm just like your father's housekeeper.' Edwin let go of her hands.

'What?'

'One thing to fuck me in private, but unthinkable to marry me.'

She slapped him.

He glared at her, holding a hand to his stinging cheek. 'At least your father had the decency to marry her.'

'It was different for him – he was a *man*!'

'I don't see how that makes a blind bit of difference,' Edwin snarled.

'You wouldn't, you're a man too.' She glowered. 'And he was a duke – dukes can do whatever the hell they like. I can't – I might be a duke's daughter, but I'm still only a woman. And you can't. You're only a—' She stopped herself.

'Only a painter,' Edwin said through clenched teeth. Canvasses and easels wavered before his eyes. He groped at the back of the chaise longue for support.

'Lanny, listen to me,' Georgina said, reaching for his face. He turned away. 'It's not fair – I know that. I wouldn't care about any of it for myself. I'd marry you and damn Francis to hell, but for Rachel . . .'

Edwin felt her hands on his back, felt sick. 'So I'm not good enough for my own daughter?'

'Lanny, please.' She tried to take his hand. 'Can't we carry on as we always have? I love you.'

'No!' He shrugged her off. 'I've felt like a nasty little secret for too long. Seeing you always on the arm of another man, seeing Rachel look up to him not me as her father, having to listen to the gossips say you have other lovers . . . The only thing that kept me sane through the worst parts was thinking one day I'd be able to go about in public with you – as your husband.'

'But we can still be together.' She reached again for his hand. 'Why do we have to marry?'

'Ha!' He stepped back, staring at her in disbelief. 'That's exactly what you said about your father and his housekeeper.'

'Lanny, please, I love you.'

'You don't. If you did, you'd let the whole world know. You'd marry me.'

'I can't,' she sobbed.

'Then get out.'

'Lanny . . .'

'Get out.'

'Lanny, please . . .'

'Get out!'

He poured one whisky after another, lost count. Didn't want to count. Didn't want to think. Didn't want to feel.

He should have listened. They'd all told him. Bell, George, even William. Arrogant idiot. Fool. Chasing a mirage. What would his father say? That's what comes of fucking another man's wife. What on earth did you think would happen? That she would actually marry you? A duchess marry a painter? And his mother . . .

There was no whisky left. Everything hurt.

Being his daughter would ruin Rachel's life.

But what was *his* life? Without her, without Georgina?

He staggered up, clinging to the wall.

There was no whisky left. But there was laudanum.

He made it to the bedroom. There was the bottle on the bedside table. Labelled with the dose in Bell's sloping hand. *Careful or you won't wake up at all.* He'd ruined everything. Had let them all down.

He gagged, swallowed, swallowed again. Closed his eyes. Curled into a ball on the bed.

The pain swirled, slowed. Stopped.

FOR A LONG WHILE, THINGS WERE CONFUSED. As though he were watching everything through dark, rippled glass.

'I feel like I'm at the wrong end of a telescope.'

'It's the pills,' said Bell.

'Oh.'

Bell's voice had been the first, after the barking. Shouting. Refusing to let him sleep. Slapping him. Making him vomit.

And someone stroking his hair. Not Georgina. Not his mother. Belinda's voice. More vomiting.

None of them would let him sleep.

'Why is my throat so sore?'

'The stomach pump,' said Bell.

'Oh.'

* * *

Other voices. Doctors. Muffled. Echoing. He wasn't sure if they were dreams.

'What happened?' said Bell.

Edwin told him.

'Promise me you will never try that again.'

'I won't. It was worse than being at sea.'

'It's no joking matter.'

'I know.'

'They've declared you temporarily insane. So you can't be prosecuted for attempted suicide.'

'Oh.'

Pause.

'The Duchess sent a message. Will you see her?'

'No.'

'Did you tell my father?'

'No. Tom thought best not to.'

'Thank you.'

*They* – he wasn't sure who 'they' were and had no energy to find out – sent him to Hastings.

Air full of screeching birds and salt breezes.

More pills.

Back to London.

The newspapers printed gossip that he and Georgina were married.

It was cruel.

* * *

*They* sent him to a friend in the countryside.

Painful golden beauty. Eyes stung by harvest dust and sun lancing off hayricks.

More pills.

Back to London.

The newspapers printed gossip about the marriage plans going awry.

*They* tried to hide them, but he found one. Read one.

A lot more pills.

*They* talked about him not to him.

Bell said let's go abroad for a while. Get you away from all this.

Don't let him work, *they* said.

What do you mean don't let me work? I'll paint if I want to . . .

No more than enough to keep his hand in.

The Duchess has sent another message, should we tell him?

No. No. No.

He and Bell would go to Belgium, the Netherlands, Germany, Switzerland.

'You can tell the Queen you've been visiting your Dutch family,' Bell said.

Edwin laughed. But it was only a laugh on the outside.

'Am I still insane?'

'Oh no, you're much better now.'

# *June 1863, London*

THE LION STRETCHES IN THE shade of the mulberry tree. Edwin's eyes burrow into its fur, meticulously noting shape, form, texture. Lying on his stomach, he's as close as he dares, as though stalking a deer, but armed with a piece of board and a clutch of pastels rather than a rifle. His fingers tingle with excitement and he squirms a few inches nearer, squinting at the mats in the fur, the pile, the way the mane tumbles like a Highland waterfall – this is what he needs – this will bring the clay to life, metaphorically speaking. This will enable him to finish the small model.

He's so close. And he's on time. He can't remember the last time he was this punctual with anything. It makes him giddy with pride.

Marochetti has leased him one of the foundry studios. He's spent the past three months shut in there with his sketches, refusing entry to everyone except Angelo, the man who comes with his bucket and sponge to moisten the clay every hour, to keep it malleable, stop it drying and cracking. Each time the man leaves, Edwin moistens his own lips from the flask in his pocket. He's like the clay, he cannot risk drying out, cracking, breaking, but he will not allow himself to dissolve either. It's a fine balance, but it seems to be working. A year has passed and there's been no return of the *delirium tremens*.

Every night, they wrap the clay – which rests on a wooden platform like a body lying in state – in a shroud of damp towels and tarpaulins. Each morning, when they unwrap it with equal care, he feels like Victor Frankenstein gazing on his creation. And the sketch he's now making, lying on his belly in the mud in his garden, should allow him to finish and show this creation to the world, before beginning the task of scaling it up to three times the size of life.

At the sound of footsteps on gravel, the lion rolls onto its front, eyelids lowered but open.

'Lanny?' Louisa Abercorn's voice. The lion blinks. 'I know you're here. Your man says you're not at home, but I know you are to me . . . Oh! God in heaven!'

'Louisa!' Edwin drops the board and, with some difficulty, levers himself up and hobbles towards her, left leg numb from lying so long on the ground. But, like her mother, she's made of stern stuff, and has recomposed herself by the time he reaches her.

'Lanny! I thought you had been mauled.'

He grins, brushing off his smock. 'Don't worry, it's perfectly safe. I've borrowed him from the zoo – he's very old. And I can sketch him better here without all those people around.' The look of concern on her face doesn't shift, so he adds, 'He's chained to the mulberry tree, can't come beyond the roses.'

'But you were lying just there – wouldn't he have been able to reach you there?'

'Perhaps. I don't know. I'm counting on the smell of paint to put him off.'

'Good grief, Lanny.'

'The keeper's around somewhere. I think he went off for a smoke. Probably gossiping with Mrs Potter.' He kisses Louisa on the cheek. 'Will you have some tea? Or how about a drink to celebrate?' He grins again.

'Celebrate what?'

'The imminent completion of my small model.'

'Lanny, that's wonderful. I knew you could do it. When may we come and see?'

'It's only the small version – I say small, it's seven foot long – but I think I might really be able to do this. It just needs a few final touches; that's what this poor old boy's here for.'

Louisa squeezes his hand and smiles.

Leaving her safely out of range of the lion, which has gone to sleep, Edwin interrupts Mrs Potter's pipe-smoking session with the zoo keeper and tells her to bring champagne and cake. She brings tea. He sends her back for wine and rattles on to Louisa about the lion. Mrs Potter brings biscuits. Edwin gives up.

'I know I'm rambling,' he says, watching Mrs Potter flounce off. 'But it's such a relief. For so long it didn't work, and then . . . you know the lions on the gates at Woburn?'

'Yes,' she says, lifting her teacup.

'I dreamt of them and realised that's exactly the pose I needed: dignified, silent, indomitable. They always reminded me in an odd way of . . .' He stops, hadn't meant to ramble this much.

'Of what?'

'Of your father.'

'Oh. I never thought of Papa as a lion. He was so . . . well, bald.'

'I did say it was odd.'

'I'm so pleased to hear you sounding positive, Lanny.' She smiles, but puts her cup down too carefully and pauses too long for Edwin's liking. 'I'm afraid I come with sad news,' she says slowly. 'But also some hope.'

'Oh.' He drops his gaze, stares into his tea. 'Best get it over with then.'

Louisa's eyes are all sympathy. 'Rachel's daughter, little Georgina, died.'

The colour leeches out of the day. 'Not the baby?' He'd never even seen her.

'I'm afraid so.'

The trilling of the blackbirds is too shrill, the hooves from the road are unbearably loud, a fly buzzes menacingly close to his ear. He swats it and brushes away a tear. At least he doesn't have to pretend with Louisa.

'How?'

'A fever. It was mercifully sudden, which is some comfort.'

Edwin wants to shout that it isn't much comfort to him, but it clearly is to Louisa, so he swallows the pain with a swig from his flask.

'Send her my love. Not that she'll want it.' He raises the flask again.

But Louisa reaches out, takes the flask, and places it on the table. She takes his hands firmly in her own, saying, 'She might. It was a terrible blow and it brought back memories of Mama's death. And,' she squeezes his hands, 'Rachel says it has made her think of you.' Edwin's heart flutters. 'She asked me to tell you she has read your letter, and to thank you for it. She knows writing it can't have been easy. I've told her how sorry you are, how hard you're trying, how proud we are of what you're doing with the lions. She is thinking on it – on all you said – but asks you to understand how hard it is for her. Can you give her more time?'

Edwin glances at the flask on the table – he will keep fighting – then back to Louisa.

He nods, hope flickering in the pit of his stomach.

Later at Marochetti's studio there is such a tumult in Edwin's veins that he's barely able to hold his hand steady as he adds the final touches to the model. He tells himself that if it gets a good reception, Rachel will think better of him, that she will let him back into her life. If he can just keep things under control. He's managed to do so for a whole year – the only lions he's seen have been made of clay or from the zoo. He will continue to do so. He will.

He washes his hands, shaking so much he has to leave the wrapping to Angelo, then steps out into the cool air beneath the walnut trees in the yard. Taking several deep breaths, he sends a silent prayer up into the canopy of serrated leaves – for poor baby Georgina and for Rachel – then turns towards the stables, and hears a familiar voice as he rounds the corner.

Caro stands there, with Marochetti on one side, and a plump, pop-eyed man on the other. Edwin recognises him as Rossetti, remembers him twenty years before as a student at the Academy – an arrogant braggart whose ambition outstripped his appetite for actual work, not to say his talent. But he's one of Ruskin's cronies, and these days praise from Ruskin is worth the patronage of ten dukes. Edwin's heard rumours that Rossetti had wormed his way in with Caro. It's the first time he's seen her in months. Hasn't even had a letter. A year ago, he'd have been fuming to have bumped into her with Rossetti like this. Now, he finds himself surprisingly unmoved.

'Sir Edwin!' cries Marochetti, embracing him. 'You are not going to tell me you have finished him, are you?'

'Finished who?' says Caro, leaning forward to offer Edwin her cheek, then awkwardly pulling herself back as he makes no move to kiss it.

Rossetti grunts and fiddles with his voluminous maroon cravat.

Edwin's mouth curls into a grin in spite of everything. 'The lion,' he says. 'And I have.'

The Baron hugs him again. Caro's face breaks into the sort of smile it used to wear when they were first friends. Rossetti looks at his watch.

'We must celebrate. Lady Baring, Signor Rossetti, you will stay for a tiny glass of champagne? This is a moment of great historical significance – the first time I have not wanted to throttle Sir Edwin in four years!' He claps his hands and embraces Edwin a third time, then, seeing Caro's face, adds, 'Don't fret, Lady Baring, it is a joke.'

Marochetti shepherds them around the corner to his house on Onslow Square, where he proposes a toast. '*Salute!* To you, Sir Edwin, and the lions. Let us hope we shall not have to wait another five years for the large ones.' He raises an eyebrow.

'May we not see the model, Sir Edwin? Baron?' asks Caro.

'I'm afraid not,' says Edwin.

'Do not be offended, dear lady,' says Marochetti in a stage whisper. 'Nobody is allowed to see it. Not even I. But I will make sure you are one of the first when it is ready.' He winks. She blushes.

Rossetti tuts. 'Whenever that is.'

Edwin is about to snap back at him, but, seeing something too familiar in his bloodshot eyes and puffy cheeks, simply raises his glass and smiles.

The bubbles of the wine burst on his tongue. Some releasing surges of hope, others pangs of sadness.

When Edwin arrives home, the sun's still bright but the shadows are lengthening. Drained, he sinks onto the bench and lets the whispering of the wind in the leaves wash over him. He shouldn't have let Marochetti pour him a brandy after the champagne. But it was only one. And they were celebrating. Something rustles in the grass beneath the mulberry tree. He thinks it's the dogs and is about to call them over for some company, then sees they're both at his feet already. He's more tired than he realised. It's the lion – of course. It emerges from a shadow, and sits, licking its paws, more active than it's been all day.

'Evening, Ned!' He turns to see Tom, squinting at him in the setting sun. 'I was hoping you'd be back. I was wondering if you fancied a pipe and a pot of ale? Lindy's gossiping with her sister and says I'm surplus cargo.'

'I can't think of anything I'd like better,' Edwin says.

They talk, light pipes.

'Look at us,' Edwin says, trying to stretch the ache out of his spine. 'A pair of old men. Makes me feel like Father.'

'Could be worse,' says Tom.

'It could be.' Edwin puffs on his pipe, the sweet smoke wafts into the garden. 'Did Jessie say when the zoo people are coming to take the lion back?'

'They came and took it while you were at Marochetti's.'

'Oh.' The smoke sours in Edwin's mouth. 'Are you sure?' He coughs.

The lion stops licking its paws, stretches, and rises, then narrows its eyes at him.

'Yes,' says Tom, puffing away. 'Why? Did you still need it?'

'No,' Edwin says, dread pooling in his stomach.

The lion passes through the rose garden and pads on towards the studio. This one is not tethered. This one can't be tethered.

# *April 1841, Ramsgate*

RACHEL HAD WRITTEN, ASKING HIM TO COME. He would have stayed away otherwise.

Rough yellow sunlight fell on the beach and the cliffs, where splashes of gorse brightened the scrubby green. On the seafront, clutching their hats, Easter invalids sought renewed health among gulls' cries, clattering ropes, and flapping sails. Edwin hesitated at the door to the Albion Hotel, envying the ease with which his luggage had been taken inside. What kind of man envied his own luggage? What kind of man couldn't walk into a hotel without his heart pounding fit to burst? He was twisting a waistcoat button again – Bell would say stop it, that's how you lost all the buttons on your coat in Switzerland: leave it alone. But it was Bell who caught a chill and spent the next fortnight laid up with a rasping sore throat.

A young man in hotel livery leapt up the steps, carrying someone else's bag.

'Excuse me, sir, sorry, sir, let me hold the door for you, sir.'

That got him into a hallway painted with another yellow. Egg yolk. The smell of eggs too. Breakfast. He asked for the Duchess, fingers button-twisting again. Was it a terrible idea? It had been almost a year. Georgina had spent most of it in Nice. Rachel had written saying they were back, would be here. Would he come and stay? Saying Dr Woolryche thought it a capital idea.

The porter said the Duchess was in the salon.

Edwin's legs carried him past walls hung with prints. Seascapes, Turner mostly; a few of his own. It felt like the originals had been painted by another Edwin Landseer, one who was keeping him from bankruptcy now he couldn't face the easel. He'd told the Queen he would start painting again after Easter. It was now Easter, but he couldn't deal with that at the moment.

Fiddling with the waistcoat button again, he followed the swell of conversations, the chink of china cups.

There.

'Lanny!'

Rachel held out her cheek for a kiss as if nothing had happened. He took the deepest breath he had ever taken, smiled like the other Edwin Landseer, and said, 'Dormouse'.

She beamed. She chattered. She told him about her tutors, about their winter in France, how sorry she was he hadn't come to see them.

'We missed you,' she said. 'I had no one to bore with my stories, and I've written two more. Mama fell asleep when I tried reading them to her.' Her eyes flicked towards Georgina, who had yet to speak. Edwin fixed his gaze on a print of Lawrence's portrait of Wellington. 'And Georgy spent all her time talking to Mr Romilly.'

'I'd love to hear the stories now,' Edwin said. 'If you have them here?'

'I was hoping you'd say that. They're in our rooms. I'll be back before you know it. I'll bring the sketches I did too.'

He watched her go. A young woman now, so little of the child left.

'Lanny . . .' Georgina reached across the table.

'Don't.' He folded his arms and stared at Wellington. 'I came for her not you.'

'But . . . it breaks my heart to see you like this.'

'Like what?'

'You're so thin. And your hair . . . it's so grey.'

'So is yours.'

Edwin called over the waiter, ordered a glass of wine, and stared silently at Wellington's hat until it arrived.

That night, after Rachel had gone to bed, he reluctantly agreed to walk along the seafront with Georgina. The water, sludgy green in daylight, was now silky black. It lapped at the boarded hulls of boats and the stone blocks that formed the quay, along the top of which cats crouched hopefully by piles of cargo.

'How much does she know?' Edwin asked as they paused, gazing out at the long dark arm of the pier.

'Only that you were very ill,' Georgina said. 'I told her it was a brain fever. Brought on by overwork.'

'That was kind of you.' He glowered at her. 'And the . . .' he swallowed, 'the wedding?'

'Nothing. I keep any newspapers that contain anything she shouldn't see away from her. And we live so very quietly these days.'

They walked a little further. She tried to link her arm through his. Silent rage boiling up inside him, Edwin turned on his heel, said he was tired and needed to go back.

During the days, Edwin sketched – donkeys, horses, fishermen – but was unable to concentrate for long before his head got out of order. It was like the first time he looked through a telescope: unable to find what he was looking for, black closing in around the edges. The slightest nudge sent everything pitching out of control. So he would sit and smoke a pipe, watching waves curling onto the sand, and ships, clunking and creaking, penned behind the grey harbour walls. And there were always gulls, wheeling, circling, screaming.

*We know what you tried to do. What you did to your family, your friends – just because you didn't get your way. Still throwing tantrums like a child.*

In the evenings, Rachel read to him, and sang and played the piano while Georgina turned the pages of her music. Edwin wished he could snap back to the way things used to be. But something in him was still broken.

On the third night, he woke from a nightmare, heart hammering, breath coming in gasps. Georgina was sitting on the edge of his bed in nightgown and shawl, repeating his name softly, stroking his hair.

'I'm sorry,' she whispered, her hand resting on his shoulder. 'Your room wasn't locked. You were screaming. I couldn't leave you like that. And you were liable to wake the whole hotel.'

Saying nothing, heart still pounding, he turned away, shaking off her hand.

It happened again two nights later. This time, though he still turned away, he clutched at her hand. 'Help me. I don't want to be like this. I don't want to be ill again.'

She gripped his hand back, so warm, so real, her voice cracking as she said, 'I will always help you.'

He wanted nothing more than to turn to her, to let her make it all right. But couldn't.

He began painting again. The Queen insisted. Or said her dogs insisted, which amounted to the same thing.

'We don't wish to put you under any undue strain,' she said, looking into the eyes of a hairy Skye terrier named Islay (the Queen herself still resembled a toy spaniel, albeit a fuller figured version than previously). 'But we read some unpleasing things in the papers saying you will never paint again and . . . well . . . we wish to show you we still believe in you. And,' she went on with a regal sniff, 'we know that Dash would have felt the same way if . . . if he were still with us.'

Edwin was so touched that he was still trying to think of an appropriate reply when she added, 'And of course, you're still working on my equestrian portrait, and the double portrait with Albert too. Islay and I were thinking we ought to enlarge that one to include Baby now. What do you think?'

Saying what he actually thought would have led to arrest and immediate incarceration, not just as a lunatic, but as a dangerous lunatic, so Edwin said it sounded like a capital idea.

'And,' she said, looking at him directly for once, 'might you paint a little something for Albert's birthday? As a surprise?'

Like a fool, he said yes. 'When is the birthday, ma'am?'

'Oh, not for a few weeks.'

It started well enough. There were times when the old ability to effortlessly conjure depth, form, and texture seemed to have returned, but these were interspersed with days of restless procrastination at best, crippling panic at worst. On bad days, everything he touched looked distorted, sketchy, amateurish.

The day before Albert's birthday, the August air was clogged with harvest dust from the fields to the north and building dirt from the new terraces taking shape to the west, intensifying

Edwin's sense of stifling horror. The picture – which he should have delivered to Victoria the day before – still sat on its easel, looking flat and monotonous. In a panic, he'd taken a palette knife and was scraping out a large section of the background when Bell let himself in.

'Stop, stop, stop!' he shouted, seizing Edwin's wrist. 'Leave it!'

'It won't do. It's no good!' Edwin tried to shake him off.

'It is good.' Bell eased the knife from his hand and gripped him by the shoulders. 'It is.'

'It's not. It's awful. Whenever I touch it, it makes it worse—'

'Don't think about it. Just paint. And don't scratch it out.'

'I need a drink.'

'No you don't. I'll have Lucy make some coffee.'

'What if I can't do it?' Edwin drew in a shaky breath.

'You can. You trust me, don't you?'

Terrified, Edwin nodded.

'Well, I say you can do it. So you can.' Bell placed a brush in his hand and held his fingers closed until he gripped it.

The Queen sent a servant to collect the overdue picture two hours before midnight.

Bell and Lucy Potter stalled him in the kitchen with tobacco and beer until two hours past midnight, when Edwin appeared with the painting, finished.

'It's still a bit wet in places,' he said, handing it over and pushing a shaking hand through his hair. 'I . . . I've attached a board to protect the paint, b-but be very careful.'

'See?' Bell smiled, putting an arm around Edwin's shoulders as the crunch of royal carriage wheels retreated into the stuffy night air. 'You can work quickly when you really want to.'

* * *

The following week, Edwin was back at Windsor for a sitting for the double portrait. Alone with the Queen, he attempted to apologise for the lateness of Albert's birthday picture, and before he knew it, found himself crying and unable to stop. The Queen, who'd been sitting on a sofa with Islay, rose with a rustle of ivory silk, dismissed the footman, and shut the door.

'Please, Mr Landseer, sit down.' She patted the sofa next to her voluminous skirts.

'I'm sorry, ma'am – it's ridiculous . . .' Edwin said, roughly wiping his eyes and trying to swallow his humiliation. 'The gossips are right. I can't do anything any more.'

'You mustn't listen to gossip, Mr Landseer,' the Queen said, placing a terrier next to him on the sofa. 'I have every faith in you or I wouldn't ask you to paint for me. People are mesmerised by tales of misfortune. Why else would the newspapers print them? And the promise of more tragedy makes a story even more compelling, even if there's not an ounce of truth in it. How could those people writing those tiny words know more about your health or your art than you do? I've admired – no, I've adored – your work since I was a girl. I have wanted to paint like you ever since I was able to hold a brush. I don't believe for a moment that a gift like yours could be gone. The gossips will forget their predictions of doom if you show them the talent is still there.'

'What if it isn't? What if I can't do it?' He couldn't look up, no matter how wretched he must seem. He'd felt fine when he walked into the room. How had he been reduced to this sobbing mess, and in front of the Queen?

'Mr Landseer, I know I'm young, but I have learnt much these past few years. And I have felt the way you do now. You should see me when *I* really cry.' She gave an embarrassed laugh, adjusting a bunch of pink peonies pinned to her bosom. 'I have felt I have no right to be here – on the throne – though I was born to be Queen as much as you were born to paint. And I've felt the lash of harsh tongues. I've also felt too afraid of failure to go on. But I've learnt that, at such times, I cannot trust the image of myself offered by my own eyes, so I must trust the eyes of others. When I look into my glass, I often see a scared little girl,' another embarrassed laugh, 'but when I look at myself reflected in Baby's eyes, I see an adored mother; in Albert's eyes, I see a beloved wife; and in the eyes of my people, I see a queen.'

Edwin felt even more contemptible. What must he look like now? Pitiful. Pathetic. No wonder Georgina didn't think him fit to be a father.

'And,' the Queen said very softly, 'when I find myself in the darkest of places, I look into the eyes of my dogs.'

Islay shuffled up to him on the sofa. Trying to swallow, Edwin ruffled the thick copper fur at the back of her neck. She rolled on to her back and he scratched her stomach, more tears rolling down his cheeks.

The Queen handed him a handkerchief.

Eventually he managed to say, 'Thank you, ma'am.'

'I'm sure a rest would do you good, dear Landseer. Help you regain strength. You are going to Scotland soon, aren't you? I wish we could go with you. I've wanted to see the Highlands since I was a little girl. Is it really as beautiful as in your pictures?'

'More beautiful, ma'am.' Edwin sniffed, trying not to think of Glenfeshie.

'We plan to visit next year, provided I am unencumbered by . . . ahem.' She cleared her throat and placed a hand on her swollen belly. 'Will you promise to meet us there and sketch with me?'

Edwin nodded.

'You are going with Lord Abercorn, I think?'

Edwin nodded again.

'Will you be visiting the Dowager Duchess of Bedford?'

Edwin shook his head, keeping his eyes firmly fixed on the dog.

'Maybe you will be deerstalking?' the Queen said hastily. 'Albert has been talking to Lord Abercorn incessantly about it. It sounds thrilling but so tragic.'

'At times, it is, ma'am. It's sublime and terrible . . .' He groped for words, failed to find any, shrugged. 'I can't describe it, ma'am, but I feel compelled to paint it. And I would rather be a stag living and dying amid the glory of the Highlands than anything else.'

'I can believe that, Mr Landseer,' said the Queen, looking into Islay's eyes again. 'But I can't help thinking how amusing it is that you, coming from such a flat country, take such delight in the mountains.'

'Ah, well, ma'am,' Edwin said, awkwardly. 'I'm not actually Dutch. I'm from north London.'

'But Lehzen told me ... we've thought for years ...' The Queen's normally pale oval face flushed the same shade as the peonies in her corsage and she began to giggle. 'All those little Dutch pancakes I ordered the kitchens to make ...'

Edwin laughed more than he had in a long time.

# *April 1864, Windsor*

THE SCREECH OF THE TRAIN whistle coincides with a blast of menthol to the roof of Edwin's mouth, making his ears ring and eyes water. It's a damned awkward time for the Queen to have demanded their first meeting in years, but he can't make excuses indefinitely. He just has to hope the lion will survive without him.

Bringing it to life is a precarious balancing act: the larger clay is exponentially more demanding than the small model. It would be like looking after a living creature, if it weren't so cold: Edwin strokes its hide, teases out tangles in its mane, massages its muscles into existence. All the while, Angelo is there with his bucket and his sponge, mopping, feeding it, stopping it drying out. And when Angelo isn't looking, one of Edwin's flasks is pressed into service. Just enough to stop the cracks widening, so he can bring this beast to life, but not so much that he gives the Other Lion control – the one he sees in every mirror, every window, every bottle. Sometimes he misjudges.

And now he's agreed to see the Queen again, for the first time in ... how long? It's more than two years since Albert died, so it must be, what, four since he's seen her? He fumbles with the tin in his pocket, manages to extract a single breath pastille without spilling the others, slips it into his mouth. Another blast of menthol. His thumb catches the black-bordered letter received that morning from Caro, thanking him for his sympathy following Baring's death. The poor old badger is gone – a blessed relief for him in the end, and for Caro. It's a good letter. No pretence. No expectation. Just friendship.

Rachel still hasn't replied. But he won't give up. Not until he's finished the lions.

'She won't care. She'll still hate you,' says the Other Lion, rippling across the grimy window of the railway carriage.

'Shut up,' Edwin says, slipping another pastille into his mouth as the train hisses and jolts, drawing up to the platform at Windsor. It reeks, but it's better than the smell of brandy.

The Queen's sitting room is so filled with floral patterns he's surprised it isn't giving him hay fever. He bows and braces himself, ready with excuses for unfinished works, for refusing to come to the palace. Lions and my health, lions and my health. Like a parrot. She's always liked parrots.

But when she appears, in black silk that's so sad and striking against the riot of chintz, she doesn't berate him; she smiles her pop-eyed smile and says, 'Sir Edwin, it really is most pleasing to see you.'

The parrot doesn't have an answer ready for that, but the Queen doesn't wait for one. She babbles as much as the first time they met, finally finishing with a blush that reaches the roots of her hair, which has lost only a little of its sheen and is still a deep brown, 'Will you have a drink, Sir Edwin? I-I usually have a little something at this time.'

He almost laughs. She's as nervous as he is. A footman enters with a tray, followed by a tall, kilted Highlander with striking blue eyes, who directs him to put it down next to the Queen, then tuts loudly when the bottles clink together. A dachshund waddles into the room behind them, looking confused. Edwin knows how it feels.

The Queen clears her throat. 'I know you are fond of whisky, Sir Edwin, but h-have you ever tried it with claret?'

'In the same glass?' He's so shocked he almost forgets to add 'ma'am'.

'Yes.' Her full, slightly fishy lips stretch into a smile. 'I find whisky on its own a little harsh, but Brown swears by it for the constitution.' Her eyes flit up to the tall Scotsman, then back to Edwin. 'You know Brown?'

'Yes.' Of course he knows Brown. Everybody knows John Brown. Edwin's known him longer than most. He wasn't keen on the blue-eyed Scot when he was an obsequious pony boy to Albert, and – from what he's heard – he suspects he won't like him any better now he's become the personal servant of the Queen.

Brown's lip curls, but not in a smile. '*Sir* Edwin.'

The Queen continues, 'Dear Brown suggested mixing the whisky with wine. He often takes it that way.'

I'll bet he does, thinks Edwin.

Brown smiles coldly and hands him a glass. Edwin smiles back, just as coldly, and sips: deuced odd, but he's had worse.

'Isn't it delicious?' says the Queen, smiling at the Highlander. 'Thank you, dear Brown, that will be all for now.'

As Brown stalks out, she takes another slug and says, 'Albert hated it, of course, but he was so very particular. Is it odd that

I often find myself crying because he's not here to disapprove of things like this now?'

'Not in the slightest, ma'am,' says Edwin, relaxing as Brown's mixture begins to blend with the brandy that kept him company on the train. It's actually surprisingly pleasant. And strong. Strong enough for them to be talking like old friends before many minutes have passed.

He'd forgotten what a surprising person she is. And still young, in spite of the widowhood in which she hides herself. About the age Georgina was when Rachel was born. And when she talks about the Highlands with Albert, her eyes brighten and her cheeks glow.

Then she says, 'We went to your huts. Did James Abercorn tell you?'

In the past year, since the last period of illness, since Rachel has still not made contact, he has refused to think of the huts. He can't watch those bubbles burst all over again. He can't think of them now. 'Did you hear the Abercorns have another grandchild?' he says, but the Queen is looking dreamily into her glass and is not to be diverted.

'Such a setting,' she says. 'Beautiful, sublime . . . And the deer you painted on the walls . . . but the buildings are falling down and the paintings are fading. I said to Albert I wished we could have rescued them – taken them to Balmoral. The best I could do was attempt to copy them. Of course, they're only poor copies, but . . . would you care to see them?'

Edwin's heart is in his mouth. There's nothing he'd rather see but nothing terrifies him more.

'Sir Edwin?'

He downs the rest of the mixture. 'Yes, ma'am.'

He'll pay for it later but damn that. And the Queen's almost certainly going to show him whatever he says.

She places a leather-bound sketchbook next to him and opens it at a page marked with a tartan ribbon. Having refilled both their glasses, she joins him on the sofa.

'The weather was against us. We only had a short time, but I couldn't help trying to place all the things in your stories – the balls, the fishing, the goats.' She smiles.

Perhaps it's the fault of Brown's mixture, but, as his eyes trace her pencil lines, Edwin finds himself repeating the stories, feeling the place once more. And she joins in with her own, of Albert and the children. By the time Brown re-enters – without knocking – both their faces are smiling and tear-stained.

An hour later, Edwin is on the train back to London, laughing to himself as he spills the entire tin of breath pastilles on the compartment floor, swearing he will never drink John Brown's mixture again. Memories of the glen still shimmer before his eyes. He was a fool to avoid the Queen for so long. He feels a stab of guilt at the thought of the unfinished Balmoral boat picture. The telescope view jerks and spoils. A chill rises up to his neck. What if he never finishes it? What if he's no longer capable? What if he's not in control at all . . . Instinctively he unscrews and upends his flask, though his head's still thick with whisky and wine. It's too loud, too dark. He needs to see out, can't breathe, but the window's dirty and stuck and – suddenly – black. Smoke and screeching darkness and ticketytock ticketytock.

Then they're out. The light is back. A tunnel. Just a tunnel. He can breathe again.

Then he remembers that he agreed to do some sketches of Brown for the Queen and curses the mix of wine and whisky to hell and back.

# *1841 to 1842*

EDWIN SPENT AUTUMN IN SCOTLAND with Abercorn. Wind, rain, and mountains brought life tingling back to his body and mind in ways no amount of English seaside quackery ever could. The glass through which he seemed to see the world grew clearer. Sometimes, watching the deer, fingers clutching ropes of old heather, lungs filling with the glistening scent of peat and bog myrtle, it was so clear he could almost forget it was there. But it clouded again when he thought of Georgina. He did not go to The Doune.

The Highland clarity remained, more or less, until spring, when it was disturbed by ripples of anxiety over submitting his first pictures for the Exhibition in two years.

'Don't be ridiculous,' William said, as they sat in the smoking room at the Athenaeum. 'You're sending in a portrait of my dog. And your Loch Maree picture is accompanied by one of my poems. You can't fail.'

Georgina had been ordered abroad by her doctors for the winter after a chest infection, and her absence on an extended visit to Nice had made it easier to keep an even keel. Rachel wrote to him frequently, signing herself Dormouse. Among other French adventures, she described her sister Georgy's wedding to Mr Romilly, joking that her mother must have taken leave of her senses since Romilly didn't have any title at all and his father was only a baronet. Superscribed crossways next to this was a comment that '*Mama instructs me to say she is more rational than ever and wishes you to know she is now of the mind that love is more important than what Society thinks (which only confirms me in my former suspicions that she is mad)*'. Georgina herself did not write, but Edwin sensed her behind Rachel's pen on several occasions.

There had also been another Landseer wedding: Emma, Edwin's youngest sister, married an Edinburgh-born doctor named Mackenzie and went with him to take up an appointment in Jersey. By sibling consensus (Dr Mackenzie had little say in the matter), Emma invited John Landseer to accompany them in the hope that a change of scene might alleviate the melancholy that had enveloped him since their mother's death and Edwin's illness.

At the same time, Bell suggested Jessie should come to live with Edwin.

'Think how useful it would be for her to keep house for you,' he said. 'Cheaper than paying a stranger. It'd be good for her painting, and she could help with the books and keep an eye on things in the studio too.'

'Keep an eye on me, you mean,' said Edwin.

'She'd be good company.' Bell shrugged, coughing. The throat infection that cut short their tour of Germany two years ago had never really left him.

'Have you seen someone about that cough?' Edwin said.

'Yes. And I have Hills worrying over me like a nanny goat. I don't need you bleating as well. Don't change the subject.'

Bell was right, as usual. It was good to have Jessie around, especially now he was working again – the Queen was keeping him extremely busy and was still delighted with him, so delighted that in May she offered him a knighthood.

In June, Georgina, who'd been back a month without contacting him, invited Edwin to Campden Hill to celebrate Rachel's birthday. Driving his gig past a row of new villas and through Georgina's gates, he found his hands shaking. How on earth had he become a forty-year-old man with a sixteen-year-old daughter?

'Lanny!' The sixteen-year-old daughter waved a lace-gloved hand. She was looking alarmingly like a grown woman but ran across the lawn with the eagerness of a child. 'Come and have some strawberries. Mama didn't think you'd come but I saved you some anyway.'

'I'm sorry I'm late. The Queen kept me – I'm painting her and Albert in fancy dress and she keeps getting the giggles.' He kissed her on both cheeks, realising with a lurch that she was nearly as tall as him. 'Happy birthday.'

She took his arm and walked him across the grass. 'So, what were they dressed as?'

'Who?' He was more affected by seeing her again than he'd expected.

'The Queen and her consorting prince, silly.'

'Well, they look like a pair of playing cards, though the Queen insists they're meant to be medieval monarchs. But I came here to pay homage to your advanced age, not talk about them. How is being old? Has your mother lined up a host of suitors for you?'

'Goodness me, no! What a question.' Rachel laughed, squeezing Edwin's arm and sending a lump into his throat. 'I couldn't think of anything duller than suitors for me. But we hear all sorts of things about you – always at balls, the Queen's favourite . . .' Her grin turned into a pout. 'And you never come to see us any more. Have you dropped us? Are you courting some mysterious beauty?'

They'd reached the tent in the middle of the lawn, where food and drink were laid out on a long flower-strewn table, next to which Georgina stood talking to William, watching them with wary, deer-like eyes.

'Only the Princess Royal.' Edwin fixed his gaze firmly on Rachel. 'And she's only just toddling. The love of my life is currently Luna. She's just had another litter, so I'm too busy with puppies to think about people.'

'Oh, lovely Luna. You must let me come and see her babies.'

Instinctively, Edwin glanced at Georgina, then wished he hadn't. William was talking airily about something, but she looked as though she was about to cry. His stomach tightened.

'Let's ask your mother.' It wasn't hard to catch her eye. 'G—Duchess . . . Your Grace.' He bit his lip. 'Would you object if Rachel came to see Luna's latest litter?' On the spur of the moment, he added, 'And chose a puppy for herself as a birthday present?'

'Lanny, really?' squeaked Rachel, definitely more dormouse than young lady.

'Of course really, provided your mother doesn't mind.'

'Why should I mind?' Georgina said, blinking rapidly and sniffing.

Edwin looked back to Rachel. 'I'm being dragged back to the palace tomorrow, but Jessie will be delighted to show them to you.'

Georgina pressed her lips together and wiped a hand across her cheek. Edwin swallowed hard. She had no right to be upset. It was all her fault. But, unable to ignore the pang of compassion twisting his stomach, he met her eyes and said, 'Or I'm sure I could put the Queen off this once if you'd like to come tomorrow – both of you?'

Georgina wiped her other cheek. With an almost imperceptible quiver in her voice, she said, 'Thank you, Lanny. That's extremely kind of you. Is your Royal Mistress well?'

'All whim and fancy, as usual,' he said, holding her gaze, determined to sound nonchalant. 'She complains to the dogs that I haven't painted Albert handsome enough, but mostly fusses about their trip to Scotland. Keeps asking me about midges and what sort of boots and bonnets she ought to bring, should she have Albert wear a kilt, and all manner of other nonsense.'

'Will you be going with them?' Georgina swallowed.

'No.' Edwin accepted a cup of tea from Rachel, holding it firmly in its saucer to stop any telltale rattling. 'I'm not grand enough or good enough at standing around looking serious.'

'Then come to us at The Doune.' Georgina flushed, quickly adding, 'If you have no other engagements.'

'Oh do!' Rachel said. 'The glen doesn't feel right without you. We've missed you since . . . since you were ill. Now you're better, you must come. I won't take no for an answer.'

'Please.' Georgina's voice quivered again.

The lump was back in Edwin's throat. He looked from Rachel's eager face to Georgina's melancholy one. An excuse was on the tip of his tongue, when Rachel placed her hands on her hips and said, 'It's my birthday, so you have to do as I say.'

Georgina shrugged and bit her lip.

Edwin agreed to go.

Perhaps he'd done something in a past life to anger an ancient god of travel plans. Edwin's train had reached Lancaster, but his luggage hadn't. Worse, he'd panicked and snapped at Claridge the valet to stay behind with Luna until the baggage turned up, while he continued by coach to Edinburgh. Now he had nothing but his own thoughts for company, too many of which were of Georgina. He wasn't going to let her break him again.

The sun had long set by the time the coach rumbled into Edinburgh, but the sky was eerily lit from below. People filled the streets, singing, shouting, gathered like moths around bonfires, because the Queen's yacht had arrived and was lying at anchor in Leith. Edwin passed unheeded through the smoke and songs and sounds of bottles clinking. Finally, he reached the inn from which the Inverness coach was scheduled to depart at dawn, bought a tankard of beer and waited, wishing he knew what to do, and that he hadn't left the dog behind.

It was almost evening by the time he reached the road approaching The Doune. Curving with the contours of the valley, it was as picturesque as ever. When the pony, who had valiantly pulled the cart for the final leg of the journey, turned in at the iron gates, Edwin couldn't help leaning forward to catch a glimpse of the pale stone house in the late afternoon light. In the stable yard, the sound of the trees murmuring over the river mingled with whistling from the larder and women chattering in the kitchen garden, but none of them was Rachel. Or Georgina.

'Mr Landseer!' The housekeeper bustled out of the laundry. 'Good to see you again, sir. It's been two years?'

'Three,' Edwin said, masking a stab of anxiety with a smile. His heart began to beat faster. 'Where is everyone?' He would have expected to see some of them on the lawn at least with the weather this fine.

'They're up the glen, gone to the huts.'

'Oh.' Disappointment washed away the tension that had kept tiredness at bay. He suddenly felt ready to collapse. 'Did they say when they'd be back?'

'They only went yesterday, so I'd guess not until tomorrow, maybe the end of the week? You know what Her Grace is like.'

All too well. 'Did she leave any message?'

'I don't think so. But they left a pony, and there's the cart with Willie, so you can join them tomorrow, I'm sure. It's a wee bit late to start now.'

Edwin walked like a ghost through the empty house, stepping softly past shadows and between dancing dust motes. With no sounds of occupation to mask them, it was as though he could hear every creak and shift of floorboards and shutters – and of the past.

There was a fire in the drawing room, though there was only the faintest hint of a chill in the air. Edwin poured himself a whisky, took it onto the lawn, and looked out towards the glen. Having seemed so desperate for him to come, Georgina might have waited, or at least left a message. Damn her.

The whisky mingled with tiredness and his annoyance mellowed. At least he didn't have to deal with his feelings immediately, and there was a soothing calm to being alone in the house with its memories.

He followed an echo of his younger self across the bright grass down to the river, passing the places where the Russell children used to play and the spot where the Duke used to sit with his straw hat, blanket, and champagne. Clouds of midges coalesced into living shadows. The river babbled, birds swooped.

After a solitary dinner spent watching a crescent moon rise in a sky tinged red with beacons to mark the Queen's visit, Edwin took a candle, another whisky, and a volume of Scott's poetry and sat by the fire. The familiar words rose from the page but few managed to slip beneath his eyelids before they drooped and closed. The fire muttered softly and sent sweet blue smoke swirling among images of Scott's deer and damsels.

The book was still in his hand when a draught made him stir and open his eyes just enough to see the candle had burned to a stump. Sinking back into a half-sleep, he shifted again as the scent of roses mixed with the smoke and an all-too-familiar dream began to play out: roses, and the warm, soft press of a kiss on his forehead. It was painfully real, but that dream was always painfully real, as was the desolation he always felt on waking to find himself alone. Clutching the book, he willed the dream to continue.

Georgina cleared her throat.

Edwin opened his eyes.

She stood in front of him, drinking the remains of his whisky.

'I thought you were in the glen . . .' He blinked away layers of drowsiness, still not sure he wasn't dreaming. In spite of everything he'd promised himself, his heart leapt.

'I was, but I couldn't neglect my duties as a hostess. I meant to come back this morning, but Alexander commandeered all the damned ponies for some madcap stalking expedition before I was awake, so I couldn't set off until they came back.'

'You should have waited until morning. I would have been fine. You must have ridden the whole way in the dark.'

'Nonsense. There's a moon.'

'A very small one.'

'Since when were you a lunar expert? It's bright enough. There are stars and Mr Collie had a lantern. And the fires of hell are burning all around thanks to your little Queen.' She upended the glass again and glared at it for being empty. Against express instructions he'd given it earlier, Edwin's face cracked into a smile.

'It must have been quite something.' He pushed himself up out of the chair and fetched the bottle.

'It was,' she said, as the gold-tinged liquid glugged into the glass. 'A little infernal, but only a little. Come out and look.'

Edwin found a second glass and filled it for himself before following her onto the terrace.

They watched the fires for a while, then she turned to him, a dark silhouette against the red-rimmed sky, and said, 'I was expecting to have to call you Sir Lanny. Why did you refuse the knighthood?'

'How did you hear about that? I only told William.'

'He arrived with all the little William Russells a week ago. I bribed him with a cigar to tell me how you were. He said you were an idiot to turn it down and I agree.'

'It's my business. Not his.' Edwin drank. 'Or yours.'

Georgina took a mouthful of her own whisky before replying. 'I only speak as a friend. William said you didn't think you deserved it. I want you to know that – as far as I'm concerned – you deserve it a thousand times over.'

'She only offered it to me because I paint her damned dogs and parrots – that's hardly great art, is it?'

'That's not why she offered it to you at all—' Georgina laid a hand on his arm.

'What the hell would you know about it?' Edwin snapped, stepping backwards.

Georgina withdrew her hand, placing it firmly on her hip. 'I know how hard you work, how beautifully you paint, what your pictures mean to—'

'You don't understand.' Edwin turned to go back inside, but Georgina caught his arm again.

'Well, tell me then,' she said, resisting his attempt to shake her off.

Edwin took a deep breath and looked to the heavens. He could kill William for telling her about this. Closing his eyes, he said softly, 'How could I go around calling myself Sir Edwin when I'm behind on so many commissions? When there are days my head is so out of order I can't even get out of bed, let alone hold a brush? All I'm fit for is pet portraits.'

'That's not true,' Georgina said, sliding her hand over his. 'If this is because of what happened between us . . . then I'm sorry. More sorry than you can ever know. But you are good enough. You always have been and you always will be. Your animals make people *feel*. They hit us in the heart in a way that words – and humans – rarely can. And if you can't see that at the moment, then take my word for it. Take William's word, or the Queen's . . . listen to your friends. And I will always be your friend, whether you like it or not.' She downed the last of her whisky and glared at him, a muscle twitching in her jaw.

'You sound just like the Queen,' Edwin said, reluctantly removing his hand from hers, but meeting her gaze and holding it.

'In that case, she has more sense than I thought,' said Georgina, her eyes not leaving his. 'But, Lanny, if I ever hear you say you're just a pet painter again, I shall … I shall box your ears. Not that painting pets is anything to be ashamed of. What would Luna say if she heard you talking like that? And where is she? I thought you were bringing her?'

Edwin sighed, then told the story of the luggage disaster.

'"The best laid schemes o' mice an' men",' Georgina smiled. 'My mother was a great friend of Burns, you know. She used to boast about having kissed him. But—'

'A kiss doesn't signify,' they both said at the same moment, eyes locking as the Queen's fires made the sky blush above them.

# *1844, London*

TIME SLIPPED AROUND HIM AS though he was standing on a rock in the middle of a river: sometimes it trickled, sometimes it raged. Usually, Edwin's head was clear, but there were moments when the mist gathered. On bad days it was a stifling fog. Things became unmoored, all sense of perspective gone. Jessie and Bell were his anchors and kept him from being swept away.

The Queen continued to demand pictures of pets and children, and stories of the Highlands. Edwin fell back into old grooves: clubs, dinners, and country houses, balls, and boxes at the theatre. Visits to Campden Hill also resumed. Edwin assured Bell there was no danger in renewed friendship. Only the dogs were privy to his raving soliloquies about how much he wanted Georgina back.

Detained at the palace again, Edwin arrived late at the last of a series of celebrations for Rachel's eighteenth birthday. The creamy canvas of a marquee glowed in the afternoon sun in the garden at Campden Hill. Next to it, the pale hide of a milch cow gleamed almost as brightly. The face of the dairy maid next to her was a hard-working red as she dispensed fresh milk to young fashionables, who were as brightly dressed as the flowers blurring in the background.

'I can't believe you actually brought in a cow,' Edwin laughed, watching with Georgina from the shade of the terrace.

'I said I would, so I did.' She fanned herself, almost as red in the face as the dairy maid. 'But if I ever say I'm holding four garden parties in a month again, lock me up until I've regained my senses.' She leant on the balustrade and closed her eyes.

'Are you all right?'

'Yes, yes, it's just . . . I think I might go inside and sit for a minute.'

He took her arm, alarmed by how heavily she leant on him, and led her to the morning room, which was cool and dark at this hour of the afternoon.

'Don't lie me down, I'm not an invalid,' she muttered, as he steered her towards a chaise longue, but, ominously, she didn't offer any physical resistance, adding, 'I'm just too old for this.'

'No, you're not,' Edwin said, perching next to her.

'I'm almost sixty-three.' She covered her eyes with a hand, her breathing heavy enough to be heard over the marble clock striking three.

'That's nothing,' Edwin said, hiding a mounting sense of concern. 'But promise not to get any older while I fetch you some water. Is Woolryche here?'

'Wait.' She gripped his hand. 'I'd rather whisky. And no doctor. Woolryche won't tell me anything new. The winter in Nice helped my chest a little, but it can't stop me getting older.

I'm not planning on shuffling off yet, but I must be realistic.' She pushed herself up into a sitting position, ignoring his protests. 'I might not be here to see Rachel married.'

'Nonsense.' His own chest tightened.

'It's not nonsense. And I know I promised to tell her that you're her father after she was married. Once she was established.'

'We don't need to talk about this now.' Old worms began to writhe in his stomach.

'We do. I've been putting it off for months, but I need to tell you. I fully intend to be around to honour that promise, don't mistake me, but . . . you know how schemes have a habit of going astray. I've written a letter. It's with my will. If you wish to tell her, the letter will confirm my side of it – if I'm not around to swear to it in person.'

'That's ridiculous. You will be around.' He gripped her hand. 'And what if someone finds it?'

'Just in case,' she said. 'I promise to burn it the minute she's married. If I'm still here.'

'Don't be so melodramatic. Burn it. Burn it now.'

'Now who's being melodramatic?'

'Georgina.' Edwin squeezed her hand, hard. 'I appreciate the gesture, deranged as it is, but please burn it.' Her breathing was almost back to normal, but still not right. 'Will you allow me to get the doctor now?'

'No.' She sat up fully and coughed. 'I've seen enough of them. They all say the same: a weak chest – winter in the sun and lose weight. Hmph. You may fetch me some milk though. I only have that cow for a few more days and I intend to make the most of her.'

'Only if you promise to burn that letter,' Edwin said, blinking to dispel the mist that was seeping in around the edges of his vision.

'If I must.' She coughed again, glaring at him. 'Now, milk please, Nurse Landseer.'

A month after Rachel's eighteenth birthday, the three of them were dining at Campden Hill. Rachel told Georgina off for packing too much for their imminent trip to Nice. Georgina retaliated by saying Rachel was bringing too little – what if they were invited to this villa or that villa? Both demanded support from him. He'd drunk more than usual, trying to muffle thoughts of them being away . . . then there was a blank.

He remembered darkness. Someone saying send for a doctor. Blind panic – had something happened to Georgina? To Rachel?

Then more voices: 'It's Landseer, the painter, isn't it? Mr Landseer, can you hear us? Goodness, there is a lot of blood. One of you fellows go for a surgeon, will you? And someone catch that horse!'

Then nothing until waking up in the blue bedroom at Campden Hill, the curtains billowing gently, revealing glimpses of warm grey clouds and a climbing pink rose nodding and tapping at the open window.

His head hurt.

At the sound of the door handle, he turned. A searing pain lanced backwards from his right temple.

'You're awake,' Georgina whispered, her brow furrowed with concern. 'How are you feeling?'

'Like someone's pushed a red-hot poker into my brain. What am I doing here?'

'You've asked that a hundred times.' She sat on the edge of the bed, lines of concern deepening.

He reached up to the spot from which the pain radiated and winced, discovering bruises and bandages.

'You fell off your horse and landed on your head. The doctor said you had a severe concussion and needed absolute quiet, so I volunteered to turn this place into a field hospital.'

'She didn't volunteer – she practically kidnapped you,' said Rachel, slipping in through the door. 'Your sister said you'd be better at home, and Mr Bell said you ought to be at his house. But Mama said you would be bothered by work at home and bothered by friends at Mr Bell's, so, after quite a battle, they let her bring you here on the basis that it will be the dullest place imaginable.' She lifted a bunch of drooping sweet peas from a vase next to his pillow and replaced them with two plump rosebuds.

'But weren't you starting for France?' He closed his eyes, which helped a little with the pounding in his head.

'Nice can wait,' Georgina said. 'I was only going in order to keep the doctors quiet about my chest, which is as sound as an opera singer's now. I shall go to The Doune instead – when I'm satisfied you're recovered.'

Edwin grimaced at another stab of pain. 'There was no need to stay behind on my account. Jessie and Bell could have looked after me.'

'Not as well as I can. As I told them, if you were at home you'd only try to get up and work.'

'Not with my head like this.' Edwin gritted his teeth.

'Is it very sore still? I'll get you something.' She squeezed his hand, which did more for the pain that he could imagine any laudanum doing. 'And when I get back – try not to ask me why you're here again.'

As Georgina pulled the door closed, the curtains billowed, revealing more of the creeping rose bush. Rachel went to close them.

'No, don't,' he said.

'Darkness and silence, doctor's orders.' She reduced the light to a chink.

'I'd rather have roses and clouds.'

'Mr Bell wouldn't have let her bring you here if she hadn't promised to make it the epitome of dark and dreary. She really had to fight. I never knew she was that keen on … nursing … One might almost think she was sweet on you.' In the gloom, he couldn't see Rachel's expression, but the tone of her voice was more than enough to make his heart quicken. 'She fought almost as hard as she did to keep the cow from my birthday party.'

'Perhaps she's sweet on the cow then?'

'Oh, there's no doubt about that.'

The slice of light coming through the curtains illuminated a broad grin on Rachel's face, then they billowed again as Georgina returned, bearing a bottle and a glass.

After three days of listening to thorns scratching at the window, Edwin succeeded in proving to Woolryche's satisfaction that he was capable of remembering who he was, where he was, and why he was there, and they let him out of bed. He sat in the breakfast room, squinting at an uneaten egg and an unread newspaper, both blindingly lit by a shard of sunlight. He felt very sick, but didn't tell the doctor, who pronounced him fit enough for a brief walk in the gardens.

'Excellent, I'll take you to visit Josephine the Second,' said Georgina.

'I thought you were sending that cow back?' Edwin tried not to wince visibly as he stood up.

'I was going to, but now we're not going to France, I thought she might like to stay a while longer. I'd keep her for good if there were space.'

They'd barely left the terrace when Edwin was overcome with dizziness.

'It's all right,' said Georgina, helping him to the bench beneath the honeysuckle, where they'd argued shortly before Rachel was born. 'The doctor said you might feel fragile for quite a while. There's no hurry. We have all the time in the world.'

Edwin leant back against the twisted plant stems, breathing slowly. Pigeons cooed, insects hummed, leaves rustled. He let his eyes trace one of the thick streaks of silver in Georgina's hair until it disappeared under her bonnet. The years had mottled her face with faint freckles and now it was firmness of character rather than firmness of flesh that was its defining element.

She was still beautiful.

'Did you really fight to bring me here?' he said.

'Of course I did.' She blushed.

'Weren't you worried what people would say?'

'No. Well, nowhere near as much as I was worried about you.'

As she described the battle with Bell, Edwin watched the curves and dimples dance in her cheeks. In spite of the headache and dizziness, he felt he was seeing clearly for the first time in years. She paused, her eyes resting on his, and he realised their fingers were entwined as firmly as the honeysuckle stems behind them.

'Now, sit still for a moment.' She squeezed his hand. 'I'm worried that's fresh blood on your bandage.'

'I am sitting still,' he said, enveloped by the scent that had once been as familiar as his own heartbeat. Twenty years telescoped in on themselves. Driven by the same impulse of tangled desire and fear he'd felt in the whisky still half a lifetime ago, he pulled her close, and kissed her. And he'd missed it so much that he carried on kissing her though his head felt it was about to split in two, and his heart was almost certainly in similar danger.

Head as mended as it would ever be, Edwin arrived at The Doune at the end of September. An early layer of snow on the tops of the hills and a hard frost in the valley made the first sunrise, which he watched, wrapped in a sheet, from Georgina's bedroom window, spectacular. Ice crystals coating the leaves and long grass turned into a shimmering golden mist as light spilled into the valley.

By the afternoon, the wind had changed and the temperature had risen. By the second morning, the thaw had filled burns, streams, and rivers to bursting point. Then it began to rain. It seeped through cracks in window frames and beneath doors. It brought a thousand more burns out of hiding – streaks of foaming white, tumbling through the heather to join the already raging river. The noise of so much raw, angry water seemed to make the house itself tremble.

When Edwin said he was going out to have a closer look, Georgina said he was mad; Rachel said she was going with him.

Wrapped in as much tweed and oil cloth as they could find, they squelched across the lawn, feet soaked before they even reached the trees that flanked the bend in the Spey. As a whole fir tree careered around the corner, Rachel stepped forward to get a better view, and slipped, perilously close to where the soft ground fell away into a short, muddy cliff. Heart in his mouth, Edwin caught her, and her fingers dug deep into his arm as he drew her back up the slope to solid ground. There they remained, wide-eyed, until every thread they wore was saturated and they were both shivering. Rachel didn't lessen her hold on his arm, nor did he loosen his grip on her.

When they made it back to the house, Georgina was furious. She ordered them both to change instantly then decreed that they weren't to move from the fire until they had drunk at least three hot whiskies and their hair had stopped steaming.

Pushing her damp curls aside and grinning through chattering teeth, Rachel told Edwin her plans to write a novel about a great flood, while the rain continued to batter the windows.

'It needs whisky stills, of course, and poachers – that goes without saying – and a tragic love story.' She twirled a pencil between her fingers, eyes shining. 'Are you listening, Lanny? I'll need you to illustrate all of this.'

'At your command, my lady.' Edwin smiled, spellbound.

By the time he entered Georgina's room that night, the clouds had cleared. She was gazing at the moon rising over the hills, casting a rippling path across the flood waters. The house was surrounded by a new lake.

'Are you sure we should be doing this again?' she said.

'No,' he said, slipping his hand around hers as the roar of a stag drifted through the open window. 'But I am sure I want to.'

'Even though we still can't marry?' She turned to him. 'Nothing has changed with Duke Francis.'

'I know. But being without you is worse.'

Beneath the window wings flapped, an owl screeched. Georgina slid her hands around his waist. 'I love you. I've never stopped loving you. I will never stop loving you. Whatever happens, you must believe that. And once Rachel is married, I will marry you a thousand times over.'

There was so little wind the trees were silent. The river was the only sound in the darkness until another stag bellowed. Long after Georgina fell asleep, her head resting heavily on his shoulder, Edwin lay awake. If only the flood would last forever, sealing them off from the rest of the world. But already the lake was draining, and a small voice was beginning to whisper that he was a fool, that this way lay madness.

*She'd marry you now if she really loved you. If you were good enough.*

You're wrong. Rachel will marry. Then we will.

*You'd better hope she marries soon.*

With a shiver, he pulled the blankets higher and drew Georgina closer, burying his face in her hair, vowing to find a way to make this work.

# *1845 to 1850*

EDWIN WAITED. AND WHILE HE WAITED, he painted. Large paintings, small paintings, pictures grand and pictures simple. Ideas and inspiration flowed. The old exhilaration was back. He stayed more regularly at Campden Hill, exploring Georgina's Rubenesque attractions from delicious, more mature angles, murmuring sleepily to her that she was his muse.

'I'm not sure that's terribly flattering,' she murmured back. 'Aren't you painting a dead horse at the moment?'

'It doesn't work like that, and you know it,' he said, and kissed her before she could argue.

There were garden parties, luncheons, and concerts, but still Rachel showed no signs of getting married or even falling in love.

There were highs – the newspapers declared he was back to his old self and the reviews glowed more brightly each year. At times he even believed them.

There were also lows, not least the death of his old antagonist and teacher, Benjamin Haydon. Overwhelmed by debt, he'd taken his own life. Edwin was shaken to the core, refusing to talk about it with anyone but Bell, much to Georgina's annoyance. He and Bell visited Haydon's widow in the house on which the rent had not been paid for months, and from which the furniture had long ago been taken by the bailiffs. Bell gave Mary Haydon over the odds for several of her husband's sketches, and Edwin overpaid considerably for one of Haydon's paintings: *The Judgment of Solomon*.

The painting had haunted his thoughts – the true mother giving up her child to save its life – ever since the Duke's ultimatum about Rachel so many years ago. It served now as a reminder of why he and Georgina couldn't marry yet. He didn't hang it, but kept it covered on an easel in a corner, occasionally taking it out when frustration threatened to overwhelm him.

'I don't see why you have to marry,' said William, in response to a now familiar line of grumbling from Edwin as they played billiards one night. 'Can't you just carry on quietly?'

'Yes, but not forever.' Edwin took a sip of claret. 'I want to be properly spliced. In the eyes of God and all that.'

'Eyes of God? I've never known a fellow avoid Church the way you do.'

'That's not the point.' Edwin pursed his lips, assessing the balls on the table. If they were married, it would silence some of the demons who still whispered to him in the small hours. 'Perhaps if I weren't living in sin, I might go more.'

'If you really want to marry her, why don't you just do the Highland thing?' William said, drawing on his cigar.

'What Highland thing?' Edwin grimaced at the lack of a workable shot.

'Irregular marriage – you must have come across it up there. No banns, no licence – no danger of Duke Francis finding out. Don't even need a clergyman if you don't want to bother God about it. Both parties declare their intention to be married, then consent to the same, and that's basically it. Can be done with or without witnesses, though it can be damned hard to prove without. But are you worried about that? In the most respectful way, I'm assuming you're not concerned with the legitimacy of any future children?'

'No.' Edwin continued to stalk the table in search of a shot. 'I don't want it to be a secret.'

'But is it really such a problem just for a few years?'

'Yes, it is. You don't understand.' Edwin miscued and failed to make contact with anything. 'Damn.'

'It was only a suggestion,' William said, calmly potting a ball from an angle Edwin hadn't considered. 'Think about it.'

'All right,' Edwin grunted, 'but enough about that. I've been meaning to ask, you don't still have that ass's head we borrowed from the Academy, do you?'

William coughed a cloud of smoke. 'That was over twenty years ago! Why on earth do you want to know?'

'I've said I'll paint a scene from *A Midsummer Night's Dream* for that engineer fellow, Brunel, and I'm woefully short on donkey parts.'

As he painted the donkey's head, Edwin's thoughts kept returning to William's suggestion. Being able to marry openly seemed as distant a prospect as ever: Georgina's continued matchmaking efforts resulted only in exhaustion for herself. The passing of each year muffled the voices that whispered she was ashamed of him, weakening his objections to keeping a marriage temporarily secret, but there was enough self-doubt left to tie his tongue every time he thought of broaching the subject with her.

Then, in the summer of 1850, the Queen repeated her offer of a knighthood.

'You will accept it this time even if I have to march you to the palace myself,' Georgina told him, hands on her hips.

On the morning of the ceremony, Edwin stared into his bedroom looking glass as his valet buckled on the ceremonial sword, brushed down the velvet breeches, and straightened the lace collar required for full court dress. The figure in the glass glared defiantly back at him. He was not merely some flash in the pan or fashionable pet. He was a senior Royal Academician. He'd been called England's greatest animal painter. He was about to become Sir Edwin Landseer. If this Edwin Landseer couldn't pull off a proposal, no Edwin Landseer could.

His father shuffled into the room, back from Jersey and staying at St John's Wood while recovering from rheumatic fever. He was followed by Jessie, who carried his ear trumpet.

'That's the wrong kind of sword,' he said.

'It's the one Colonel Phipps told me to wear.' Edwin raised an eyebrow at Jessie's reflection, which smirked back.

'Well, Colonel Phipps ought to know better,' sniffed John Landseer.

'Good luck, Ned,' said Jessie. 'You look every inch a knight.'

As soon as it was over, he took a cab to Campden Hill, fingertips running over and over a rose pattern engraving on his sword hilt.

'Sir Edwin!' Georgina curtseyed, beaming and blushing. 'I must say, you look very dashing. The sword suits you. And so do the breeches. How was it?

'You were right. I should have accepted the first time. I'm getting too old for all this kneeling,' Edwin said, heart thumping as he discarded his cocked hat and gloves on a side table. 'And now I have to do it again.'

'What on earth are you talking about? And what on earth are you doing?'

Kicking his sword to one side and flicking out his black velvet coattails, Edwin gingerly placed one knee on the floor, looking fixedly at her. 'Do you remember the last time I knelt before you in breeches? About twenty-five years ago. You were wearing white silk and kept kicking me in the ribs. George Hayter was furious.'

'Yes . . .' she said, a flicker of understanding kindling in her eyes. 'What are you—'

'At least these don't have fleas.' He winced as his knee cracked.

Flushing, she picked up her skirts and bent stiffly to join him on the floor, 'Lanny . . .'

'That was the day I realised I was in love with you,' he said, taking her hands. 'And I'm more in love with you now than ever. So, I'm asking you on bended – and really quite uncomfortable – knee: will you be my wife?'

'Lanny . . . what about Duke Francis?'

'Let me finish. We marry secretly now – Francis will be none the wiser – then have it solemnised when it's safe.'

'But you said you didn't want a secret wedding—'

'Things are different now. And I'm sick of waiting. I want all the world to know we're married, but I'd rather be married to you in secret than not married to you at all. So, please say yes, and put my knees out of their misery—'

She cut him off, eyes shining. 'Yes, Sir Edwin, Sir Lanny, Sir Endymion . . . yes, yes, yes, yes—' and she went on saying yes until he kissed her.

# *1865, London*

'SIR EDWIN, I'M SORRY BUT you can't smoke in here. Will I carry your glass to the smoking room, sir?'

'S'my house, s'my cigar. I'll smoke where I damn well like.'

'I'm sorry, Sir Edwin, but this is the Athenaeum Club.'

'Hell it is! Go away.'

Eyes closed. Chair leather. Cigar smoke. Rough on the tongue, on the cheeks. To sleep . . . Too much damned talking. Damn them.

'Mr Landseer, your brother is a little . . . unwell.'

Which brother? Whose brother? He isn't Mr Landseer. Not Mr . . .

'There have been complaints. From other members.'

'Damn the complaints,' he growls. Drops his cigar. Tries to pick it up. Misses. Laughs.

'Come on, Ned.'

Charles. Of course. Laughs again. Forgetful fool. Charles, Charles, Charles. Charles is here. Charles is Mr Landseer now. Now that he is Sir Edwin. Sir Edwin the . . . the what?

'Come on, Ned, let's go home.'

'Sir Edwin,' he snarls at his brother's blurred face. 'Sir Edwin. *Sir.* Not Ned. You should all show more respect, damn you. Nobody ever takes me seriously. It's *Sir Edwin*!'

In the corner of the room, the Other Lion yawns.

*You're pathetic, Sir Edwin. Sir Edwin the drunkard.*

The Other Lion has been sitting at his bedroom door for three days. It's quiet now. The memory of claws in his flesh is fading, but, as the air clears, the memories of shouting at his brothers, at Jessie, at Lindy, are horribly vivid.

Over the hammering of his heart, he can hear them talking about him in the hall with Tuke – the mad doctor.

Tuke: 'I strongly advise that you let me take him to Chiswick.'

Not Chiswick. Not the madhouse. Edwin grits his teeth, hauls himself back, back into the room, back into his mind.

Charles says something he doesn't catch.

Tuke again: 'I understand, but if he doesn't stop, it will kill him. It may already be too late.'

Edwin grips the sheets and closes his eyes, but he can still feel the Other Lion's stare boring into him. Louisa said Rachel will be in London soon, said she has a scheme for them to meet. He must be well enough to see Rachel. He must not be mad.

Charles: 'Surely it's not that serious? He's been much better recently. This is the first bad spell for over a year. He's just had a difficult month. There was a fuss about one of his pictures for the Exhibition, but that's all rectified now.'

Tuke: 'The demon eats away at the patient from the inside. Once the addiction has progressed to a certain level, the body and mind are permanently affected. Even then, the patient may still appear well. Let me take him for a month – even a fortnight could make a difference. We can reduce the drinking, help him.'

Edwin glares at the beast pacing at the foot of the bed.

Charles, sighing: 'Can it wait until he's finished the lions? If it were to get out that he were in an asylum, even voluntarily, they'd take the commission away. It would finish him off. He'd never be able to live with the failure.'

The Other Lion narrows its eyes, growls. Edwin would throw a pillow at it. But he mustn't move the pillows.

Tuke, sighing, tutting: 'How much longer will the lions take?'

The Other Lion has come close, its muzzle is inches from his face. Edwin could touch its whiskers – if he wanted to. Could run his finger along the scar beneath its eye.

Charles: 'All he has to do is finish the large models. Scaling up. Nothing new – and they're almost done. Marochetti will take the lead on casting.'

Tuke: 'Very well. I shall examine him and we will wait. But you know he cannot continue like this.'

Edwin stares at the ceiling, refuses to look at the Other Lion, tells himself he can't smell it, can't feel its hot, rancid breath prickling his neck.

Tuke enters, followed by Lassie. Takes hold of Edwin's wrist, feels for a pulse with cold, cold fingers. 'How are you feeling this morning, Sir Edwin?'

He wants to vomit. He wants to sleep. He wants to plunge into cold water. He wants to curl up and die. He wants to breathe Highland air and feel the wind and the sun and the rain. He wants a drink.

But he must not be mad.

He says: 'Much. Better. Thank you.'

After completing his examination – such inane questions – Tuke leaves, closes the door. How considerate. No one can see him now. Edwin reaches for the bottle hidden under the pillow, upends it. The warmth slips down his throat, seeps through his bones – balance returns, panic recedes as he strokes Lassie and tells her what a good girl she is.

He needs it. Not forever. Just for now. Just until the lions are done.

'Do you really think you're still in control?' purrs the Other Lion.

'I've told you,' Edwin snarls. 'I can hold you off until they're finished. Then we can both go to the devil.'

'You'd better work quickly.' The Other Lion licks its teeth. 'You won't last much longer, not at the rate you're going.'

When he is better – or better enough to be seen in public – Edwin goes to the Isle of Wight, to Osborne House, where the Queen wants him to paint her youngest daughter on a pony. It takes only an hour of whisky and claret before she says she also wants him to make a large picture of herself and Albert, happy in the Highlands. And one of Brown and herself now, in sorrow. It's a terrible idea. Even Edwin, half-drunk and only half-recovered, can see that. Even the Other Lion can see that. It's worse than her damned Van Amburgh painting.

But she will not be told.

Plump and petulant, she says: 'I need a reminder of those happy times, and you ought to understand better than anybody. You were so much a part of them. I wouldn't dream of having anyone else make the picture.'

'It's not the Highland subject I object to, ma'am, but the picture you want with Mr Brown.' Edwin inspects a button he has just pulled off his waistcoat.

'Why shouldn't I have a testament to the goodness of dear Brown? In my great sorrow?' Her eyes flash beneath lids that are heavier than they used to be as she smooths her stiff black skirts. 'I am aware that people think our friendship improper, but they don't understand.'

They understand that Brown is an arrogant ass who bullies everyone from footmen to field marshals, thinks Edwin, drinking to make sure the words don't accidentally make their way out of his mouth. It's going to be hard to get out of this one.

Lifting a terrier named Boz, whom Edwin has been idly sketching, the Queen adds, 'They say it's not fitting for a forty-five-year-old widow to have a close friendship with a man her inferior in age and rank. If I had been born a man, none of them would make the slightest fuss.'

From what Edwin has heard, Brown is so obnoxious people would make a fuss whether the Queen had been born man, woman, or elephant.

Still addressing the dog, she says, 'And we so hoped you would understand, Sir Edwin, better than all those others,' she turns those rounded eyes to him, pleading, 'because of your duchess.'

It hits him right in the chest, harder even than the claret-whisky mixture. He'd known she'd known – she had her network of royal gossips, and George Hayter. But she never referred explicitly to his relationship with Georgina. Even immediately after her death – the last time he'd been here – the Queen avoided mentioning her. That had been a large part of the problem.

And she is nothing like Georgina, and – surely – he is nothing like Brown? But . . . He swirls the contents of his glass and clutches the button, eyes falling on the Glenfeshie sketch-book and its tartan ribbon.

'All right, ma'am.' He swallows, batting away the shade of Van Amburgh. 'But it will be for Your Majesty only. Absolutely not to be exhibited.'

'Oh, thank you, Sir Edwin, we are so grateful. We knew you would understand.' She beams at the dog, momentarily the girl-Queen he first knew in spite of the crows' feet and sprinkling of grey hairs beneath her mourning cap. Then she lays a hand on his arm and asks softly, 'I hope you didn't mind me mentioning your duchess?'

'No.' He can't exactly say anything else.

'You loved her to the end, didn't you?'

Edwin nods, biting his lip.

'Have you been back there? To the huts? Since our last talk?'

'No. I . . . no. I don't think I could without her.' Why must she always come back to this? Can't she see how hard it is?

'I understand,' she says.

Edwin wants to scream that she doesn't. He can't go back. If he goes back and finds Georgina not there, it will destroy him.

But the Queen continues: 'I felt the same about the places Albert loved. I couldn't face the thought of his absence beside me in a place where he used to be so present. Then I came to see that it wasn't his absence that was with me, but his memory. Go back to your huts, Sir Edwin, while you still can.'

There are two colossal clay lions now. The tail of one curls to the left, the other to the right. Their expressions differ slightly. This pair will be cast in parts and the casts used to create four individual beasts. One clay is complete. The second, only the head needs work, but it requires endless moistening; he's been working on it so long it will set in the wrong state if he's not quick. But it's so nearly there – towering above him.

The Other Lion looks on, stalks around the base of the platform on which Edwin works. It breathes down the back of his neck, drips doubt into his ear, but he will not listen. Not today. Today, when he's finished with the clay, he's going to tea with Louisa Abercorn. And Rachel will be there.

He gets the cabman to drop him by the mews behind the Abercorns' house, where no one can see him tip the contents of his flask down his throat; where he can swallow the nausea and the crackling fear that fills his lungs.

The Other Lion laughs. Tells him he's pathetic.

Edwin tells it to boil its head. Tells it to stay outside.

'This way, Sir Edwin, they are in the garden,' says a footman, showing him through the drawing room, indicating open French windows.

William's is the first voice he hears. 'Get off me! You rascal, James! And you too Gracey! I thought you were my trusted ally?'

Edwin steps out onto the ornate iron steps and there they are: a freckled, flaxen-haired boy of around seven or eight and a girl with darker hair, perhaps slightly younger, giggling and attacking William with what look to be napkins. Across the grass on a blanket sits Louisa's youngest daughter, Maud, blowing bubbles through a clay pipe for a delighted, dribbling baby. Behind them, laughing with Louisa, is Rachel.

Her face turns white as she notices him. Edwin's breath catches in his throat. He can't do this. It's too much. A dark circle appears around the scene and the figures – his and Georgina's grandchildren – grow small and indistinct …

'Lanny,' calls Louisa, firmly. 'Lanny, come and have some tea.'

The black recedes.

He breathes.

He drinks tea.

Why must teacups be made of china? It rattles so much.

'Lady Rachel.'

'Sir Edwin.'

She drinks tea.

She wrinkles her nose.

Her cup rattles too. 'Louisa didn't tell me you were coming.'

'I can't be expected to tell everybody everything all the time,' says Louisa, pointedly pouring more tea. 'And I thought Grace and James might like to meet a famous artist. Grace is particularly fond of drawing, aren't you, Gracey?'

The children turn, allowing William to escape from his table linen bonds.

'I'll see you later, Lanny,' he mutters. 'I'm too damned old for this. I only came to talk to Abercorn about a dog.'

William forgotten, the boy – James – says, 'I'm good at drawing too! Papa says I'm already better than he is.'

'Well, you're not as good as Mama or me,' says the girl, hands on her hips, pouting as a bubble floats close to her snub nose.

They glare at each other, picking their way through the heap of discarded napkins, and come to stand by their mother's side.

'James Butler, sir, how do you do?' The boy holds out his hand, his sky-blue eyes meeting Edwin's.

Edwin blinks and solemnly shakes the small hand, swallowing a large lump in his throat just in time to say 'Sir Edwin Landseer' without sounding too gruff.

'You're Landseer? The Landseer?' says Grace, stopping her curtsey halfway, hands returning to her hips.

Edwin nods, heart swelling.

Another bubble from Maud's pipe floats past. If only Rachel would look at him, but her gaze is fixed on the baby – another grandson? – who is now giggling and wet as he tries to catch the bubbles and they pop in his face.

Questions from the older children fill the air.

'Will you paint us like you've painted our cousins?'

'Why don't you ever come to Ireland?'

'Aunt Louisa says you don't like sailing.'

'Uncle Abercorn says the Queen keeps you a prisoner in a tower with a lion.'

'Is that clay on your coat?'

'Is it lion clay?'

'Do you really keep a lion in your garden? Aunt Louisa says you do.'

'She says she met it. Can we meet it? Do you ride it?'

Edwin blinks as a stream of bubbles drifts across his face, unable to keep from smiling, just about keeping from crying. 'I don't have the lion any more, only a goat,' he says. 'But I should be delighted to take you to the zoo and introduce you to the lions there. If your mother has no objection.'

There is a crescendo of 'Mama, Mama please say yes!' then the sound of breaking china. And silence.

'James!' cries Rachel. 'Why must you be so careless? You've covered Lanny in tea. And you've broken Maud's bubble bowl.'

Rachel kneels to gather the shards. Not meeting his eye, she hands Edwin one of the napkins recently used to bind William, saying, 'You must forgive James. He's very excitable.'

'I'm sure he didn't mean it.' Edwin mops the tea from his trousers, smiling apologetically at the boy, whose lower lip is quivering. 'And I was only thinking just now how they shouldn't make teacups out of china. I should use wood, or India rubber.'

The children laugh. Rachel wrinkles her nose. For a glorious moment, what could be a smile flickers on her face, but then she shakes her head.

'I really am sorry, Mama.' The poor boy looks distraught. His sister mutters 'crybaby' at him but, undaunted, he asks, 'But may we go to the zoo and see the lions? Please may we?'

One of Maud's last bubbles drifts past his nose.

'What a wonderful idea,' says Louisa.

Rachel glances briefly at Edwin.

'No,' she says.

The last two bubbles drift towards a rosebush.

'But you have a few more days. The children have seen so little of Lan— of London.' says Louisa.

'No,' says Rachel. 'We don't have time. And there's a perfectly good zoo in Dublin.'

The first bubble hits a thorn and bursts.

Edwin clutches the tea-stained napkin. The second bubble sits, half an inch from another thorn, quivering on the petals of a white rose.

Rachel takes a deep breath, glancing again at Edwin, and adds, 'But perhaps – I'm not saying we will, but perhaps – maybe next time we come to London. If Sir Edwin finishes his lion sculptures. Now I'm afraid we must go. Your papa will be wondering what has become of us.'

# *1865 to 1866*

EDWIN CLINGS TO THE MEMORY of the rose, the bubble, and the children in the garden. He redoubles his efforts. He strives to never be drunk, even if he's rarely sober.

Casting begins. Marochetti's men make the moulds – too large to be cast as single pieces, the lions must be made in segments. Each one must fit perfectly with the others. Watching them pour the writhing, molten metal stretches and twists what's left of his nerves. It seems never-ending. But, even though his face burns in the heat, he will not step away until every last drop of bronze has been safely captured.

In between these fiery sessions, he diligently attends Academy meetings, sends pictures to exhibitions, and performs the role of a respectable member of his profession: he goes to dinners, country houses, shooting parties; he dines with his brothers and sisters and stares into the fire as Lindy shrieks at Charles's puns, and he eats sugarplums with Jessie and Tom. He does everything right – but still the blue devils come, and when they do, he claws himself back, swearing and cursing at the Other Lion until it slinks back into the shadows.

He waits for a word from Rachel as 1865 slides into 1866. He will not give up hope. Not yet. He just needs to finish the lions.

In March, he's elected President of the Royal Academy. He declines. He might appear well enough on the outside, but he knows he's not. The Other Lion mocks him for bursting into tears in front of all the other RAs. He tells it to go to hell and hurls a bottle at it.

In April, the Queen comes to St John's Wood to sit for the picture of herself and Brown. She brings one of her ladies, who talks with Jessie in the drawing room, and Brown, who strolls about the studio picking things up without asking, peering at canvases that are turned to the wall, tutting. Then, opening a tin of Edwin's tobacco and filling his pipe, he announces that he's going into the garden for a smoke. The bastard has also shortened his beard by half, which means Edwin will have to redo part of the picture. It would serve Brown right if the Other Lion ate him while he was out there.

Claridge brings in a tray containing whisky and claret. Before long, like the determined terrier she is, the Queen is back on the subject of Glenfeshie.

'Have you been back yet?' she asks.

'No.'

'How many times must I tell you? One would think a queen wouldn't have to repeat herself so often. You must go, Sir Edwin. It would be good for you. It always helps when I visit the places Albert and I held most dearly in our hearts. Brown comes with me; he understands. He lets me weep and helps keep the memories alive. He can be remarkably gentle, you know. He is like a dog my mother once had, a cairn terrier, who was terribly disobedient and fierce with everyone but me, and knew exactly when I needed him most.'

'Yes, ma'am,' Edwin says. 'If you wouldn't mind putting the glass down for a moment and looking at the letter, just so I can get the angle of your eyes.' He makes a light chalk mark on the likeness of the Queen's face, then another to soften the expression he's given Brown. Perhaps he has some redeeming features.

'Brown told me something the other day.' The Queen sneaks a sip, glancing at Edwin before resuming her pose with the letter. 'He heard a rumour about a secret wedding in the Highlands.'

Edwin's tempted to return Brown's expression to the truculent scowl he'd originally drawn, but he doesn't. He puts down the chalk, picks up his glass, washes the sweet, fiery mixture around his mouth as the deepest currents stir in his blood.

'Such a romantic notion,' the Queen says, sliding him another sidelong glance. 'It sounds heavenly.'

'It was, ma'am.' Edwin's voice cracks. He hasn't told anyone before. Has barely allowed himself to think of it for over a decade.

* * *

They make no more progress with the picture that afternoon, and Edwin soaks another royal handkerchief.

When the Queen has gone, he takes Lassie and Tracker, the quiet, long-haired pup he's kept from her last litter, and wanders a little unsteadily through the gardens until he comes to the silver birch he brought back from Glenfeshie as a sapling. It's where the others are buried. Brutus, Bran, Angus, Luna, Topsey . . . so many friends. He lets his eyes trace the stems of a rambling rose that has wound itself around the tree, then lowers himself to the ground, leans against the peeling bark. And weeps.

Georgina is buried in Nice. He's never seen her grave, never got to say goodbye. He saw her for the last time through the smoky glass of a train window at Victoria Station as she and Rachel set off for Dover. Smiling, waving, shouting something he couldn't hear above the shrieks of steam and iron, of meetings and partings. It was just over two years after their wedding.

The doctors were strict about her needing a warm winter. She wanted Edwin to go too, but he had too much work, was under pressure to make progress with the Balmoral boat picture. He'd struggled to get back into the rhythm of things after his father's death the year before and was already behind. He begged her not to go abroad – he didn't see why Brighton wouldn't do, as it had the year before, then he could have visited easily. But the doctors were insistent. Damn the doctors. Damn everything.

Woolryche's first letter came on a cold February morning.

Influenza, he said, had fallen on her chest. She was dangerously ill.

*'This night is the great crisis. I will write again tomorrow.'*

The following day, a second letter arrived, *Immediate*, scrawled on the corner of the envelope. Edwin's hands were shaking so much he could barely open it. He made it as far as the words '*at 2 p.m. the Duchess resigned her spirit to him who made it . . .*' before everything blurred – the words, the sitting room, old Luna. The world clouded, filled with a freezing fog.

It had never quite come back into focus.

He continued working for the 1853 Exhibition like an automaton, throwing himself into large pictures of deer in the mist, as he'd painted them in the glen. At times, half-delirious, he was convinced that if he could make the picture good enough, she would come back. That it would all have been a mistake. Or that he could follow the deer into the mist, where she would be waiting.

Once the pictures were sent in, he'd fallen apart.

The one ray of hope had been Rachel. But Georgina's executors had found the damned letter – why hadn't she burnt it? – and told Rachel she wasn't a duke's daughter after all. Duke Francis agreed not to make it public. As far as he was concerned, Georgina had kept her side of the bargain. But that made no difference. Rachel hated him for making her life a lie.

Edwin promised Bell he wouldn't repeat the trick with the laudanum. He chose a different bottle.

A breeze stirs the air, sets the catkins swaying, flutters the young rose leaves. Too much in the shadow of the birch, the plant hasn't flowered in years but doggedly puts out new growth every spring. A stem reaches out, catches in his hair. Fumbling to unhook it, he stops, feels a slender swelling on the stalk. Hardly daring to breathe, he teases out the tangles, works the stem loose, trembling as he tries not to break it – he must remember to brush his hair more often – and there, free, resting on his paint-stained fingertip, is a tiny rosebud.

They round the final bend in the track, emerging from the trees into the clearing. The babble of the Feshie is muffled by the tall pines, mixed with the whispering of young aspens, golden in the October sun. The shadowed hills seem angled differently from how he used to paint them. Perhaps they've changed over the years – rocks fallen, trees grown – or perhaps his memory is faulty. Perhaps both. Edwin reaches into his breast pocket: the flask is there, of course, but his fingers close on the sketch-book next to it, the pages of which protect the rose that flowered beneath the birch tree, now carefully dried and pressed.

The ghillie, a grandson of Anna Mhòr, leads the ponies and they pick their way on foot across clumps of waxy grass and tangled heather. The huts are ahead. Their wall planks are bleached and bowed. In some places, the roofs are overgrown with moss, in others, whole sections have fallen away.

'I'll leave you to it, Sir Edwin,' says the ghillie, settling himself on a rock with pipe and tobacco tin.

Silently, Edwin enters the largest of the buildings, the old hall that served as sitting room by day, dining room and dancing floor by night. The walls lean wearily, pierced by spears of daylight, but on the plaster of the stone chimney breast, the deer he painted are still clear, even if cracks have begun to grow beneath their hooves. He traces their delicate legs, antlers, ears, the surface rough and cool beneath his finger tip. Here's one he added the year of the kippers – he can almost smell the fish. And another – he flattens his palm against it – the first one Rachel added. A calf, round eyes staring back at him as clearly as the day he held his hand over hers, gently guiding her slender brush. And the mountain hare she painted all by herself. White in its winter coat.

A breeze coming through a hole in the roof stirs the hairs on the back of his neck. He drifts. The sounds of reeling feet and fiddle music seem no more than a heartbeat away. Old laughter lingers in the shadows and makes him smile.

He greets the ghosts in the other huts, then, finally, pushes open the door of Georgina's. Dust motes dance as soft light streams in. The old boards creak under his feet. His fingers feel echoes in the air, tingling with longing and loss. And there, above the fireplace, are the three deer. The family: faded and cracked, but still together.

The next morning, he rises at dawn and rides up along the high road beneath a canopy of amber-leaved oak, beech, and bright-berried rowans. The mist-streaked air is already turning golden with the sunrise as he reaches the gate to the small churchyard that nestles on the hill above The Doune. The house is let to an English lawyer, but there's unlikely to be anyone up here at this hour, and he needs to do this alone.

It was just as early and even mistier the day they were married.

Boots glistening with dew, he steps inside the church for the first time since that morning, walks solemnly through the shadows, then sinks onto a bench at the west end, and, the cold stone wall at his back, lets himself remember.

Georgina arrived in a simple plaid cape; she wore no jewels, but her bonnet was spangled with mist, setting off the silver streaks in her hair. Though both of them were shaking with nerves, she'd never gripped his hands more firmly than she did then, as they declared they would be man and wife from that day forward. The witnesses were Annie Rose, a local girl of whom Georgina was particularly fond, and William. Annie cried and sniffed loudly. William pretended he was coughing but mopped his eyes, not his mouth, with his handkerchief. They'd kissed as briefly as that first time in the whisky still and it signified everything.

He can still feel it now. Can taste it along with the salt of fresh tears. He watches the scene again and again until a ray of sunlight creeps through the east window, then he stands and follows his own ghost out through the side door.

Before returning to Kinrara, he pauses at the gate leading into The Doune's parkland. The sound of hooves on the path makes him stiffen. Damn it. Someone is out early after all. But there's a softness, a lightness to the sound he can't place. Then a sharp bark issues from the trees to his right: it's not a pony – it's a deer. While he scans the trunks and shadows to catch a glimpse, it barks again, and, from his left, comes another in answer. He holds his breath. There's a faint rustling, then a roe doe darts out and leaps away in the direction of the house. From the other side, a buck appears, briefly staring in Edwin's direction, before bounding after her into the mist.

# *January 1867, Trafalgar Square, London*

IT IS DONE.

Edwin has supervised, losing countless waistcoat buttons, as the lions have been cast and cooled and riveted and sanded and polished. He's watched them being wrapped in enough canvas to make a fleet's worth of sails, loaded onto wagons and rolled through the streets, then hauled and heaved and winched onto their pedestals, still covered in their winding sheets. Herding them here took four days. Four days of the foulest, coldest January weather.

And now here they are. Back where it all began.

Small groups of people whose curiosity is stronger than their fear of catching their death of damp have gathered to watch the unveiling, but there's no ceremony. Just fog. Charles, Tom, and Lindy are here though, with Hills. Jessie and Mrs Potter are in bed with influenza. But George Hayter has come and is inspecting his gloves. With a pang of guilt, Edwin realises he can't remember how long it's been since they last saw each other.

Edwin himself stands between Marochetti and William.

He and the Baron paid two guineas to have the bells of St Martin's rung and a flag flown from the spire. The flag is invisible in the mist. The bells are muffled and flat. The lions' canvas wrappings are so saturated and heavy that Marochetti's men struggle to remove them and a few members of the public step in to help. Lord John Manners taps his foot. For a moment, Edwin thinks Manners might lend them a hand, but he simply takes out his watch and tuts. At his side, George Russell catches his father's eye and shrugs apologetically.

Finally, just as all the cloths are off, the watery yellow light turns to white gold as the sun glimmers through a break in the fog. The frost glitters briefly on the beasts' black flanks, before the clouds close and all is dull again.

'Thank you, Sir Edwin,' Manners says with a thin-lipped smile. 'Better late than never.'

'They're magnificent,' adds George Russell, with an emphatic flash of his eyebrows.

The unseen bells of St Martin's ring noon as the lions' winding sheets are loaded onto a wagon and taken away. Marochetti leaves with them, calling out, 'We will celebrate later, Sir Edwin!'

With a curt nod, Manners marches back to the office, George Russell trailing in his wake.

There's a brief shaking of hands with the few friends and family who have made it, and the little crowd melts away.

Edwin feels numb.

Then William passes him a slim package.

'I was instructed to hand this over once the beasts were in place and not a moment before. Gracey chose it. It's her new favourite book, apparently.'

Grace: Rachel's daughter with Georgina's eyes ... Hardly daring to hope, fingers trembling, Edwin gets the string off on the third attempt, then unfolds the brown paper. It's a book, bound in red cloth. On the front, picked out in gold, is a girl holding a pig, on the back is a grinning cat, on the spine are the words: *Alice's Adventures in Wonderland.*

But these details pale into insignificance when he sees, written inside:

*Lanny. With love. Dormouse.*

Edwin's heart swells so much it nearly chokes him. It's all he can do to wrench his handkerchief from a pocket in time to hide a sudden flood of tears. While he composes himself, William whistles and looks closely at the lion's paws.

'Well, that was ... err ... foggy,' William says, once the handkerchief is back in the pocket. 'Drink?'

Edwin nods. Ignores the Other Lion. Clutches the book.

They slip through the fog, past the fountains that gurgle like hidden mountain streams, up the steps towards Pall Mall, pausing at the top, William wheezing.

'Damned cheap cigars,' William mutters.

Edwin leans on his cane and gazes down at the lions, sitting in the sea of fog. He takes out his sketchbook, gently removes the dried rose and lays it inside Rachel's gift, next to the words, *With love. Dormouse*, then returns both books to his breast pocket.

After a minute or two, breath recovered, William points his own cane at the empty plinth next to them. 'I hear this one's looking for an occupant. Fancy making another lion?'

'No.' Edwin smiles, watching a roebuck pick his way past oblivious figures in the mist to join a doe, who stands with a well-grown calf at the spot where he once waited for a coach to Woburn.

# Epilogue

Edwin Landseer was certified as a lunatic in July 1872, just over five years after finishing the Trafalgar Square lions. He died in October of the following year.

* * *

# Author's Note

This is a work of fiction but is inspired by real people, places, and events. Where possible, I have stuck closely to the historical narrative, though have had to tweak some timelines and employ a touch of artistic licence to cram fifty years into a single volume. I have tried at all times to remain within the realms of possibility.

Some names have been changed to minimise confusion: this period contained an unhelpful surfeit of Georges, Georginas, Georgianas, Williams, and Louisas. The historical figures behind 'Caro' and 'Baring' are Louisa Caroline Stewart Mackenzie (known as 'Loo') (1827–1903) and William Bingham Baring, second Baron Ashburton (1799–1864). 'Amelia', the not-quite-wife of Sir George Hayter (1792–1871), was another Louisa, this time Louisa Cauty.

From the 1820s onwards, fashionable circles were filled with rumours about the relationship between Edwin Landseer (1802–1873) and Georgina Russell (née Gordon), Duchess of Bedford (1781–1853), and that Lady Rachel Russell, Georgina's youngest child, was Landseer's daughter. As is so often the way, it is impossible to know the truth, but the duchess and the painter were certainly extremely close, and the sheer volume of gossip makes a romance seem highly likely. This novel explores what might have happened if those rumours were true.

Landseer's mental and physical collapse in the summer of 1840 is on firmer historical ground. Contemporaries cited various causes and, as in the novel, newspapers ran stories of a failed elopement with the recently widowed Georgina. The precise nature of Landseer's illness is not known, but some papers reported that he was initially not expected to live. The suicide attempt is speculation on my part. Landseer suffered a second severe breakdown after Georgina's death in 1853, from which he never fully recovered. Landseer received news of her demise by post and the text given here is taken from the letter itself. In real life, the sender was not Woolryche but another friend, Captain Leslie. Landseer's ongoing struggles with addiction and his mental health are also based on the historical record, as is his disastrous proposal to Louisa Stewart Mackenzie ('Caro').

Edwin's elder sister, Jane, did marry an animal painter named Charles Christmas at Christmas, and, tragically, died a year later in childbirth. She was a gifted artist in her own right, becoming an exhibitor at the Royal Academy before any of her now better-known brothers. Two of Edwin's other sisters, Jessie and Emma, also became painters. I greatly regret not being able to give them all more space here. Likewise, apologies are due to a fourth sister, Anna Maria, an aunt, Barbara Potts, and an uncle, Henry Landseer, who have been asked to wait politely in the wings for lack of narrative room. I hope to redress these slights in a non-fiction work on the Landseer family in the future.

The accusations of adultery brought against Belinda Landseer are also based on fact. The case was indeed made painfully public thanks to John Landseer's inability to let it lie. Tom and

Belinda remained together in spite of everything and their son, George Landseer, went on to become a successful artist in his own right, spending several years in India.

Rather than risk making this note as long as the novel itself, I have included below some suggestions for further reading on various aspects of the novel for those interested.

The best accounts of Edwin Landseer's life and works are contained in Richard Ormond's exhibition catalogues, *Sir Edwin Landseer* (Tate Gallery, 1981) and *The Monarch of the Glen: Landseer in the Highlands* (National Galleries of Scotland, 2005), and in his more recent *Edwin Landseer: The Private Drawings* (Unicorn Press, 2009).

For an account of Georgina on her own, see Rachel Trethewey's biography *Mistress of the Arts: The Passionate Life of Georgina, Duchess of Bedford* (Review, 2002). For a really deep dive, try Keir Davidson's double biography of Georgina and the Duke, *Improbable Pioneers of the Romantic Age* (Pimpernel Press, 2022).

For more on 'Caro' or Louisa Stewart Mackenzie, a fascinating figure in her own right, see Virginia Surtees's *The Ludovisi Goddess* (Michael Russell Press, 1984).

There are numerous biographies of Queen Victoria to choose from, but my personal favourite is A. N. Wilson's 2014 *Victoria* (Atlantic Books). Victoria's own *Leaves from the Journal of our Life in the Highlands*, in which she describes visiting the ruined Glenfeshie huts, is also illuminating.

The history of the Highlands during the nineteenth century was complex and was, for many, fraught with hardship and the pain of forced dispossession. This is not the subject of this novel, but it is highly advisable to read the idealised view of the Highlands presented here in its broader historical context. For anyone interested, in particular in the Badenoch region in which Glenfeshie and The Doune are situated, David Taylor's *The People Are Not There* (Birlinn, 2022) offers an excellent, highly readable and nuanced account, and illustrates the genuine affection local people held for Georgina and her family. T. C. Smout gives an excellent summary of what is likely to have been evident to Landseer in *The Monarch of the Glen: Landseer in the Highlands* (National Galleries of Scotland, 2005). T. M. Devine's *The Scottish Nation* (Allen Lane, 1999) and *The Scottish Clearances: A History of the Dispossessed* (Allen Lane, 2018) give the picture at national level. If you can put up with print-on-demand, you can also read Rachel's novel, *Jessie Cameron; A Highland Story* for some wonderful descriptions of life in the glen, published in 1856 under her married name, Lady Rachel Butler.

Edwin's house in St John's Wood was demolished in the 1890s, but you can still walk along the canal tow path that marked the bottom of his garden from the Maida Hill Tunnel to Regent's Park and the zoo. Tom's house, across Cunningham Place from the site of Edwin's, is still there, now named 'Landseer Studios'.

The Doune still stands. At the time of writing it is possible to visit by arrangement. The huts in Glenfeshie are all but gone. A bothy, elements of which may date back to Landseer's time, is maintained where they once stood at Ruigh Aiteachain in Glenfeshie. It's a wonderful place to stay, provided you don't mind trekking a few miles through the glen. Nearby, stands a lone chimney stack that once bore paintings of deer, which is what inspired this novel.

The lions are still in Trafalgar Square and would be delighted if you were to give them a nod next time you're passing.

# Acknowledgements

Heartfelt thanks to everyone who has helped and listened to me talking about Landseer over the years in which this novel took shape.

To my agent, Sharon Bowers, for taking a chance on Edwin and his lions, and for excellent, Guinness-fuelled book chat.

To my editor, Rachel Morrell, for her brilliant combination of calm, enthusiasm, and insight, and to the entire team at Black & White for giving this book a home.

To Richard Ormond, who knows more about Landseer than any man alive, for sharing his expertise, and also to his wife, Leonée, for hospitality, kindness, and stories.

To James Hamilton, 5th Duke of Abercorn, for support, wisdom, and the warmest of welcomes.

To Rachel Trethewey, whose vivid and moving biography of Georgina sent me down this rabbit hole in the first place.

To my favourite contemporary painter, Ben Sullivan, for putting up with more dogs and fewer beards than he bargained for, along with endless questions.

To Peter Benson, my Faber Academy tutor, for the invaluable advice to 'just write the bloody thing', and to all my Faber classmates: your feedback on the early chapters was invaluable, and your company was excellent.

To Sara Cox and the judges at the Cheshire Novel Prize for shortlisting an unfinished first draft and giving me the kick I needed to get to the end, and for introducing me to the best writing group anyone could wish for.

To Lucy Steeds for putting up with my pedantry and returning it in the best possible way: toast lions and champagne forever.

To my early readers Julie O'Sullivan, Hayley King, and Terri Mullholland, for your incredible support and insight, for making me laugh, and for keeping me going.

To the Cheshire Cats. You are The Best.

To Sarah Steegar, for coffee, company, and generally getting it.

To all the authors I've met while making this book who have been so generous with encouragement, expertise, and expectation management. It makes such a huge difference.

To my family, for putting up with me, cheering me on, and wading through clouds of midges in the pursuit of Landseer relics.

To Florrie, for putting up with more than most and for not hating it.

To all the dogs and deer who showed up when I needed them most.

And to you, the reader, if you've read this far. Thank you.